LAST STOP
SALINA CRUZ

ALMA BOOKS LTD
London House
243–253 Lower Mortlake Road
Richmond
Surrey TW9 2LL
United Kingdom
www.almabooks.com

First published by Alma Books Limited in 2007
Copyright © David Lalé, 2007

This is a work of fiction. Names, characters, places and incidents either are
the product of the author's imagination or are used fictitiously, and any
resemblance to actual persons, living or dead, business establishments,
events or locales is entirely coincidental.

Printed in Great Britain by TJ International, Padstow, Cornwall

ISBN-13 (HARDBACK): 978-1-84688-032-2
ISBN-10 (HARDBACK): 1-84688-032-7

ISBN-13 (SPECIAL EDITION): 978-1-84688-047-6
ISBN-10 (SPECIAL EDITION): 1-84688-047-5

ISBN-13 (PAPERBACK US AND AUS): 978-1-84688-044-5
ISBN-10 (PAPERBACK US AND AUS): 1-84688-044-0

LAST STOP
SALINA CRUZ

DAVID LALÉ

ALMA BOOKS

LAST STOP
SALINA CRUZ

PART ONE

PARIS

"I am the prophet of a new life, and
only I am living it."

– *Arthur Cravan*

I let myself in quietly so I wouldn't wake the dog. It was midday and the flat was still and empty. I stood on the threshold to our bedroom for a few moments, taking in the leaden silence. The only sound came from a fly battering itself against the window pane.

I felt funny being there when I shouldn't be. The place looked different, too, and it wasn't just the light that was unfamiliar. It almost felt as if this wasn't our flat at all, but a stranger's. I picked a fag end out of the ashtray on the mantelpiece and sniffed for Cathy's breath on the stub. In the kitchen she'd left her cereal bowl unwashed by the sink, and now I ran my finger slowly around the rim, over the flaky residue of breakfast.

I changed out of my suit and packed some things into a bag. Clothes, my notebook, medication, various other items. I hesitated over the picture of Cathy. For a moment I wondered whether it would be best not to take it. I stared at the picture long and hard, and then I poked it into my wallet. I knew immediately that was a mistake.

It all happened just as I had planned it, until I turned to go. There, resolute in the doorway, sat the dog. He knew something was up. He was staring at me with such curious intensity that my head swirled with guilt. As I stepped over the dog I tried to avoid his unblinking black eyes and their terrible glare of accusation.

I had to put a bowl of Chum down for him so he wouldn't scratch after me at the door when I let myself out. I dropped my latch key into a drain round the back of Budgens. Then I walked to a lay-by near the bypass and stuck out my thumb. I'd known for a long time that I had to do it, but that's how I finally got away. I didn't leave a note.

* * *

I was there for about an hour, I suppose, before someone stopped. The car, which seemed to be listing over to one side, pulled up jerkily and the engine cut out. I wasn't sure if it was stopping for me, or if it had just happened to break down.

I opened the passenger door and looked inside: a man in his forties with a gold earring, wearing a vest and correctional glasses with round lenses tinted different colours. As he cranked the ignition, to anticipate my gratitude he said straight off:

"It's all right. Used to do a bit of hitching meself – know what it's like, mate."

I couldn't get in because the seat was occupied by a quantity of Lucozade bottles and packets of Superkings. Once he had the engine started he set about clearing all the stuff away.

"Make yourself useful," he said, "You can empty that." He handed me the ashtray from the dashboard. I shook the contents out over the long grass, and the wind took the fag butts in a cloud of dust and scattered them into the ditch. Funnily enough, it had been at a similar spot on the M40 that I had disposed of the earthly remains of my father nearly three years before: on a motorway verge just like this one I had watched him join the mud at the roadside in a brief flourish of white ash. As I got into the car and slid the ashtray into its recess, it occurred to me that the strange symmetry of this had something of a portent about it.

"Where you going?" the man said.

"To Dover."

"The ferry is it?"

"That's right."

"M- m- m- m- m- m- m- m- muh," he said, appearing to go into some kind of seizure, "'scuse me, I've got a bit of a ster- ster- ster- ster—" his mouth yawned open wide, but no sound came out for a long while.

"Bit of a stutter," he said at last.

I shot him a flinty look. As we merged with the traffic on the motorway, I considered telling him to let me out on the hard shoulder. But I knew it might be hours before I got another lift.

"I was saying, I can drop you off at the terminal if you like, cos I'm headed for Deal. Come all the way from Bristol today, taken me just over an hour. She goes like a beauty, this." His hand gave the dashboard a light caress. "N-reg. Rover," he said. "Got her last week. How much, you reckon?"

The car smelt like it had gone off, and the suspension certainly was lazy on the one side. I didn't value it at much, but I got the impression he wanted me to suggest a vastly inflated price, and since he was giving me a lift it would perhaps be the right thing to do.

"Five hundred?"

There was a moment's silence.

"Yeah," he said.

I watched the M25 reel by and I felt a strange twinge of nostalgia at the thought that I would never see it again.

"Look at that beauty," he said, tapping the speedometer. "Seventy, that is, and I've not even opened her up yet."

I tried to make sounds of admiration.

"Course I shouldn't go any faster, cos the steering wobbles a bit over seventy," he said.

He reached over for an opened pack of Superkings and managed to pull one out and light it with one hand. When he drew on it, he immediately started wheezing great gouts of blue smoke into the car. With each wrenching cough, his convulsions sent the car veering across the road, while between hacks he was steady long enough to swerve back into the lane. We were tossed first this way, then that, and I caught myself gripping on to the door handle for dear life.

Strange, this instinct for self-preservation. It made me think of my father again. The nurses had told me he'd fought until the very end – funny that, since he had made it perfectly clear, right from when I was a boy, that the end couldn't come soon enough.

As the car veered towards the central reservation, I released my grip on the door handle. Watching the crash barrier coming up to meet us, I folded my hands in my lap and relaxed. There are worse ways to go.

But by now the man had regained control of the car and his face was fading to a normal colour.

"The wife passed away three weeks ago."

He squashed his cigarette end into the ashtray and lit another one. The old cigarette wasn't quite out, and a thread of smoke extended from it up towards the rear-view mirror.

"She – wuh- wuh- wuh- wuh—"

He took a drag on his Superking, rearranged himself in the driver's seat and started again.

"She wuh- wuh- wuh- wuh—" he was making frantic little stirring gestures in the air with his free hand, the one with the fag in it.

"Wuh- wuh—" it was no use, he just couldn't get the word out.

He put the fag in his mouth again and glanced out of the side window at traffic going the other way. A long moment passed, and then suddenly, as if he were trying to catch himself off-guard, he was at it again.

"She – she wuh- wuh—"

He appeared to be trapped in a strange limbo somewhere between words, and I could see the pressure building up inside him, the panic opening his eyes wide. After a while it began to sound like gagging.

Things carried on in this vein for some time, until it struck me there was something ridiculous and unsettling about the repetitiveness of this man, the monotony.

"Wuh- wuh- wuh—" he said.

At last, out of frustration, I think, he gave a short, sharp kick at the accelerator, and the car lurched violently forwards.

The steering did indeed begin to wobble, but it seemed to do the trick – it shook loose the words that had been clotting in his gullet. They came out all at once, in a yell:

"*She was only thirty-seven!*" he shouted.

He nodded grimly to anticipate my disbelief.

"Asthma attack, only thirty-seven."

He took another drag on his cigarette, but it had burnt down, so he went to light another one. In the lengthy silence that followed as he fumbled to spark the lighter, the car drifted towards the verge, the lane markers drumming insistently against the tyres. The man's thumb grated nervily at the flint.

"Yeah, thirty-seven years old," he said at last with a deep intake of smoke. "That was a shock, I tell you. Left me with—" he reached behind him to feel around for something on the back seat. "Left me with three babies," he said, handing me his wallet, which he'd flipped open. In the plastic window was a photograph of three little boys.

"I can't work, so I've got to bring 'em up by meself on disability. Ain't easy that."

An articulated lorry drew abreast of us on the inside lane and began slowly to overtake.

"Can't even sing any more," he went on. "That's what hurts the most. I just had a lump taken off me throat. Used to do pubs and clubs, took the guitar everywhere. Even got it in the back here."

He directed my attention to the back with a jerk of his thumb. There was a white plastic guitar case wedged into the space between the seats.

"Ovation Matrix. Nineteen seventy-one. Only thirty of 'em made. Take it with me everywhere. Course, I can't play it any more – not since I broke the hand."

He let go of the steering wheel for a moment and turned his palm over for me. His first three fingers were swollen and twisted at the joints.

"I – yer- yer- yer—" and he was off again.

I gazed out of the window and tried to ignore him. The gagging went on in spasms with the regularity of a machine. By the time he'd got over it we were coming into Dover and, thank God, he had forgotten what he was trying to say. The stuttering trailed off into silence, and he swallowed down the rest of the words, leaving the sentence hanging unfinished in the air between us. The cigarette he had resting in the ashtray must have slipped his mind because he lit another one, and smoked it through clenched teeth. Then he put it out, half-finished, with a sigh.

He stopped the car at the terminal, and the engine spluttered out. I thanked him and walked towards the ticket office, leaving the car and the wheezy stuttering of the dead ignition somewhere behind.

I'm sure you've had one of those days where everything seems to go wrong. But imagine, if you can, a whole life where nothing goes your way. If you're going to understand me, this is where you'll have to begin: a lifetime of umbrellas buckling inside out in the wind; heaps of dog shit puréeing softly beneath each footfall; shopping discharged in all directions from the tatters of a prolapsed polythene bag; parking tickets spread out like a fan of playing cards under the windscreen wipers; Jehovah's Witnesses on the doorstep day after day; a war of attrition with insurance salesmen and old ladies collecting for charity; running sores around the runny nose of a perpetual cold; and the mere *idea* of haemorrhoids at my age…

Over a lifetime things like this really start to take their toll, let me tell you. There comes a point when it dawns on you that things aren't ever going to get better, and most people surrender all hope then and there – it's easier if you don't fight it. Stop struggling, keep taking the pills, start taking pride in office-desk paraphernalia, discover the healing power of television, let your mind slip out of focus, lie back and take it. But there is another way. You do have a choice.

I distinctly remember the moment I first came across the name of Arthur Cravan. It was on the train somewhere between Streatham and Loughborough Junction, just after a gang of baseball-capped adolescents had filed into the carriage and started to harass an elderly woman. Everyone in the compartment produced dog-eared paperbacks and became engrossed. For the past few weeks I had been reading a book about suicide on the way to the office – I found it used to put me in the right state of mind for the day ahead. As I slid out the bookmark that morning, right there on the page underneath was his name. From the very first sentence Cravan's story captivated me, and I was never quite the same again. That's when all this began – everything that's happened since I can trace back to that moment on the train.

I read that by way of introduction he gave new acquaintances a business card with the inscription: "Arthur Cravan, captain of industry, sailor of the Pacific, muleteer, orange-picker in California, snake charmer, hotel thief, nephew of Oscar Wilde, lumberjack in the great forests, ex-champion boxer of France, godson of the Queen's Chancellor, chauffeur in Berlin, burglar, etc. etc. etc." The mysterious Cravan claimed, "I am all things, all people and all animals," but because of his reluctance to decide who he really was, he very nearly became nobody.

Somewhere along the carriage the old woman's whimpering went up a notch amidst a gargling of delinquent laughter. I turned the page and read on.

Cravan was the ultimate self-made man and, being his own creator, he reserved the right to unmake himself, to unpick his existence stitch by stitch. His was a life dedicated to wanton destruction, to the extent that he elevated scandal and humiliation into an art form. In this endeavour, Cravan turned out to be his own greatest artefact, and in the revolutions that followed throughout the twentieth century he was the inspiration for successive generations who sought to reshape the world by tearing it apart.

Leaving nothing but destruction behind him, Cravan would surely have slipped unnoticed into the obscurity of the past if it hadn't been for an infamous movement in modern art which claimed him for a figurehead. The book's author identified Cravan's life – and his strange death – as the point in history at which art began to strangle itself.

I was so absorbed by Cravan's tale that I missed my stop, overshooting to King's Cross, and I got into work half an hour late. No one seemed to notice. I wondered if they would notice if I never turned up again. I wondered if they would bat an eyelid if I got up from my desk, walked over to the corner by the fax, and began to feed myself into the shredder.

The tedium at the office that day was profound and re-lentless, and periodically my wandering mind returned to Cravan. In the following months he became a regular fixture in my thoughts, recurring in daydreams and odd fantasies, and soon those fantasies occupied every idle moment spent sitting on the toilet or watching the darkness beyond the windows of the underground train. I realized he had become an all-consuming obsession when I started spending my lunch hour in the library scouring books and old newspapers for any mention of him.

It didn't take long for Cravan to impinge on my home life too, and soon enough he had moved in permanently with me and my girlfriend. He became my companion throughout the long nights of insomnia as Cathy snored next to me, and when my mind wandered at the dinner table Cravan was always there to meet me. Poor Cathy, she had no idea of the black thoughts that took shape as she slept, she knew nothing of the plan that was slowly forming in my brain. Of course on the surface there was no sign that anything was wrong. In fact – apart from the time Cathy and I were courting, and the romantic holiday we spent in Anglesey the previous summer – I enjoyed these last months of our relationship more than any in our three years together, perhaps because I already knew how it would all end.

The ferry was crowded with throngs of people who felt obliged to stand on deck just because the sun was out. They huddled round, grimacing against the cold wind and squinting up at the sky, which was pale and cloudless.

Booze cruisers. Down-at-heel salesmen. Ugly young families in matching tracksuits. Hordes of smugly excitable students from the University of Leeds. A package tour of middle-aged ladies with improbable perms. And a gang of teenage East European lads sitting angled away from each other on the orange plastic seats, all of them smoking with such determination that it suggested it was their first time. I sat at the back of the boat to get the best view of the country disappearing.

A family group came to stand against the railings in front of me with the express intention of obstructing my field of vision. I eyed the corpulent infant as he hoisted himself up on the guard rails. His father, stepping back to take a picture, trod heavily on my foot. The flash didn't go off the first try, and the man brooded over the camera for a time. Meanwhile his son clambered further up the railings: it looked as if he was about to throw himself over. His father lined him up in the viewfinder. This time the flash went off and the man got the child by the collar of his coat and pulled him back down to the deck.

It was then that I allowed myself a little cry, sitting there. With all the excitement I had forgotten to take my tablet at lunchtime, and now, out on the deck, things were catching up with me. I made no attempt to hide the misery. One woman came to sit down nearby, but then, thinking better of it, she moved quickly away. I held nothing back, I let it all out – sobs, whimpers, snivelling moans, the lot – and I didn't give a damn who saw.

When the moment passed I wandered around a bit, went inside and around the snack bars. I saw lorry drivers amassed in lines, blowing smoke over the one-armed bandits, row upon row of hangdog faces turning red and yellow in the flickering lights. Along the windows people sprawled in the chairs looked absently into the salt-encrusted glass. In the shop a great number of people were browsing out of sheer boredom, prodding the distended bellies of cuddly toys, gingerly inspecting the magnum bottles of perfume, pooling their resources to purchase a carton of cigarettes and a litre of London Dry. Their restless eyes, pinched with shame and defeat, then moved reluctantly towards the slabs of chocolate displayed on racks by the checkout queue.

I wandered back to the observation deck and came to rest against the railings, to consider the water below. It was a long way down, there'd be no chance of rescue.

That night I was standing by a deserted tollbooth that guarded the mouth of the A26 near Calais. Haloes of fog were gathering around the lights overhead, and my sign was beginning to wilt in the damp air. I was staring along the length of the road, down the corridor made by the lights, into the darkness where they came to an end. It was only six o'clock, but there was no traffic at all.

Hours passed, and nothing happened other than the slow, tortuous tightening of the cold, and the gradual spreading of the numbness. The darkness sprawled all around like the pitch walls of a vast pit, and the black sky seemed as dense as earth piled on remorselessly by the shovelful from somewhere high overhead.

At some point I was joined by a nagging voice in my head, and as the evening dragged on it grew in prominence. Soon I found myself concentrating on the cold, taking note of every ache and pain, clinging on to anything that might distract me from that voice, but still it wittered on. Since I couldn't stifle it altogether, it had to be endured, like a bitter drunk pontificating at a wedding.

What the bloody hell are you doing? The voice was saying.

Go back. It's not yet too late to go back…

After another hour, having lost all sensation in my body, I started walking along the road. It was a futile effort from the outset. I headed miserably into the descending mist, leaving the glow of the motorway lights somewhere behind. The only life I came across for a long while was a group of shell-suited youths in baseball caps who were smoking reefers in a burnt-out bus shelter.

Then, not very far along the road, I came to a standstill.

Fatigue overtook me, and I saw no sense in going further. The road ahead stretched on into the darkness, there was no way out. I turned and traipsed back, crossing the road to avoid the kids smoking reefers. As I crept past, the spark of a cigarette lighter caught them silhouetted in the graffiti-misted perspex. Soaking my shoes in the wet grass along the verge, I wandered back to the lonely patch of light before the empty motorway. The place had a strange atmosphere of familiarity about it.

I found a deserted toilet behind the outbuildings of the tollbooth, unrolled my sleeping bag on the concrete under a urinal, and lay down to get some sleep.

I spent the next two days there by the tollbooth. I spent so many hours with my thumb out that I forgot what the purpose of it was. I eventually abandoned all hope of being offered a lift, and just stood there like a redundant signpost, watching all manner of vehicles drive past. I became deeply mesmerized by the procession of faces, glimpsed for an instant through dirty windscreens.

Once I saw a head shaking in acknowledgement of me, a hand half-lifted from the steering wheel to make some slight apologetic gesture. My spirits soared.

On one occasion someone gave me the thumbs up as he went by, and I was left smiling to myself for a long time.

Once a white van actually appeared to be pulling over for me. I ran after it dragging my luggage behind, and just as I reached for the handle on the passenger door I saw reflected in the wing mirror a grin breaking across the face of the driver. The tyres spun a few times before they gripped the tarmac, and the engine roared as he pulled away into the distance.

It should come as no surprise that by the second day I was taking it all quite personally. Each car, appearing from the profound emptiness of the road, each lorry emerging from the silent tedium, inflicted a new humiliation. All of my awareness was focused upon their long, almost endless approach. The cycle of their engines reverberated through me, the pattern of changing gears dropping down through my soul. Through the windscreens I watched each head passing pitilessly by, imperiously po-faced in profile like the plaster bust of a little Napoleon.

What finally tore it was that last car. Barrelling out of the fog it came: a lime-green Deux Chevaux pitching from side to side on its elastic suspension, the panic whine of its two-stroke engine as it slowed for the barrier sounding like a bomb falling out of the sky. A 2CV – the car that, legend has it, is incapable of passing a hitch-hiker by.

It's not possible that the driver didn't see me there, because I fell to my knees almost across his path and he had to swerve to clear me. The car's acceleration was so puny that I ran abreast of the vehicle for several seconds after it pulled away from the barrier, landing a few blows with the flat of my hand against the bodywork. I nearly buckled one of the wheel arches, but it made no impression on the driver, who didn't hesitate for a moment.

I flung my cardboard sign after him and it wheeled once in the air and then plunged into the ditch at the roadside. Then I marched off in a ravening fury. My guts were screwed tight in my chest, my tendons drawn taut, muscles clenched and trembling in anger, the pulpy matter of the brain pulsing, the eyes rolling over in their orbits, emotions raging off the scale of sensation. I spat every kind of obscenity at the concrete verge, the barbed wire. I kicked a petrified flake of road kill across two lanes.

It didn't last, that feeling. The fury turned quickly flaccid and subsided. My organs unravelled their knots and gorged themselves fat on self-pity.

I wandered lost in a wasteland of industrial installations where chimney stacks spumed yellow vapours to feed the dismal sky. From darkened hangars there came a chugging of vast machines, rusty dump trucks crawling from their orifices.

How do they go on living? I asked out loud, addressing myself to the corrugated iron wall streaked with rust water, the spooled miles of razor wire and anything else that would listen.

How have they made it this far?

It was around that moment that one of the trucks turned out of a plant exit and pulled up next to me with a hiss of pneumatics. For the first few seconds I really didn't understand what the driver meant: he was a heavy-set man with a Freddie Mercury moustache, and he was making hand signals. There was still an edge of murder in me, and a stray remark, composed in an earlier and particularly sour moment, fluttered back into my head. I filled my lungs to scream it and looked around under the truck tyres for a piece of wood to brandish or something to throw.

The man had reached over to open the passenger door and in a gruff smoker's voice was saying: "*Hé! Où vas-tu mec?*"

I stared out of the passenger window at the outskirts of Calais dropping away, the clapboard hypermarkets and discount booze wholesalers giving way to the sprawling acres of nothingness along the A26. I rebuffed the driver's attempts at small talk and we sat in sullen silence for the duration of the journey to Paris.

The Cimetière du Père Lachaise covers forty-four hectares in the twentieth *arrondissement* of Paris. It is more like a miniature city than a graveyard. The tombs are great buildings, some of them two storeys in height, carved out of slabs of dark stone, each of them constructed according to the elaborate designs of an architect, each of them furnished according to the peculiar tastes of the deceased. The tombs stand in lines, divided by avenues into blocks in a vast grid system like Milton Keynes.

Oscar Wilde's final resting place is at the corner of block 89, near the perimeter wall, and I came to pay my respects just as Arthur Cravan had done so many years before. The tomb's monumental sandstone face, sheer and smooth, has the grandeur of an Egyptian pyramid. A ten-foot art-deco angel thrusts out of the stonework, sculpted with squared edges, the lines of its wings converging in false perspective to give a sense of speed. It resembles the kind of silver figurine that can be found stuck to the bonnets of vintage British cars. But it's a castrated angel, hacked at by moral crusaders in the decades after Wilde's death.

When he first arrived in Paris in the winter of 1909, Arthur Cravan found that his blood tie with Oscar Wilde was his most bankable asset in the pursuit of literary fame, and he continued to trade off it for the rest of his life. The epithet "nephew of Oscar Wilde" would follow his name wherever it appeared. Those who knew Cravan in Paris acknowledged that this was more than pretence – he had much in common with Wilde. Blaise Cendrars was struck by Cravan's "unstable mind, ruled by vanity, ambition, greed, lust, the craving for fame and scandal, as well as a vicious congenital childishness – the inevitable price of being the beautiful nephew of Oscar Wilde!"

The rest of Cravan's family were ashamed to be related to a convicted sodomite, and they did all they could to distance themselves from Wilde – including changing their surname. So it was to spite them – and their petty Puritanism – that Cravan embraced everything that his uncle represented. He went so far as to hint at an even closer connection still: "There is an unspoken mystery surrounding my birth," Cravan wrote darkly. "It has always led me to wonder: might Oscar Wilde be my true father?"

Père Lachaise is the most visited cemetery in France, drawing even more visitors than the vast graveyards of the Somme that contain the innumerable dead of the First World War. Tour groups traipsed listlessly in all directions, snaking Indian file amongst the tombstones. A throng of drivers had gathered to kick their heels and smoke cigarettes as their coaches slumbered in ranks by the crematorium, waiting for their tourist loads. I wandered past them, ankle-deep in fallen leaves.

Towards the ancient centre of the cemetery the precise pattern of avenues began to deteriorate into a labyrinthine cobweb of paths that spiralled in on themselves. The great tombs here were subsiding, their inscriptions effaced by a rime of black mould, the lids of some split and staved in.

I became disoriented. The pathways meandered aimlessly, then tapered into sudden switchbacks or crumbling flights of steps that descended into a dark chaos of graves. Somewhere here were the corpses of people like Ledru-Rollin – the heroic defender of republican ideals against the extremists of the Revolution – Molière, Chopin and Marcel Proust. Their tombs have sunk into the damp earth, or have been consumed by weeds, or have just lapsed into obscurity.

As the paths dwindled away, overspilling with rubble, and as the slimy mouldering walls of the tombs drew in closer, I felt the panic mounting inside my skull. None of the other visitors had penetrated this far, there hadn't been a sign of another living person for a long time. I hurried on, taking turns at random, looking for the way out. And as I came full circle to the same familiar snarls of bramble, the same ruined graves, I began to imagine I had wandered into a closed circuit of pathways lost to the world.

Then I came across an intersection of trails. Tendrils of incense uncoiled across the tomb tops. The cold afternoon air reeked of sandalwood, and there was the strange refrain of a bell or a wind chime coming from somewhere nearby. As I went on, I became aware of a low warbling that seemed to come from all directions, that seemed to emanate from inside the verdigris-slathered walls of the tombs themselves. Around the next corner I stumbled into the midst of a crowd of tourists. They were kneeling at the foot of a tomb adorned with tea lights and great welts of fresh flowers in bouquets. These people were consumed by a hushed reverence, the only sound was a murmur of sobbed incantations. Taking pride of place at the centre of the shrine was the sleeve of a record by The Doors depicting Jim Morrison pouting like the Messiah.

I backed off. I walked away as quickly as I could, but the sandalwood stench followed me wherever I went. At every turn I ran into tourists consulting fold-out maps and asking me where Morrison's grave was. The first few I just ignored, but – thinking better of it – the next group to flag me over I misdirected into the inwardly collapsing vortex at the centre of Père Lachaise. This had a tremendous balming effect on my mind.

The Morrison thing made perfect sense, though – it all fitted in. He might as well have been Cravan in another incarnation, just another corpse in the time-honoured tradition of the poet-visionary taken from us by premature death. A seedy overdose in a bath and Morrison somehow crossed over into sainthood. We like to think he died for us: he died rather than carry on into the mediocrity of middle age. He was by no means the first to seal his immortality by capping a reckless life with an untimely death. He followed the template of Arthur Rimbaud, the original hellraiser, sexual experimenter and drug-addled martyr.

Rimbaud was an idol of Cravan's. He was the reason why as an adolescent Cravan decided to become a poet. The myth of Rimbaud was the lure that drew Cravan irresistibly to Paris as soon as he came of age. And perhaps it was the example of Rimbaud that inspired Cravan to look for fame by flirting with death, rather than by writing half-decent poetry.

Born Fabian Avenarius Lloyd, the young Cravan pursued his ambition to seek fame as a poet with the obstinate single-mindedness that characterized his strange and short-lived existence. Fabian had been expelled from numerous secondary schools in Switzerland and England for his glaring disrespect for authority. His teachers went to increasingly desperate lengths to rein in his rebellious nature but, despite their efforts, institutional discipline made no impression at all. Finally Fabian was ejected from a Birmingham military college for bending his schoolmaster over his knee during a maths lesson and beating him with the heel of a shoe.

When he arrived in Paris, Fabian sought to make a name for himself by any means necessary. His first act was to rechristen himself under a pseudonym: this was the end of Fabian Lloyd the delinquent, and the beginning of "Arthur Cravan", poet and provocateur. With his new name Cravan seemed to take on a new identity, the first of many. So began a career of deceptions and confidence tricks, the fortuitous rise and catastrophic fall of a man who hid behind disguises and tall stories.

Cravan's life seems to have been deliberately conceived to test the sanity of his biographers, to thwart all attempts to pin him down. He left so many suspect clues, so many false trails and red herrings, so little in the way of concrete fact, that it is practically impossible to tie up the loose ends of his chaotic trajectory, or salvage something of the real man from the skins he had discarded, the disparate identities, the apocryphal stories that comprise the legend of Cravan.

That there is a legend at all, not to mention the cult that has sprung up around him, is perhaps due to the tantalizing indications Cravan gave that he had anticipated the strange course of his life. Indeed, considering all the evidence, it's difficult not to imagine his story unfolded according to some devious and overarching strategy to fix his name in history. All these indications can be found in the auspicious beginnings of his career: consider the obsessive commitment he gave to his work on his arrival in Paris, the all-engrossing self-confidence that drove him to doorstep every literary academic in the city and demand that they listen to his poetry. But above all there was the telltale element of duplicity in his fervent self-promotion.

In a letter written shortly after his arrival in Paris, Cravan declared himself on the brink of fame. He told his mother that he had devised a novel way to launch his career, for which he would only need one hundred francs of her money. "The scheme is quite simple and wonderful and no one has ever thought of it before," he wrote. "I will fake my own death and then publish a book as a posthumous work." Perhaps he had learnt from the example of Rimbaud. In any case, Cravan understood that premature death was the easiest and most certain means for an artist to gain status and, more importantly, to sell some copies. He didn't carry out his scheme – at least not quite yet. But the mere fact of it is telling, since it carried an implicit acknowledgement that his poetry was atrocious. Cravan was a talentless poet but an inspired publicist, and in this respect he set the precedent for the course of modern art ever since.

A supercilious waiter placed the bill on the table in front of me, and then next to it, as an afterthought, my espresso. The Bal Bullier café is all that's left of the great Bullier ballroom that stood on the corner of the Avenue de l'Observatoire before it burned to the ground in the Thirties. Looking around me, it was hard to imagine that this place had ever teemed with the chic and affluent of Montparnasse, or that Cravan had come here every Friday night to dance the tango and rub shoulders with celebrities.

They hadn't troubled to arrange tables on the pavement, because it was too cold to sit outside. There was a smattering of customers within the glazed terrace, but it was still too early for lunch and the place was dead. Without touching the espresso I sat there for a long time, soaking up the tawdry atmosphere. A pair of fifty-something ladies were discoursing at a table by the windows. I watched cigarettes burning down in their hands, occasionally to be waved in a conversational flourish. In the corner, by a potted palm, an elderly husband and wife were looking past each other through bottle-thick spectacles, all topics of conversation long since exhausted. Outside the rain pattered drearily against the awning.

I looked more closely at the bill, to make certain I'd read it correctly. Then I opened my wallet and emptied out the contents on the table top. I spent a while sorting the English coins and the French coins into separate piles. I did the same with the paper money. Then I went through the receipts and business cards, screwing them up one by one and depositing them in the ashtray. It was while I was doing this that I came across the piece of newspaper. It had been so long since I'd read it that I'd forgotten it was even there. The discovery of this frayed and dog-eared shred of paper brought with it a potent sensation of bitterness – but at the same time an odd nostalgia. It was a review of my novel.

There had been a time when I had dreams, when I had aspirations. There had been a time when I had a sense of a future. It is ironic that this misconception should have sprung from my infirmity. Perhaps it is apt that my literary ambitions turned out to be just another symptom of my illness.

In the summer of my sixteenth year, my mother took an overdose of my father's pills and was found dead in the en-suite bathroom. Consequently, for the most part of my adolescent life I was confined to my room. For months on end I languished in a sickbed, seized with a terrible affliction of morbid idleness. I couldn't muster the enthusiasm to get up, and to cope with the inexpressible tedium I started writing.

I started with journals, pouring my frustration and my loathing into lengthy tracts of unrestrained prose. Gradually, as I grew more confident, I moved on to poetry – the Sylvia Plath kind, seething with pubescent rage and obtrusive metaphors. I never showed these writings to a soul, but for some reason I got it into my head that I was good. From then on I told myself that writing would be my thing. One day I would write a great book, I would become a successful novelist.

It was nearly ten years before I got round to writing that novel. Despite all that had happened in the meantime, the idea still lingered in the back of my head that I had a calling, that it was my destiny to achieve distinction as a writer. I started writing the book at weekends and in the evenings after work. I devoted every free moment to it, and it proved an effective distraction from the fact that I had no friends and no life to speak of. The book comfortably displaced the social and sexual vacancies in my pitiful existence. The book gave my days meaning, in its gradual progress I could measure my own contentment. For as long as it lasted, life was good, I was practically happy. But then one day I found that I had finished it.

"*Quelque chose à manger, monsieur?*" It was the waiter, standing over me. "You want somezing else, monsieur?"

I covered the piece of folded newspaper with my fingers and told him no. The waiter stood there a moment longer looking at me and then looking at the coins and the bill on the table. Then, reluctantly, he moved away. Behind the bar, two other waiters in immaculate whites were polishing glasses and eyeing me over the counter. When I returned their stare the two of them averted their faces in unison.

I had hoped in my own way to find Arthur Cravan. But sitting there in the sparse remains of the Bal Bullier, I was beginning to wonder if there was anything left of him. It had taken barely one morning traipsing around Montparnasse to discover that his trail had long gone cold. The landmarks of Cravan's life in Paris seemed to have been systematically removed, and going around the city, following the clues he left, I began to despair that anything at all survived.

Cravan had established himself here in what was once the bohemian centre of Paris. He had resided not far from the Bal Bullier at the convergence of wide tree-lined boulevards that extend plumb into the distance with an unwavering geometric precision. The Avenue de l'Observatoire is the long boulevard that connects the Jardins du Luxembourg with the Observatory, and Cravan's apartment was found at number 29, near the intersection of the Boulevards Saint-Michel and Port-Royal. These were the lodgings belonging to Renée Bouchet, the secretary of a respected art collector, a local beauty seven years Cravan's senior who was known for her elegant wardrobe, and rumoured to have slept with all of Montparnasse. These lodgings became Cravan's permanent address when he insinuated himself into her life, managing to take a residence and a lover in one fell swoop.

Even though Cravan's elder brother Otho dismissed Renée as little more than a sheer sexual necessity, theirs seems to have been a relationship of tenderness and intimacy that lasted throughout Cravan's life in Paris, and that persisted even after they had exhausted Renée's inheritance. In fact the relationship continued in their secret correspondence until the very end.

That morning I had found that not only their apartment at number 29, but the entire block, had been utterly obliterated. The buildings had been cleared to make room for the Port-Royal Métro station, which is sunk below the level of the pavement, leaving a dark hole, fringed with sharpened iron railings and barbed wire to prevent suicides from leaping onto the tracks below. Where Cravan lived during his Paris years, nothing remains but a gaping void.

The same goes for the studio of Kees van Dongen, where Cravan had first encountered Renée. It seems that Van Dongen – the most important of the Fauvist painters – was the only artist in Paris whose work Cravan didn't loathe, and one of the few people whom he could call a friend. At number 5 Rue Denfert-Rochereau, the workshop was within striking distance of Cravan's flat, and he could often be found here, whiling away the long afternoons of a life of idleness. Today there's no trace of it – the building was levelled in the Fifties to accommodate a medical school that has since fallen into an unsanitary state of disrepair.

The morning had been a dead loss: I'd found nothing that brought me closer to Cravan. Now the lacklustre state of the Bullier was the final straw. Prints of the place in its glory days hung over the stairs to the toilet, a desultory commemoration of its decline. They showed men in top hats dancing the tango with corseted women, ostrich feathers lolling from their heads. In 1912, when Cravan had been a regular here, the Bal Bullier had not only been the venue of choice for the in-crowd of Montparnasse, it also played host to international celebrities during their visits to the city. It is likely that it was across the nightclub floor at the Bullier that Cravan had glimpsed Jack Johnson for the first time.

The heavyweight boxing champion was in exile from the United States for his ignominies with white women, and he was now touring Europe to stage high-profile exhibition fights. Although he was past his prime, Johnson possessed a princely aura, and wherever he went the crowds parted for him, the ladies fawned. Cravan might have watched him dance the tango here, his diamond rings scattering splinters of light across the walls and ceiling. "After Poe, Whitman and Emerson he is the greatest glory of America," Cravan declared. "If there is a revolution I shall fight to have him crowned King of the United States." Soon the trajectories of the two men would collide, and Johnson would play a decisive role in the turning point of Cravan's life. But that night at the Bullier they were strangers, Johnson a celebrity and Cravan not yet anyone.

After this encounter Cravan became a face at the Bullier, and acquaintances noted that as the weeks passed he developed a taste for lavish outfits and a keen appetite for the ladies, to whom he boasted that he was a skilful boxer. His ungainly bearing straightened, and the physique that he had carried so awkwardly now took on an impression of nobility, even arrogance. He began to keep extravagant company, making an avant-garde trio with the poet Blaise Cendrars and the painter Robert Delaunay. On Friday nights at the Bullier, the three of them would dance the tango in bizarre and colourful costumes that made the men resemble abstract artworks. According to Cendrars, Cravan dressed all in black, with obscene tattoos showing through holes cut out of his trousers. Sometimes he would adorn himself with smears of lurid colour by wiping his behind on Delaunay's freshly painted canvases.

The atmosphere in the Bullier today is much more sedate. I noticed that one of the waiters had come out from behind the bar and had taken up a position by the entrance door, where he now stood with his arms crossed, watching me. I looked down at the table top, at the scrap of dog-eared paper I'd found in my wallet. When I unfolded it, it sent up a tiny breath of fine dust. Between my fingers I gently smoothed out the creases. This was a page torn from a parochial newspaper, a review of my novel. It was for moments just like this that I had saved it. The reviewer, who gave no name, wrote:

It is a requirement of this job to read every book featured for the Gazette's *Arts page from cover to cover, no matter how hackneyed, tedious and offensive. But never have I resented the time wasted quite as much as the five hours it took me to get through this self-indulgent wodge of ordure. Five precious hours of my life that I could have spent washing dishes, clipping my toenails or staring into space! Quite why the author thinks anyone should be interested in this story of a man who discovers he has an identical twin is a mystery, but evidently he is so sure of its import that he has himself financed the vanity publication of one thousand copies.*

Born Unlucky narrates the tale of Clifford, a suicidal binman who happens to stumble across long-lost twin brother Frank, a self-made millionaire and raconteur extra-ordinaire, whom women find irresistible. In a plot which strains credulity as well as patience, Clifford kills his success-ful brother and assumes his identity. For a few weeks he lives the high life he has always dreamt about, before somehow managing to bankrupt his brother's business and alienate everyone around him.

Clearly revelling in this riches-to-rags conceit, the writer seems to offer the reader one petty morsel of satisfaction in the final suicide scene. But adding insult to injury, in the end his protagonist doesn't go through with it, and instead finds "something to live for". This conclusion seemed to me preposterous after having been brought to the verge of suicide myself by such nightmarishly unmitigated dross.

I made myself read it through again, slowly, taking it all in, until my spirits could plunge no further. Behind the counter now I sensed the waiters were gathering themselves for something. I smoked another cigarette and looked obstinately out of the window at the grey street. When I noticed the waiter by the door start towards me on his solemn approach, I quickly knocked back the cold espresso, left the right money on the table and walked out.

I went back over the road, walking across four lanes during a lull in the traffic to the fading Fifties' prefab of the Jean Sarrailh medical school. I went in through the front entrance, where the reflective polymer was peeling in strips from the windows, between the BacoFoil ventilation tubes spooling out of the air ducts, under the name of the building that was mounted on yellowed urinal tiling with the telltale gaps of missing plastic lettering. In the basement was the "Restaurant Bullier", a sterile-plastic canteen named in honour of the illustrious establishment opposite. The resemblance ended there.

I carried a plate of curry and rice from the till to a plastic table and ate it while I watched the sluggish charlady mopping herself into a corner of the lino.

The glamour and notoriety of visitors such as Jack Johnson no doubt had much to do with the vogue for boxing that erupted in Paris at the time. The new style had none of the brutality that had previously brought the sport into disrepute: since fights were now judged by a referee, the object was no longer to drub an opponent senseless but to outclass him through technical prowess and fancy footwork. For a brief time, boxing was the height of fashion and, having seen the adulation that Papa Jack received, Cravan decided there and then that he too would become a boxer.

The Rue du Faubourg du Temple is a narrow road that crosses the canal at République, where sightseeing *bateaux mouches* lurch downwards through the stepped locks towards the Seine. The road winds its way up the hill. Its cracked pavements, where Parisian ladies bring their lapdogs to defecate, are lined with tiny shops, from halal butchers to exorbitant shoe stores and Chinese herbalists. At number 99 there is a solid wooden gateway firmly locked to the street. I had to wait outside for half an hour before it opened to let a car out and I was able to slip inside. Beyond the gate I found a collection of whitewashed ateliers, home now to small architects' offices and warehouses for trendy clothing labels. Nothing remains of the Club Cluny, where Cravan spent so many hours in training.

In a local library I had come across a faded sepia photograph of the club's masters and students, so old that the enamel was flaking away. They were arranged in ranks for the picture: scrawny boys sat cross-legged at the front, then lines of pigeon-chested young men wearing stripy singlets and handlebar moustaches. They looked stiff, like men standing against the wall to be shot. The students were all wiry little men, with the exception of Cravan, who stood conspicuously in the middle of the back row, a head and shoulders taller than the rest.

In March 1910 Cravan entered the 8th Boxing Championship Meeting organized by the French Federation of Boxing Societies. This turned out to be one of the most uneventful competitions in the history of boxing. Plagued by clerical cock-ups and an outbreak of illness amongst the competitors, it was in fact an utter washout from which Cravan was the only person to derive any satisfaction. His first opponent was overcome by pre-fight nerves and forfeited the match. The following two fights were called in Cravan's favour when his rivals fell victim to administrative incompetence and were directed to the wrong venue. Cravan progressed through the tournament unchallenged and found himself in the final rounds. His semi-final opponent, Gaumier, sprained his ankle as he vaulted into the ring and promptly withdrew limpingly from the competition, allowing Cravan to go through to the championship bout. On 14th March he claimed victory in a blaze of glory when his opponent, Pecquerieux, was confined to his bed with a nasty cold. Cravan was pronounced Heavyweight Champion of France without having thrown a single punch.

Even though he hadn't earned it, Cravan exploited his new-found reputation to the full, assimilating it as a definitive part of his persona: henceforth he would introduce himself as "Arthur Cravan, poet and boxer". He sketched out a ring in the studio of his friend, Kees van Dongen, and this became a regular fixture of the painter's bohemian parties, where Cravan exhibited himself every Thursday night. He also recognized the financial value of his title, and set about organizing lucrative exhibition fights to cash in on his success.

Today the Rue du Faubourg Saint-Honoré on the right bank of the Seine is festooned with haute-couture boutiques stocking designer tat – it is reputed to be the most expensive shopping street in Europe. I found that a featureless Ministry of Justice building now stands in the place of the Cirque de Paris, the grand venue where Cravan followed the glory of his triumph-by-forfeit with a resounding defeat.

In April 1910 he squared up to a boxer called Ricaux in a contest that was sourly ridiculed in the sporting press. An article in *La Boxe et les boxeurs* likens the fighters to contestants in a gurning competition, for "they did little more than stand opposite one another in ungainly, warlike postures. From time to time, they might sniff and blow with the enthusiasm of sperm whales". At the beginning of the second round, in a sudden flash of inspiration, Ricaux started hitting his opponent and, landing a blow to Cravan's stomach, immediately laid him out on the canvas.

Just down the street, in the staid grandeur of the Place du Palais-Royal, I came across a man sprawled on the ground having his chest pumped by a green-bibbed paramedic. This was the high point in an otherwise tedious afternoon. A small crowd of overdressed shoppers burdened with design-er purchases had assembled around the body. It looked like this man had been window-shopping and had simply packed it in there and then, and who could blame him. The onlookers were drawn to his example. They stared down at his corpse, wondering if this wasn't in fact the thing to do.

In April 1912 Cravan had brought out the first issue of his literary periodical, *Maintenant*. Paris was awash with revues and journals at the time, but what made *Maintenant* unique was the fact that it was written entirely by Cravan himself: the "contributors", such as Robert Miradique, W. Cooper and Marie Lowitska existed only as pseudonyms for Arthur Cravan, which of course was itself a pseudonym.

He didn't bother with the frills and niceties that preoccupied other revues: *Maintenant* was printed on the cheapest possible paper and caught the eye with all the artistic flare of a bistro menu. What appealed to Cravan about the form was its potential to shock and outrage on a grand scale: he saw *Maintenant* as a way of airing his dirty laundry in front of a large audience. "It's quite simple," Cravan admitted: "I write in order to infuriate my colleagues, to get myself talked about and to make a name for myself. A name helps you to succeed with women and in business."

The first edition of *Maintenant* had been unremarkable, containing only a few of Cravan's least distinguished poems, and a tribute to his late uncle, Oscar Wilde. The magazine came into its own, however, with its next edition. *Maintenant* number two was dedicated to an irreverent hatchet job on André Gide, the great man of letters and pillar of the French literary establishment. Gide was an old acquaintance of Cravan's late uncle, and together the two of them had travelled around Algeria in search of sex with young boys. It seems it was some disparaging remarks that he had recently made about Wilde that incurred Cravan's scorn. Gide had claimed that it was Wilde who first introduced him to carnal vice, showing a teenage boy into Gide's bedroom and locking the door behind him with "a sonorous, maniacal laughter...

for it is the pleasure of the debauchee to draw others into his debauchery".

Now in his middle age, Gide's moral ambivalence had ripened into utter depravity. He had by this time refined his sexual tastes into a bizarre ritual involving an ice pick and a rat in a cage by the bedside: at the point of orgasm he would turn away from the young boy, take up the ice pick and viciously stab the rat to pieces. Through aesthetic appreciation, the simultaneous experience of sex and death apparently sent him into throes of ecstasy.

Cravan's sexual proclivities were rather conventional by comparison, yet his philosophy on wider matters seems to have a lot in common with that of Gide. In his novel *The Immoralist*, Gide posed the fundamental problem: "Knowing how to free oneself is nothing; the difficult thing is knowing how to live with that freedom". This might as well be the moral of Cravan's own story.

It was in 1914, with the fourth instalment of *Maintenant,* that he was to seal his reputation.

In the first decades of the twentieth century, Paris – the centre of fashion and culture, the undisputed capital of the art world – was experiencing the first twinges of modernism. Aspiring artists of all nationalities were flocking here because Paris was the place where reputations were established, fortunes made and revolutions set in motion. In March the Salon des Artistes Indépendants set out to challenge the conservatism of the Paris establishment by holding an exhibition devoted to the radical fringe of the art world. It was Cravan's review of the Exposition des Indépendants that would make him famous.

In the fourth number of *Maintenant* he attacked the most distinguished names of the day with gross sarcasm. "If I mention a lot of names," he wrote, "it's a trick of mine to sell more copies... They will buy a copy... for the sole pleasure of seeing their name in print." And in this article

Cravan does indeed go through the roll-call of exhibiting artists, dismissing each of them in the most ruthless and petulant manner:

"*Boussingault*, I've seen it a hundred times before... *Einhorn, Lucien Laforge, Szobotka, Valmier*, they're all talentless Cubists. *Suzanne Valadon* knows her little recipes, but to simplify is not to make simple, you old bitch!... *Metzinger*, a failure who has attached himself to cubism. His colours have a German accent to them. He disgusts me. *K. Malevitch*, you fake! *Alfred Hagin*, sad, sad. *Peske*, you're ugly! *Luce* has no talent. *Signac*, I'll say nothing of him because so much has already been written about his work... *Deltombe*, what a fool!..."

Cravan dismisses the majority of the exhibiting artists in this manner, with offhand, disdainful remarks. But Cravan's own friend Robert Delaunay is singled out for special attention and subjected to a bitter tirade. "*Robert Delaunay*, I am cautious to speak about him. We have quarrelled in the past, and I am anxious that anyone should think my criticism impartial. I am not bothered with petty hatreds or personal friendships... Delaunay has a face like an inflamed pig or the coachman of a great estate... But I probably exaggerate if I have suggested that his remarkable appearance is anything to be admired. With the physique of a soft cheese, I'd be surprised if he didn't have trouble running or throwing a pebble thirty metres... He cuts such a vulgar figure that he resembles more than anything else a great red fart."

Cravan considered it his personal mission to shock the establishment out of its lifeless conventions at a time when art was the preserve of the bourgeois. "It is to outrage Art," Cravan wrote, "that I declare that to be an artist you must begin by drinking and eating." Of Marie Laurencin – an exhibiting painter, a woman of considerable refinement, and the lover of Apollinaire – he wrote: "(I didn't see her work.) But here's someone who's in sore need of having her skirts lifted over her head and being shown a good seeing-to with a great big... somewhere to teach her that art is not a pretty little pose in front of the mirror... Painting is walking, running, drinking, eating, sleeping and moving your bowels. You'll call me disgusting, but it's true."

To be accepted within the Paris milieu at this time, it was first necessary for an artist to demonstrate his credentials as a superior being of exquisite tastes, to prove himself genteel and highly cultured. But with *Maintenant* Cravan, ever perverse, was declaring himself to be wholly lacking in taste, refinement and restraint. "I declare once and for all: I will never be civilized!"

The impact of *Maintenant* number 4 was seismic. Delaunay began legal proceedings for slander. Cravan himself was assaulted by a band of slighted artists out for vengeance. He was even challenged to a duel. His notoriety was sealed.

Word of the revue spread quickly, and the first print run sold out almost immediately. Members of the cultured classes fought each other to get hold of a copy. Cravan had a further two editions printed, and the copies of each disappeared as soon as they were released.

Everyone agreed that it was a disgrace, but at the same time they couldn't conceal their delight. Instead of affronting good manners, Cravan's publication was considered frightfully droll, and was snapped up by the very people he sought to offend. The offhand elegance with which he delivered the deadliest of insults became for a while the most popular topic of conversation at dinner parties. And briefly Cravan himself was held up as an idol by those who wished they too had the guts to let their colleagues know exactly what they thought of them.

Cravan sold his revue from a wheelbarrow outside the exhibition rooms on the Place de Clichy. It was here that a dozen or so of the slighted painters got a lynch mob together and stood waiting for him one morning.

I wandered off in search of the Galeries de Clichy, the grand rooms where the Exposition des Indépendants was staged. The Place de Clichy is now a congested intersection, a bastion of low culture, heaving with tourists, overhung with great illuminated billboards, saturated with noisy bars and chain restaurants. It lies at the end of the Boulevard de Rochechouart in the district of Pigalle, once famous for its mixture of high and low taste as epitomized by the Moulin Rouge. That establishment is still there, although now its flashing plastic windmill looks like it has been salvaged from the liquidation of a Disney theme park.

Pigalle has become a strange two-headed beast, on the one hand playing off its rich history as the seamy side of Paris to draw coachloads of tourists, and on the other catering for the obscure tastes of lonely and sexually perverted men.

Amongst the many *steak-frites* franchises and multi-storey megastores there are the unmistakably blank shop fronts of the peep shows, strip joints, and dirty-book emporia. I discovered that the Galeries have been converted in the same vein. The façade has been painted black, its windows tinted, and with a great signboard over the sunken entrance it has been rechristened in luminous lettering: GALERIES-X. In daylight hours it is closed, and the effect of its decor is unimpressive without the ultraviolet illumination.

It was on this spot that the band of enraged painter-vigilantes confronted Cravan and his wheelbarrow. Despite his six-foot-four height, and a physique impressively honed from his boxing training, against such an onslaught by furious artists he didn't stand a chance. With long swipes of his mighty arms Cravan batted the painters off like flies, but they overcame him by force of numbers. The artists clung to his great legs, they pulled at his hair and hung from around his neck. They kicked at him with their pointed shoes and beat him repeatedly over the head with their walking canes. The brawl was finally broken up by the police, who were not sympathetic to Cravan's point of view. He spent that night and the whole following week in a police cell, nursing his wounds.

The next day Apollinaire, known for his gallantry, sent his seconds to challenge Cravan to a duel to defend his honour and the good name of his lover, Marie Laurencin. What was more, mutual friends confided to Cravan that Apollinaire had enrolled in an intensive course of fencing lessons. He scoffed at the challenge, but secretly he was terrified. When his friend Cendrars informed him that Apollinaire had been seen practising with a rapier and a leg of lamb nailed to a post, Cravan turned deathly pale. "He was a great coward," Cendrars affirmed, "despite his bluster." Luckily for Cravan, his own chest-puffing bravado had given Apollinaire the impression that he would be a formidable adversary, and he was just as scared. Both men spent the days leading up to the confrontation in a state of dread, toying with excuses, desperately searching for a way to back out of the whole thing without losing face.

Cravan was the first to blink. He issued a public statement of apology for the offence he had given: "I'm not the least bit frightened of Apollinaire's big sword," the published statement read. "But because I don't have much self-respect I am ready to rectify all my mistakes and to say that, contrary to what I implied in my article on the Exposition des Indépendants as it appeared in my revue *Maintenant*, Monsieur Guillaume Apollinaire is not a Jew at all, but is in fact Roman Catholic. In order to avoid any further such misunderstandings in the future I would just like to add that Monsieur Apollinaire, who has a grossly fat stomach, resembles a rhinoceros more than a giraffe and, as for his head, he looks more like a tapir than a lion, and with his long beak he's more like a vulture than a stork. Taking this opportunity to put everything in order, I would also like to amend a certain phrase about Madame Laurencin which was misconstrued. When I said *here's someone who's in sore need of having her skirts lifted over her head and being shown a good seeing-to with a great big... somewhere*, it literally means that *she needs someone to lift up her skirts and give her a good seeing-to with a big astronomy at the Théâtre des Variétés.*"

Cravan was beginning to make a reputation for himself. The calculated provocation of *Maintenant* brought him a taste of the attention he craved: his name was splashed across the front pages of all the Parisian newspapers that week. He basked in his newfound infamy during the eight long days and nights he spent in prison, waiting to answer the charges of slander brought by Delaunay. He made productive use of the incarceration, recuperating from his injuries and planning a comeback appearance that would make the bourgeois establishment retch with distaste. He had realized the power of scandal, and on his release he put into action a strategy for consummating his notoriety once and for all.

I should explain a bit about the pills. It was Cathy who encouraged me to visit the doctor, but it took several weeks of needling on her part before I finally gave in.

It might seem incredible but I'd had the cold, on and off, for nearly twenty years. I mentioned this to the doctor after he'd examined me, and he claimed that he could find nothing physically wrong, said it was probably psychosomatic. Cathy, too, was convinced that the symptoms were conjured out of nowhere whenever the mood took me, and could disappear again, if I willed them to, just as quickly as they had materialized. But I knew better than that – I could hardly fail to, having endured those symptoms since I was a teenager. I knew for a fact that the affliction had always been with me, only sometimes I could distract myself from its discomforts, and sometimes there was no escaping them.

It usually starts at night, when I'm lying awake in the dark with insomnia. That's when I begin to notice the first tickling soreness in the sinal tracts, followed by a sudden stabbing pain in my temples as clear and resounding, as predictable as the chime of a carriage clock. The next day comes the irritation of the nasal passageways and the beginnings of rapid congestion. By the third day my nose has begun to stream more or less continually, so that the next symptom is the materialization of abundant swathes of tissue paper that trail from pullover sleeves, accumulate in pockets, and mass around waste-paper baskets in straggling, soggy heaps.

When it gets really bad I become aware of a leaden sluggishness in my body, my limbs start to ache dully, it becomes an unbearable effort to move, and I lie in bed incapacitated for days on end. My mind too becomes congested with morbid thoughts that swarm and multiply with a viral keenness. The final proof that this isn't an elaborate hypochondria is that the condition is highly infectious. There are always people foolish enough to rally around ailing acquaintances, impinging on their miserable seclusion to offer cups of tea and words of encouragement – and with my own rheum-filled eyes I have observed their simperingly condescending good health swiftly deteriorate. On numerous occasions I have seen Cathy weaken at my bedside, I've actually seen the illness take her. The funny thing is that once others go down with it, I often begin to notice a marked improvement in my own condition.

It's no mystery really, a flawed constitution runs in the family. I remember my father was frequently beset by a catalogue of complaints for which he had an exhaustive supply of medicines and treatments, little plastic vials of brightly coloured capsules, eye drops, and restoratives. There was certainly a strong ritual element to his regime of tablets and medicaments: he would place the dose reverently on his prostrate tongue as if it were a communion wafer, then follow it with a gulp of water and an automatic toss of the head like a supplicant swilling the blood of Christ. For him each had its own special significance, the green and red capsules held a mystical power quite apart from the white tablets. Most sacred of all were the dull yellow pills that he stockpiled in the bottom drawer of his bedside table, hidden away beneath folded underpants as if they possessed a holiness so terrible that their name could not be spoken.

The doctor prescribed me a course of drugs to be taken daily. At first there were no noticeable effects other than mild nausea and occasionally an uneven heart rate. But in the coming months I became aware of a subtle change. I knew from the start that the pills weren't a treatment so much as a diversion. It's true that they did make me feel better: if taken strictly every lunchtime I found they kept me stable, made things bearable. But with this came an odd sensation, almost as if the world around me had ceased to be quite real, that things lacked depth somehow. Still underneath it all the dark feelings persisted, the pills just took the edge off them, and while the medication provided a distraction, the thoughts lingered on in the back of my mind like the memory of something terrible that you can never outlive, something that has become an indispensable part of your soul.

When he came out of prison, Cravan discovered himself to be poor for the first time in his life. Copies of his revue had found their way to his mother in Lausanne, and she was appalled by what she read. For Mrs Lloyd the embarrassment of *Maintenant* was the final straw in the fraught relationship with her wayward son. Now she disowned Cravan and cut him loose of his living allowance. Facing destitution, he was forced to devote his singular talents to earning his own keep, and he set about devising scams and confidence tricks, anything to scrape a living.

In the gospel of Cravan biography, it is assumed that Cravan made an inept confidence man. This judgement is based on the fact that he tended to draw his quarry from his own circle of acquaintances instead of grooming victims from further afield.

Cravan started with what he knew best – writing grovelling letters to acquaintances and distant relations, tapping second cousins and great-uncles for small sums of money. He said he must raise a hundred francs within a week to get his fiancée's jewellery out of hock; he claimed he'd got his hands on a genuine Lautrec worth a thousand francs but couldn't afford the fee to have it verified; he had fallen gravely ill and needed fifty francs for specialist treatment… Cravan got by on hard-luck stories. But when he happened to meet a client of his brother, the painter Otho Lloyd, he knew he was about to hit the mother lode.

His brother Otho had so far had experienced little success in Paris. His apartment was stacked from floor to ceiling with paintings he couldn't get rid of, and if it hadn't been for the regular allowance from his mother in Switzerland he wouldn't have survived. He saw a way of turning his luck round when he was introduced to Philippe Garonne, a young country aristocrat who had recently inherited his father's title and estate. The man was flirting with the idea of starting a collection, and had come on his first jaunt to the capital to educate himself in the art of the day. He was to sit for a portrait at Otho's that coming weekend, and while he was there Otho hoped to interest him in a series of watercolours. He was determined to close this deal – if necessary he was even prepared to throw in a couple of nudes and a still life.

But Cravan had seen an opportunity of his own. He offered to show his brother's client some of the sights of Paris the following afternoon, and as they walked by the Seine he let him in on a highly secret project. Cravan produced a roll of paper, and made Garonne swear not to breathe a word of what he was about to see. Then he unrolled the blueprint for a rubber push-bicycle that he claimed could be deflated and stowed conveniently in a trouser pocket. This was the shape of things to come: he was sitting on a gold mine of potential, he told Garonne – all he needed was a business partner with vision, someone to pay for the construction of a scale prototype. Cravan walked away that afternoon with a cheque for a sizeable sum, and went directly to his bank to cash it.

That weekend Otho prepared his easel and oils and waited for Garonne to arrive for his sitting. But when the doorbell rang, he opened the door to see a delivery boy with a note. "Due to this unfortunate affair with your brother," Garonne wrote, "I regret that I have changed my mind about the portrait." Otho was furious, and he went at once to confront his brother. Cravan, however, showed no remorse.

47

He explained to Otho: "Garonne had the audacity to ask for his money back. I showed him my contempt by not responding in the slightest to the silly fuss he was making. You can tell him from me that he should consider himself honoured to lend me a packet without having to worry about reimbursement."

The dispute turned ugly and public when the brothers were arrested for brawling in a posh restaurant. Their mother wrote to her favoured older son: "That which I feared would happen has at last happened. You have lost a brother and I a son. Unjustly he hates us and makes us suffer. I hope that in the demonstration neither of you were too badly hurt. I shudder to think what you might have done to one another. It is fortunate that he chose to confront you in a public place – despite the bad taste of brawling in a restaurant like a couple of barbarians – so that at least you could be separated."

Despite appearances, Cravan was far from being a reckless or clumsy con artist. The incident with his brother's client was not a result of naivety or ill discipline – in fact it is a testimony to both his deviousness and his spite. This was a shrewd, calculated exercise that had more than a touch of vengeance to it: for Cravan there was a certain poetic justice in punishing his mother's favourite for the poverty to which she had condemned him.

That night I cooked pasta in a dented, soot-caked saucepan in the galley kitchen of the hostel. The air was dense with the reek of old Camembert and the rancid accretions of years of spoilt dinners. The microwave was buzzing discordantly in the corner, and after a while a Japanese teenager came in to stand and stare at a Tupperware pot that was rotating slowly inside. I offered the obligatory grunt of acknowledgement and turned back to my saucepan in extreme boredom. My attention wandered, time passed, and when my eyes came back into focus I saw that the pasta had turned flaccid and was bubbling in a gluey mass resembling wallpaper paste. I took it out into the little courtyard, sat down on the steps and ate without enthusiasm.

Lonely souls started to congregate around a table by the door to the Turkish toilet. Owen was an afro-haired Canadian wearing sandals, who looked like the forgotten member of a '70s psychedelic rock band. He was on his way to the south of France to work on an organic farm, and he had a deadpan languor about him that I found unsettling. He was acquainted with a plump, prematurely balding kid from Kentucky called Karl. This one was trying to push the cork into a bottle of cheap wine and had devised a technique for this purpose which involved hammering the handle of a wooden spoon into the neck of the bottle with a frying pan. He didn't seem to be having much success, but he persevered nonetheless. They were soon joined by the Japanese boy, who emerged apologetically from the kitchen with his steaming Tupperware pot.

From the steps I half-listened to their stilted conversation. By way of introduction they went through the particulars of where they were from and where they were going, and they appeared to be almost as sickened by the conversation as I was. Their sentences trailed off at the end into barely concealed sighs. Even the Japanese boy was showing the symptoms of a terrible boredom, the pain becoming evident as his clenched-teeth grin began to weaken. Very soon they could go on no longer, the effort of it was too demanding, and they lapsed into silence. The Japanese boy bowed his head into his pot and sucked noodles rapidly into his face. Karl was absorbed in the task of opening the bottle of wine, and Owen was drumming his fingers on the table top, from time to time slamming down the flat of his hand to relieve some pent-up frustration.

Then an attractive unaccompanied girl emerged from a dormitory. The boys stiffened. She sashayed languidly over, closely followed by a man in his late twenties who wore a battered trilby hat and a corduroy blazer buttoned across the chest. She walked quickly a few paces in front, giving the impression that she was trying to shake him off.

The boys watched her pull up a chair across the table, and all of a sudden they seemed to recall a long-forgotten reason for carrying on, a purpose emerged from the loins of their sorry existences. At that moment the fat boy, Karl, succeeded in knocking in the cork, squirting a plume of vinegary wine into the cold air. There was a chorus of approval all round and I chose my moment to insinuate myself.

They seemed dubious at first, perhaps a little taken aback by my appearance and the habit I had of dabbing the rheum from my eyes with a crusted knot of toilet paper. But the courtyard was so small that there was nowhere for them to go, and after a few plastic cups of wine their concern lapsed. Somehow the wine ended up in my hands and I took a long swig from the bottle. They were obliged to let me hold on to it because of the risk of contagion, and Karl wearily set about opening another.

As a rule I would never allow myself to drink alcohol. I

51

always found that it brought out the least endearing facets of my personality. Under the influence of alcohol it was more difficult than usual to restrain my darker inclinations, and evenings such as this would invariably end in tears for all involved. Remaining perpetually sober was my best chance of preserving the illusion of normality. But tonight I felt that I had nothing more to lose, and I allowed myself to grow steadily drunk. It didn't matter what I said to these people, what atrocities I committed against them, for I would see none of them ever again.

Martin, the effete Englishman in the trilby hat, was in the middle of a speech with his voice raised to ensure that everyone could hear. With a toss of the head he was saying: "Yes, I'm writing a travel novel. It's kind of a beat-generation thing."

Owen said, "Oh yeah?"

I noticed Karl's tongue poke between his lips as he watched the girl light another cigarette.

Martin – oblivious to the fact that no one was in the least interested – went on: "Of course you need a gimmick these days. Travelling across the Sahara in drag, that sort of thing. Around the world without bathing." Martin laughed with a jerk of his torso.

"Right." Owen had started to drum his fingers again, more softly this time.

"Or, you know, in search of the hotel with the worst sanitary conditions in the world." He laughed again with a sneer. I despised Martin. "But my book is about the very superficiality of our global culture. My gimmick is a kind of ironic gimmick, sort of a *post-gimmick* gimmick…"

At this moment a peel of derisive giggling erupted from the pit of my stomach like a fit of uncontrollable retching. It came so suddenly that the whole table fell silent and all of them turned to look at me. I gave the table a number of sharp blows with my balled-up fist, and as the laughter exhausted the last of the breath from my lungs it shuddered itself out with one final sobbing honk.

Mercifully the ensuing silence was broken by the arrival of an Italian couple, and this distracted the party around the table with pleasantries and introductions.

We had gone through four bottles of wine, and I felt the colour come into my cheeks and my spirits lift. The newly arrived Italian man had sat down next to me, and because his English was poor I was speaking to him slowly and loudly, careful to enunciate each syllable.

"You know, *Society* – with a fucking capital fucking *S* – calls it an 'illness'. Bollocks!" I told him. "That's only because they're all so terrified of what's inside them."

He was frowning with the effort it took to comprehend. When I put an arm around his shoulders he grew tense. I reassured him: "You musn't be ashamed! It's perfectly normal – in fact I'd say there was something deeply wrong with you if you *didn't* seriously contemplate suicide at least once in your lifetime."

I was just starting to get through to him when I was interrupted by the keening sound of a harmonica. My spirits plunged when I saw what was about to happen. Owen had produced and distributed a number of musical instruments. The lazy-eyed impresario had persuaded the Italian woman to play a couple of spoons like castanets, and her enthusiasm concerned me. With convulsive stomps of his foot Owen now began to play the same riff over and over again.

They had a knees-up of sorts. Their combined efforts on the harmonica, the spoons and Tupperware percussion created a kind of music that raked into the mind and sickened the senses.

At midnight for some reason I followed them out into the street. They headed along the Boulevard de Rochechouart, and I followed at a distance, not wanting to be associated with them. By now the music had deteriorated completely into a cacophonous clatter of discordant noises. Owen kept time lurchingly with the same two notes of the harmonica, while the others trailed after him in a melancholy cortège.

Pigalle lay before us, a lurid confusion of neon *XXX* and *Girls Girls Girls* signs and leather-jacketed little men with scarred faces beckoning towards the curtained doorways of strip clubs. The pavements were awash with great herds of tourists waiting to be shooed back to their coaches.

We came to a standstill on a street corner. By this time everyone was feeling the disorienting effects of too much horrible wine, and the spirit was beginning to abandon them. I was feeling tearful and found it didn't take much to tip the others towards despondency.

"You know who you remind me of?" I asked Owen.

He shrugged my hand from his shoulder and then turned to look at me with a face full of pity and revulsion.

"*Me!*" I told him. "You remind me of *me* when I was younger!"

He gave me a little shove away from him and I staggered and fell against the Italian girl. She'd had far too much to drink, and when she saw my tears she put her arm around my waist and gave me a hug. Over her shoulder I saw her boyfriend, a little worse for wear, muttering under his breath, and staring at us. When she withdrew I noticed I had left a snail trail of saliva on her lapel. Nodding earnestly at me she declared in poor English, "Any time-a you need somebody to talk-a-to I am your friend okay?"

Pulling her towards me I tried to slide my tongue into her mouth, but I wasn't quite quick enough. She managed to wriggle out of the way and my tongue glanced off her cheek. Then there were exclamations of outrage and I felt someone dragging me roughly off her from behind. I clutched the girl even tighter and she gave a little yelp of alarm or pain. The next thing I knew, I was on the pavement and there were kicks and punches raining down on me from all sides. I think everyone took the opportunity to put the boot in – even the Japanese boy who contributed a single, exploratory jab to the kidney.

"Stop it!" someone was shouting. "Stop it for fuck's sake!" Rolling over onto my back I saw that it was Martin. He was trying to restrain Owen.

"*Don't!*" I screamed. "*Don't stop!*"

Martin positioned himself between me and the angry mob, with his arms stretched out to shield me. "For fuck's sake stop it!" he was stammering.

Gathering all that remained of my strength I took a swing at the back of Martin's legs, but I missed and my face connected with the paving stones.

After what seemed a long time I heard the harmonica pipe up again. The clatter of the spoons faded into the traffic noise and soon there was no longer any sign of them. I lay in a stupor for a while longer and then climbed unsteadily to my feet.

I wandered the streets of Pigalle until I found myself outside the Galerie-X, looking up at its fluorescent exterior, the strobing *peep-show* signs. In his glass kiosk the morose black doorman pulled my money lethargically under the screen without lifting his eyes from the newspaper. Sighing like a pneumatic brake he tiresomely fingered a plastic token and slid it to me through the opening.

As I pulled the door open, the gaudy shop fronts of Pigalle flashed their reflection in the smoked glass. Behind lay a long mirrored corridor lined with purple strip lights. The place was filled with the alarming sound of a pack of dogs at the peak of excitement – the frenzied barking and squealing of a hundred women on a hundred video screens all perpetually at the climax of the most improbable and upsetting orgasms. Ahead of me, kaleidoscoped by the reflective surfaces, a red carpet led onwards into the dark.

I made my way inside, bracing myself against a mirror

until I got my bearings. With the astringent wine sitting indigestibly on my stomach, and the high-voltage buzzing of the strip lights, and the closeness of the air which was fetid and saturated with the odour of disinfectant, I felt the swift onset of nausea.

I fed my token into the slot by the first vacant booth I came to, and sat up against the wall inside. On the screen an obese woman in heavy make-up and military regalia was in the middle of a curious sex act. She was wearing an eighteenth-century tricorne hat with a black rubber dildo mounted on each of its three points. She had taken it upon herself to see to two other women and a small bald man simultaneously. It involved an ingenious motion of the head that reminded me of the circus noddings of a performing seal. Despite the effort that this demanded, not to mention the appreciative noises coming from those on the receiving ends, she seemed to be afflicted with a crushing boredom, and made no attempt to modulate the monotony of her grunting.

I can't say what happened in the end because I didn't stay long enough to find out. I walked back to the hostel and lay perfectly still in my bunk. Some time later I heard the far-off sound of the harmonica growing slowly louder along the street outside. By now those same two notes had fallen melancholy, the spoons had a mournful ring to them, and the girl's singing had become subdued and was lapsing out of time.

On his release from prison, Cravan advertised that he would present a series of "lectures" across Paris. The news was greeted with puzzlement by those who knew him, especially since he had not specified what the topic of his lectures would be. Indeed, anyone arriving in earnest at one of Cravan's conferences would soon discover that he had very little to say on any subject. He made no pretence of wanting to spread ideas; he had no message to share with his audience: the sole point of his appearances was to cause an almighty stink, and to get his name in the headlines.

One conference was billed for 5th July 1914. The flyer read:

COME AND SEE
the poet
ARTHUR CRAVAN
(Oscar Wilde's nephew)
boxing champion, 125 kg, 2 metres in height
THE BRUTAL CRITIC.
HE'LL SPEAK!
HE'LL BOX!
HE'LL DANCE!
The new Boxing Dance.

Under the headline, "Nephew of Oscar Wilde", a report of the performance appeared in the *Paris Midi* newspaper the following day: "Arthur Cravan, who never fails to write 'nephew of Oscar Wilde' after his name, yesterday evening performed a spectacle in front of several hundred Englishmen, Americans and Germans, amongst whom one or two unsuspecting Frenchmen had strayed. This Arthur Cravan is a huge, blond, beardless young man who was wearing a shirt with a plunging neckline... Before speaking he fired several pistol shots over the heads of the audience and then began to expound – half smiling, half serious – the grossest insanities against art and life. He praised sportsmen, homosexuals, robbers of the Louvre and madmen, pronouncing them all superior to the artist. He stood there swaying from side to side, and from time to time ranted at the crowd with powerful abuse. At first people seemed amused by all of this. But then things took an unpleasant turn when Cravan felt the need to hurl a box of paints at full force into the first row of spectators... This Englishman's burlesque demonstration, this elaborately mounted farce lacked spirit, and its contrived flamboyance went down like a lead balloon. Our own thugs could do better."

It seems that such excesses were typical of Cravan's lectures. He had another "literary presentation" scheduled at the Société des Savantes at the heart of the Latin Quarter, now derelict and boarded up for renovation, and surrounded on all sides by bookshops supplying textbooks to the students of the Sorbonne. Cravan turned up for the gig in nothing but a butcher's apron. He climbed onto the platform and discharged a pistol into the ceiling. Then he spoke to the crowd, expressing his contempt for artists, demanding complete silence from the audience with repeated cudgel blows on the lectern, occasionally singling out a face in the auditorium on whom to unleash a torrent of obscenities. To conclude this "happening", Cravan took a solemn bow, his backside turned to the audience so that they could clearly see he wore no underwear.

The prospect of failure did not seem to concern him, indeed it was something he grew to relish. Failure was, in the end, the point. Boasts and threats, gratuitous profanity, outlandish conduct, all culminating in disaster and disappointment: failure was ingrained in him. It was part of his persona, and the main draw of his act.

There was a reckless defiance in his exhibitionism that was designed to fire the antipathy of his audience, to goad them to the brink of riot. He was keen on audience participation and he encouraged spectators to take an active part in his public humiliations. Before one show he is reported to have set up a stall by the entrance from which he sold rotten fruit and vegetables and punnets of gravel to the audience as they filed in.

There was a curious chemistry between the performer and his public, because the more he invited them to despise him, the more appreciative they became of the masochistic spectacle that he made of himself. He took his strategy to its logical conclusion when he announced that for his final conference he would kill himself in front of a paying audience. Tellingly, this event sold out almost immediately, and on the night the queue for returns extended halfway down the street. Blaise Cendrars reported that for the performance, instead of the usual carafe of water Cravan took swigs from a bottle of absinthe and, with a nod to the ladies, he wore only a G-string, delivering his suicide speech with his balls proffered upon the table. This time, though, he didn't go through with it, despite the protests of the spectators, nor did he refund the price of admission.

Whilst this was the only occasion I could unearth on which Cravan made suicide a part of his act, the whole of his career was tainted with this instinct towards self-destruction. I think that the scant celebrity he achieved in his lifetime had a lot to do with the kind of morbid infatuation we feel driving by a nasty car crash, or watching a drunken colleague at the office Christmas party ruining their prospects for career advancement.

The following afternoon something strange happened. I was wandering along a nondescript street and I saw Martin, the fop from the hostel who reckoned he was writing the next *On the Road*. Martin was standing in the middle of the pavement with a notebook in one hand, sucking the end of a pencil and gazing up at the sky. I experienced a jolt of revulsion and got off the street and out of sight as quickly as possible. I don't think he saw me.

I lunged into a small café and decided to stay there until the danger had passed. There was a group of flat-capped old men propped around the bar. I stood at the opposite end and ordered a coffee. By the door into the kitchen I could see the backside of an old man on his knees mending the fridge. The men around the counter paid me no attention, their heads were tilted up towards the television in the corner. There was a wildlife programme on.

Earlier that morning at the hostel I had caught the tail end of a measly breakfast. Martin had paused at the foot of the stairs to survey the room. Even though I was careful not to acknowledge him, he had headed straight for my table and to my dismay sat down opposite me.

I said nothing, but I couldn't help noticing the way Martin spread jam over a tartine. He did it with a definite smugness, as if to emphasize the fact that he didn't have a hangover.

"Strange night last night, wasn't it," he said.

I said, "Mm-hm," and noticed that he held his butter knife like a pencil, a trait I abhor.

There was a moment's silence. Martin didn't mention my black eye. He slid the baguette in between his lips and had trouble biting off a piece of the dense plasticky bread.

The two jam sandwiches I'd been making were lying on a plate in front of me, but now I had lost my appetite.

"What are you up to today then?" he asked.

I ignored him.

Martin flipped open a small notepad and lay it on the table in front of him, saying: "You don't mind if I take notes?"

I looked at him.

"*What?*"

"It's for my writing."

I narrowed my eyes, and then averted them altogether. Behind the counter, the hostile girl who worked the morning shift was fiddling with the stereo. She put on The Doors and smoked a cigarette, contemptuously watching a couple of guests deposit their soiled plates next to the sink.

"What are you doing here, are you on holiday, working?..." Martin discarded the remains of his baguette and glanced around for somewhere to wipe his fingers.

"A working holiday."

"Oh right," he said, wiping his hands on the tablecloth. "And what work do you do then?"

"It's uh..." Martin had picked up his pencil and was now poised with it. "It's a project I'm doing. A private project."

"Oh right. That's interesting mm." Martin shifted buttocks in his seat. I could see him gather himself for something. "That sounds a lot like what I'm doing."

He picked up his coffee and drank some of it. There was a long pause and I let it drag on, hoping that it would go on for ever.

"I'm working on a novel here in Paris."

I looked out of the window at the dreary street for a long time. He had finished his coffee, but seemed determined to persist with this line of conversation. He handled his tartine again, just as a pretext for sitting there longer.

"Yeah," he said after a while. "I'm writing a novel." I felt him looking at me expectantly. In the corner of the window a large fly was drubbing its head remorselessly against the glass. I sighed long and hard.

"What's your novel about Martin?"

Martin laid his pencil down with relief and took a deep breath. I knew I would regret opening the floodgates, but some small, insignificant part of me was curious, if only to understand the full horror of his enterprise.

"Well it's not *about* anything, I don't think you can productively reduce any book to what it's *about*," he said with a moue. "But it takes in a lot of different influences and ideas. It's essentially a travel novel, of course…"

I cast my eyes around the room, to acquaint myself with the exits.

"But I'm just using that as a way of exploring a whole range of issues."

"I think I'm going to get some more coffee," I said, standing up.

"Good idea." Martin got up and followed me without missing a beat. "It's funny that you asked me what it's about because that's my whole point, really. It's not about *anything*."

Martin let this sink in.

"That's where my gimmick comes in."

I had filled my cup with coffee and, looking around, I realized that there was nowhere to go except back to the table.

"Gimmick, eh?"

He followed me back to the table.

"Yes. What I'm doing, the *hook*, if you like, is travelling with an *empty suitcase*."

"Really." I could feel the part of my brain which deals with sarcasm sitting up in my head.

"A suitcase with nothing whatsoever inside it," Martin said nodding. "I hate gimmicks. I hate the whole *idea* of gimmicks, but you've got to have one. So I've developed this kind of anti-gimmick." He stirred his coffee very quickly and showed no sign of stopping. He said: "It's ironic."

"Oh sweet Jesus," I said.

"What's wrong?"

"It's nothing." I massaged my temples forcefully. "Nothing. I just came over all... I just don't really think I can sort of handle..." I let out a deep, heavy sigh.

Sometimes, when things are particularly difficult, I get a funny kind of premonition in the morning. Almost as if I can sense that the day ahead is going to be unbearable. At these times I have an overwhelming wish that I had never woken up.

"I'm telling you," Martin said, resting a hand on my shoulder, "it's that terrible wine. It's just criminal to buy fifty-fucking-centime pesticide wine in Paris when you can get an incredible Côtes-du-Rhône or a great Merlot in any corner-shop for like three euros, it's ridiculous."

I shook that day's pill out of the vial and stared at it there, sitting in the palm of my hand. Then I knocked it back with a swill of tepid coffee. Martin watched this carefully and then made a note of it in his pad. He wrote very quickly, his shoulders hunched forwards, the nib of the pencil scratching sharply.

"So where was I..." Martin continued a moment later, putting his pencil down. "The point of the suitcase as a device, if you know what I mean, is as a kind of metaphor for the modern kind of *global* soul." He gave me a level look. "It's *empty*."

I took a deep breath and the sickness seemed to subside a fraction.

"Where is your suitcase?" I said.

"Ah. I don't have it."

"What do you mean?"

"Someone pinched it."

I swilled the dregs of coffee around in my cup and became engrossed in the rainbow patterns of grease on the surface.

"Yeah," Martin said. "Someone stole it from the hostel in Berlin."

"Right."

"Incredible isn't it."

"So you don't in fact carry it around with you."

"Well, not now, no." He looked thoughtful. "It's just a metaphor."

Even Martin was looking bored.

"What are you going to do today, Martin?"

He looked out of the window.

"Well I don't know. I'm just going to sort of walk. Just walk around, you know. Just sort of collect material." He shrugged and drank more coffee.

Until then I had been wondering whether Martin had made the whole story up. He seemed to be the kind of person who would come up with a lie like this to impress people or just to assuage his boredom. But looking at him then, I knew that he was serious. This was all he had. This is what lifted him clear of the realm of ordinary, run-of-the-mill beings.

As I parted company with him that morning he said, quite offhand: "You don't mind if I use you, do you?"

"*What?*"

"In my book. Can I include you?"

My lip curled up as I looked at him. I said, "I'd rather you didn't," quite firmly, and walked away. I thought that I had made myself clear, but as I opened the door to the street I glanced back and saw him scribbling avidly in his notebook. I was in half a mind to go back over to the table, snatch his pencil from him and trample it underfoot.

Now in the café there was a wildlife programme on. Two young elephants were feeding their trunks into each other's mouths. Everyone in the café watched intently as they ground their faces together with blissfully expressive gestures of their ears. The repairman had turned away from his work and was leaning out of the kitchen door to see. The deep-voiced

65

narrator was rasping, "*Les deux jeunes frères se partagent un moment intime d'affection joyeuse.*" One of the men took his cap off and shook his head. The credits came up on the screen and all of them, as if synchronized, rotated on their stools to face the bar and poked cigarettes between the stiff fronds of their moustaches.

Running into Martin in the street like that had been more than a strange coincidence, and it worried me. I sat worrying in the café. Then, when I left, I left gingerly, peering in either direction before stepping into the street. I had the unsettling feeling that I was going to run into Martin again at some point that day, that no matter which direction I set out in, that's where I would end up.

I headed along the Rue des Martyrs, a wide attractive street that swooped downhill from Montmartre, furnished with exquisite window displays of brightly coloured patisserie, and grocers' abundant spreads of shiny prize vegetables. This was the quarter of choice for art collectors in the first decades of the twentieth century. On the corner of the Rue des Martyrs and the Rue d'Orsel is a drab office of peculiar beigeness. Through the window it is possible to see broken-looking desk clerks in collars and ties surrounded by huge quantities of paperwork. Above the door an insipid brown sign says "G. Aubrey, Accountants". In Cravan's day this was the boutique of Georges Aubrey, art dealer.

At that time Paris was at the centre of a thriving art trade, and dealers such as Aubrey were making a small fortune selling paintings to rich collectors. Seeing an opportunity to make some money, Cravan got in on the act. In the newspapers he publicized the "Galerie Isaac Cravan", exclusive supplier of works by Modigliani, van Dongen and the Mexican painter Diego Rivera. He boasted to friends that he had come across a clutch of Cezannes that would make him a small fortune. However, an acquaintance of Cravan's, André Level, in his memoir of the Paris art world, *Souvenirs d'un collectionneur*, tells a different story: "Cravan was making a very bad living, as it happened, off the occasional brokering jobs that he managed to get away with."

It seems that the Galerie Isaac Cravan never existed. In fact Cravan was often to be found hanging around at the Aubrey boutique, trying to persuade Aubrey to take his canvases. It's possible that Cravan even tried to get shot of some work of his own here.

Édouard Archinard was an obscure painter who apparently experienced a massive spurt of productivity at this time, knocking out a series of hastily rendered canvases in a naive pointillist style. A brief entry in the Bénézit *Dictionary of Artists* mentions that "this painter's colours are highly personal, and merely represent a quest for harmony, with no regard for the truth." A handful of these paintings survive, and a postcard signed by Archinard, apparently sent from the South Pacific, turned up for auction in Paris in the Nineties. Other than this, there is little evidence of his existence. The Bénézit entry puts Archinard's disappearance down to the carnage of the War, in which countless young Frenchmen went missing in action. But the fact that this entry was written by a close friend of Cravan's points to the possibility that Archinard never existed at all: he is now widely presumed to be another of Cravan's alternative identities. This would explain why the several Archinard paintings that Blaise Cendrars counted in his collection came with a bill of sale signed by Cravan. There was one retrospective exhibition of Archinard's works in Paris a few years after Cravan's departure, but close inspection of the programme reveals that the curator was another old friend, and the whole thing has about it the malodorous whiff of a practical joke.

I hadn't gone more than fifty yards from G. Aubrey's when I passed an old woman meandering behind an elderly Pomeranian. The dog was wearing a tartan jacket and glared at me with a pert expression. I returned its stare as I walked past, determined not to be the first to break eye contact, and immediately I sank my left shoe plumb into a soft pile of crap.

After a week in Paris I was so inured to this kind of thing that I felt almost no bitterness. I looked down at my feet and saw that I was standing at the centre of a constellation of small nuggets of excrement. Evidently I had not been the first to wander into it, for just ahead there was a fresh shoeprint left by someone else. He had left the trace of his next footfall a yard further on, and the smears led along the pavement for about fifteen paces. My eyes followed his path across the paving stones. And there at the end of the pavement, braced against the side of a delivery van parked on the corner, stood Martin, vigorously scraping his shoe on the edge of the kerb.

I crossed the road without looking, barely noticing the Doppler whine of a moped horn swerving round me. I carried on, half-running, taking turns at random. I put block after block between us. I went on and on without stopping, until I panted with exertion, and my shirt was sodden through with sweat.

By the time I stopped to rest, night was falling and I found myself over the Seine. I was standing in one of the recesses on the Pont Neuf. I was leaning over the side looking down at the black morass of the fast-flowing river. Below, the traffic streamed unabated in and out of the tunnels on the François Mitterand bypass. A fog was beginning to diffuse the lights from the far bank. And once in a while a sparsely populated *bateau mouche* went by, a handful of forlorn tourists in woollen hats standing on deck. As it passed, the distorted voice of the tour guide blared from the tannoy echoing in the darkness around the concrete jetties.

Eventually my teeth started to chatter with the cold, so I wandered on. Crossing the river to the Île de la Cité, I came under the sneering gargoyles and the looming buttresses of the Cathédrale de Notre-Dame. It wasn't much warmer inside. The mass was under way and the place was filled with the sound of the requiem. The singer was a young woman in a blue surplice, and I watched her from the shadows by the pillars. In my state of exhaustion, the sweet sound of her voice sent me into a reverie.

After a few minutes a group of middle-aged Japanese men kitted out like war photographers set up their tripods next to me and started videoing everything. I moved quickly away and found a seat in the middle. I tried to concentrate on the woman's singing, and the cloying sweetness of her voice began to pacify me, until after a few minutes my clenched jaw loosened and the shaking of my hands was no longer noticeable.

Banks of votive candles flickered white and red in the recesses. Above hung the gurning face of the crucified Jesus, rivulets of blood spidering his cheeks. My eyes wandered along the high arcs of the stonework, towards the great black void of the stained-glass window. The chorister came suddenly to the end of her song and stepped back from the music stand. I noticed that beneath the surplice she was wearing a pair of running shoes.

One of the priests stood in front of the lectern and began his incantations. The other took up the chain of the censer, and with great swings he sent blue clouds of incense wafting up to the ceiling. The Latin chanting went on monotonously. The priests accompanied the droning voice with spasmodic bows and crossings of the chest. The voice resounded from the high ceilings and came back altered, ringing in the air all around long after he had finished speaking.

I must have been there a quarter of an hour before I realized that Martin was sitting in the front row. He was sucking the end of a pencil, his head cocked to one side in rapt contemplation.

* * *

The nine hundred and eighty-two unsold copies of my novel had been stacked in my father's garage for years, to gather cement dust and be pissed upon by generations of rats. Finally I carted them out in a wheelbarrow, down to the bottom of his garden, where I intended to burn every last one in a ritual of purgation.

But during the years of storage the books had become damp and mildewed, and they burned reticently, giving off a bitter green smoke. Even with the addition of a gallon can of paraffin they failed to come alight. They smouldered there for two days before finally choking the fire. I raked through the pile of blackened and partially carbonized books, and left them for the autumn, to be rained on and to rot.

The following year my father used the remains of them for compost on his vegetable patch, and that season their corrupted ashes miscarried three sickly and inedible Savoy cabbages. The garden was barren ever afterwards, and its wretched drabness mocked me whenever I went over to visit.

Stoically insistent on doing the washing-up, my father would stand bent over a blackened grill pan in the sink, staring grimly out of the kitchen window at his desolate garden. He was resolved never to mention it, although he exuded resentment with his every glance towards me, with every perfunctory handshake upon meeting ever afterwards.

I could hardly bear to set foot in that garden. The black and mouldering earth reeked of cheap bulk paper and incinerated lamination. My father couldn't die soon enough so that I could sell the house and be rid of it once and for all.

The moment I stepped out into the street the next morning the dark sky slouched closer overhead and I felt the first insistent peckings of a torrential downpour. Lurid posters on walls turned to papier mâché and oozed down the brickwork. A heap of last night's vomit sluiced languidly across the pavement towards the gutter. People in transparent plastic rain hoods scurried by in the opposite direction. Clusters of men in suits jostled for shelter under shop awnings, holding wilting newspapers up against the sky.

I took the Métro to the Place Denfert-Rochereau to look for Cravan's last known Paris address. The steps out of the subway broke the surface on an island in the middle of gridlocked traffic. The Rue du Faubourg Saint-Jacques was one of the many radials of avenues leading off in every direction from this point, and I had to walk all the way round to find it, making infuriatingly slow progress through a complex system of zebra crossings, waiting in the rain for the lights to change, after a while not even bothering to dodge the spray from speeding cars. It was somewhere here that Cravan spent his final months in Paris in the summer of 1914.

That year in the east of Europe war was brewing. At first news of the crisis in Belgrade barely reached Paris, but as it began to encroach upon western politics, day by day the newspapers devoted more and more column inches to the build up of hostilities in the east. Loyalties were being tested, old scores and enmities aroused, and one by one the world powers were drawn into taking sides. There was no longer any hope that the conflict would be isolated to the Balkans, and it spread now like an epidemic.

Russia was the first to mobilize its forces in the defence of Serbia. On 1st August 1914 Germany declared war against

Russia, and France declared war against Germany. Two days later Germany declared war against France, and then invaded Belgium. Committed to the defence of Belgium, Great Britain declared war against Germany the following day. Austria-Hungary declared war against Russia on 5th August. Serbia declared war against Germany on the 6th. Montenegro did the same against Austria-Hungary on 7th August and against Germany on the 10th. On 12th August France and Great Britain declared war against Austria-Hungary. Then on the 23rd Japan declared war against Germany, Austria-Hungary against Japan on the 25th and against Belgium on the 28th.

In Paris the propaganda effort began. The War was sold as an idealistic struggle to defend the moral purity of the civilized world, and when France joined in, the capital greeted the news with a wave of patriotic feeling, even jubilation. The Parisians believed that their side would be victorious within a matter of months. Cravan, however, took the news with a mixture of dismay and ironic detachment: for him the War was a serious setback in his pursuit of notoriety. Blaise Cendrars joked that Cravan believed the World War was being waged against him alone, just to spite him.

Just as the Parisians did not understand how long and bloody the conflict would be, Cravan could have had little prescience of the catastrophic impact the coming war would have on the course of his life. It was the War that started him on the chaotic trajectory that would lead him to the other side of the world, and the strange fate that awaited him there.

Of course I found no trace of number 67, the cramped apartment which Cravan had left in a hurry, with several months' rent outstanding when he fled the city. The house numbers stopped at 54, for some reason, and number 54 was a blank new development called the Société Technico-Commerciale des Machines Automatiques.

I stood in a puddle for a few minutes, wondering what to do with the rest of the day. Standing there with the rain falling all around, it was immediately apparent that there was nothing at all to do. I turned and stared back down the street towards the Métro station. The only conceivable option was to traipse back to the hostel and crawl into bed.

I wandered back the way I'd come, and it was then that I saw it. Through a momentary rent in the cloud cover a single, slender beam of sunlight fell beyond the intersection and found there the hoarding indicating the entrance to the Catacombes. For a second picked out of the surrounding monotony, the sign twinkled long enough to catch my eye before it was engulfed once again by the greyness. I followed the zebra crossings around the Place Denfert-Rochereau towards the gloomy stairwell that led into the strangest of the tourist attractions of Paris.

The tight spiral staircase descended thirty metres below the surface of the street. This place would ordinarily have been infested with sightseers, but that morning the incessant drizzle had kept them away, and it now seemed abandoned. The tunnel extended a kilometre into the rock beneath the city. It was perfectly straight, the occasional electric lights forming a line that dwindled without deviation into a distant vanishing point. Other than the soft grinding of my footfalls the only sound was the drip-drop of water from the ceilings. The experience of moving along the passages, with their lime-streaked walls larded all around with slimy concretions, recalled the videos we were shown in biology lessons at school, the footage of a keyhole camera probing the bowels of a cancer patient.

The light in the chamber was so dim that at first I didn't notice the bones. They were stacked from floor to ceiling, lining either wall for as far as I could see. They were arranged with meticulous regularity, arm bones criss-crossed over the neat little chevrons of femur joints. There were layers of human skulls, their pallid domes placed in intricate patterns. Craniums bulged out of the walls all around, some of them with gaping cracks, or turned with the black maws of the eye sockets staring outwards. Occasionally a spare pelvis had been propped up on top of the stack like the crowning adornment of a grotesque cake. The passageway followed a pattern of delicate symmetry, forking around elegantly curving islands of mounded human remains. At every corner the faces of skulls were worn smooth from the touch of curious fingers, or by the passing hips of obese tourists.

I remembered when I first became aware of the skull beneath the flesh of my father's face. It was in the last months of his illness, when he was growing sallow and frail and the bones were becoming apparent beneath the thinning veneer of life.

He had stopped responding to human contact and appeared to be utterly insensible. The nurses, however, assured me that this dissociation was purely voluntary. He just couldn't be bothered any more: the weariness, the loathing that had always been with him, had now taken full possession of his faculties.

Not only did he refuse to eat, but he no longer cooperated when they tried to feed him. He would lie there unmoving, his eyes half-open and focused somewhere in the middle distance beyond the ceiling. The only sign of sentience was the slow, deliberate thrusting of the tongue that gently pumped the soft food back out of his mouth. The stuff oozed down the sides of his face faster than the nurse could scrape it back in with the spoon. Whenever I had the privilege of observing this ritual I couldn't help thinking I saw a spark of elation then in his otherwise deadened eyes.

Despite the grave, confidential tones of the doctors, the assurances that *it might be any day now*, he persisted for an improbable duration. For months and months he lay there, growing steadily thinner, paler, more insubstantial.

Apparently he did try to end it all on several occasions: the nurses reported that he managed to pick the drip out of his arm once or twice. But I was never convinced by this, I felt he was going through the motions, his heart wasn't really in it. In any case the nurses on their rounds would simply reconnect him. No, I became convinced in the course of my regular visits that he had no intention of leaving me. I saw in the darkening lines of his face a grim determination to hang on for as long as he possibly could.

Sitting there at his bedside, reaching to replace the mouldy satsumas with fresh ones, as I listened to the tedious bleeping of the pulse-rate monitor, I became convinced that this was all part of his legacy to me. It wasn't just bloody-mindedness keeping him here: there was a perverse logic to it all. He was trying, in his own way, to *teach* me something.

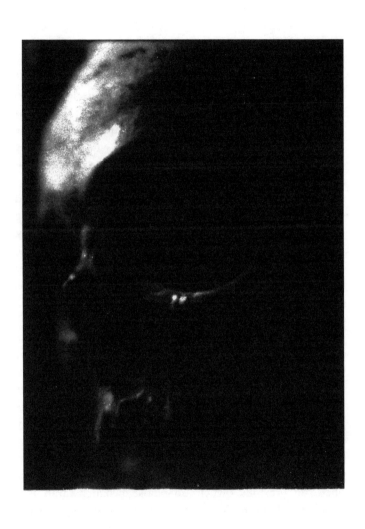

The cold reality of war settled quickly over Paris. The city's motor vehicles had disappeared overnight, requisitioned by the War Office. Crowds of reservists clutching bundles of belongings and farewell bunches of flowers disappeared on train after train from the Gare de l'Est, leaving the streets eerily silent in their wake. The gallant Apollinaire was the first of the intellectuals to throw in his lot with the patriotic cause, marching off to join the infantry with his sword drawn and the ends of his moustache waxed to points. The spirit of exuberance had entirely abandoned the literary gatherings and soon the cafés grew desolate. With the German armies massing on the Western Front, Cravan found himself without money, amongst chronic shortages, with his friends abandoning the country in droves. The prospect of being mobilized terrified him, and he knew it would not be long before he received his conscription papers. He applied himself to gather funds as quickly as possible in order to get out of France.

The means of his escape turned out to be André Level, the credulous art collector whom Cravan had met one day at George Aubrey's boutique. In his *Souvenirs d'un collection-neur*, Level recalls the meeting: "Cravan's distress, together with his undeniable gifts as a poet, moved me, and I was happy to give him some business. He brought me a relatively old Matisse and a Picasso that I found quite singular, an early cubist piece, he assured me. He sold these paintings to me on the understanding that his name should not be made known, since the previous owner, on whose behalf Cravan was working, didn't want his identity to be revealed. I took part in the affair because of my trust for Cravan, justified until then, despite his violence when he took up the pen as an art critic, because he had shown much sensibility and taste."

Cravan couldn't wait to get out of Montparnasse. He told Level that he hated it there: "In Montparnasse art is nothing but theft, con tricks and schemes," he said. "In Montparnasse forgery is calculated, tenderness is replaced with syntax and heart with reason. In Montparnasse there is not a single noble artist alive." But this was also an environment in which Cravan's singular talents thrived, and the irony was that art and con-artistry would be his very means of escaping it. The money that Level paid him was enough to get him out of France, and it was only after he was long gone that Level discovered the paintings were fakes, that his friend Cravan was a fraud.

Ignoring the call of his native land, Cravan headed south, on the run from the authorities. It was no longer emaciated intellectuals with whom he would have to contend: he had a new and ruthless enemy in the form of the military police, and the danger of being outmanoeuvred in a snide exchange of cocktail-party put-downs now seemed trivial next to this new threat of summary execution. Cravan was a wanted man, and this was the beginning of a wild flight that would last for four long years.

I felt like an idiot standing outside McDonald's on the Péripherique with my thumb out again. It grew dark. Countless people went inside and then came out perceptibly fatter and nearer to death. The traffic poured past me, no one showed any sign of stopping. They locked the doors at McDonald's, at last the lights were turned out.

It was past midnight and I'd long since given up all hope when I was offered a lift by a man heading south in an unmarked van. The driver was a small laconic Algerian called Brahim, who sat dwarfed behind the steering wheel.

After introductions there was a long period of silence, when neither of us said anything. Brahim picked his way through the suburbs, changing lanes to overtake on the inside, cutting up other drivers, occasionally fisting his horn and making obscene gestures which must have been purely rhetorical, for they were lost in the darkness.

Roads converged, we sped under flyovers, merged with the traffic on the autoroute. Driving at night felt like being inside a computer game – sliding through the passageways of bright light, the acute geometries, the inhuman night world of the motorway.

Brahim weaved across lanes of fast-moving traffic.

"I'm turning off for a second," he said. We took a slip road off the motorway. "I've got to pick something up from the depot."

We slowed into a single lane and pulled up to an automatic barrier. Brahim unfastened his seatbelt and said to me: "Promise me something. If anyone asks, you're my friend, right? You're a family friend of Mr Brahim, got it?"

When the barrier lifted, we turned into a sprawling warehouse complex. There were unmarked white vehicles of various sizes parked in ranks. Small vans, trucks, articulated lorries. There was no one about. Brahim stopped the van and reversed up to the pale glow of the loading platform.

"Do me a favour," he said opening the door. "Don't get out. While I'm loading stay in the van. Do that for me please. We'll be here for less than an hour." He climbed out and slammed the door after him. I sat in the van listening to boxes being shoved into the back, watching the occasional lorry come and go in the wing mirror.

When we got going again, Brahim took a cigarette off me and went on for a time about how stupid it was to hitch-hike in France.

"No one will stop for you," he said. "Simple as that. Maybe in the old days you could get away with hitching, but not now. The problem is France is full of foreigners. All the time these damned immigrants are pouring in from Eastern Europe, from Turkey, Afghanistan, Ukraine, from all over the place." The cigarette lighter popped out of the dashboard.

"They come to France with nothing, they think they'll find work here, but there's nothing. And there's no way to keep them out. In England you're okay because you've got the sea to protect you, but in Europe they can just walk across the border. If you're hitch-hiking, people will assume you're one of these people and they won't ever stop for you, because they're afraid of being robbed, raped and stabbed."

He took quick, impatient pulls on the cigarette as he spoke, bringing it up to his mouth each time and hesitating as if he couldn't make up his mind about it.

"These days everyone's scared. I mean *I'm* scared to pick people up. You never know who people are – you could be anyone for all I know. And for all *you* know *I* could be a murderer, a serial killer, whatever, you couldn't know. You never know."

He pulled off the motorway without indicating and reached to put his cigarette out in the ashtray.

"Have you got any money?" he said.

We came into a service station that was closed, all the lights off, the car park deserted except for a single lorry with the curtains drawn around the cab.

"Um, no. Just some change."

He stopped the van by the front of the service station.

"There's a cash machine there. Take out fifty euros."

I looked at him and he looked back, cool as you like.

"There's no such thing as a free ride," he said, turning back to the windscreen. "You can pay me for it, or you can get out here. As you choose."

The fury lifted a clammy flipper in my stomach, and then let it fall again weakly. I got out of the van, looked despairingly around the car park, then went over to the cash machine.

The motorway went on and on. Brahim turned up the radio and reached over to get his own pack of cigarettes from the glove compartment.

"Have you got a coat?" he said. "Better wear it – I drive with the window open. So I don't fall asleep."

The radio DJ put on a Cyndi Lauper record.

"It's going to get cold," Brahim said.

PART TWO

BARCELONA

"I am perhaps the king of failures, since I must surely be the king of something."

– *Arthur Cravan*

Arthur Cravan, now wanted by the French authorities as a deserter, fled south towards the frontier. According to various reports he either swam to the Cap de Creus at nightfall or was smuggled into Spain in the trunk of a millionaire's automobile, whilst a stamp on his French residential permit suggests he crossed the border on foot at Puigcerdà in early September.

Spain had declared itself neutral in the war, and its bitter political infighting made it seem certain it would remain that way. Cravan made for Barcelona because he'd heard that the sport of boxing was gaining ground in Catalonia, and he hoped there might be a living to be made for someone with his credentials. The city was also known for its love of French culture, and for this reason Parisian artists who opposed the war sought refuge here in their dozens, along with deserters from many other warring nations. But after the creative freedoms they had enjoyed before the war, these artists soon felt stifled by Barcelona's deep-rooted conservatism. In his own way, this was something Cravan would relish: his first act on arrival was to ask a troupe of Carmelite nuns for directions to the nearest brothel.

The town was undergoing huge social changes. The industrial sector was exploiting Spanish neutrality to sell arms and munitions to both sides in the war and, to satisfy demand, the factories were bringing in thousands of migrant workers from the countryside. To accommodate them, sprawling barracks were being constructed in the hills to the north of the city. Cravan too was drawn to the new and inhospitable colony of Vallcarca by the prospect of low rents, and he found a cheap flat on the arid footslopes of the Güell Hill, far from the crowds, the noise and activity of the centre.

Vallcarca has since been swallowed by Barcelona's abundant suburbs, and today it is no more than an extension of the town centre, only a steep walk up from the Passeig de Gracia and the frosty exteriors of its expensive shops. But in those days, before the viaduct spanned the river, it felt estranged from the city. It was a place where the locals came to escape the pressures of the town, and Cravan often mingled with the workers who filled the bars on weekends. His fellow foreigners, however, noted his fondness for the more vulgar haunts of Vallcarca with a certain disdain.

Expat intellectual life revolved around the stately apartment of the painter Francis Picabia, which was once found on the Avinguda de la República Argentina. I followed the road as it wound its way around the rim of the Turó del Putget hill, and I noticed that amongst the dilapidated minimalist tenements put up in the Fifties there are still clear remnants of the modernist era in the faded grandeur of this street. The two-tone brickwork patterns have been obscured by a rime of lead deposit, but the butterfly-winged, steel-filigreed balconies are unmistakable, with their floral ornamentations in twisted black metal. The high balconies of these buildings overlook the valley and the dense clutter of decaying habitations that crawl up the steep slopes of the hills on all sides.

Picabia was in the process of weaning himself off an opium habit that had left him with a nervous condition, and he had come to Barcelona seeking the peace and quiet he needed to recuperate. But he soon found himself at the centre of a crowd of uprooted émigrés that sought refuge here in the opening months of the war. This was an eccentric assortment of artists, aesthetes and pacifists that included the painter Albert Gleizes and his wife, and the poet Max Goth, as well as Marie Laurencin, whose lover, the gallant Apollinaire, had recently died on the Western front having contracted the flu. Drawn together by their common sense of isolation in this foreign city, and by nostalgia for their lost Paris, they formed a tight-knit group. They idled away their afternoons at a café on the Rambla, and spent their evenings lounging in the apartment that Picabia shared with his wife Gabrielle, the daughter of a French senator. Theirs was an odd, liminal existence, spent waiting for events to take their course, and Cravan soon found himself on the periphery of their frequent meetings.

Nearby, at the bottom of the Avinguda de la República Argentina, as the road begins to descend over the cusp of the hill, there stands the viaduct spanning the river to Vallcarca. This district comprises a chaotic web of narrow alleys veering back and forth across the contour of the hill. The Carrer dels Albigesos is a short, abrupt road on a gradient so steep that I felt seasick when I turned onto it. I walked down past the unremarkable residential blocks that line the street on either side.

Number 10 is a peeling green gate set in a sheer, featureless wall, a gate of solid iron with no cracks or keyholes to offer the slightest glimpse of what lies behind. The wall outside is fifteen feet high and streaked with dirt, the brickwork showing in places where the stucco has crumbled away. There was no answer when I knocked on the gate. I stood breathless for a long time with my ear pressed against it, but I detected no sign of life inside. Finally I climbed the scaffolding holding up the front of the building opposite to try to get a look over that wall at the house in which Cravan had once lived.

Behind the gate there seemed to be a tiny courtyard cast into perpetual gloom by the high walls all around. Beyond was a concrete front of unyielding blankness, and set into this the two windows of Cravan's lodgings, each of them walled in with crudely cemented breeze blocks. The building looked long condemned.

An iron frame riveted to the stonework provided the lacklustre illusion of a small balcony beneath each window, with room enough to accommodate a small child perhaps, but certainly without sufficient sturdiness to support someone of Cravan's stature. Overhanging the windows was an iron joist that jutted three feet out of the lintel, and from the end of it dangled a noose of thick steel rope. The view over the rooftops was towards the urban conglomeration, and through the evening haze I could make out the configuration of cranes that loomed like totems over a city being slowly dismantled.

I was sitting on the esplanade at midnight. It curved into obscurity on either side, sterile and empty in the yellow floodlamps that recalled so many deserted motorways in the dead of night. Under the lights, other-worldly palm trees stood out incandescent against the darkness. There was the sound of nothing but the hush of pale fringes of breaking waves and the tick-ticking out of time of a single cleat against a masthead somewhere.

I had walked here along the beach, and the sand had been lit every few dozen metres in pools of bright light that showed up footprints left over from a day at the seaside. The only sign of life along the way had been the retinal flare of a black dog's eyes from the porch of a tent under the elevations of the boardwalk.

I was sitting there waiting for time to pass. I was hoping I could slip into the darkened dormitory room after everyone else had fallen asleep. I was hoping I would be spared the lapses in their inane conversations as they watched me clambering onto the top bunk, my testicles flapping into plain view through the leg holes of my boxer shorts as I went up the ladder.

Earlier that evening I had found myself wandering back to the hostel out of boredom, with the intention of getting some peace on the stained mattress. I'd walked in on a group of Irish gap-year students with eyebrow piercings who were ensconced in the room with a gallon bottle of Bull's Blood wine. They'd fallen silent when they saw me, the laughter draining out of their faces. I'd backed out of the doorway and sat in a toilet cubicle until I lost all sensation in my buttocks. For an hour and a half I'd stared at the graffiti on the inside of the door, trying to ignore the sounds of other people's evacuations in the neighbouring stall, the melancholy kerplonk of displaced water.

Then, drifting aimlessly out to the street again, I'd become deliberately lost in the labyrinths of the Barri Gòtic. I sleepwalked through the honeycomb of dilapidated buildings that make up the medieval old town. The alleyways threading amongst the densely packed tenements were so claustrophobic that the balconies overhead, and their abundance of laundry displayed on lines, seemed about to collapse upon me at any minute. The place was dark and stagnant, blind alleys offered dead ends occupied by malicious loitering figures, and set the heart racing. And then the paths turned hidden corners onto bustling tourist streets noisy with tapas bars, letting everything subside into familiarity and disappointment.

Wandering was a habit I'd picked up from my father. On Wednesday afternoons we'd walk into town for the shopping, and on the way back from the supermarket he'd take me for a wander. I don't think he had any particular fondness for walking – he'd never take me to the common, for instance, or for a stroll along the canal – it was more likely a way of stringing out the afternoon, of deferring the inevitable return to the house. He'd never wander the same way, not if he could help it. Each week he would set off in a different direction, down an unfamiliar road, with me following a few paces behind.

Wednesday afternoons were always the same. The bags of shopping would grow immensely heavy after half an hour of wandering, and the polythene handles would almost cheesewire my hands off. No matter how eccentric a route we took, no matter how many twists and turns and ventures along obscure and unfamiliar streets, we always emerged beneath the towering blankness of the multi-storey car park. When it was working, we'd take the lift, otherwise it was ten flights of concrete steps to the top. There we'd stand by the edge, me dropping seedless grapes over the side to watch their precipitous fall, him frowning off into space.

Of course I knew now what the wandering was all about, I understood why he used to do it. He had been trying to escape, somehow, to shrug off whatever it was that haunted him.

I did the same thing now, taking turns at random through narrow alleys that ran according to no apparent logic or design. The Barri Gòtic played tricks with my mind. After an hour of wandering I found that time and space began to rupture. The streets and the tapas bars bled into an amorphous familiarity. The more I tried to escape the peculiar gravities of these streets, the more I had the impression of travelling in circles. The alleyways divided repeatedly into forking paths, they tapered off narrower and narrower, delivering me time and again back to the place where I had started.

Barcelona was just the same as Paris. If it hadn't been for the long days of crossing frontiers, I might have moved from one quarter to another in the same city. And the people here knew it too, even though they denied it to themselves. It was written in the long faces of the backpackers at the youth hostel – the slow, sure recognition that it was all a waste of time. One place is no different from another. You can run away from your home, your job, your somnolent and tawdry existence, you can take yourself off to somewhere distant. But before long you'll find you've gone nowhere. It's just a momentary distraction, and sooner or later you'll have to resume your place in the scheme of things and abandon all hope. You'll find you've packed all your problems along with your sunblock and your sleeping bag. Your neuroses are waiting patiently for you there in the dark when you lay down to sleep.

I could read it in the lines of anxiety scored into the faces at the hostel: the chubby man by the shower smothering rolls of flab with a towel; the whiny American girl in the dormitory scouring her hair with a stiff brush. There was a telltale hunch of the shoulders, a certain mumpish languor to their expressions, a clear sense that they had surrendered themselves to the conclusion reached time after time: *I can never change.*

It was a year of radicalism and violence in the city. Whilst the owners of the munitions factories were becoming fabulously wealthy catering for the insatiable appetite of the war, the armies of factory-hands newly arrived from the country-side were growing restless. The workers represented a huge new underclass increasingly unhappy with their lot. They protested their deplorable living conditions, their miserable wages, but they soon found that their complaints fell on deaf ears.

The workers began to organize into unions, and the unions started to flex their muscles with strike actions. Seeing their profit margins drop, the factory owners paid for the assassination of the labour leaders and fanned the flames of working-class resentment. Rioting broke out on the streets and, when the government declared martial law, the strikes turned into armed confrontations. By the summer, the sporadic outbursts of violence had grown so fierce that the city was brought to a standstill.

The unions were inevitably a breeding ground of radical politics, and in this volatile atmosphere the town quickly became a hotbed of anarchist agitation. Soon the cry of dissent was no longer just for improved working conditions: the scope of the struggle had extended, and people were now beginning to demand armed uprising against the factory owners, the overthrow of the ruling classes and the right to self-government.

Cravan's relationship to the anarchist cause was an ambiguous one. It seems he should have been sympathetic to the workers' plight, since their struggle reflected his own personal revolution. He had slipped the leash of polite society, and had nothing but contempt for the tyranny of civil behaviour that turned natural instincts into guilty secrets, primal urges into perversions, and made hypocrites of all men. He embodied the questioning nature of a godless time riddled with doubt and insecurity. In the crucible of war-torn Europe, the moralities of a passed age were left standing like exotic follies in a wasteland.

These were the times that gave birth to Dadaism. It sprung from the same spirit of nihilism, in defiance of the values of the past. Dada was a violent revolt against bourgeois piety, and who better to enact this revolt than Cravan, the scandal-artist with a love for the puerile and the profane and a natural-born gift for causing offence – the human spectacle who inspired admiration and loathing in equal measure and was ready to drop his underpants at a moment's notice?

The Dada rebellion began in the summer of 1916 with the crucial meeting of the impoverished Arthur Cravan and the Spanish-born artist Francis Picabia. These men came together during an excursion to the coastal resort of Tossa de Mar, and whilst their paths crossed for little more than a month, the affinity between them was immediate and catastrophic. Picabia's wife Gabrielle wrote of this meeting that, "Without premeditated intention it let loose, from one shore of the Atlantic to another, a wave of negation and revolt which for several years would throw disorder into the minds, acts, works of men."

Other than a devastating venereal infection, I can think of nothing more miserable than a holiday town in the off-season. Tossa de Mar is a small beach resort on the Costa Brava about forty kilometres north of Barcelona, and when I went there in the wintertime the place was worse than dead: it was not quite dead, still twitching, and praying to be put out of its misery.

I was on the cliff top at night, standing by the crenellated walls of the crumbling fortress that cradles one flank of the village. Below I could make out the pale shreds of foam swelling against the rocks, and then the dark presence of the ocean that extended infinitely into the void. There was no hint of a horizon, the sea stretched onwards into the sky. The sweeping beam of the lighthouse on the headland gestured weakly over the apartments a kilometre across the bay, then turned its attention to the Atlantic, to be quickly lost in the blackness.

I walked back along the coastal path, passing the modulations of a lonesome cicada, and came to the head of the spiral cobbled track that led down to the village. The floodlights at the base of the fortress cast my shadow into space, a black hole in the pissing rain. Somewhere below, wave after inconsolable wave dashed itself against the rocks.

The rain had been coming down in a desultory fashion since that morning. I had hoped to spend the day in aimless wandering, but the village was so tiny I covered almost everything within an hour, and grew deeply bored.

I had crossed the pockmarked, coarse sand beach, found the rocky outcrop on which Cravan had been photographed many decades earlier. When the heat of the summer became stifling and the demonstrations in the city became violent, the odd collection of outsiders came to Tossa de Mar to get away from it all. In the pictures they are perched on the rock or sitting around on the sand, some of them fully dressed, suits and hats for the men, all-enveloping dresses with excessive skirts for the ladies; others are in antiquated bathing costumes, the off-the-shoulder all-in-ones and rubber caps, or just stripy trunks with their bellies sucked in for the more free-spirited of them. Picabia is there in the holiday snaps, fixing the camera with a penetrating stare.

In the pictures there is also a glimpse of Renée Bouchet, Cravan's Parisian mistress. Deeply in love, Renée had followed Cravan to Spain, where she hoped to stay with him permanently. That day at the beach she was wearing a wide-brimmed sun hat and a long white dress belted so high around her chest, according to the fashion of the day, that it gives the impression of unfeasibly long legs, or that her torso has been hammered into her waist. And sniffing around in the background is her ugly black dog Tam Tam, which seems in one picture to be stranded at the very summit of the rock. Shortly after the photograph was taken, she received news that her sister had suffered a miscarriage and fallen seriously ill. Renée had been reunited with her lover for little more than a week before she was called back to Paris. She would never set eyes upon Cravan again.

I had been woken abruptly in my hotel bed that morning. At 8 a.m., with a sudden revving of big engines and a great wrenching and smashing of brickwork, the village had turned into a monumental building site. All morning the sound of drills and hammers reverberated along the pretty streets. Around every corner there was a hotel gutted for renovation, or a new complex going up in a cleared lot, scheduled for completion in time for the first tourist arrivals the next summer.

Then, just as suddenly as the work had begun, at the stroke of twelve from the little church tower, the machines fell silent, the tools were downed, the dust subsided on the deserted building sites, and the place turned into a ghost town.

I walked past the vast whitewashed hotels that stood empty and shuttered. The only sound was the groan of the wind in the scaffolding. In the gutter a neon sign for the "Restaurant Minerva" stuck out of a pile of rubble. The doors to the little church stood open, and on the threshold there was a sign that read "This is a place for prayer" in six languages. But there was nothing inside except for a parked JCB, with its mechanical arm bowed before the crucified Jesus.

For this eerie lunch hour, Tossa de Mar lay hushed and motionless as if under a vow of silence. There was no one around. Despite the incessant rain, the river bed that ran out to the sea was dried up, the stream had shrunk to a trickle of dirty water that picked its way between the plastic bottles and old cigarette packets deposited there. Down by the beach the fishing boats were laid out under tarpaulins like draped bodies in a morgue.

Now, coming down the spiral track from the cliff top, the haloes of the lights of the village were glimmering through the rain. I went down, passing the Bar Don Pepe, boarded up, with a picture of a Spanish guitar on the sign outside and the words "*Flamenco y Rumba*". A few doors down was the Excelsior Cocktail Bar, locked, with its windows nailed shut. The streets lay comatose, it seemed their inhabitants had long since abandoned them to the hush of the rain and the soft gargling of water in the drains.

Further on I came across an enclave of activity in the general desolation of this town. Here was a restaurant that was open for business. A waiter in a tailcoat stood by the doorway in minute inspection of his fingernails, the proprietor had his head in his hands at the bar, there were no customers in sight. Up ahead, through the acrid smoke of coal fires, I saw an open *cervecería* with lights on inside, and I went in for a nightcap.

There were three skinheads bent over a bar littered with empty shot glasses. The barman looked over at me listlessly from behind his moustache. His face was so old and weather-beaten I doubted that it was still capable of expression. His flesh had the colour and consistency of smoke-cured ham. When I ordered a whisky in broken Spanish I became aware of the skinheads' pale faces turning towards me.

"Ee," the closest one said to me. "Are yae England?"

I looked around and met his gimlet eyes.

"I beg your pardon?"

"*Ah seed*, are yae England?"

The skinhead flexed his knuckles on the counter.

"I'm from England, yes," I answered.

"He is, ay," the one on the end said. The skinhead in-between was only half-conscious; some reflex must have lifted his head towards me, and the whites of his eyes were showing under his faltering eyelids.

"England, eh?" said the man nearest by. "That's greet, that is."

"You're Scottish?" I said, tasting the unpleasant Spanish whisky.

"Scotland, ay." He hiked up the sleeve of his terylene shirt to expose a pasty shoulder. His fingers felt around on the blank flesh, searching for something. After a moment, a sudden look of comprehension crossed his face and he peeled back the sleeve on his other arm to reveal a saltire tattooed there. "Scotland," he said, prodding it, relieved to see it was still there.

His friend said, "Ay pal," and raised an empty glass.

The man's eyes came up to my face and he stared at me so intensely that he began to pitch forwards on the bar stool. Finally he looked away, saying, "S'alreet, thoo. We're all streengers here, eh? Yull survive the night, man."

The two of them collapsed over the bar with laughter, and the one on the end soon broke into an uncontrollable hacking cough. His face turned the colour of beetroot and he started slapping his half-conscious friend hard on the back, just as a wrestler in a stranglehold beats the canvas. The slapped man woke from his stupor with a start and stared around him as if seeing the world for the first time. I saw the look of horror come over his face when he remembered where he was.

I downed the whisky and felt it strip the lining of my gullet. The old barman was sitting on a stool watching us without interest. Behind him there were Catholic icons stuck up amongst the bottles behind the bar. Next to the vintage Coca-Cola sign, a stony-faced Jesus had his eyes rolled back into his head.

When the skinhead's coughing had run its course and he had fallen into silent recuperation, and the third man had bowed his head once more to the bar, the one closest said to me in confidential tones:

"Fuck'n spics everywheer, man. Have you seen 'em?"

I nodded.

"Every fuck'n wheer, ah tell yeh." He nodded at the barman. "S'alreet," he whispered to me, "he cannae understand a fuck'n word."

I flicked the ash off my cigarette.

"What brings you to Tossa de Mar?" I said.

"Thomas *bastarrrd* Cook," he snapped, pursing his lips. He cast a scowl into the corner of the room. "One week in the Coasta Brava. Three-star hotel. Sun, sex and sodd'n sangria."

"Sex," declared the third man suddenly, without quite waking.

"Sangria's fuck'n shite and all," mumbled the one on the end, looking for stray flecks of phlegm on his football shirt. "Tosser de ars'n Mar. It's fuck'n deid, man."

"It's a nice enough place though, eh," his mate said.

"Ay, man." He looked thoughtful for an instant. "But fuck'n deid, eh."

I paid for a round of whiskies, and the arthritic barman clambered down off his stool and poured them with a trembling hand so that whisky spilt over the lip of the glass. I was about to propose a toast to intoxication and oblivion when I noticed that the two of them had already throated their drinks without a moment's hesitation. I did the same.

The fourth shot sat on the bar in front of the sleeper, and at the smell of it he came suddenly to his senses. His eyes settled on the glass and, taking it in his hands with such gentleness that you might have thought he was handling a rare bird's egg, he slowly drained it. The whisky caught in his neck on the way down, and it was touch-and-go for a moment if he'd bring it back up. He looked at his surroundings, his sluggish sloe eyes trailing behind the turning of his head. There were heavy bags weighting down his eyes, and his face was ruddy and swollen, the flesh sagging off the bones as if his muscles had atrophied beyond hope.

It took a while for him to focus on me. Then he made as if he was about to stand up but, unable to marshal his limbs, he remained seated.

"Eh!" he said in alarm, pointing.

"Easy, Jackie." The man on the far side of him clamped a hand over his bald head to steady him.

"*Eh!*" Jackie pointed at me and looked first at the one on the left, then the skinhead on the right of him.

"S'alreet man, we're in Speen."

"Who's he for?" Jackie said, growing more agitated with every passing moment.

The man next to me said, "He wants eh knoo which team you support."

All eyes were on me, even the cloudy, uncomprehending eyes of the old barman, who hadn't a clue what they were talking about.

"Romford Town," I told them, and the face nearest me split open to laugh. But he stopped short and the smile faded when he saw in my eyes that I wasn't joking. The three shaved heads were turned to me, the six narrowed eyes were giving me a long searching look. An expression of sudden sobriety had fallen across their faces. There was silence for a time, broken at last by Jackie's hoarse cry:

"FUCK'N REEN-GERS, MAN!"

He threw a fist in the air and nearly toppled from his stool.

"FUCK'N COME ON YOU REEN-GERS!"

And then he fell abruptly forwards, his forehead striking the bar with a coconut-shy sound, and he lay there perfectly still.

After a while the man next to me asked, "What'r *you* doin' here then?"

"I'm on business."

"Is that it. You looked a wee bit like a sex tourist, man," he reached across to put a hand on my shoulder. He had to take a second swipe, having missed the first time. "And ah mean neh offence by that, pal. Did it myself last year in Thailand, eh." He took his hand away from me, had second thoughts and replaced it. "Gotta watch oot for the fuck'n leedieboys, though, eh?"

The one on the end said, "Ay," and raised his glass in salute.

"Eh. You're no a handbag, are yeh?" he said, quickly reclaiming his arm. I shook my head.

"Neh offence, pal. Man's neh seef anywheer these dees."

His mate said, "Ay, man," and went to raise his glass again, but it slipped out of his fingers and smashed on the floor.

"Gonnee have neh luck here, anywee. Fuck'n taches on all the leedies roond here."

Jackie started snoring. I could hear his lips flapping wetly on the bar top. The barman slipped a coaster under his face, and went to find a broom for the broken glass. It was time for me to leave.

I got up and said goodbye. The talkative one tried to get to his feet too, but he couldn't quite make it. He fell back onto the stool and beckoned me over to him. I looked round at the door to the street. He beckoned me over again, more authoritatively this time.

"Come *here*, pal," he said.

Reluctantly I went over to where he was sitting.

"Ay, that's it, pal."

When I was within reach he swung for me with both arms, and I flinched. He grabbed me around the waist and pulled me to him. I hesitated to put my hands on his shoulders, which were cold and clammy. He ground his face against my chest in an embrace. It didn't occur to me at the time, but later I remembered that he had patted me on the back in a tender, almost consoling way.

"S'alreet," he said softly. "Ah *knoo* hoo it as, pal."

I stood at my hotel-room window for a long time, turning the pill between my fingers as I stared out. I could see the empty car park around the back, the tarmac slick with rain. Further off there were the flashing lights of a one-armed bandit in a deserted bar. I swallowed the pill down with a glass of tap water.

Before going to sleep I took out the dog-eared passport photograph of Cathy and, holding it up to my face, I inspected it closely. The flash of the photo booth made her look flat and pale. Her expression was rigid and expectant, she seemed uncomfortable posing for the picture. I tried to remember the details of her face and the way her eyes looked at me. I felt like I was about to cry, but I didn't. I shoved the picture back into my wallet.

I didn't quite catch my father's last words to me. The nurse had briefed me outside the ward that death was very close now, this might be the last time I saw him alive.

There he lay, as pale as the sheets around him. I decided to try and put aside my feelings: anything that had happened in the past was unimportant now he was going to die. I waited patiently, and after a few hours he at last seemed to rouse himself from his torpor. He appeared to be summoning the last of his energies from somewhere deep inside. His eyes rolled as he gathered the strength to speak. I leant in to put my ear by his pallid lips which were blistered like pork scratchings. It wasn't clear, I couldn't be certain, but what he said sounded strangely like "I love you".

I sat by his bedside for the rest of the afternoon, the rest of the evening, waiting hopefully. I even stayed overnight, stretched out on the seats. But he was still there in the morning. He was still there for months. Perhaps if he had died then, those words would have held some significance. As it happened their meaning waned with every week he clung on. And as for putting aside our differences, the longer he persisted the more my resentment grew. Staring into his collapsing face I could not find an ounce of repentance in him.

Deathbed protocol generally dictates some measure of conciliation. Death is supposed to throw one's life into perspective, and in this new light even the most heinous sins are forgiven and forgotten. Prostrate, withered, as helpless as a newborn baby, a dying man seems to relapse to a state of purity and innocence. But lying there before me, gaunt and deathly, my father appeared the very essence of himself. He was relishing this.

I wondered what he could have meant by those last words of his. I couldn't be sure that I had correctly interpreted the pops and guttural crackles of his voice box. Had I, after all, merely heard what I wanted to hear?

At the time I didn't think much of it. I assumed that whatever his words had been, they were without meaning, merely a last gasp of senility. But later I found that as time cleared out my memory, discarding the trivia of the past, that moment remained.

That mute flapping of his dry tongue came back to me at the coffin side. The funeral speeches were short and perfunctory. There wasn't really too much to say. Everyone agreed that it was all best forgotten. Barely a dozen people had turned out, and I suspected those who were there had come to make sure he was really gone. Nobody wanted to get too close to the coffin. They lingered long enough to be certain he was dead, and there was an audible sigh of relief when the doors of the furnace finally closed on him.

I'd noted that it was probably a trainee mortician who had done him, because there was a little too much enthusiasm about the job. His hair, instead of being brylcreemed back the way he always had it, had been blow-dried and brushed absurdly to one side, and this had the effect of softening his features. A ruddy bloom had been added to his cheeks with blusher, and the muscles of his face were drawn up around the mouth to produce the distinct impression of a smile.

It seemed a sick practical joke. Everyone had remarked upon it in whispered tones, a scoff had resounded around the chapel. Then, remembering where they were, faces were quickly downcast, looks guiltily averted when they met my eyes. But I could see the joke, the irony wasn't lost on me. That was the first time I had seen him smile.

Francis Picabia was a man with a strange, stunted, hairless body. In old photographs of the group of émigrés at the beach in Tossa de Mar, Picabia stands obstinately in a minuscule pair of bathing trunks and a fedora, resembling nothing more than an indulged child with a future of obesity before him.

Picabia was blessed with great wealth, whilst his marriage provided him the privilege of senatorial protection, and this independence allowed him to lead a life of gratuitous creativity. In sharp contrast to Cravan's nonchalant, slowed-down nature, this pugnacious little man lived at a hyperactive pace, with a quick tongue, darting eyes and a nervous, edgy manner.

Picabia's life and work reflected the strange contradiction which ruled him. "What I like," he said, "is to invent, to imagine, to make a new man of myself at every moment – and then to forget him, forget everything." He was a cruel paradox, a born artist with sublime gifts of invention, and at the very same time a sceptic who despised these gifts. Even as he produced a masterpiece, he knew full well that art was a petty waste of time in a world without meaning.

Picabia was perhaps one of the most frivolous people who ever lived, and yet he conducted his buffoonery in a spirit of chilling sobriety. He was at all times deadly serious, and acquaintances likened a conversation with Picabia to "an experience of death". Nevertheless, the lonely expatriates were drawn to his perverse magnetism, he was the empty centre around which they gathered.

Hans Richter was a painter who passed through this milieu in 1916, and in his book *Art and Anti-Art* he recalls Picabia: "He was very strange, very magnetic, very challenging and intimidating. Picabia had his own inexhaustible arsenal of destructive weapons: he could provide negations, contradictions and paradoxes of all kinds, from ridicule to downright slander. All this at the service of a negation of life that was exuberant." Richter was struck by Picabia's curious personality, the terrible cynicism that, far from crippling him with apathy and depression, actually seemed to drive him forwards. Richter observed how the exiles fell under the spell of the anti-life impulse that Picabia so virulently expressed; even he felt the pull of this negative attraction: "I remember the moments of despair when I went round kicking holes in my mutely staring paintings," he wrote.

It was inevitable that art should bear the brunt of this cynicism, for art itself, not just its artefacts, represented the mechanisms of repression that shored up the social order.

"ART – a parrot word replaced by Dada... Art needs an operation. Art is a pretension, warmed by the timidity of the urinary tract, hysteria born in the studio." From Picabia's perspective the whole tradition of past art was corrupted with a false ideal, every painting in the great galleries of the Western world reproduced the same beautiful lies. The antidote, he proclaimed, was Dada.

When Cravan crossed paths with Picabia on the sunny beaches of Tossa de Mar, a darkness fell over the enclave of émigrés. In Picabia, Cravan had met someone with a mind as rebellious and degenerate as his own, and in Dada he had found his calling. Although Cravan produced nothing during his time in Barcelona, there is no doubt that he was an inspiration for the provocations wrought by Picabia and his entourage – not to mention the atrocities committed against art that were to follow the world over.

Seven years earlier Barcelona had seen a full-blown anarchist revolt in which civil disorder took on the complexion of rampant chaos. The "Tragic Week" had been a blunt reminder of the entropy that lurked beneath the social veneer: police stations were overrun, convents were burnt to the ground, graves were desecrated, and one man led the skeleton of a long-dead nun in a profane tango. All the decorum and taste which maintained polite society had been overturned, and it was a riot like this that the Dadaists wanted to instigate; they wanted to set the world against itself in a carnival of organized lunacy. They declared, "We are circus directors whistling amid the winds of sideshows convents bawdy houses theatres realities sentiments restaurants Ho Hi HoHo Bang." They envisaged a revolution of their own, but instead of tearing down the class system it was meant to change the way people thought: this was to be a revolution in the sphere of art.

The sixth issue of the *Dada* periodical was printed in red and black, the colours of anarchism. But that was the extent of the group's political commitment, and in truth the

Dadaists had little sympathy for the struggle of the workers' unions in Barcelona. Whilst the city rang with the clamour of popular protest, Cravan and the rest of the émigrés couldn't care less about the plight of the working man. They turned a blind eye to the factory labourers who marched without rest below the high windows of their cloistered studios. They soon tired of the endless demonstrations that spoilt otherwise peaceful afternoons at the café playing billiards and discussing intellectual trifles.

Whilst they drew their spirit from the political agitation going on around them, the Dadaists did all they could to distance themselves from it. They existed in a hermetic bubble, whiling away the days plotting deeds of riotous nonsense that would be comprehensible only to the other members of their own little clique. Not everyone in Picabia's circle played along – the socialists amongst them watched the activities of the Dadaists with dismay. The painter Albert Gleizes considered his former colleagues to be afflicted with a pathological childishness: "They confuse excrement with the products of the mind," he declared. "Never has a group gone to such lengths to reach the public and then bring them nothing."

Dada was a rebellion purely for rebellion's sake, it was two fingers held up to anything and everything. Its perpetrators sought to maintain at all costs the essential inanity and silliness at its core, because they understood that the spirit of revolution would survive only as long as it remained utterly pointless. All they wanted was to tear off their clothes and run gibbering through the streets, just for the hell of it. "*Dada means nothing*," the Dada manifesto stated. "*We wish to change the world with nothing!*"

If Francis Picabia was the driving force behind the revolt, then Cravan embodied the negative principle, he enacted the deeds of anarchy that were promised in the profligate theorizing. Cravan's singular achievement was to take the struggle out of the intellectual sphere – out of the cabaret, out of the idle little debates in coffee shops, out of inaccessible polemics in obscure little magazines – and to put it into practice in the real world. Dada embraced Cravan because he led his life as if his life itself was a work of art: something to be exhibited and defiled. Even his strange demise had the feel of a piece of absurdist theatre done in the worst possible taste.

Dada was a prophecy and Cravan was its prophet. But he didn't stop to consider what he was prophesying. The fact is, he didn't care.

It was a day of signs, of small indications, all signalling the despair permeating the fabric of things. I walked along La Rambla, the interminable tourist drag leading to the seafront, where bereted caricaturists pestered passers-by to taunt them with their likenesses, and exotic birds trilled listlessly from cages stacked like freight containers at the shipping depot. I saw malicious infants running across plazas thick with pigeons, swiping at them, making them rise into the air in great numbers. I passed a pisshead busker who, for lack of a talent for anything else, was begging for spare change in a cardboard bird hat. His routine, which consisted of jumping on the spot and flapping his cardboard wings, had drawn a crowd of jeering teenagers.

Turning off the main drag, the warmth of the morning sun was eclipsed by the damp chill of densely packed alleyways. Slumped in a dismal doorway, a sickly-looking youth in a tattered tracksuit pulled his sallow face out of a bag of solvents as I passed and shouted something at me, his voice dissolving into a long hacking giggle of despair. I was looking for the Dalmau gallery, another important reference point of Cravan's Barcelona. I knew it was to be found on the Carrer Portaferrissa, somewhere amidst the gloomy rat runs of the Old Town.

Past the rear goods entrance of the fish market I came upon the city's red-light district. I walked hurriedly by some of the most unappetizing prostitutes I had ever laid eyes upon: aged bodies shoehorned into hot pants, spilling flaccidly out of boob tubes, drooping breasts erupting from sequinned halter tops. I hastily avoided the unsightly gyrations of a shaven-haired tart dancing in the gutter outside a peeling bordello, her high-heeled boots stamping drifts of fluorescent rat poison into a thick yellow mud. Toothless hairy pimps jeered from the doorways as I passed, and one sizeable prostitute in laddered tights bent forwards and shook her tremendous buttocks at me. I fled amidst a chorus of catcalls that sounded like the frenzy of jungle primitives.

With relief I found my way back into a street of legitimate businesses, and the window display of an acne-treatment clinic marked my return to civilization. I paused to look in the window display at blown-up photographs of the afflicted, pictured before and after their miraculous therapeutic cure. Terrible skin conditions magnified to overwhelming proportions, pus welling up from each welt, cheeks lubed with Vaseline to accentuate their inflammations, human beings cruelly mocked by creation, and condemned to life with a face like the inside of a pork pie. There was no hope for the wretched souls drawn here out of desperation, and compelled to hand over their life savings to a con man with a pot-scourer.

When at last I found it, I saw that the Portaferrissa was a narrow alley feeding back into the Rambla. These days all that is exhibited here are the window displays of trendy clothes stores stocking useless and overpriced tat. A boutique selling baby-doll crop tops with obscene logos printed on them now occupies the premises of the old Dalmau Gallery.

The Dalmau had been a little antiques shop that was a haven for radical artists out on their uppers in this town of conventional tastes. The owner, Josep Dalmau, made his living from stocking musty old furniture and reproductions of the Old Masters, but at the rear of the shop, next to the water closet, was a doorway concealed behind a curtain. Customers looking to relieve themselves might accidentally pull back this curtain and stumble into another dimension, for Dalmau had turned his tiny backroom into an illicit gallery for the most radical works of modern art.

For Dalmau this turned out to be a loss-making venture – not only because he never managed to sell a single canvas, but also because he felt compelled to loan money to the painters themselves. Indeed he was such an easy touch for artists seeking handouts that it seemed the whole of Europe's displaced avant-garde lived out of his pocket. His generosity did not come without personal sacrifice: there was the unmistakable look of starvation about him, the sunken cheeks and bloodless complexion of a cadaver, and his clothes hung off him in loose folds as if several sizes too big. So many bankrupt artists were dossing down in his apartment that he had even taken to sleeping on the shop floor. Dalmau's masochist streak made him the target for the flock of radical artists that descended on Barcelona during the summer of 1916, and the Portaferrissa Gallery soon became the nerve centre of the Dada enterprise.

When they claimed that their goal was "New art in a new-found freedom", it seemed the Dadaists had taken up the burden of creating meaning for themselves in a universe of chaos. And yet from the beginning Cravan and his friends seemed more interested in wanton destruction than in creating anything new. They claimed: "Our follies and our deeds of heroism, our provocations, however polemical and aggressive they may be, are all part of a quest for an anti-art, a new way of thinking, feeling and knowing." But this quest for an anti-art, on the whole, consisted of reckless defiance of moral values, puerile trouncing of tradition, and farting in the face of authority.

Dada aspired to a world released from all values, all conventions, all restraints. But it was towards the darker implications of this freedom that it was inexorably drawn. In 1999, during the excavation of a site for a new shopping mall in the outskirts of the city, construction workers unearthed a series of strange cells. These detention rooms were built during the Spanish Civil War as part of the workers' losing battle against the Fascists. The design was curious in the extreme: the beds were pitched at a twenty-degree angle to make them almost impossible to sleep on; the floors of the cells were scattered with sharp-edged obstacles to prevent prisoners from pacing back and forth; a stone bench sloped in such a way that the prisoner would be sent sliding to the floor when he sat on it. There were no windows, and no distraction from the optical illusions and mind-altering tricks of perspective painted over the walls. The effect was confusion, distress and ultimately psychosis. The rooms were the work of an artist who had joined the anarchists' struggle, and in his trial after the defeat of the workers' militia, he confessed that he had been inspired by the work of the Dadaists.

This was perhaps the first time that modern art was used deliberately as an instrument of torture. Before Dada, art had existed for its own sake. Now it seemed the Dadaists had at last found a practical purpose for it. Their insight was that art has the unique capacity to show us horrors, to cause boredom, disorientation, pain, and even to induce a suicidal malaise.

The turn of the twentieth century may have ushered in a new age of liberty, but it brought with it an awareness of just how close this newfound freedom is to nothingness. With a reckless courage that few others possessed, Cravan threw himself headlong into the moral vacuum. He lived out the ironies of this new condition, seizing the endless possibilities it opened up, even as the glaring pointlessness of all human activity began to paralyse him. While his complete works number a mere dozen derivative poems, the real Dada masterpiece was Arthur Cravan himself.

Cravan's story bears many similarities to that of Jacques Vaché, another character who walked the fine line between genius and certifiable insanity, and whose strange life made him the poster boy for the nihilism of subsequent generations. The story of his short existence was so absurd that he was considered an honorary Dadaist – like Cravan, a Dada artefact in himself.

Until his death Vaché had been known principally for interrupting the premiere of a play by Apollinaire, where he invaded the stage dressed as an English aviator and threatened the actors with a revolver. He had spent much of his brief life walking tirelessly through the streets dressed in ladies' clothing or military costumes from the Napoleonic era and steadfastly ignoring any acquaintances he might run into. Like Cravan he was a self-proclaimed artist who in fact produced no palpable works of art. Vaché's life came to a premature end at the age of twenty-seven when he invited two naive friends to an opium parlour and, with a perfectly straight face, administered a lethal dose to his unsuspecting companions before overdosing himself. His suicide and double murder was a chilling act, a practical joke taken far beyond the limits of sense. And for this the Dadaists and the Surrealists after them considered him a hero: his example had revealed to them the only possible answer to the intolerable ironies of life.

The comic suicide was an apt archetype on which Dada should choose to model itself. This destructive impulse is the true essence of Dada. This cynical humour, entirely disengaged from any ethical end, proved so virulent that it would corrupt the minds of succeeding generations. It would infect popular culture with an acute self-loathing, and breed the neuroses of modern society.

All those implicated in the excesses of Dadaism have conspired to ensure that history remembers them kindly. Whilst some have portrayed the movement as a kind of harmless clowning, and others have cast it as a protest against its time, they all agree that it could only be a righteous exercise, for it had its origins in a sense of outrage at the futility of the First World War. But in fact, the Dadaists shared that same consuming force. Perversely, they relished the carnage of the war, and their own scandals aspired to a similar conflagration of everything that had gone before.

The erasure of the past was, of course, a vain effort. In the end the Dadaists succeeded only in perpetuating the legacy of the past they sought to annihilate. It was a pattern that would recur time after time throughout the course of the century. Revolutionaries everywhere struggled to dethrone one dictator only to install another in his place, just as each and every one of us ceased to be children that moment we stared into the mirror to see there the father we so despised.

I'd turned nineteen and, after a long period of inactivity following my A-levels, I had recently started work as a clerk at Bradford & Bingley. Earlier that day over dinner I had told my father that Bernard the cashier had a spare room in his flat above the takeaway on Carvey Road, and so I would be moving out the following week.

That night he came into my bedroom and shook me awake. He told me to get up, quickly, and get dressed. As I got into my clothes he paced up and down the corridor. I could hear him jangling his car keys impatiently.

It was pitch-dark out and raining. He didn't answer when I asked him what was going on. He told me to just get in the car and shut up. The clock on the dashboard read quarter-past two in the morning.

As he drove I noticed his hands clamping and unclamping around the steering wheel. I didn't say anything, I was still half-asleep, and all kinds of things were running through my mind. I could see he was in a state of some anxiety. I was sure he was working himself up to tell me something. I glanced at his face illuminated by the eerie green glow of the instrument panel. From the rigid set of his jaw I knew that whatever it was he was about to tell me, it was of the utmost importance.

He turned onto an A road heading west and put his foot down. I watched the needle on the speedometer pass sixty and carry on up towards seventy. I was about to ask where he was taking me, but there seemed no point, I would find out soon enough.

The aureoles of oncoming headlamps bloomed in the windscreen. I saw the light slide across my father's face before the driver dipped his full beams. The engine changed in pitch and the needle on the speedometer climbed up to eighty. Frowning the light out of his eyes, my father hunched forwards, his knuckles turning white around the wheel. The drumming of the rain seemed to build to a crescendo. I watched the headlamps growing rapidly as the car rushed towards us.

My father didn't say a word, and after a while he seemed to crumple and sink back against the headrest. I listened to the soughing of the windscreen wipers, and the monotony of it made me nod off. I woke up again as we were turning into our front drive. When he turned the engine off, the clock on the dashboard read quarter-past three.

The silence in the car seemed impenetrable. In the ignition the car keys swung gently to and fro. At last he whispered that I should go upstairs to my room. I didn't say anything. I changed back into my pyjamas and before getting into bed I parted the curtains to look out. Down in the driveway I saw he hadn't moved from the front seat of the car.

My relationship with the other inmates of the dormitory in Barcelona had been frosty to say the least, and the situation had only got worse once they contracted my infection. There had been a day when two of them languished in their bunks until the afternoon, coughing miserably and blowing thick gouts of mucus out of their noses. I could see the bitter resentment in their bloodshot eyes that blinked rheumily at me when I came in whistling from the shower.

For some reason I had felt elated that morning. I even did some callisthenics right there in the room – toe-touching, squat thrusts, press-ups, that sort of thing – and the two of them watched me for a while and then turned heavily to face the wall. Now they seemed to have moved out.

I was sitting on the edge of my bed in the afternoon, taking the air and its unpleasant edge of rotting feet. I was staring at the cracked floor tiles, and my eyes had drifted out of focus. Weakly I was trying to muster some measure of enthusiasm for life. Then from somewhere outside in the corridor there came the sound of doors thrown open, and the bellowed "*BWEN-ASS DEE-ASS!*" that announced the arrival of an American.

There was a mighty stomping down the corridor, and the door to the room was flung back to allow a short, broad-shouldered man in wraparound shades and a baseball cap to come spilling in.

"Wassup man," he shouted, his face blank through a dark goatee. "I just got here, how 'bout you?"

He didn't wait for an answer, but threw his hefty backpack at the nearest bed.

"Jeez Louise, that's some heavy shit know what I'm sayin'?" He swaggered over and put his hand out to me. "I can see you do brother – backpacker's burden, eh? Name's Kevin, how-ya doin'."

I saw his left eye narrow with exertion as he clenched my hand and mashed it in his fist. I let my arm go dead as a sign of deference, and he sent it swinging limply back to me. Then he moved about the room checking everything out.

"This place fuckin' *stinks* man," he said after a moment. "I'm not saying it's you, it's just I think something *died* in here. *Fuck* man that's some rancid shit." He threw open the doors to the little balcony and poked his head out. "Hmmah… Been in worse places. This ain't so bad."

He punched his fist into the drawstring sphincter of his pack and pulled out a guidebook the size and shape of a house brick. It said "Europe" on the cover.

"I've just got into town from Belgium. Night train. I've done Paris, Italy, Amsterdam, Berlin, Amsterdam again cos it's so damn crazy, now here. Next I'm gonna do Madrid, maybe Monaco, probably Amsterdam again if I've got time. So much to do, so little time to do it, you know what I'm sayin'."

Kevin moved his short, stocky frame around in his shorts. He had a definite air of self-satisfaction about him, even though his face bore those telltale lines, the traces of long nights spent entertaining thoughts of self-destruction.

He pulled off his shirt to reveal an array of rigidly packed abdominals.

"So what's there to do in this town?"

He pulled on a new shirt just the same as the old one, and set about taking things out of his rucksack and shoving them forcefully into a smaller bag, half-listening to me. I said I'd just wandered around, hadn't really seen anything worth recommending.

He said: "Oh yeah? Uh huh."

He threw me a level look, and for the first time came to a dead stop as he stared across the room at me. Then he viciously garrotted his bag shut.

"Okay man, I will definitely have to check that place out. Now I'm gonna have to love you and leave you cos I got shit to do today."

When he was halfway out of the door he leant back in and made a little pistol out of his thumb and index finger, aimed at my head.

"And if you find some weed, save some for me cos I'm clean out, you hear?" He pulled the trigger and, like that, he was gone.

An hour later the obese black cleaner waddled in and ranted at me in Spanish. When I didn't move, she went about her business, tearing the sheets off the beds with some violence, and muttering under her breath. My eyes had slipped out of focus again.

The cleaner went out and returned with a mop and bucket. She gave the grime-encrusted floor a token once-over, making a point of mopping around my legs meticulously, even vigorously scrubbing at a stain under the bunk that might have been blood or mattress rust from an old bed-wetting. I didn't bother to move, and she muttered in an increasingly disgruntled fashion, then made an acerbic speech in the doorway before disappearing. I didn't understand a word, though I think I caught the gist of it.

After another hour had passed I heard the sound of Kevin the American barking at someone in the corridor. Kevin's return was just the impetus I required, and I succeeded in heaving myself to my feet and sleepwalking out of the building.

I wandered for a while, then sat in a bar. I drank the first beer without stopping for breath. Later, after four more, my stomach had begun to turn, and my last cigarette had burnt down in the ashtray. The passport photograph of Cathy was lying on the bar top in front of me. I had been staring at it for some time, and there was a dull spot by her shoulder where a single tear had dissolved the emulsion. Just to demonstrate how cold I could be, I took a chewed biro and very carefully gave her a handlebar moustache and a beauty spot with a hair sprouting out of it. As an afterthought, I drew a Gorbachev wine stain below her hairline.

It was the first and only time I had gone with Cathy to the clinic. It had been a long time since I'd been to the hospital, but walking through the automatic doors into the antiseptic lobby I had the strange sensation of coming home. Going arm in arm with Cathy along the corridor I recalled the countless afternoon visits to see my father on the wards.

We turned a corner and went through swing doors into the Blue Wing. We passed a man lying stupefied on a gurney, apparently abandoned. Further on a couple of African orderlies in green scrubs high-fived one another with rubber-gloved hands and erupted into a fit of shrill laughter.

As we came into the clinic we had to stand back to let a woman in a wheelchair be manoeuvred outside by her husband. She was sobbing in dry convulsions, and Cathy and I both cast our eyes towards the far end of the corridor and pretended we didn't see.

Nurses are terrific at small talk, I suspect it may form part of their training. The nurse that was seeing to Cathy chatted amiably about the weather in her country, and it nearly took my mind off things whilst Cathy changed into her hospital gown. She kept it up throughout the whole procedure of preparing the machinery, and helping Cathy up onto the table. She barely stopped for breath as she snapped the gloves on, and parted Cathy's gown to expose her abdomen. Her mouth carried on moving whilst she smeared a glutinous substance over Cathy's stomach, but I was no longer hearing a word that she said.

The screen showed a sea of static the colour of cigarette ash. Dark swirls throbbed and squirmed amongst the flecks of light like strange creatures rising from the depths, then plunged back into obscurity. The knots in my stomach had turned into a dizzy sick feeling. The nurse drew the probe slowly across the camber of Cathy's belly, and the sweat turned cold in the cleft of my back.

"There's its head there, can you see?" The nurse said, pointing at a shadow on the screen.

"And do you see, that's its heart beating."

Cathy squeezed my hand and looked up at me. I smiled back. Her eyes searched mine for a second before she turned back to the screen.

Cravan was up to his old tricks in Barcelona. Spending much of his time holed up in bars, he would embark on lengthy drunken discourses, enthralling all present with exaggerated tales of his boxing career. One night, after a glass too many of pastis, he happened to meet the director of the most exclusive boxing club in the city.

"You've probably heard of me," he declared, offering his hand, "Arthur Cravan – nephew of Oscar Wilde, poet and boxer."

The man appeared nonplussed.

"Arthur Cravan – the shortest-haired poet in the world?" Cravan tried as an afterthought.

With another pastis inside him, he was soon well into his stride: his arm slung around the director's neck, Cravan expounded on his own unique style of boxing, a synthesis of the English and American techniques. As the man tried to uncoil himself from his grip, muttering something about a prior engagement, Cravan reminisced about his close friendship with Jack Johnson, recalling the times they had sparred together in Paris. To top it all, he gave a rousing blow-by-blow account of the fight that had won him the French title. By this time the man had stopped struggling, and had fallen under Cravan's spell. Stupefied by his extraordinary claims, he seemed reluctant to be released from his new friend's embrace. Pressing his business card into his hand, he invited Cravan to call on him at the club the following day.

The Reial Club Marítim looks much as it did a century ago, although the landscape surrounding it has been transformed. Today this yellowing modernist compound that squats on the quayside has fallen under the shadow of a vast new IMAX cinema. The club remains the preserve of the rich, the owners of the bulging super-yachts that are moored in the harbour. In 1916 the Club Marítim was still young, but its reputation was already established, so when the director offered Cravan the job of boxing instructor he was bestowing upon him a post of some status.

His rise to the elite circles of the Spanish boxing fraternity had been so precipitous that Cravan had begun to think of himself as untouchable. A strange twist of fate was soon to bring him back to earth. Barely two weeks into the job, he was called into the director's office once again, and there he found the boss at his desk with his head in a newspaper. On the inside pages of *La Vanguardia* was a story under the headline, "Ex-World Champion to Visit Barcelona". It read that Jack Johnson was on his way to the city, and was looking for a worthy opponent for a boxing match. The director clapped Cravan on the shoulder and declared:

"It will be my honour to recommend you!"

Jack Johnson is one of the most illustrious fighters in the history of boxing. He was the first black boxer to wrest the world heavyweight championship title from the white race when he defeated Tommy Burns in Australia in 1908. His match against James J. Jeffries, who had come out of retirement to reclaim the title for the whites in Reno, Nevada, two years later, was the first great fight of the twentieth century. He now came to Barcelona to play a cameo role in an adventure movie, the beginning of a long, slow decline in his career that would see him taking any job that was offered, from self-parodying appearances in burlesque stage shows, to wrestling in a mask and cape.

Racial politics dominated Johnson's career. He too was a fugitive, on the run from the United States authorities for sleeping with white women. Johnson had been criminalized under the Mann Act, which forbade black men from transporting white women across state lines. Even though the woman in question was his wife, he was convicted, and when he was released on bond pending appeal he disguised himself as a member of a black baseball team and escaped to Canada and then Europe. His persistent affairs with white girls became a way of insulting the race that fed off his success yet refused to accept him as a human being.

Johnson was a true champion for the downtrodden blacks of segregated America. The newspapers had billed his confrontation with Jeffries as the fight that would decide once and for all the superiority of the white race. But Johnson not only beat Jeffries, he humiliated him, announcing after the fight, "He was the easiest man I ever met! I could've put him away quicker, but I wanted to punish him." During his exile the white supremacists' hue and cry for a "Great White Hope" provided him with numerous opponents, and when he lost his title to Jess Willard in twenty-six rounds in Havana in April 1915, it was widely believed that he had thrown the fight in the mistaken understanding that the charge against him would be dropped. Later, when he visited Mexico on the restless trajectory that brought him finally homewards, he would be welcomed as a hero for his attacks on racism in the States.

In March 1916, Johnson stepped off the morning express and struck a pose, fixing his brilliant white smile for the waiting flash-bulb cameraman. With his glistening bald pate and the Palm Beach suit buttoned tight over his chest, he appeared in person exactly as he did in the society pages. He was ageing now, and padded out with excess flesh, and his reputation had been diminished by the loss of his title the previous year. But, whilst he was not all he once was, he still possessed the impressive figure of the champion heavy-weight. Now the newspaper reporters moved in on him with their pads and pencils at the ready, and Johnson obliged them with quick-fire sound bites reeled off as if he were tossing breadcrumbs for the ducks. With a deep melodic voice he spoke in a kind of poetry that prefigured Muhammad

Ali's freestyle ramblings five decades later. He was a man for whom introductions were a tiresome formality, and he greeted the reception committee one by one with a glancing handshake and a moment's fleeting attention. Then, swinging his diamond-topped cane, he strode off along the platform with a motley entourage in tow: the cigar-chewing manager, a leggy chorus-line redhead, the pug-nose sparring partner, and the champion's wife, Lucille, trailing with the baggage.

Johnson's arrival caused a stir in Barcelona. He was given a frosty reception by those who still thought of boxing as barbaric and didn't welcome the prospect of a fight being staged in their city. The provincial mayor in particular wanted no such violent spectacle and prohibited the contest. Only after the fight promoter had explained to him that the haemorrhages caused by boxing injuries were rarely fatal did he finally relent.

On the 26th a press release announced that a contract had been signed for a match between Johnson and Cravan. Soon afterwards it was reported that Cravan had left his post at the Club Marítim so that he could concentrate on his training. The contest was advertised like a bullfight, with fly-posters plastered all over the streets of Barcelona. In the effort to persuade the media that the unknown Cravan was a serious challenger, a series of public appearances were scheduled: he was presented to the crowd at the corrida, he performed a boxing demonstration during half-time at a football match, and was even carried on a float during the carnival parade, flanked by dancing girls. For the next two weeks his name appeared in the newspapers on an almost daily basis, and only once the atmosphere of excitement had reached its peak did the promoter finally release tickets for sale, at an inflated price.

On 12th April, to continue building anticipation, a great boxing evening was arranged with Johnson and Cravan acting as referees. All that's left of the Gymnase Sole today is a crumbling façade held aloft by scaffolding and draped in wafting green mesh. I scattered a clot of limping pigeons and looked through a crack in the fence at the demolition site inside, the skeleton of red girders, the hard-hatted workmen ushering the arms of cranes into position. This was the site of Cravan's first public appearance with Johnson, the hero whom he had admired in the Paris cabarets. Cravan had been nobody then, but now he was fast becoming a celebrity in his own right, Johnson's opponent and equal.

The following week the papers reported a spectacular training session put on to sustain the momentum of the publicity campaign. Expectations of the match were so high that the session was documented by the motion-picture pioneers, the Baños brothers. The film reels still exist, although time has severely warped the celluloid with blisters and disfigurations.

Until now Cravan had existed for me as a composite character, a shadowy figure emerging from the conflicting accounts of numerous biographers, from dubious second-hand testimonies, and from his own correspondence of highly questionable veracity. Now, on the screen of an old Moviola in the hushed basement of the visual-archive office, Cravan materialized for the first time; here he began to take form even as he seemed to dissolve before my eyes.

Flickering above a tumult of static, the vague shape of a heavily built man stands cross-armed in a pair of stripy trunks. Grinning proudly at the camera, his outline bleeds into the grain of the film, shimmering on the brink of dissolution. Next he is seen tossing medicine balls around the sandpit, then allowing a midget to pound his stomach.

The sixteen-millimetre projector ran the film at a hyperactive speed, giving the images an air of cartoon-like absurdity. The decades have bleached the print, and at intervals there appears only the ghost of an image. At other times the cracks and discolorations explode into a black hole that threatens to engulf the frame.

In the final shot Cravan, moving at an accelerated pace, appears to run straight out of a Benny Hill sketch. Dancing past the camera with a skipping rope, he at last plunges into a rapidly spreading void that swallows him whole.

The press lavished him with praise for his training performances, whilst the bookmakers took so many bets on Cravan to win that the odds began to tip in his favour. But from the beginning Cravan didn't stand a chance. Cravan the boxer was nothing but bluff and bluster, it was a role he played to seduce women and to intimidate intellectual rivals. Under the influence of alcohol he was always keen to throw himself into bar-room brawls that never progressed beyond a few glancing blows before they were broken up by his friends. But facing Johnson in the ring his strutting theatrics would count for nothing. Cravan had a mere handful of amateur bouts to his name, whilst Johnson had won dozens of matches and had been knocked out only twice in a career that spanned more than two decades. Even though Johnson was nearing retirement and in physical decline, the pairing was absurd.

There was talk of a set-up. This would certainly be in keeping with Cravan's history of con-artistry, and Johnson too was not above suspicion. But it appears that on the eve of the great fight the amicable relations between the two men turned sour. Johnson heard that his opponent had gone behind his back to sell the film rights to the fight, with no intention of cutting him in on the deal. This was a smarting blow to Johnson's vanity, and he set off in a fury to confront his adversary. He marched along the Rambla towards Cravan's gym, the promoter running along behind, trying to talk him down pleadingly.

Cravan was clearly rattled when Johnson burst into the dressing room. The ex-champion squared up to him, his fists balled, his chest inflated, and Cravan stutteringly tried to deny everything. The promoter stepped in to diffuse the situation, but Johnson merely brushed him aside. He took a swipe at Cravan, catching him on the nose, and Cravan fled into the gym. Johnson chased him in circles around the ring, whilst the promoter could do nothing but watch, the tears welling in his eyes. Cornered at last, Cravan confessed to everything. Then, pressing a discarded jockstrap to his nose to stem the flow of blood, he declared the match was off and stormed out into the street.

Fearful for his investment, the promoter sent a search party out to look for Cravan, and they finally found him in a whisky bar later that night, dead drunk and still wearing his training shorts. He was sobered up and put to bed, whilst Johnson was placated with the promise of an extra percentage.

The match was back on but, with a personal vendetta coming into the contest, any secret arrangement to fix the course of the fight would now be forfeited. Perhaps this goes some way to explaining what happened next.

The promoter envisaged the fight as a great spectacle, and to give it the proper grandeur of scale it was staged in a bullring. The scaffold was erected in the middle of an arena that seated twenty thousand, and the boxing ring sat there dwarfed into insignificance by the sheer size of the place.

The Plaza de Toros Monumental is a hulking red-brick structure covering an entire city block. It is still used for bullfights today, but when I came here in the wintertime it was acting as the temporary home to the Gran Festival del Circo. A banner over the entrance advertised "Cocodrilos Gigantes!" with pictures of a grotesquely grinning clown and of a dark man in a turban cranking open the jaws of a crocodile.

On 23rd April 1916 the atmosphere in the arena was cold, and the five thousand spectators that had turned out sat scattered across the ranks of seats, giving the vast place the miserable impression of emptiness. Blaise Cendrars was at his friend's side before the fight, and recalls seeing him tremble uncontrollably. There were rumours that Cravan had got himself drunk before the match. At precisely three o'clock that afternoon he entered the ring and sat in the corner opposite Johnson to have his gloves laced.

From the very first round Cravan gave the impression of being daunted by his opponent. Having been frightened by Johnson's first assault, he was on the back foot from the outset. He held his guard high, his head tucked in. He didn't throw a single punch, didn't even feint. According to Cendrars, Cravan merely turned on the spot whilst Johnson prowled around him "like a great black rat stalking a Dutch cheese". After circling him several times, Johnson moved in for his first strikes, which Cravan avoided by lunging at him, and clinging onto his opponent's torso until the referee pulled the two men apart. These clinches quickly exhausted Cravan, and when Johnson landed three successive blows to his stomach at the end of the opening round, it looked for a moment as if he would collapse.

He slumped in the corner, letting the ropes take his weight, and gazed blearily around the auditorium. The bell barely woke him from this stupor, and his seconds had to shove him back into the ring. Johnson skipped around his adversary, laughing at him, shouting insults and egging him on. During five rounds Cravan increasingly showed his fatigue. Johnson outclassed him without effort, but allowed himself to be struck once or twice for the benefit of the sixteen-millimetre film that was being shot.

The fact that Cravan lasted this long was interpreted by some commentators as evidence of a fix. "Finally after scandalous and despicable propaganda, there took place what some have dubbed the Great Johnson-Cravan Fight, which should have been entitled The Racket or The Great

Swindle," wrote *El Poble Catalan*. But *El Mundo Deportivo* put the fight's length down to the private feud between the two men: "The fight was a real disaster. It is believed that, if Johnson drew it out, it's because he wanted to play with his opponent. He must have realized very quickly that he faced an unthreatening individual, more terrified than anything else. Cravan was treated as a ridiculous spectacle by Johnson who, from the very first blow to the eye, didn't take him seriously and mocked him cruelly. But for the incident that passed between them behind the scenes, Johnson would have had the grace to knock him out in the first round, and spare him the sad humiliation."

In the sixth round Johnson cuffed him with a left jab, followed by a right hook which knocked him to the floor. The referee counted him out and the gong sounded the end of the fight. Cravan's seconds didn't have time to revive him with a bucket of cold water, but dragged him unconscious from the ring as the spectators erupted in immediate and clamouring protest. Hundreds invaded the arena, screaming for their money back and setting the barricades on fire. The following day the fight was universally denounced in the newspapers, who accused the promoter of being a fraud and cast Cravan as his hapless stooge.

Quite why Cravan would take part in such a highly publicized confrontation with a fighter far his superior – and risk the reputation he had so artfully established – is uncertain. It is possible that Cravan had started to believe in his own hype: he was living up to the image he promoted, the invented persona, the French Champion, the legend based on an elaborate collection of lies and exaggerations.

But it is likely that Cravan's motivations also owed much to sheer desperation brought on by the approaching War. The previous month he had received a curt letter from the British Consulate requesting that he report to the military attaché at his earliest possible convenience. Cravan never responded to the letter, realizing that it was a prelude to his conscription in the British army. It looked as if he couldn't hide for much longer behind Spanish neutrality.

The situation in Europe was growing worse by the day. The German invasion forces were making steady ground in their advance on Paris, and every passing day soldiers on both sides were falling by the thousands in the Somme. Only weeks earlier, in a gesture of solidarity with the Alliance, one thousand Catalan volunteers had left Barcelona to help the French army. Countries on the fringes of the conflict were becoming drawn into taking sides as new fronts opened up and the war steadily engulfed much of the continent.

Cravan was growing anxious to gather funds for his passage to America, where he could at last put himself beyond the reach of the War. The purse of the boxing contest may have been reason enough to take such a risk: "By my reckoning," he wrote in a letter to his brother, "this will really bring the money rolling in, and if everything goes according to plan I should make a packet out of the deal. And I'll be in America before they notice I've left the ring." This too was the view held by the Barcelona newspaper, *Illustracio Catalana*, which discussed the noble sport in the most disdainful terms: "There is a haul of 50,000 francs for the winner. For such an amount perhaps it is worth getting your face smashed in."

The night after my father died I had a strange new feeling. It was a big bright feeling that made me want to throw an uproarious party. I felt like stripping to the waist and doing ridiculous dances on tables. I felt like sucking shots of tequila from the belly buttons of young women. I felt like tossing canapés into the air like confetti. I didn't have a party, though, my problem being that I didn't have any friends, not really even any acquaintances to invite.

Instead I put on a Donna Summer cassette and gyrated around the living room by myself for a while. On the sixth play-through I took the tape out halfway into the song. I stood there in silence, panting. It was no good. I had to *do* something, I had to follow this terrible urge. That's when I remembered the beer mat.

I threw open the wardrobe and went through my jacket pockets. Just when I began to despair that I'd thrown it away, or put it through the washing machine, I found it underneath wads of old tissue in my corduroy blazer. The telephone number was still there, scrawled on the underside.

Cathy and I hit it off immediately. She told me she'd been surprised to hear my voice on the phone, she hadn't expected to see me ever again. A pleasant surprise, she said.

I didn't know where to take her, so we went to the theatre. Fifteen minutes into it, I grabbed her by the hand and dragged her along the row of seats towards the aisle. I tried to suppress a fit of giggling as the other audience members, with a communal hiss of indignation, got to their feet in a Mexican wave to let us pass. We stood outside bowing with laughter, and then we set off on a wanton excursion through the West End, careening headlong through any pub we came across. We sunk flaming sambucas in the Fez nightclub and then did the funky chicken so violently that the dance floor emptied. Soon after that I was asked to leave for dropping my trousers and Cathy had to drag me away from a scuffle with some Crystal Palace supporters outside. We ended up having sex on the back seat of a night bus to Southend, where we watched the sun come up over the water.

I'd never been in love before. Of course I was on the rebound from my father's death, so my defences were down, and that's undoubtedly why I fell for her so badly. The world seemed transformed or regenerated. Suddenly I could avert my eyes from the shabby details that had always preoccupied me. It wasn't until I came across an old photograph whilst clearing out my father's house that I regained some sense of perspective.

It was a picture of my parents. They looked very young, him with long hair and sideburns, her with her eyes ringed thickly with eyeliner as was the fashion in those days. The picture must have been taken soon after they first met. It showed them sitting on a park bench somewhere, their legs crossed towards each other, their hands clasped together on her knee. They were smiling. There was nothing extraordinary about the photograph, but as I looked at it the hairs stood up on the nape of my neck and my heart sank.

Cravan's new life in Spain didn't last long, his freedom was merely an illusion. For a brief respite he had held off the War, pretended that it no longer existed, when in fact all the time it continued its remorseless progress, consuming everything in its path.

After the Johnson fight there is little evidence of Cravan's activities in Barcelona. Whereas on his arrival he had been a focal point of gossip on the social circuit, following the Johnson fight, his biography becomes corrupted with mysterious blank spots where he seems to disappear, retreating into seclusion. It seems that Cravan was growing increasingly distant from the group, spending more and more time by himself, no longer showing up at their gatherings or answering their correspondence. There had always been this strange side to his behaviour, the odd stretch when he would seclude himself, when his thoughts would become elusive, a shadow pass over his features, but now this dark aspect seemed to be wholly displacing the familiar Cravan. It would not be long before he faded from their lives altogether.

With the War closing in on all sides, the closeted little world of the émigrés came under threat. Difficulties with entry visas and doubts over residence permits led to trouble with the Spanish police. The suspicions of the authorities were first alerted by irregularities about Francis Picabia's residential status. He had entered Spain as an agent of the French government sent to buy supplies for the army. But six months had now passed and it was clear he had no intention of purchasing anything at all. His case was not helped by the dubious company he kept, not least the down-at-heel alcoholic Cravan, whom the police had been keeping an eye on ever since he flashed a group of schoolgirls on a class outing in the summer. Picabia's situation grew worse still when he started a torrid affair with Marie Laurencin.

The French consulate posted a man outside Picabia's apartment to observe his movements. The man reported that Picabia received clandestine visits on a nightly basis from Laurencin, a German national, who left in the early hours, often carrying away documents. Matters came to a head in November when the authorities arranged for Laurencin to be intercepted as she accompanied her husband, a German baron, on a trip to France. Searching her luggage, Customs officers found a gift from Picabia – one of his machine drawings, a portrait of Laurencin herself in the style of a ventilator fan. The border police, however, interpreted this as a blueprint for a military engine-cooling system and arrested them both on suspicion of espionage.

The group of exiles was coming to pieces. The final blow was the sudden disappearance of Cravan himself, without warning or explanation.

On my last night I walked around the deserted perimeter of Montjuïc Castle on the headland and came to rest against the railings on the far side. A great yellow glow rose from beyond the edge of the cliff, and when I looked over I saw the vast expanse of the docks laid out below: a landscape of faceless towers and immense hangars; of jetty roadways arcing far out into the void of the ocean; acres of freight containers stacked in mile-long columns; tanker trailers parked in rows, pale and minuscule as insect pupae.

This tarmac world was bathed in the lonely yellow light that had grown familiar to me from the many nights spent on empty roads. The wind off the ocean carried to me the bass drone of colossal engines turning over, the grinding and squealing of strange machines. Out at sea there were the blinking beacons of ships making their glacial approach, or setting off on journeys to distant ports.

It was here on Christmas Day 1916 that Arthur Cravan, having purchased a one-way fare with his takings from the Johnson fight, boarded the cruise liner *Montserrat* and, without telling anyone, set sail for the United States.

Also onboard the *Montserrat* was Leon Trotsky, about whom the French magazine *La Revue de l'époque* had recently claimed, "The grand master of Dadaism is in fact a Jew called Trotsky". He had travelled to Paris to be reunited at last with his wife and son after a long estrangement, and was now embarking on a trajectory that would take him back to Russia, where he would lead the Bolshevik armies to victory in the Russian Revolution the following year.

In his diaries Trotsky described his motley collection of fellow passengers: "The liner *Montserrat* was to deliver its cargo, dead or alive, in seventeen days' time in New York...

The composition of the ship's population was varied and as a whole rather unattractive. There were a number of deserters from different countries, including a boxer, occasional man of letters, and cousin of Oscar Wilde, who frankly admitted that he preferred to break a Yankee's jaw in a noble sport to being brained by a German."

The ship was gripped by a mood of smouldering anxiety for the duration of the transatlantic crossing. This was the time of unrestricted naval warfare, in which German U-boats prowled the deep waters of the Atlantic targeting civilian vessels. This was also before the inception of the convoy system, so the *Montserrat* made its crossing alone and unprotected. The passengers spent their long days staring out over the railings at the inscrutable face of the ocean.

I was lying awake in bed, not even bothering to stop my alarm. I was lying perfectly still, as I had done all night. I hadn't slept at all, I hadn't even moved. I had just lain there listening to the others return in the early hours, the squeals of the rusted hinges on the locker doors, the rustling through bags in the dark, the groans of the bed springs that amplified every tiny movement, and then the deep breathing of sleepers.

Daylight crept through the shutters and now I listened to the others waking, unzipping their sleeping bags, taking themselves off to the shower, applying deodorants, leaving for breakfast.

If I'd had the energy I would have thrown back the covers, climbed up onto the railings around the balcony and swallow-dived into the pavement three floors below. Instead I just lay there staring into the pillow, wishing I could go to sleep, hoping for days and days to pass. I never wanted to get up again. I wanted to dissolve into the mattress, to percolate through the springs, drain into the cracks between the tiles.

One by one the rest of them gathered their things and left for the day. At eleven the girl from reception knocked on the door and came in. I was dimly aware of her standing there looking at me.

"Meester," she said in a gravely Catalan accent.

I pretended to be sound asleep and she started tapping the bed frame with her fingernails.

"Ay! Meester! You leaving now."

I grunted my disapproval.

"You don't pay for tonight," she said in a raised voice, as if speaking to the hard-of-hearing. "You must leave now. Eleven o'clock."

I told her: "I want to die."

"Not here," she persisted. "We close the rooms." She started knocking the bed frame again, more insistently this time.

She stood there, hands on hips. She watched me crawl out of the sheets and achieve a sitting position on the edge of the bed. I looked up at her imploringly.

"Go now," she barked.

I found my feet and got hold of the stacked lockers by the bed for support whilst I worked the blood back into my legs. At this moment Kevin, the goateed American, came in brashly and swung his backpack down onto a bunk across the room. She turned and fixed him with cold unblinking eyes.

"Ay!" she told him. "Room closed now. You must go. *You must all go!*"

"Yeah lady," Kevin said, pointing his gun hand at her and cocking the hammer. "No sweat, I'm just dropping off my shit. I'm outta here man."

She scowled at me once again and then marched off.

"Jesus. Fuckin' Nazi hostel woman, ah?" Kevin said. "You been out all night? I hear that." He had a smug air of gloating about him. The volume of his voice was overwhelming, it seemed intended to aggravate someone with a hangover.

"Stayed out all night partying, ah? I done that a coupla times believe me. But I'm too old for that shit now brother."

I pulled my pyjama bottoms down, let them drop around my ankles, and I stood there, hunched against the lockers, stark naked and glaring at him. Kevin seemed unfazed by this. He started thrusting things violently into a bag.

"Good times, ah? I'm gonna hit the town, bro. Shit to do today, know what I'm sayin'? This town's crazy." Kevin hoisted his pack on and swaggered to the door. I was giving my haemorrhoids a good scratching – they had scabbed over during the night and itched like the devil.

"Listen, have a great day now you hear. Catcha later man." He left noisily, and I heard him shouting *How's it goin' man* to someone in the corridor before slamming the front door.

After a while the hostel girl came in again wearing a pair of rubber gloves. She stood cross-armed in the doorway with a pert expression.

"I tell you. Go now okay!" She put her hand out. "Give me key for locker please."

Weakly I protested: "My things are in there."

"Take out okay? Must go. *Now.*"

I tried to find it in me to launch into some kind of tirade. I wanted to show her the full horror of her life. God knows she was a miserable cow: the long face, haggard before its time; the knotted enmity of her body; those cold blue eyes, the penetrating pin-prick pupils closed over some hidden, insurmountable pain that gripped her mind like a pair of salad tongs. But there was nothing left in me, and instead I merely sighed and scratched my testicles. Unimpressed, she refused to leave until I'd handed over the key, which I eventually did with resentment. She snatched it from me and declared as she left, "You people – *you all same.*"

I dressed myself mechanically, and dragged my bag down the stairs. I sat on a doorstep outside and took no notice of passers-by.

After half an hour I became aware of the smell. By the time it had seeped through to my skin it occurred to me that I had sat in a pool of congealing urine. It may have been piss from a dog, but the quantity of it suggested a man, and from the rich smell I suspected probably a wino. I felt the fury flare up within me like cheap nylon curtains in a house fire.

This was no ordinary anger. It sprang from a long-buried core of revulsion, the culmination of years of silent submission to indignity and degradation. This anger demanded some spontaneous act of destruction. In fact it would be satisfied with nothing less than murder.

The pigeons had come down from the rooftops to congregate around me. With one exception they were fat, healthy things, scuttling in circles, the chests of the males pumped up proudly to intimidate the females. But amongst them there was one sickly, withered specimen that hobbled painfully on a mangled leg. Its head was pecked bald and it crouched in front of me, blinking its pathetic clotted eyes. It came willingly, offering me its paltry life. Looking at one another like that we shared a moment. Something passed between us.

It didn't take much to stamp the life out of it. It made no attempt to save itself. I felt its straw bones give under the sole of my shoe. There was no blood, its head was slightly flattened, that's all, and one eye stared out with an expression of peace at last. As I walked away I looked back over my shoulder and saw the strong ones gathering for the first curious pecks at it.

I had to take a budget airline back to London to catch my connecting flight to New York. I knew this was dangerous, that it was tempting fate, but it was the only flight I could afford.

I had learnt from watching films that it is customary for fugitives to be apprehended in the airport as they try to flee the country. It occurred to me as I came through arrivals that the police might be there waiting for me. But oddly enough, what happened to me from there on didn't seem important. I found I could no longer muster the enthusiasm to care.

For a night I found myself back at Gatwick, sitting under the shelter of an overpass as the rain pissed down in sheets all around. Behind me automatic doors kept jerking noisily open to let little groups of people heave their luggage out to the taxi rank. I took drags on a damp cigarette between coughs and tried to let my mind drift. Some travellers talk of their relief in coming home, to be surrounded once again by the familiar accents of their own people. But I think I liked it better when I didn't understand a word anyone was saying.

Fat, sunburnt couples returning from exotic holidays were trying to hide their misery from one another. There they stood on a Gatwick kerb after midnight, staring into the rain and putting on a brave face. A week together had exhausted all conversation between them, laboured weekends of romance had stripped off the veneer; the overfamiliarity of a cramped double in a Caribbean resort had bred contempt. They stooped against the cold, sneering morosely into the puddles, grimly reassessing their relationship, trying not to think about the job they had to go back to on Monday morning.

The following day I caught a train, joining the grey army of morning commuters that scrambled for the empty seats. In the carriage there was rank upon rank of long faces yearning for the weekend, dozens of clenched, hostile bodies sitting with their arms crossed in languorous fury. And then there were the ones without seats, who stood face-to-armpit with the next man, their raincoats dripping disconsolately onto the floor of the train. Their bloodless faces hung in rows like sides of beef in a meat locker, the minds behind them craving oblivion, and dreading the day ahead that would be identical to the day before and the day after. Perhaps like me they prayed for a train wreck to bring it all to a swift and painless conclusion.

The train windows offered no consolation. Outside the suburbs of London crawled past, everything shrouded in wintry desolation. The windows looked out over a landscape of unparalleled dreariness, coloured in monotonous shades of bruise. Every so often another train would draw level with us, obscuring the view with its dirty rain-streaked flank. From these other trains the same hard-set faces stared desperately back at us.

The whole thing was like a memory replayed from my own life. It was as if for a time I had picked up just where I'd left off. The train even stopped at my old station, and out of habit I moved over to take pole position by the opening doors. The commuters all folded their papers, clenched the handles of their briefcases, and primed their umbrellas with bitter resolve. When the doors sprung open they streamed past me and in a whirlwind were gone.

A robotic voice repeated its mantra: *Mind the Gap Mind the Gap Mind the Gap*. I teetered on the threshold, with half a mind to get off with the rest of them, to follow the familiar pavements to the office, and sit down at my old desk as if nothing had changed. I had half a mind to do it, just to see if anyone would notice.

The doors shut and I watched the platform drop away. It was just me alone in the carriage now, alone with the patterns left by the hair of commuters in the condensation on the windows.

My pulse quickened on arrival at Heathrow. At nine in the morning the terminal was already teeming. People trundled their excessive luggage around on trolleys, they clustered around the screens like cattle at the trough. I joined a seemingly endless queue that jack-knifed through rope cordons towards the check-in desks.

As the queue inched forwards, I was overcome by a tremendous sensation of guilt. I could feel people's eyes on me, and I was sure it wasn't just because of my unkempt appearance and the strong odour I was giving off. An airport policeman cradling an automatic weapon passed by and looked me up and down. He said something into his radio on his way past, and my chest tightened with anxiety. I was trapped, hemmed in on all sides, there would be no way through the hordes of an extended Indian family with their suitcase barricades behind me, or the trolleys of the British nuclear variety blocking off the exits in front. I began to sweat more than usual, I could feel it crawling down the cleft of my back.

When I got to the front of the queue, I followed the flashing arrow to a vacant desk. I presented myself to the girl behind the counter like an outlaw giving himself up. It was over. There was no point in running. How stupid of me to think I could escape the consequences of what I had done.

The girl took my passport, then handed it back with a cursory glance. She called out, "Next."

As I made my way towards the boarding gates, the airport police I passed didn't show the slightest interest either. It crossed my mind that perhaps Cathy hadn't even reported me missing. At the thought of this I felt a strange twinge of resentment.

At the end of the gangway, the stewardesses were assembled for a lacklustre welcome, their tortured eyes, dilated with caffeine tablets, staring out from behind larded-on smiles. Shuffling onto the plane, I realized that I would have to see this through to the end after all.

PART THREE

NEW YORK

"The world has always exploited
the Artist – it is time for the Artist
to exploit the world!"

– *Arthur Cravan*

It was the dead of winter when I came to New York. The sun broke out of the clouds in the morning, cast the city into a brilliant clear light for an hour or so, and was gutted by the onset of night at around four in the afternoon. The people of the city lived like troglodytes, emerging from their apartment buildings swathed in mufflers and Bolshevik hats, then scurrying directly to the nearest entrance to the subterranean passageways. Drivers cruised the streets restlessly in a vain search for somewhere to park amidst the sagging heaps of black bin bags spilling over the kerbs, and the week-old snowdrifts that had turned to great slag heaps of dirty ice in the gutters.

On his release by the Spanish authorities, Francis Picabia soon learnt of Cravan's departure. In his journal *391*, Picabia reported his friend's imminent arrival in New York: "Arthur Cravan too has taken the transatlantic liner. He will deliver talks; will he be dressed as a gentleman or a cowboy? Before he left he was in favour of the second outfit and intended to make an impressive entry on the scene: on horseback with his revolver drawn and firing three shots at the bourgeois chandeliers."

On Cravan's behalf Picabia forwarded a letter of introduction to his acquaintance, Walter Arensberg. Collector, philanthropist, bon viveur and affluent industrialist, Arensberg had set himself up as a patron of the arts. He opened his home day and night to the artists and intellectuals that were floating around the city, and he could ensure Cravan's admittance to the circle of New York bohemia. However, Cravan would find he needed no introduction.

Number 33, 67th Street was once a town house on the Upper West Side of Central Park, in the staid, airy, moneyed quarter of the city, far from the noise and restless activity of downtown, and from the uptown sprawl of Harlem and the immigrant ghettos. Today the house has been carved up into expensive apartments, and even the polished brass fittings around the buzzer have an air of haughty exclusivity.

It was the middle of the day and there was no answer from the flats on the lower floors. Up on the fourth floor, however, I heard an indistinct voice coming through the hiss of static. The nameplate said: "Miss L. Rosen". To my surprise the electric tone sounded and the door yielded without resistance.

At the top of the stairs there was a tiny geriatric waiting in the doorway. She was wearing an immaculate woollen suit and pearl earrings. She was dressed as neat as a button, but her hair was rather wild and unkempt, and the black dye was growing out at the roots.

"Lionel!" She threw her hands in the air, bracelets jangling loose on her skinny wrists. "How wonderful!" she cried in delight.

I started to introduce myself, and she appeared to take it in, beaming all the while, the translucent flesh draped over her cheekbones pulled to wrinkles around the myopic eyes. But before I could finish she disappeared into the apartment muttering, "Come, come!"

I stood on the threshold, reluctant to go any further.

"Excuse me," I said, poking my head around the door frame. Paying me no attention, she was walking away, moving unsteadily on needle-thin legs.

Now she was plumping a satin cushion and ushering me over to the chaise longue.

"Come and sit down, darling," she croaked. "What can I get you, coffee, cognac, whisky soda?"

Holding on to the rim of the coffee table she lowered herself stiffly onto the sofa, crossed her legs demurely and patted the seat next to her. I hovered uncomfortably by the door, looked out into the hallway, then back at her.

"*Well!*" she said, clasping her bony hands together.

I eased myself dubiously onto the very edge of the sofa.

The room had a mouldering grandeur about it. It was furnished richly with antiques, and filled with a great clutter of ornaments and collectibles, the accumulations of a lifetime. It was such a confusion that my eyes couldn't take it all in. The walls were carpeted with flock paper, deep red with gilt floral patterns, and it was worn and fraying in places. On the walnut veneer dresser there was a vase of desiccated flowers and a large framed photograph of a black poodle in soft focus.

I sat as far away from her as I could, leaning against the armrest of the settee. She was looking at me and smiling. Her face was drawing gradually closer, and I began to feel intimidated under this filmy-eyed scrutiny.

"I wondered if I could just have a look round your apartment," I said.

"Oh!" she exclaimed. "How *simply* wonderful."

The smile continued. The face was a foot from mine now, and I could see the tightness of the flesh, paper-thin it was, and drawn taut over her bones by some surgical procedure. Her cloudy eyes gazed dimly through me. They must at one time have been lustrous eyes, set in a face of great beauty. Now the cheeks were rosy and filigreed with the cobwebs of burst corpuscles. Her hands were folded in her lap, she turned a thick gold ring restlessly between her fingers.

"How long will you stay dear?"

"I'm not staying," I said. "I really just wanted to see inside."

"Wonderful!" she declared.

"I only want to find out about the history of this house," I told her. "A man called Walter Arensberg used to live here."

"Oh!" she peeped. "How *marvellous*." And she beamed, her face looming only inches from me now.

Walter Arensberg was the son of a Pittsburg steel tycoon, but he had no interest in business: he had always fancied himself as a great poet. However, it came as a shock to him to discover that he had little talent. His verses received a tepid response, and he realized that they would never win him the admiration he craved. But he found another way to satisfy his aspirations: he bought the respect of his peers. Arensberg's readiness to open his chequebook ensured that he quickly became one of the most fawned-over figures in the New York avant-garde. He lavished money on the boldest of the young artists, using his wife's fortune to buy their paintings in bulk, and this way he established himself as the city's first collector of modern art. But he was also a collector of colourful personalities, and in his townhouse on 67th Street he gathered around him a menagerie of eccentrics.

As well as cash-strapped painters and poets, the Arensberg salon attracted a strange assortment of Harvard old-boys, dandyish businessmen and titled Europeans rubbing shoulders with anarchist poseurs, suffragettes, birth-controllers and several reporters from the communist gazette *The Masses*. These radical elements also drew the occasional visit by undercover agents of the police. Despite their many differences, Arensberg's guests were united by a common sense of their own individualism – a trait which expressed itself mainly in little affectations of dress and speech – and they gravitated to Arensberg because he indulged the precious disorder of their lives. He plied them with cake and cocktails, he set the scene for pretentious conversations without end, periodically wheeling around a trolley of nibbles whilst they languished over games of chess that dragged on remorselessly until the small hours, perhaps in this very room. According to one visitor, Arensberg's gatherings "turned night into day, with conscientious objectors of all walks of life living in an inconceivable orgy of sexuality, jazz and alcohol."

Cravan's first appearances set the regulars astir. His reputation was well established amongst the New York artists and, even before his arrival, stories of his achievements and rumours of his eccentricities had spread infectiously amongst them. Cravan hovered uncomfortably on the fringes of their gatherings, standing at a distance, and this gave him an air of mystery that added to his appeal for the bohemian set. It quickly became "the thing" to be seen with Cravan. For a while he was a distraction from the idle discussions of art and politics – all the talk was about Cravan: everyone was asking, "But haven't you met the prizefighter who writes poetry?"

Miss Rosen lit an extra-long menthol cigarette and, holding it in the crook of her skeletal hand, she let it waver in the air beside her head with an accomplished elegance. She emitted two sharp giggles and then cast her smile contentedly over the room.

"*Well*!" she said, exhaling an interminable plume of sickly-sweet smoke.

We sat in silence for five minutes or so. Every so often she would turn and smile warmly in my direction. She smoked her cigarette down to the filter and poked it gently out in a cut-glass ashtray. Then she softly patted her hair, attempting vainly to smooth down an obstinate tuft that stuck out of her head at a right angle.

"May I look around the apartment, please, Miss Rosen?" I asked.

"Oh!" she cried. "Delightful, delightful." She began to scratch at a mark on the table top with a chipped lacquered fingernail.

"*I SAID*, MAY I LOOK AROUND MISS ROSEN."

She gave a little twitter of laughter, pitching back and forth on the settee and shooting a coy look at me.

"You *are* terrible!"

We sat in silence for another minute or so, Miss Rosen

drummed her fingers on her lap and smiled. I watched her sidelong with a frown.

Heavily I got up and crossed the room to a door at the far side, next to a standing piano with brass candle fixtures. I turned the handle and looked over at Miss Rosen to see what her reaction might be. She smiled back, unperturbed.

On the other side of the door was a scene of rampant chaos. Just across the threshold from the elegance of the living room, things tended towards entropy. Because of the darkness and the general disorder, my first thought was that I had opened the door into a store cupboard. But there was a pale glow of daylight from somewhere inside, and I saw that this was in fact a corridor leading into the wild hinterland of the apartment. I was hesitant to go though the door, and I glanced back at Miss Rosen, who was lighting another cigarette and squinting.

The corridor was stacked from floor to ceiling with old newspapers and magazines that came spilling out of the rooms leading off either side. They were stored here in such huge quantities that there was barely room to move along the corridor, and they blocked out almost all the light from the window at the end, giving the place a gloomy, claustrophobic atmosphere. Weak daylight, the colour of dishwater, was diffused through the thick dust rising from the decaying paper. I had to climb over a pile of *Vanity Fairs* from the Eighties, and the whole stack of them overbalanced and threatened to collapse on top of me. The place smelt of mouse piss; it was probably infested.

The door at the end of the corridor opened into a minuscule toilet that was thick with mildew. The pipes from the cistern were encrusted with flakes of yellowing lime scale. I climbed back towards the lounge and stopped by an open doorway to poke my head into a room. The newspapers began in neat stacks by the far wall and then subsided into a great amorphous heap that slumped out into the hallway. I saw that amidst it all there was a double bed and, lying across it like a corpse, a set of golf clubs draped with cobwebs. On the walls there were old photographs, bleached by time. They showed Miss Rosen in the bloom of her youth: a bridesmaid clutching the bouquet; standing in jodhpurs by a saddled thoroughbred; smiling from the passenger seat of an open-top sports car; lounging under a parasol at the beach with a handsome young man who smoked a pipe. And exhibited in pride of place above the headboard was a large portrait of the pruned black poodle.

Back in the lounge I found Miss Rosen still sitting where I had left her.

"You must excuse the disorder," she said. "I've been meaning to sort through my things."

"Do you mind me asking what they're for?"

Miss Rosen looked at me uncertainly, then she clapped her hands together and exclaimed: "Oh! How wonderful." When she smiled I could see her full set of yellowing dentures.

"I'm going to kill myself, Miss Rosen," I told her.

She giggled and looked out across the room.

"YOU'RE DEAF AS A POST AREN'T YOU DEAR."

"Oh!" she said. "Marvellous."

Sensing that this conversation had run its course, I got up and went over to the front door. When I looked back at her I saw that one of her stockings had slipped down around her ankle.

I frowned one last time and went out.

As well as locals such as William Carlos Williams, the American poet, the Arensberg circle included a good number of foreigners, especially French artists who had fled from the War in search of refuge in a neutral country. Amongst the regulars was Edgar Varèse, the composer who made melodies from the sounds of the metropolis, the streetcars and the foghorns of tugboats on the Hudson, and Man Ray, the surrealist photographer. The émigrés brought with them the germ of Dadaism, and the New York movement would soon be established with the arrival of Francis and Gabrielle Picabia, the ambassadors of the European avant-garde.

A few months after Cravan's disappearance from Barcelona, the Picabias also abandoned Spain for America. Upon their arrival in New York they were immediately drawn into the Arensberg circle, and this is where they encountered Cravan again. In her memoir, *Rencontres*, Gabrielle Picabia recalls finding Cravan in desperate straits, utterly without money or any source of income, living off the sympathy of more fortunate friends.

Cravan seemed to be seized with a profound and irresistible lethargy. He would lie on the Arensbergs' couch with his enormous feet in somebody's lap. He would doze for hours, it didn't matter what was going on around him. One evening a drunken ingénue was chased screaming around the room by a man brandishing a live duck: Cravan snored through the whole thing. On another occasion, as the group soberly discussed the War, Cravan rose suddenly to his feet and, without quite waking, proceeded to urinate into an antique vase standing in the corner. When he felt more lively, he would tell anyone who happened to be sitting nearby that he had twice experienced the delirium tremens. His conversation apparently left much to be desired, consisting of little more than crude puns and profane French rhymes about prostitutes. The lolling figure of Cravan became part of the furniture in the Arensberg house, where non-conformism was prized above all else. Indeed, regulars at the salon not only tolerated Cravan's behaviour, they felt honoured by his presence – as one acquaintance put it, "he despised humanity so much that humanity was always very pleased if he'd come near any of them."

The reunion with his Barcelona friends should have given Cravan a new lease of life. With a missionary zeal, Francis Picabia began preaching the necessity of the modernist revolution, and soon the spirit of Dada had established a fully fledged movement in New York. But as the principle actor of Dadaism, Cravan was now to be usurped.

Marcel Duchamp had arrived in New York in 1915. As a present for his friend Walter Arensberg he brought with him a glass ball containing Paris air. Duchamp had already earned a certain notoriety because of his *Nude Descending a Staircase, No. 2*. This cubist painting had been rejected by the curator of the Paris Exposition des Indépendants on the grounds that "Nudes stand or recline, they do not walk down stairs". The painting then caused controversy in the New York art world, where it was described variously as "an explosion in a brick factory", "a pile of old golf clubs" and a masterpiece.

As the favourite of Arensberg, Duchamp received the full benefits of his patronage. Arensberg set him up in the basement of the house on 67th Street, and here Duchamp was given total freedom in which to work. But instead of con-centrating on his painting, Duchamp spent his time pacing the studio. The canvases that he produced were few and far between, and they hardly did justice to his considerable gifts as a painter. Indeed a bitter sarcasm was creeping into his style, and soon his paintings began to ridicule the activity of painting itself. Duchamp was losing his faith in art, and at the age of twenty-five, even as his *Nude* garnered more and more extravagant praise, Duchamp gave up painting altogether.

Duchamp's unusual temperament made him a kindred spirit of Cravan and Picabia. He occupied the centre of his own universe: for him there was no higher power to answer to, no standards against which he would be judged. Utterly unfettered by any sense of propriety, he valued nothing but himself. Declared unfit for military service due to a weak heart, he had the body of a malnourished child, his hair was ginger and his complexion pallid, and his thin lips and sunken eyes had abandoned all expression to a deadpan blankness. Duchamp's striking features seemed to be physical symptoms of his chronic nihilism. He understood that any search for meaning in life was fatally misguided, that there was at the bottom of it all only a bitter sense of the absurd. But being party to the joke, Duchamp somehow managed to hold himself aloof of it, and this cynicism became the backbone of his art. In the basement of the Arensberg town house Duchamp systematically stripped his work of all its frills, all its pretence, all its lofty aspirations.

At the first public viewing of his new work, he exhibited a single bicycle wheel mounted on a stool and a bottle rack fresh out of its department-store packaging. Although the audience of art connoisseurs didn't quite know what to make of these objects, they politely applauded, made appreciative noises and invented forthright opinions on the spot, as is the custom at exhibition openings. But Duchamp's Readymades not only ridiculed the stuffy sophisticates who comprised the art world, they made a mockery of the whole idea of art.

Duchamp's point was that an object like a bicycle wheel or a bottle rack became a work of art as soon as he said it was. When he chose such an object it was lifted clean out of the mundane world of inert objects and plunged whole into the aesthetic dimension: just looking at it made it into art.

However trivial it may now seem, Duchamp's exhibition was a revelation, one of those rare moments in history where consciousness is seen to evolve – and yet it is a revelation that the entire modern world has since lived to regret. Little did he know it, but Duchamp was licensing generations of students ever afterwards to spout hot air in theme pubs, to pontificate in raised voices about *What is art?* Duchamp had given birth to the Concept, the vaunting of the idea at the expense of form and content, that would come to dominate the twentieth century. Little did he know it, but by cranking open the gaping emptiness where art's soul should be, Duchamp made this emptiness the very subject of art for decades to come.

The bicycle wheel was just the beginning of an all-out assault on art and the establishment. Duchamp's pièce de résistance – the work that he will always be remembered for – was a urinal.

In 1917, New York was feverishly anticipating the opening of the Independents' Exhibition, the showcase of the van-guard of art to be held in the magnificent galleries of the newly built Grand Central Terminal. Duchamp was a founding member of the Independents' Society and held a position on the jury, but just before the inauguration he purchased a porcelain urinal from the showroom of J.L. Mott's sanitary engineers, took it out of its packaging, signed it with the name "R. Mutt" and submitted it for exhibition.

The basic premise of the Independents' Exhibition was its independence. The curators declared that the whole point was to extend the principles of democracy to the art world, too long dominated by a conservative elite. The artworks would be displayed in alphabetical order so as to eliminate the insidious hierarchies of classification. What was more, to rid themselves of the bias of a selection committee, every work that was submitted would be exhibited so long as the artist paid the $1 registration fee. However, despite all the lofty ideals of the Society, its board members were outraged by Duchamp's *Fountain* and called an emergency meeting to block its exhibition. An eyewitness, Beatrice Wood, reported that behind the scenes of the great exhibition, the organizers were bitterly divided, and an absurd dispute broke out over the urinal. Walter Arensberg, Duchamp's chief defender, stressed the urinal's aesthetic qualities, pointing out "its striking, sweeping lines": "If this is an artist's expression of beauty," he argued, "we can do nothing but accept his choice."

This did nothing to placate the other board members: "You mean to say, if a man sent in horse manure glued to a canvas, that we would have to accept it!"

"I'm afraid we would," said Arensberg weakly.

The majority voted against him, stating "The *Fountain* may be a very useful object in its place, but its place is not an art exhibition, and it is, by no definition, a work of art".

This is exactly what Duchamp had planned: the Society had played right into his hands. Having demonstrated just how independent the Independents' exhibition really was, he triumphantly resigned from the judging panel.

Duchamp's signed toilet was a definitive statement about the nature of art. Just as his bicycle wheel collapsed the distinction between art and rubbish, the *Fountain* declared that art was nothing more than a puerile joke. But the scope of Duchamp's irony extended far beyond the art world: his Readymades exposed the hypocrisy that he saw all around him. On the brink of America's entry into the War, Duchamp was challenging its supposed moral superiority: the *Fountain* was a lurid skid-mark smeared across the country's conceited image of itself.

At the turn of 1917, a few weeks after Cravan's arrival, the refugee tide from Europe brought another exotic character onto the shores of New York. Mina Loy was a fugitive from personal crises. Running from a ruined marriage, the beautiful English poet had left behind an estranged husband and their two children and embarked for the New World.

Loy was part of the mass emigration of artists abandoning Europe. She was one of many to arrive in America carrying the contagion of modernist ideas that would gradually take hold here, prefiguring the gradual creep of the War to these new territories. She came with her head full of money-making schemes that she hoped would solve her financial problems: she would sell her poems to the *Little Review*, start a business in ornamental lampshades and design sets for the stage. Above all, in New York she hoped to find colleagues with whom to discuss "the new consciousness about things that is beginning to formulate in some of us".

Loy's impact was profound and immediate. In February 1917 the *New York Evening Sun* ran a feature proclaiming her the archetypal "Modern Woman". Feminist circles in the Village held her up as the prototype of the emancipated female. She was welcomed as a guest of honour by the New York literary cliques, who took her as an icon of the European avant-garde. Djuna Barnes described her reciting poetry "in that divine and ethereal voice for which she was noted, the voice of one whose ankles are nibbled by the cherubs". If she had not found fame as a poet, the American writer William Carlos Williams noted, it reflected not the quality of her poems, so much as the quality of the literary public: "When she puts a word down on paper, it is clean – that forces her fellows to shy away from it, because they are not clean and will be contaminated by her cleanliness... Her metaphors, when they can be detected, are of the quality of the sunlight". Wherever she went she was treated with a certain awe as a woman on the very threshold of the future – as the *Evening Sun* wrote, "This woman is halfway through the door into Tomorrow".

Mina possessed a strange and subtle beauty that arrested the attentions of the quickly enamoured – and even sooner bored – libertines of New York bohemia. She met new acquaintances with a measuring gaze from cool grey eyes, her nose lifted enquiringly in a manner that gave those she addressed the sense of being looked down upon. She had the gliding posture of a ballerina and seemed to move from pose to pose like a tableau vivant. Well aware that she looked most impressive in profile, she had an unsettling habit of looking at people sidelong. Marcel Duchamp was smitten at first sight, and lost no time in persuading her to work with him. Of all her peculiar mannerisms, he was especially intrigued by her tendency to turn away in the middle of a conversation, her lips mouthing a thread of poetry that she had just conceived.

It was at the Arensberg salon that she and Cravan first met. Mina recalled that even though meeting the poet-boxer was "the thing" at the time, she had little interest in him. Robert Coady had dedicated the first edition of his New York art review, *The Soil*, to Cravan, publishing some of his poems together with a photograph of him posing on the couch of his Paris apartment with a pair of Siamese kittens. Seeing this portrait, Mina interpreted the way he crossed his legs as a clear indication that Cravan was gay.

She admitted that she was anxious about meeting Cravan, because the legends that surrounded him were so far-fetched, but when Arensberg introduced them, Mina was disappointed: trussed up in a tweed suit, Cravan gave the impression of being decidedly dull. He turned out not to be a homosexual, but he wasn't handsome either: she observed that he had the drab appearance of a farmer. It may have been an inauspicious meeting, but of this first encounter she later wrote: "I felt no premonition of the psychological infinity he would offer my curiosity as to the mechanism of man".

Her second meeting with Cravan took place once again in the town house on 67th Street. After Marcel Duchamp's urinal was rejected by the curators of the Independents' Exhibition, Loy joined him and other budding Dadaists to publish *The Blind Man*, a radical art journal. On 25th May 1917 they held a promotional Blind Man's Ball, which was billed as "Ultra-Bohemian, Prehistoric and Post-Alcoholic", and was conceived principally to fleece the wealthy young New Yorkers keen to display an interest in all things Modern. Before the ball, the initiates gathered at Arensberg's house, and it was here, Mina recalled, that she first perceived of Cravan as beautiful. She was struck by "his huge bulk, his empty stare". For the occasion Cravan was wearing a bed sheet with a bath towel tied around his head, and "this white encasement," Mina wrote in her typically pompous fashion, "gave the perfect construction of his face the significance of sculpture".

When he spotted her, Cravan pressed a paper into Mina's hand and urged her to read it. She was outraged and a little intrigued by its contents: he had given her a letter from his Paris lover, Renée, "a woman of whom I had never heard, throwing a jealous fit on account of *my* relationship with this creature Cravan, with whom I had not yet exchanged a word!"

Mina did her best to appear unperturbed. She casually handed the letter back to him. Then she struck a disinterested pose by the window, where the light was most flattering.

Webster Hall is a great Gothic monstrosity of red-brick charmlessness. Today the place still squats on East 11th

Street – its sheer, featureless façade blotting out the sky and threatening to pitch forwards onto the pavement. By day it is boarded up and seems to have been left derelict for years, but on Friday evenings floodlights transform the dreary walls, the front doors are thrown open and a dirty red carpet lolls down the steps to the street. The affluent twenty-somethings of Manhattan queue in their hundreds to be arraigned and insulted by crew-cut bouncers, and anxiously await the parting of the velvet rope.

Inside was awash with ultraviolet, and as soon as I walked in I could feel the flare coming off the dandruff on my shoulders. The music pounded relentlessly, the walls resonated with the monotonous house beat. Strobes flickered all around, big banks of lights were lurching and revolving, and sweeping lurid colours across the vast open space of the club. In the obscurity, the place churned with the restless movement of people, who spread across every open surface like a voracious mould.

This was the venue for the Blind Man's Ball in May 1917. Cravan had arrived in a state of advanced intoxication, and there was a slight lull in the murmur of conversations when he came in. His bed sheet was soiled from a small accident outside, and he exuded the sickly aroma of impending scandal. After a few drinks Cravan stripped to the waist, and then spent the next hour standing in the corner, scornfully watching the society couples dance and chatter.

Mina's party was posed around a table, looking fashionably bored. Duchamp had gone down on his knees to beg Mina to accompany him to the Ball, but now he was drunk and had his hands all over a giggling blonde. So she and Cravan were brought together that night by their mutual disdain.

Loy recalled that Cravan came over to the table after a while and collapsed into the seat next to her. They sat in silence for a long time. Mina tried to appear uninterested by Duchamp's absurd charade of romance across the table.

Cravan, sinking slowly in his chair, looked on sneeringly. Loy felt the sheer, unbridled contempt rising from him like a cloud of newly hatched blowflies. He'd had too much to drink, and he occasionally gave a little jolt as his stomach flipped over. After a while he turned to Mina as if to say something, but didn't. He swallowed down an indiscreet belch, and then slowly laid his heavy bare arm around her shoulders.

The story of Loy and Cravan is certainly not one of love at first sight: there is nothing of the fairy tale in it. Their relationship was tainted from the very beginning by a prescience of its demise. "I had never been encircled by a stranger or by anyone who revolted me before," Loy wrote. "It was only satisfying to rise and leave him."

I was pressed into the corner, with five whiskies in a line on top of the breath-mint machine. I had bought them all at once, to save me having to go back to the bar. I ignored the No Smoking sign and lit a cigarette.

Watching the writhing bodies on the dance floor below, I began to reminisce about the night I first met Cathy. I had been invited to a stag night by someone in the office, presumably out of pity, or for a joke. I was already far gone by the time we ran into a hen party in a cheap nightclub serving watered-down lager in plastic cups. And there was Cathy, standing apart from the rest with one broken high heel and a learner sign hung askew around her neck. From the far end of the bar I watched her. Taking little nervous nips from a vodka and coke, she eyed the other women feeling up the lads with a certain weariness.

It took me half an hour to work up the courage to talk to her. She asked me to dance, and facing her there I was astonished by how quickly my long-held fear of dancing receded. It might as well have been just the two of us moving on the tacky floor.

But then, just as we were about to kiss, the lads lifted me clear of the ground by the elastic of my boxer shorts, so that the gusset bit viciously into my crotch. Then they released me, and as I reeled with dizziness and nausea they tore down my trousers and underpants and left me standing there stark naked in the middle of the dance floor.

Cathy led me out of the nightclub. On the way, cheers and shrill laughter drowned out a Rick Astley song, and I was prodded several times and patted roughly around the back and shoulders. Mortified, I let Cathy pull me by the hand like an infant. In the taxi we sat at either ends of the seat, staring out of our respective windows. When she got out at her place, she leant back in and gave me an awkward smile of condolence. Then she pressed something quickly into my hand and slammed the door. The taxi carried on towards Hounslow. In the back seat I unknotted my fist and saw there in the palm of my hand the beer mat she'd given me and the phone number scrawled on the back.

I shrugged off the memory and stubbed my cigarette out on the No Smoking sign. Then I downed the five shots grimly, one after another, looking out over the mezzanine balcony at the mêlée of dancing bodies below. Sinuous blondes in cocktail dresses writhed with yuppies in open-collared shirts. Along the sides of the room newly acquainted couples ground against one another with expressions of deadpan seriousness. Up on the podiums club kids in moronic outfits twirled glow-sticks and tossed their hair about. I bit back the whisky and scowled. I hated everything. Looking around for the bouncers, I lit another cigarette and inhaled it between fits of coughing.

I had drunk too much and I felt my stomach tightening. I staggered down the stairs to the toilet, holding on to the wall for support. I slipped near the bottom and went down the last few steps on my backside.

It was a huge, open-plan unisex toilet. There was a DJ down there and throngs of people stood around the mirrors by the sink chatting, pruning themselves and wiping cocaine from their nostrils. I went straight to a cubicle and shouldered the door. It was locked. A chorus of angry voices rose from the lengthy queue behind me.

"Hey! Buddy!" one of them said.

"Join the line, man," said another.

From behind the cubicle door I could hear giggling and the rat-tat of a credit card cutting lines on the cistern.

I staggered over to a urinal, barged someone out of the way and bowed my head into it. I vomited profusely. There was a plastic mesh to keep the deodorant blocks out of the drain and I noticed that this sieved out all the solid matter. I wiped my chin with the back of my sleeve, and went down on my hands and knees to look for my cigarette end, which had fallen to the floor in all the commotion. I had to reach between the legs of a man at a nearby urinal to retrieve it. At the door to the toilets, a large bouncer plucked the fag out of my lips, got hold of me by the collar and showed me the way out of the back entrance with a kick.

At the end of the Blind Man's Ball, Mina came across Cravan once again. By this time he was totally gone, dead drunk and veering aggressively through the crowd. He was stopping any women in his path and scrawling their phone numbers on the back of his hand. "You may give me yours," he told Mina. "I will ring you *if* I find the time. So many other women desire me..." He went out into the street and disappeared. For want of anything better to do, Loy followed the rest of the group back to Duchamp's studio, where there was talk of an orgy.

I'd got up early just so I wouldn't have to mingle with the other guests during the breakfast rush, and I was sitting at a table by myself when the Christians came in: a group of a dozen or so teenagers in baggy shorts, sun visors and T-shirts bearing the slogan *Jesus Rocks*. They could have sat at any of the empty tables, but they deliberately came over to mine.

"Hey man," said a boy with an ugly outbreak of acne whom I recognized from my room. "Can we sit here?"

I shot him a savage look. "*Why?*" I said.

He thought I was joking. Each of them grabbed a plastic chair and sat noisily down all around me. They had seen that I was weak. They had me marked as easy pickings. Now they had me cornered.

They passed round plastic bowls, a gallon bottle of milk and a family-sized box of sugar-frosted Cheerios. They chattered and laughed hollowly amongst themselves and gave the impression of righteously neutered adolescence. They were the kind of teenagers who spend their time discussing the afterlife, or strumming guitar and singing worship songs when they should be out abusing alcohol, doing their first drugs and getting as much sex as they can.

"Will you say grace with us?" the boy with the acne asked me.

I wasn't going to dignify this with an answer, but seeing them all crowded around, pointing their inanely sympathetic expressions at me, frankly I felt intimidated.

"No," I replied, and I immediately felt an odd twinge of guilt.

"No problem, man," the boy said, undeterred. "Sometimes I feel a little weird praying with strangers too. I like totally understand."

When they'd finished praying, the boy with acne, whom I knew as Jefferson, put his arm around me. I flinched away from him, but he took no notice. He said:

"I hope I didn't come on too strong last night, dude." He retracted his arm and then scooped a sloppy spoonful of cereal into his face. A squirt of milk ran out of the corner of his mouth.

The night before, finding myself suddenly wide awake, I had become aware of people standing around my bed in the dark. I'd been weeping into my pillow for some time, but I'd been careful not to whinny loud enough for anyone in the room to hear. But now I was sure that there was someone standing over me in the darkness. I lay motionless, listening and not breathing. There came the sound of whispering from close by, and a whispered answer from the foot of the bed.

I heard the strip lamps flutter on, and the room was suddenly awash with light. I didn't open my eyes, I pretended to be asleep. Then there was more whispering, and the grating of metal dragged across the floor. There was the sound of bare feet walking over to my bed, and a shadow fell over me. I could feel my heart thumping in my throat.

"Hey, dude," came a voice by my right ear. "You asleep?"

I kept utterly still, my eyes squeezed shut against the light and whoever it was leaning over me. A hand pressed against my shoulder.

"Are you asleep, dude?" he said shaking me.

"Is he awake?" whispered someone else, further away.

It took a moment for my eyes to adjust to the light. Jefferson was sitting on a chair pulled up by my bedside, and standing guard by the door was Allan. Jefferson took his hand away from my shoulder.

"Are you asleep, man?" He asked softly.

"Of course I'm not bloody asleep, you just woke me up!"

"You were crying," he said.

"Like a baby," said Allan, nodding by the door.

"Do you wanna talk, man?" said Jefferson, with an earnest look.

"Why?" I said.

"I think we should talk."

"I'll leave you guys alone," said Allan, opening the door.

I looked from one to the other uncertainly.

"Can't I go back to sleep, please?" I called out. There was an edge of panic in my voice.

Allan smiled reassuringly as he backed out of the room and pulled the door softly to behind him.

"We need to talk, man," Jefferson started. "I can understand it's difficult sometimes to open up, but please, man, do it for me?"

"Do we have to do this now? It's the middle of the night." I was propped on one elbow, reluctant to sit up and commit myself to this situation.

"I know, dude. But I've been wanting to talk for ages, and I heard you crying and I couldn't wait any longer. I want you to know…" He reached his hand and squeezed my shoulder warmly. "I feel your pain man."

I looked edgily about the room at the empty beds. There was no one to help me.

"I had to talk. I had to talk to you about Jesus." He gave me a long, searching look, nodding slowly all the while, his eyebrows slanted with sincerity.

"Do you know what it's like to have something in your life, to *know* something that's so fucking *essential*, dude, that you just have to let people know about it?" His eyes bore into me relentlessly, exuding sheer righteousness.

"Look, it's half-past two—"

"It's like I've got this burning *secret* that I've got to tell people about, you know?" He was staring around the ceiling shaking his head as if overwhelmed with earnestness. "Sometimes, when I see people suffering," he said, his eyes turning all starry, "I just feel so sorry for them because they don't know about Our Lord." He leant back and stared at me for a long time. I frowned back at him, then consulted my wristwatch.

He hissed: "*Jesus Christ Our Lord the Saviour.*"

"Look, Jefferson. I do know of Jesus Christ. That piece of cultural trivia has not escaped me."

"But there's a difference, man," Jefferson said, "between like knowing *about* Jesus and like *knowing* Him. You can't know Him just by like knowing *about* Him – you get to know Him, man, by, like—" he was staring around the walls looking for the right words. "You get to know Him by *being* with Him, dude."

I ground the palm of my hand into the socket of my eye.

"*I've* been with Him, man. And let me tell you, He *rocks.*"

"Fine, Jefferson. Look, I'd really like to hear about it, but now's not the time. If you've got a brochure, some promotional material or what have you, leave it with me. I'll have a look in the morning and get back to you, all right?"

I lay back on the pillow, turned over to face the wall and pretended to fall immediately asleep. I heard Jefferson saying:

"I'm gonna pray for you, I hope you don't object. I'm gonna pray that Jesus finds you soon the way He found me, and I'm gonna pray that when you're ready you're gonna let His love into your life, man, cos I just can't imagine life without Him."

The chair scraped against the floor when he got up. I heard him walking over to the door and opening it. There was a moment's hesitation before the snap of the light switch and the sound of the door closing behind him. I lay there in the dark, my heart beating hard against the mattress. From outside in the corridor there came a low murmur of voices. First thing in the morning I would demand to be moved to a different room.

Now the Christians ate their sugary cereals like animals.

Flecks of milk spattered all around, fragments of Cheerios ricocheted off the table top. Jefferson was saying, "Sorry to wake you up like that, man. But some news is worth waking *up* for, dude."

"Amen to that, man," said Allan, who was sitting across the table. They gave each other high fives.

I needed to get out of there at once.

"So, Jefferson got to you last night?" Allan said.

"What are you people *doing* here?" I asked shortly.

"We're on a field trip for college," said the kid opposite.

"What college?"

"We're at evangelical school, in third semester."

I stared at him. He nodded and scraped cereal accretions from his bowl.

"So we're like doing an East Coast trip, spreading the Word you know," he said. "So what do you think?"

"About what?" I was still staring at him. He was pouring the last of the Cheerios into his bowl, and they gushed to an end in an avalanche of orange dust.

"Do you believe or what?"

"In what?"

"*Jesus*, dude. That's what Jefferson was prepping you about, right? So are you sold or what?"

At half-past eight in the morning a metaphysical debate with a roomful of American teenagers on a sugar rush was the last thing I could stomach. My sense of outrage gave a final spasm and then subsided in apathy and resignation.

"Absolutely," I mumbled.

"No way, dude!" Allan said, glancing at Jefferson.

"I realized there is a gaping void in my life," I said, and my entire body crumpled under the weight of a tremendous sigh. "I realized Jesus is what's missing."

"I like totally *hear* you, man. My life was totally empty, dude, until He found me. I was a *loser*, man, I was getting wasted with beer and drugs. Ran away from home cos my old man was beating on me. And I got in with a bad crowd. I didn't know what love was, man, until I found the Lord and now I'm like a totally new *person*. If it wasn't for Jesus Christ Our Lord, I probably wouldn't even *be* here dude."

"Well," I muttered, "at least He didn't die in vain."

"I'm so stoked for you. You're just not gonna believe what He's gonna do for you now you've let Him into your life, man."

"I can't wait." I started gathering my things to go.

"Jefferson, dude, all right!"

Jefferson, turning away from a conversation with someone else, put his hand out uncertainly for Allan to high-five.

"What, man?"

"You *scored* one, dude! I can't believe it, on *day two*, man."

"You serious?"

"Yeah, dude. This guy's like totally tuned in."

Jefferson looked round at me. "You serious?" he said. I had stood up from the table. "Hey, will you sign a testimonial for my grade book?"

He was pulling a ring binder out of his backpack as I walked quickly away. I ducked out of the door without looking back and headed directly to reception to see about changing my room.

Despite her initial dislike for Cravan, as the winter drew on Mina Loy found herself straying into an odd kind of intimacy with him. It happened gradually, without them noticing it. They often fell into each other's company simply because they were the most detached members of the group. They existed on its fringes, not quite belonging, yet kept there by the fear of isolation. Cravan would sit next to her on the Arensbergs' divan and barely utter a word. When he did speak Mina found it almost impossible to follow: one moment she strained to hear his mumbling, the next she recoiled at some theatrical outburst that left her ears ringing. And yet without fail, day after day the unfathomable logic of his conversation would return to the same blunt demand: "Let me come home with you".

For a long time Loy pitied Cravan: only some unspoken trauma could explain the discrepancy between his spectacular reputation and the sluggish, subdued reality of him. "I remember feeling as if I were lounging on the flanks of an indolent mountain whose summit was lost in heavy clouds," she said of their time together. There were mutterings among the Arensberg regulars that this man was not in fact the poet-boxer they had heard so much about, but an impostor. Cravan, however, seemed oblivious of how quickly the initial excitement at his arrival had turned to disappointment. Mina came to the conclusion that he must be a halfwit, that his boxing career had left him with brain damage.

Cravan was persistent in his advances, despite her coldness. "Do let me come home with you," he begged her one evening. "The mere idea of sleeping in my own place makes me neurasthenic – do."

"I have no extra bed," she replied.

"But a table, surely? I will sleep on the table and swear I will not address a single word to you."

In New York, Cravan's seduction routine proved to be sorely lacking. In Europe women had thrown themselves at him – all it required was a pinch on the arse, a declaration of love and a secluded alleyway. But here courtship was a matter of mind games and manipulation, women demanded wordplay and soft persuasion.

Marcel Duchamp was himself determined to possess Loy, and even as she repelled the ham-fisted advances of Cravan, Duchamp would be hovering nearby, always ready with his whispered sweet nothings and a clammy hand picking at the laces of her bustier. Whereas Cravan was torpid, the impetuous Duchamp oozed charm and wit. "If Cravan was lumbering," she recalls, "Marcel was slick as a prestidigitator; he could insinuate his hand under a woman's bodice and caress her with utter grace."

One evening at the Arensbergs', Duchamp had Mina in a corner and was bearing down on her with increasingly bold double entendres.

"Will you come *away* from that *petit calecot*," Cravan interrupted, grabbing Mina by the arm and dragging her away from Duchamp. Hustling her into a quiet room at the end of the hall, he pulled her down to his knees and fixed her with an ardent stare.

"Why not let me show you what life can be in the embrace of my boundless love," he whispered. "My one desire," Cravan told her, plucking at the diaphanous frills dangling from her hat, "is to be so very tender to you that you will smile without irony."

Mina was bored of the sex lives of the Modernists. She channelled her distaste into her "Love Poems" and their erotic imagery of pigs rooting through garbage. All winter long she'd heard the men planning their conquests, whilst with affected nonchalance the women quibbled over who was most admired. The arrival of a new initiate always set the men aflutter – they would follow her around the room in an excited cluster, hanging on her every word as if she were the only female in existence. But this infatuation only lasted until she allowed herself to be seduced. Mina observed that the emancipated "Modern" woman differed from the ordinary, downtrodden variety only in the extent to which she had to be wheedled, cajoled and conned into bed.

But Cravan seemed to have nothing of the modern spirit. "This granite lump – although he held no magnetism – might prove affectionate." So romance bloomed out of boredom.

That night, back at her apartment, she found sex with Cravan an alienated, deadening experience. "He possessed me with an icy inertia, contriving the illusion that he was not, himself, involved in the curt, chill, passive union of flesh, and that had I stirred he would have tossed me out of bed like so much flesh that wearied his spirit."

Despite his initial impression of imbecility, as they became better acquainted, Mina now came to suspect that Cravan's apparent vacuity concealed a shrewd and conniving mind. "I began to realize that to most of those early encounters he had come as an entirely different persona. I began to wonder how I had been able to recognize any identity behind his frequent transformations."

The next morning she awoke to find Cravan in the kitchen amongst the remains of an enormous breakfast. He had emptied her larder and was looking through the other cupboards in case he had missed anything.

"I feel like a walk," he told her.

She followed him down the stairs and into the street. It was cold out and a close fog hung in the air.

Cravan strode ahead, leading her by the arm through the crowds on Fifth Avenue.

"Fear not," he told her, "you have the Christ with you."

As they traipsed about the city, Cravan sung an obscene French song about venereal disease while Mina, already exhibiting the first symptoms of love, marvelled at "the magic carpet of the Elevated Train sailing across the sky, trailing its filaments of iron fringe along the avenue".

Then Cravan walked into the road and brought the traffic to a halt with an outstretched hand. Over the blaring of the klaxons he made this solemn pronouncement: "The world has always exploited the Artist – it is time for the Artist to exploit the world!"

As the days went by, I had watched the medication slowly dwindling. That morning there was the lonely rattling of one remaining pill in the bottle. Apprehensively I looked at it through the dim plastic. It signified the final loss of all control.

I swallowed the pill morosely, staring at my reflection. My lip tightened into a sneer as I looked myself over. I was disfigured by the scratches and little welts of rust bubbling on the surface of the mirror. It was made of steel like the ones they have in prison bathrooms. Unbreakable, to prevent the gouging-open of veins.

The pill stuck uncomfortably in my throat, and no amount of water gulped down could dislodge it. It remained there, and for the rest of the day I could feel it disintegrating in my neck, a nagging reminder of the darkness that would soon descend.

The first dizzy, weightless elation of the manic phase came over me two mornings later.

I was coming down the stairs from the dormitory when I ran into Jefferson. I gave him a high five, a low five, and I went for a double-reverse five, but, already confused, this last gesture proved too much for him.

"So you want to talk to me about Our Lord do you?" I exclaimed.

"Uh…" he said. I'd caught him coming out of the showers, in flip-flops with a towel around his waist.

"You want to tell me about the righteous J.C. do you?"

"Uh, only if you're like *ready*, dude," he said, backing up against the wall in the corridor.

"I've never been more ready. I need saving at once."

I crossed my arms intently and cocked my head to listen.

"Well, let's see…"

"Hit me with some psalms or something. Or a parable."

"Uh…"

I propped my hands on hips.

"Haven't you got a quick pitch?" I prompted. "What do they teach you at evangelical school?"

He looked at me, then looked around for assistance.

"Haven't you got a thirty-second sales spiel to get your foot in the door?"

His mouth was shaping to speak, but he couldn't decide on a word. His hands gripped tightly where the towel was fastened around his waist.

"Let me tell you what *I* think shall I?"

"I guess," he said.

"If you want to know what *I* think, I think you are sorely mistaken."

He smiled, but there was a wide unblinking look in his eyes.

"I think that Jesus is up there right now *laughing at you.*"

Red patches appeared on Jefferson's cheeks.

"He's falling about *pissing himself.*"

Jefferson's smile had tightened. He swallowed hard.

"It's all a big joke!" I told him. "Think about it."

I waved a hand at the yellowing walls of the hostel corridor, at the black mould infesting the corner by the barred window, at the aroma of putrefaction coming from the toilets.

"Look around you. Look at the fucking world we live in! Tell me – is this the work of a beneficent God?"

I let him ponder this for an instant.

"And what about you? Look at the hand he's dealt you, look at your *life.*" I cast my eyes over him, from his mottled cheeks to the knock knees poking out below his towel. "And to add insult to injury, now he's got you running around singing his praises, doing his *promotions!*"

Jefferson was no longer smiling, but he was making a point of keeping eye contact, of betraying no fear.

"And then of course there's *me*. If it's hard evidence you need for the Almighty's depraved sense of humour – look no further."

I repositioned myself to stop him edging away.

"A throwaway gag, but I'm stuck with it for life!"

The kid had put a hand out in front of him vaguely as if to ask for time out.

"Behold His creations! Pattern baldness. Botulism. Blocked U-bends. Officious bureaucrats. Infections of the urinary tract. Traffic jams. The taxman. Flat-pack furniture. Sir Cliff Richard. Genocide. Check-out queues. Karaoke. Canteen food. Christmas. Chronic constipation. Corruption. Inflation. Eurovision. Fascism. Perversion involving animals or children. Wars. Nil-nil draws. Celebrity memoirs. Mosquitoes. Stubbed toes. Mobile ringtones. The inevitable decay of love, life and everything that you might come to care about—"

I stopped for a moment, noticing that the boy was inching away. I saw that his outstretched hand had turned into a weak gesture of self-defence.

"You want to spread the Word," I said gravely, stopping him in his tracks. "I too consider myself to be a kind of missionary. I consider it my *mission* to give people like you a slap around the face, to wake you up. To stop you deluding yourself and other idiots. Take a look around you!"

I gestured sweepingly and he ducked as if I might strike him.

"Don't draw it out any longer! *Put yourself out of your misery!*"

He had turned and was beginning to walk away with some semblance of dignity.

"Did we choose to be born in the first place?" I called after him. "Did I *ask* to be born? I can tell you categorically: I WISH I NEVER HAD BEEN!"

He broke into a run before he reached the corner. One of his flip-flops fell off, but he didn't turn back for it. I could hear him take the stairs two at a time back up to his room, one bare foot flapping against the linoleum.

I barely noticed that it was coming on to rain. I was marching along the street with a grin plastered across my face for no apparent reason. I shouted "HELLO" to a complete stranger. I was dimly remembering the hilarity underneath it all and I felt like giggling. As I walked on, gaining speed all the time, I gazed about me, taking in the shapes and textures of things all around. I was afraid to blink in case I missed something.

I started running, and the sensation of the cold air and the pinpricks of icy rain grazing my face was intensely pleasurable. The DON'T WALK sign was flashing but I ran across the road anyway, and a white stretch limo had to brake suddenly. The car horns sounded like a chorus of approval, and I jumped in the air and whooped in triumph. I found that I could run almost as fast as the traffic going by, and I veered into the road and weaved from lane to lane with my arms out like fighter-plane wings. I felt like a footballer doing a victory run after scoring a goal: the din of foghorns going off in adulation, all around the screaming and shouting of the spectators!

19th April 1917: the eve of the opening of the Exhibition of the Society of Independent Artists. Already blighted by the publicity over Duchamp's urinal, the ill-fated Exhibition would now be soiled on its very inaugural day by a scandal of Cravan's making.

On the strength of the reputation he had brought from Paris as an outspoken critic of the Arts, Cravan had been invited to inaugurate the exhibition with a lecture on the subject of "The Independent Artists of France and America". The lavish hall of the newly constructed Grand Central Palace was brimming with the bourgeoisie of New York – the Fifth Avenue hostesses, socialites, naïfs waiting to be initiated into the new fad of modernism, the idle rich in search of new fodder for dinner-party conversation. They gathered in their hundreds, murmuring excitedly. And they waited.

Cravan arrived twenty minutes late. He pushed his way through the smartly dressed crowds. He was blind drunk, and it took him a moment to find the lecture platform. He didn't see the steps and was trying to shin his way up the side of the stage. He struggled, hanging off the edge of the platform, and someone in the front row had to give him a shove from behind. There was silence in the hall. The rows of faces watched, dumbstruck. But the audience was prepared to tolerate the odd idiosyncrasy: a reporter covering the opening for the *New York Sun* wrote, "The thoughtful crowd understood that artists may be highly strung... This Monsieur Cravan was temperamental, but of course he was independent. Was that not the subject of his lecture?"

There was a collective drawing of breath as Cravan staggered and fell heavily on his face. He climbed to his feet and began to undress. A canvas by the American painter Sterner was displayed on an easel behind him, and as he writhed out of his shirt he put an elbow through it, then knocked it to the floor. From the audience there was a low murmuring and a single scream.

When he unfastened his belt and pulled his trousers down, the hushed muttering of the audience was immediately drowned out by jeers and hoots of indignation. Chaperones shielded the eyes of their debutante charges. In the attempt to extricate his foot from the trouser leg, Cravan tripped and went down on his knees. He crawled across the platform, shedding the trousers as he went. He finally kicked them off into the crowd. In his underpants, shoes and socks he walked up to the lectern, slowly looked the crowd over in disdain and opened his mouth to address them.

But before he could say a word, he was set upon by five security guards, who attacked him from behind. Cravan managed to get a few punches in before he was overpowered and dragged to the floor. He pulled the smallest of the guards down with him and they rolled around the stage until the other men succeeded in prizing Cravan loose. In a parting gesture of defiance he tore the seat of the little security guard's trousers clean off.

Handcuffed, Cravan was at last escorted out, screaming the grossest of obscenities at his assailants and at the cheering audience as he went. He would have been thrown in jail if it wasn't for Arensberg, who intervened on his behalf, put up his bail and drove him to the house on 67th Street, where the others were waiting.

Francis Picabia gave him a standing ovation when he came in.

"What a wonderful lecture!" Duchamp declared.

Cravan sulked in a corner, feeling the effects of a crushing hangover. Picabia and his associates had a celebratory drink. The scandal was complete.

I couldn't run any more. I staggered to a halt by the kerb and turned my face up to the sky. My whole body was beating a frantic pulse, and with each convulsion I could feel the serotonin surging prodigiously into my brain. The rain streamed down on me, caressing my face, running a cold hand inside my shirt and along the cleft of my back. I laughed breathlessly, and tears welled up in my eyes. Passersby kept a wide berth, but they smiled at the sight of me. There seemed to be heat coming off them.

I got my breath back and things subsided, they slowed down a fraction. I was standing on the pavement outside a cigar shop, and I went up close to the wall. I stood right up against the wall for what seemed like a long time, although it was probably about a minute. Then I knotted my fingers into a fist, so tight that the knuckles went white, and purposefully, ponderously, I punched the wall.

I punched it, just once, and left my fist there for a moment, half-ground into the brickwork. When I relaxed my hand and brought it up close to my face, I saw there was a large chunk taken out of the middle knuckle, and it hung there by a flap of skin. The raw flesh was pale and dry, but I watched the blood gathering in tiny spots from the severed vessels. The blood came up slowly, bulged there for a second, then spilt over, running in tracks down my wrist and dripping off my elbow. The deep red of it was astonishing.

Cravan's lecture at the Independent's is acknowledged to be the decisive Dada event. But it was also the beginning of the end for Dada.

According to Gabrielle Picabia, it was her husband and Duchamp who masterminded the scandal. They chose Cravan for the occasion, because they knew he was capable of delivering the *coup de grâce* to the complacent New York art establishment, just as he had in Paris. Before the main event they helped Cravan limber up: they took him to a bar, bought a bottle of pastis and got him dead, stinking drunk. Then he was ready to be unleashed onto the stage of the Grand Central. When it was all over, they announced triumphantly that the lecture had been nothing less than a smarting blow to the upturned nose of bourgeois inhibition. Picabia and Duchamp had plucked Cravan from the mundane world and turned him into a work of art.

Cravan maintained a scowling silence after the performance. Even once his terrible hangover had dissipated, he refused to discuss what he had done. Without his colleagues' enthusiastic endorsement, the Independents' scandal would have been quickly forgotten – but perhaps Cravan would have preferred it that way. It seems that the lecture had not gone quite as he had intended: too drunk to deliver a single word of his speech, he'd come out of it looking a fool. One biographer has gone so far as to suggest that Cravan had fallen victim to a conspiracy by his former friends: Picabia and Duchamp hadn't orchestrated his lecture so much as sabotaged it.

Whether or not they planned Cravan's embarrassment, his friends certainly revelled in it. For Duchamp there was the sore point of Mina Loy, the woman he had failed to ensnare, the woman who Cravan had stolen from under his nose. Years later, when he was asked in a magazine interview about his friendship with the poet-boxer, Duchamp curtly replied that Cravan had never been his friend. Even after all that time the mere mention of his name had touched a raw nerve. But beyond personal jealousies, there was something altogether more powerful driving them apart, something that emanated from the combustible nature of Dada itself.

The truth is that the paths of the three men had diverged, they no longer shared the same vision of the world. From the very beginning Dada had carried its death within itself, a central paradox that could not be resolved. Now that the loose assemblage of volatile personalities that made up Dada was coming unstuck, its leaders were turning against one another. The peculiar tensions underlying the Independents' scandal were a taste of the bickering that was to come – the resignations, denouncements and recriminations that would soon spell the end of the movement. Dada's self-loathing was the seed of its demise. An art movement that sought to destroy art: it was inevitable that Dada would come to a fork in the road, and that the Dadaists would have to choose where their loyalties truly lay – to art or to destruction.

"Art is a pharmaceutical product for idiots!" Picabia declared, but secretly he too had become dependent on it. Somehow he had gained heroic status in New York, and wealthy collectors were rewarding him handsomely for his work. Duchamp, especially, was developing a taste for success – when he was presented with a bill for dental work, he casually drew a cheque on the back of an envelope in felt-tip pen. His dentist had it framed. All their talk about overthrowing the bourgeois establishment was nothing but a great song and dance, and Dada had become an empty slogan. Picabia and Duchamp had taken the joke as far as they were prepared to go. But Cravan – whether he realized it or not – was on the path to utter destruction, and it was too late to turn back.

At last came the pain, a jagged, searing explosion of pain. And my hand began to throb heavily. *That's right*, I thought. *It's still there. It's all still there.*

The wounded hand was red and swollen, it was useless, so I had to reach round with the other one to get the wallet out of my pocket. It was tricky getting it open with the one hand. I had to clamp it to my chest with my right forearm so that I could pull the photo out with my good hand. There was Cathy, with the spot of smeared emulsion and the smudged imprint of the biro over her face. I could feel the familiar tugging inside me, the sinking coldness of it. It was almost like nausea, the kind you get on fairground rides.

The rain had turned to snow. It fell all around in heavy misshapen clumps, and soon began to settle on the pavements. I felt the need to walk, and I did so, through the tumbling snowfall, for the rest of the afternoon. My legs started to ache, yet I resisted the temptation to stop off at a café to rest. All the running, the chafing of buttock against buttock, had aggravated my piles and I knew that if I sat down to rest the maddening, terrible itching would begin. Instead I kept walking, through the thickening snow of the pavements, and after a while I found that the walking lulled me into a kind of trance in which the sight and sound of things washed over me, making no sense and leaving no impression.

I went down into the subway, and found the tunnels deserted. I followed the empty corridors for what seemed like miles. The first sign of life I came across was the reverberations of a guitar repeating the same chords over and over again. The sound grew louder as I went on until, turning a corner, I saw a lone busker at the end of an interminable, empty corridor.

The figure was emitting a strange whining sound. It was a long, agonizing approach, and the guitarist could not have been oblivious to it, because my footsteps resounded along the length of the tunnel. As I grew nearer, I began to discern the scale of him, which was rather small, even stunted. When I was within twenty metres, he picked up his act. In an indeterminate Eastern European accent he wailed:

"*Nobody told me it'd be like diiiss!*"

Screwing up his sallow face with soulfulness he wailed:

"*Nobody told me I'd be like diiiss!*"

He tried to make eye contact, and I looked away a fraction too late. Perhaps he sensed that I intended to ignore him, because he suddenly cranked his performance up a gear: violently he machine-gun-strummed his guitar, then kicked out a leg and dropped theatrically to the ground. But somewhere the manoeuvre must have gone awry, because I heard the resounding clomp as his kneecap struck the tiling. He let out a howl of pain, but managed to pass it off as a James Brown "*Ow*".

As I drew abreast of him, he pulled himself together and carried on the manic strumming from where he had left off, flashing me a glare of desperation. I had to stop in the empty tunnel and work my fingers into my trouser pocket to find some change, and as soon as he saw this he stopped playing with relief and rubbed his knee. I regretted it immediately, because I was wearing the skintight cords I'd had since the Nineties, and my hand had become tightly wedged into the pocket. It took a long time to dislodge the trapped fingers, and as I did so the busker stood awkwardly by, flexing his bad leg.

"Thenkyou, men," he said, looking along the empty tunnel that curved into the distance on either side.

I had managed to get hold of a little collection of coins in the depths of my pocket, and now I was endeavouring to pull them free before I lost all feeling in my hand. The man waited impatiently, drumming his fingers on the guitar. I turned my glowering eyes up at him.

All of a sudden my numbed hand twisted free of the pocket. I held sixty-one cents in my palm. He said, "Thenks" again when I tossed the coins into his guitar case.

I had just taken the first step away when I heard him say, "End cheer up, men…"

I let it ride. But then came the clincher:

"Might-a never heppen," he said.

I had taken two more steps before the words sunk in, and there I stopped in my tracks. Slowly I turned to look at him. His plectrum was poised to start strumming his guitar again.

"*What?*" I said.

The sound of a single misstruck chord echoed along the tunnel.

"I said…" he was a little taken aback. "I said, cheer up because it might-a…"

His smile faded as I walked back over to him. He watched me stoop to pick my two quarters, one dime and one penny out of his guitar case.

The subway train emerged from underground and climbed onto the elevated tracks over Brooklyn. Rooftops blanketed with snow fell beneath me, and the skyline of Manhattan rose up beyond, as bleached and faint as a watermark on office stationery. The train rattled on for a long time through the suburbs, finally slowing and coasting to the end of the line.

Cravan often came to Coney Island to spend days by the sea or to show Mina the wonders of the octopus at the Aquarium. Now the snow fell over the boarded-up fast-food stalls, it collected in powdery drifts around the corpse of a sofa discarded on the pavement, it frosted the scaffolds of the rollercoaster, locked up behind barbed-wire fences for the winter. The snow spread over the open miles of the Boardwalk, drained all colour from the beach and the sky and the ashen sea. It quietly covered the benches along the front, all around it fell in the deliberate effort to efface all memory of life. There was not a soul in sight, not a single footprint spoilt the surface of the snow. All around this landscape was flat and bleak – it not only surrounded me, but seemed to be part of me. For a moment it seemed the dead world inside encompassed all I saw.

I'd been standing on the stoop of the Arensberg house for nearly a quarter of an hour, poking the doorbell at regular intervals as the snow collected on my head and shoulders. There was no answer from the apartment on the top floor, and I began to worry that Miss Rosen might have taken a fall or had a stroke or something. I was just reassessing my accommodation options when the speaker crackled with static and the door-release tone sounded.

I hauled my suitcase up the four flights of stairs, and there waiting at the top was Miss Rosen in a dressing gown squinting from her doorway to see who it was. When I appeared before her, she clapped her hands on either cheek and exclaimed, "*Well!*" But she was just going through the hostess routine, and behind her well-rehearsed smile I could see the glimmer of confusion in her clouded eyes, the frayed machinery of her brain struggling to remember who I was.

"Come, come!" she muttered, with a weakly welcoming gesture. I walked past her into the flat and she followed me with her eyes. Then she closed the door, locked it with the deadbolt and put the chain on.

Miss Rosen stood at the threshold of the spare room watching me as I cleared bundles of newspaper from the bed. I shoved them into a great heap in one corner and stamped at a clutch of small mice scurrying from their disrupted nest. Then I shook the dust from the bedspread and started unpacking my things.

Miss Rosen observed the whole thing from the doorway with an expression of curiosity, whilst all the while patting down her hair on one side. I thought it best not to try to explain things to her. I would say nothing and trust that somewhere in the depths of her dementia she'd find her own explanations. And, so it seemed, she did.

The next morning I woke to the smell of something burning. Miss Rosen had gone to the trouble of preparing breakfast for me. She had laid the table in the living room with silver cutlery that had lost its lustre long ago. She shuffled in from the kitchen with a tray of boiled eggs and an array of carbonized sausages that glistened darkly from blackened pools of cooking oil. She sat down opposite me with a smile of contentment as she poured the tea, and she had filled the saucer before I could reposition the cup under the spout. She looked at me again and shot me a smile that revealed the full extent of her dentures. I noticed that she had painted her cheeks clumsily with rouge, and a false eyelash drooped precariously from her left eyelid. There was also the distinct smell of singed hair, perhaps from when she leant into the pan to see if the sausages were done.

"Well!" she said.

When I went out that morning, she followed me to the door and stood waiting on the threshold. I stopped and stared at her for a moment, and she stood there staring back expectantly. Slowly, uncertainly, I leant down to her level and lightly, gingerly, I kissed her once on the cheek.

Washington Square Park is the playground of nickel-bag hoods and grey squirrels too fat for the branches of the withered trees to support them. I sat down on a bench to peel a boiled egg with my good hand.

"Hey! White! Play a game?"

It was a gangling, bearded, starved-looking black man in a parka jacket, who was gesturing in my direction. He was standing in a small clearing where the various pathways intersected, beckoning me over to a stone table set for a game of chess.

"Hey! Take a seat! Have some courage!" he shouted, bidding so frantically for my attention that the tassels dangling from his woollen hat flicked about in his face.

I finished peeling my egg, then ate it without relish. It was insufficiently boiled, and the yolk was gluey and unpleasant.

The tall man's attention had moved on to other passers-by, and I could hear him saying, "Hey! Lady! Play a game?"

It had been so long since I had exchanged intelligible words with another human that my brain was beginning to digest itself. For many days now I had wandered the city, lost in my own mind. The same thoughts had been churning around in my head, feeding back endlessly, distorted and sharpened. Cathy with a moustache; the black dog watching attentively from the doorway of our empty flat; the gaunt, bloodless husk of my father sneering from his deathbed; the computer screen in the office, and its streams of meaningless data; the patterns of static on the display of the ultrasound... The images writhed in my head, they paraded themselves across my mind's eye, reduced and abstracted eventually into pure tones of loathing and disgust.

I needed to talk to someone. I needed to talk – to anyone, even if it was just to exchange inanities about the weather. Anything to escape myself for a time.

"Hey! Step up, White!" the chess hustler called to me. "Hey! That's it, take a seat! There's a man with *courage*."

The park clearing had the impression of a penitentiary recreation yard. Men hung around aimlessly, swathed in thick coats, scarves and fur hats. They sat facing each other across the stone tables, grimly engaging one another in games of chess. Occasionally passers-by from the street would take a short cut across the park and would quicken their step, fearful of what they had stumbled into.

He dusted off the seat for me and sat down across the table making quick, anxious adjustments to the alignment of the pieces.

191

"You play fast or slow?"

"Slowly," I told him.

"Five-dollar stake for a slow game," he said rapidly.

"Do we have to play for money?"

"What you think this is?"

He picked impatiently at a knot in his beard.

"Like I said, five dollars."

I unwrinkled a note and put it down on the table.

"Okay. I'm black. You can be white, because you're white, right? Your move."

I moved my pieces cautiously, and he no sooner devoured them, seemingly without thought or conviction. As I pondered my next move he would look nervily over my shoulder and pick at his facial hair, occasionally sighing heavily with impatience.

"So," I said, hoping to distract him with some conversation. "Do you play here often?"

"Every day. This park is my office. Chess is my *business*, know what I'm saying?" His fingers were drumming the table top frenetically. I moved a rook, and he immediately took it with his queen.

"Have you played all of these people here?"

"Yeah, you know, over the years I played 'em." There was a tiresome edge to his voice, as if he'd been through all this before and it bored him. "Like I said, chess is my *business*. I don't play for amusement."

"Who's the champion, then"

He pointed behind me.

"See the Russian. Over in the corner." There was a squat man at one of the tables, only a pair of steady charcoal eyes showing through a huge grey beard.

He took my queen and started drumming his fingers again. I didn't have many pieces left now.

Behind him a fat grey squirrel edged along a branch. The whole tree was leaning over, about to buckle under its weight.

"I'm going to kill myself,' I said quietly.

At this the man sat back and started to shake his head. "Buddy, buddy, buddy," the man said with a smile. "I don't give *nobody* no discount."

Suddenly he shouted, "Hey! Jewish!" He was addressing someone passing behind me. "Play a game, Jewish?"

It was an old Hasidic Jew in a black overcoat who carried his own pieces in a walnut veneer box. Jewish ignored him and went over to a table on the other side of the clearing.

"Jewish don't play for money," he muttered contemptuously.

With a profound sigh I knocked over my king, which was cornered and helpless.

The man looked me over and then cocked his head slightly with an expression approaching compassion. "'Tween you and me," he whispered, his eyes scanning the park, "For ten dollars, I'll letcha win." He looked me in the eye for a second and then leant back in his chair. His long bony hand drifted back to his chin, where it resumed the attempt to unravel a knot of beard. "So what do you say, White?" he said. "I got other customers queuing up, know what I'm sayin'?"

I took the ball of screwed-up notes from my pocket and unpicked them to see how much I had left. He shouted at someone over my shoulder:

"Hey! Paraplegic! Play a game? Wheel your seat over here, have some *courage*!"

I laid out two five-dollar bills and he set about rearranging the pieces with a machine-like efficiency.

Marcel Duchamp himself had been a regular visitor to this park. After New York Dada had blown over, he withdrew from the spotlight to the seclusion of his studio and to the consolations of chess.

He poured his energies into his great work, *The Large Glass*, also known as *The Bride Stripped Bare by Her Bachelors*. It was a huge folly of radiating geometries engraved on plate glass. Duchamp laboured on it for decades, and over the years it began to resemble a blueprint for a strange machine, a symbolic apparatus that embodied his ideas about Man, Woman and Love. It developed incrementally, aimlessly, he didn't know what to do with it. Duchamp abandoned and returned to the *Glass* many times. There in his studio he let it gather dust, and after a while he decided that the dust was part of the composition. Finally he left it permanently unfinished. In transit to its first public exhibition, the couriers dropped *The Large Glass*, and it shattered into many pieces.

Duchamp had by this time given up art altogether, so now he abandoned himself to chess. Clean, scientific, logical: chess had nothing of the dirty impurity of art. "I feel I am ready to become a chess maniac," he wrote to Walter Arensberg. "Everything around me takes the shape of the Knight or Queen, and the exterior world has no interest for me other than its transformation to winning or losing positions." For Duchamp, chess was not only more straightforward than life, it provided an alternative to it: on his honeymoon he analysed chess problems until his bride, out of desperation, glued the pieces to the board. Although it ruined his marriage, Duchamp's obsession with chess survived the relationship, and every day he would sit in Washington Square and play game after game with strangers.

The anarchist artists didn't accomplish the revolution they had set out to achieve. Despite the infamy of the Independents' Exhibition, their intended victims were not insulted in the slightest. Instead of taking offence, the bourgeoisie thought it was a hoot: they embraced the spirit of rebellion, and in so doing they neutered it entirely. Duchamp's *Fountain* turned up thirty years later mounted over the entrance of a retrospective exhibition at the Sidney Janis Gallery: it had been filled with soil and planted with geraniums.

Little by little Mina was initiated into the mystery of Cravan's existence in New York. The more she saw of him, the more fascinated she became. But their burgeoning romance had an abstract quality: it was a meeting of intellects, not bodies. Mina described her lover as "an utterly unprecedented biographical and psychological enigma". Her attraction to him seems to have been a cerebral one, driven out of a scientific curiosity. He would lead her on aimless excursions around the city, and she would use these occasions to try "to excavate my way into his consciousness".

It seems that Cravan had hit upon the very means of ensnaring Loy. Aloof and distant, she was immune to the pretence of romance, and she had a been-there-done-that attitude to sexual experimentation. Jaded and wary, the old seduction routines, the pseudo-poetry, even the machismo had little effect. It was the mystery, the challenge of probing uncharted territory that appealed to her. Instead of accompanying Mina to the theatre or buying her dinner, Cravan would take her to wander by the Hudson River, or to visit a railroad siding. Once he came across a frozen puddle in the meat-packing district and squatted staring into it for a full half-hour. Mina watched him, enchanted. She started keeping notes on Cravan's behaviour, recording every pebble and bottle top that he plucked from the sidewalk to examine, and tracing his path through the city on a fold-out map in an attempt to deduce the logic of his wanderings. She explained, "He was so simple in his extraordinariness one would, to explain him, write an analytical treatise."

Colossus, Loy's unfinished novel about their affair, is perhaps the only extensive first-hand source on Cravan. In this she describes her slow discovery of his past and present life, and the painstaking piecing-together of the puzzle of his existence from the scraps of information he let slip. Because there's so little else to go on, it's tempting to take Mina's insights at face value. And yet there is considerable cause to doubt the validity of her observations: one cannot help feeling that she has been hoodwinked by Cravan's act.

None of the New York set were familiar with Cravan, not even Picabia, who had after all only been acquainted with him for a few months in Spain, and knew little of his history. In New York Cravan had given the impression that he lived a life of idle luxury, and many assumed that he must be considerably rich. He often referred to his "bungalow", and even Loy believed for some time that he must keep a furnished room somewhere in the city. In fact he had been sleeping in Central Park through the winter weeks following his arrival, before moving into a lean-to reclaimed from the pigeons on the roof of Penn Station.

Whilst he liked to maintain an illusion of affluence, in reality he had spent his last sou on the fare to America. Now he was flat broke and, without any source of income, he was forced to live off his wits. It seems he soon proved adept at finding shelter in the beds of successive female acquaintances: his reputation being his sole asset, he exploited it to con girlfriends into lending him money, and he relied upon them for his survival. It is likely that he first sought the acquaintance of Mina Loy for this purpose, and in the early days of their relationship she was suspicious of Cravan's motives. However, her suspicions soon waned as the intuition grew of something more meaningful in their union.

On Cravan's frequent visits to her pokey two-room apartment, Loy would hurriedly hide her jewellery and anything else of value, because he had boasted to her of his exploits as a hotel thief in Switzerland. But despite her initial misgivings, Cravan soon moved in, and once he had his foot in the door of her home he also gained access to her heart.

One day she returned to her flat to find Cravan asleep in her bath, and for Mina this was a sight so sublime it brought a tear to her eye. She admits that "I had magnified his being to such proportions that all comparisons vanished, which is the trick of falling in love". In no time all her wariness had evaporated and she was beyond hope.

Years later, after it was all over, Loy returned to New York a broken woman. She found it difficult to adjust to life as an object of pity, and the cooing sympathy of her old friends soon drove her to shun them altogether. She struggled to find any point in life, and on several occasions she seriously considered jumping under a train.

The Arensberg salon still met, albeit in diminished form, a lacklustre and rather melancholy imitation of its former self. Prohibition had taken the wind out of proceedings, and the hosts were already thinking about relocating to Hollywood. Mina Loy did not go back, and carefully avoided the habits and associations of her former life. In her absence, her eccentricities became a favourite talking point in the salons, and Mina herself the butt of jokes by her old acquaintances.

Mina's travels with Cravan in Mexico had changed her, but it seems she nevertheless retained her tendency for melodrama. Natalie Barney, the salon hostess, reported that Loy turned up unannounced one evening to recite a poem she had just completed: "This ethereal creature no longer seemed to belong to humanity. She appeared for five minutes, just long enough to assert her detachment. Then, with the air of a sleepwalker that reality cannot wake, she read her poem in a dreamlike voice – a poem full of negro jazz and drunken dancers which ended with the sudden, piercing cry: '*Husband! why do you cuckold me with death?*'" And then, as suddenly as she had materialized, she disappeared again into the ether.

Loy found refuge in prayer meetings at the Church of Christ the Scientist, where they preached the healing powers of the Holy Scriptures. She became a regular volunteer for the Church's missions of mercy, ladling soup into the beggars' bowls of the city's homeless. Before long she was spending much of her time on the streets, amongst the bag ladies and beggars of the Bowery district.

Today the long wide road of the Bowery marks the outer-most frontier of Chinatown, where the virulent expansion of Asian eateries, doss-house tenements and sweatshop garment factories deadlocks with the high-rent upmarket side streets of fashionable Soho. The Bowery has an out-of-the-way feel about it. It's a conduit for fast-moving traffic, and I found its potholed pavements desolate and lonely after the teeming activity of Bleecker Street. There are few shops here, only the occasional Chinese restaurant where slabs of half-cooked animal hang on hooks in the windows, dripping profusely with fat. The walls of the buildings are blackened with exhaust lead and encrusted with years of fly-posting. Any spare inch of brickwork is claimed by the curlicued letters of graffiti tags that sprawl and tangle and ingest one another.

For years Loy lived in the company of the homeless and destitute here in the Bowery. At first she had come to lead them in prayer, but before long she was following their example. She romanticized the hardship she found on the streets. She believed the tramps had chosen a higher path – their suffering brought them closer to redemption, and their daily struggles humbly re-enacted the lives of the saints. Accompanying them on their forays to scavenge back alleys and abandoned lots for rubbish, from their example she hoped to find the path to peace and absolution.

The simple compulsion of a hand-to-mouth life proved an effective distraction from the memory of Cravan and the inconsolable pain he had left her with. For a long time she couldn't bear anything that reminded her of him. When she gave birth to his child, she couldn't stand to look at it, and so left it in the care of a nanny in Europe. It was many years before she could come to terms with what had happened in Mexico.

When I went back to the Arensberg house that night, Miss Rosen had my dinner waiting for me. I suspect she had nodded off, because I stood on the stoop for a long time ringing the bell before she finally answered the door on the fifth or sixth ring. When I walked past her into the living room, I saw that the dinner table was laid with doilies and a large serving dish of chicken soup. It must have been sitting there for quite some time, because it was lukewarm and had formed a skin over the surface. I noticed that amidst the pristine order of the set table, the only thing out of place was the bottle of sherry that had moved over to her side and stood there now half-empty.

After dinner we retired to the chaise longue, where we smoked cigarettes in silence and drank the rest of the sherry. With Cathy the TV would have been there to fill the void between us, to occupy the silence, but a careful search through all the armoires and cabinets of Miss Rosen's living room had failed to turn up anything of the sort. We sat with heads turned resolutely towards the wall carpeting, sucking on cigarette after cigarette. Occasionally Miss Rosen would turn towards me and smile, and once or twice I felt her feathery hand stray onto my knee.

After a while a wistful look overtook her wrinkled face and a strange rasping sound began to emanate from her scrawny throat. She was humming an old tune, and giving my leg one last squeeze she glanced across to show me a few teeth, her eyes twinkling dewily.

"La-da-dee-dar," she said. And then, in a reverie, the old woman heaved herself to her feet and walked drunkenly over to the standing piano, pausing on the way to smooth down her skirt and to steady herself against the table. She lowered herself onto the piano stool, lifted the lid and put her cigarette out in the pot of a small dead plant that she had mistaken for an ashtray.

The sound of her voice soared as her bony fingers fluttered across the keys.

"Lar-dee-da-dar," she sang hoarsely.

Her feet kicked at the pedals and the mechanism clattered inside, reverberating with the eerie tones of the old piano, her clumsy fingers prodding at deadened keys, the hammers striking untuned wires.

"Dee-da-da-dar-dee," she sang, and her faltering voice was soon completely swallowed by the awful din resounding from the worm-eaten carcass of that ruined instrument.

I closed the living-room door behind me, and as I climbed over the stacks of newspapers towards my room I stopped and for a moment soberly considered letting the end of my cigarette fall into that great heap of tinder, starting an almighty conflagration. I put my fag out in the cut-glass ashtray by the bed and turned off the lamp.

I couldn't sleep. For a while lying there I wondered who Miss Rosen had imagined was sitting opposite her at dinner. I had often had the same sensation as I sat across the table from Cathy. How quickly we had run out of things to talk about, how soon the silence had displaced conversation. Sometimes during our evenings together Cathy would catch me staring at her and she would smile, and in those moments I'd understand how little she knew me. I'd been a figment of her imagination; towards the end I was nothing more than what she projected onto me.

Her belly softly rounded, she grew increasingly preoccupied with preparations for the birth, and she never noticed that I was growing increasingly distant. She busied herself getting the house in order and arranging cover at work, and plotting the quickest route to the hospital, and thinking about godparents and so on. Meanwhile, I was thinking about how I could put an end to it all.

In Mrs Rosen's spare room I could hear the last of the mice rustling in a corner. Sometime around midnight the cacophony of the off-key piano ended with the final jarring discord of a body slumping across the keys. The terrible sound rang for a long time in the stale air of the apartment. Then I listened to it receding into the heavy stillness between the stacked magazines and mouldering furniture.

Cravan soon found that he had not put himself beyond the reach of the War. It was spreading like a cancer across the face of the planet: it followed him even to the New World.

The sinking of the *Lusitania*, the most opulent cruise liner in existence, had shifted the opinion of the majority of Americans in favour of entering the conflict. As it sailed from Manhattan, the ship had been torpedoed by a German U-boat, and it went down in eighteen minutes, killing almost twelve hundred civilian passengers, most of whom were American citizens.

Propaganda began to appear in New York, in preparation for the imminent conscription of soldiers. The War was sold to the people as a fight to defend culture and higher values. The Germans were vilified in the press as barbarians, Huns who vandalized artistic monuments and raped the women of Belgium. The image of a slavering gorilla in a pointed helmet leered from billboards all over town under the rallying caption "Destroy this mad brute – Enlist!". Pretty girls were posted outside enrolment offices to recruit heroes for the cause with the promise of a kiss. On 14th July the first regiment of American soldiers paraded past the cheering crowds of Fifth Avenue, and then marched off to Europe in high spirits to defend liberty and righteousness. There they would bury themselves alive in the trenches and wait to be slaughtered like cattle, demoralized and doubting. The French army, already decimated by the unending carnage, was on the verge of mutiny. Now the Americans joined the waste and futility of a war that had never seemed so pointless.

Cravan was as elusive as ever. He boasted to Mina Loy that he would never fall for the Great War, just as he would never fall for Modern Art. Yet it was not out of principle that he refused to fight. He grew furious at the accusation that he was a conscientious objector. "But I don't object!" he would say. "They may *all* allow themselves to be murdered for all I care, only they need not expect me to follow suit. If their collective insanity suggests to them that they must sacrifice their lives for my sake, I will not trouble to stop them."

Cravan regarded the whole endeavour as a scam on a grand scale, and he considered himself too wary to be taken in. He would not be one of the millions herded to their deaths by a sly handful of politicians. He refused all affiliations, just as he himself refused to be defined.

"Out of the whole political bunch," he decided, "there is only one who is sincere – Trotsky – poor lunatic! He really loves humanity, and he actually imagines war is to be done away with... But even he is trying to put one over – on *himself.*"

Loy dismissed Cravan's diatribes as the idle rantings of a man who loved the sound of his own voice. "He sounded preposterous," she recalls, "an uncultured heretic shooting the farcical arrows of his predictions into the glorious holocaust of heroism."

His discourses on Trotsky were particular sources of ridicule. Cravan told Mina about the time he had spent with him on the Atlantic. He remembered most vividly the afternoon he'd come across Trotsky's infant son playing with toy soldiers in the sunlight on deck. Cravan had squatted beside him and commandeered a battalion of White Russians. After a while the boy's father came to lean on the railings and

smoke a cigarette, keeping a suspicious eye on Cravan. The
boy had left his flank undefended, and Cravan now set about
a massacre of his troops, but soon lost interest. He turned
his attention instead to Trotsky, quizzing him about his plans
for revolution. The Bolshevik leader told his son to pack up
his soldiers and hurry back to the cabin.

"It was useless my telling him that his revolution will result
in the founding of a Red Army to protect the Red liberty,"
Cravan recalled with a shrug. "Or that he, because he is
sincere, will be turned upon by his followers. But he no more
believed me than I believe him..."

Mina thought it a joke that he should expect Trotsky
the visionary to heed the advice of a drunkard-deserter he
had met on the deck of a ship. And yet, in hindsight, Mina
admitted, "How I regret having paid so little attention to
these predictions."

The war was closing in on Cravan, and when America
recoursed to conscription he knew his days in New York were
numbered. Ever since the scandal at the Independents' opening, Cravan was convinced that he was under surveillance.
The situation suddenly grew more serious with the passing
of the Espionage Act on 15th June 1917, which proclaimed
any expression of dissent to be an act of high treason. Cravan
and the other foreigners of the Arensberg circle now found
themselves in danger of being jailed – or worse deported to
face charges of desertion in their native countries.

The Arensberg salon harboured some of the most outspoken pacifists in America. Several of the regulars had
already been taken in for questioning by the Committee on
Public Information for their connections to the communist
publication *The Masses*. The magazine had recently displayed its contempt for government policy with a front
page cartoon showing a skeleton standing in a pool of gore
with its arms around three terrified boys – the caption read,
"Come on in, America – the Blood's Fine!" In an article

entitled 'Whose War?', the magazine warned that America's intervention would soon result in brutal repression at home: "The War means an ugly mob-madness, crucifying the truth-tellers, choking the artists, sidetracking reforms, revolutions and the working of social forces". And sure enough, in the following weeks the pacifists were blacklisted as traitors, *The Masses* was closed down, the headquarters of the Socialist Party were raided, whilst a march by the No-Conscription League was broken up by vigilante attacks and its organizers jailed.

With the late summer heat trapped by the skyscrapers and city blocks, the pro-war feeling of New Yorkers now became overpowering. By August the pretty young bohemians who had once flaunted themselves in the most daring of fashions were now smothering their charms under Red Cross uniforms. Hamburgers were renamed "Liberty sandwiches". Performances of Mozart and Beethoven were banned, and a dachshund taken for a walk in Central Park was kicked to death by a mob of hysterical nationalists.

Most worrying of all, Government agents had started infiltrating bohemian hang-outs in search of draft dodgers, and soon Cravan began to feel uncomfortable even in the bars where he spent much of his time. The proprietor of Arnie's All-Hours had stopped serving German pilsner, and his regulars no longer talked of anything but the War. When they'd had too much to drink, they tried to outdo one another with shows of patriotism, and anyone who joined in half-heartedly was accused of siding with the enemy. Cravan soon grew sick of singing the Star Spangled Banner, and found himself taking refuge in the back room, where the other dissenters met to talk in hushed voices about plans of escape.

Cravan seized the first opportunity to make his getaway. This opportunity presented itself after a night of alcohol and excess with the painter Arthur Burdett Frost Jr. In the early hours, Cravan accompanied his friend back to his apartment, and here Frost promptly suffered a tubercular haemorrhage. Cravan watched the young man choke to death in front of him, then carefully relieved him of his identity papers.

Wearing a moth-holed soldier's uniform several sizes too small for him, he headed south. He hoped the disguise would make it easier to get lifts from patriotic drivers and avoid arousing the suspicion of the police. Picabia was quick to point out the contradictions of his friend's character: "Arthur Cravan disguised himself as a soldier to escape becoming a soldier, like all our friends who disguised themselves as honest men in order to be dishonest."

Cravan left Mina behind in New York with a hurried promise that he would send word for her to join him in South America. Once again he demonstrated that he was loyal only to his own whims. He accepted no responsibilities, honoured no debts. The modern world was one vast confidence trick, and he would never be taken in. "As soon as I could speak," he declared, "I knew that everything people told me was a lie. All they say – all they do is an attempt to drag me down to their own level."

He was on the road again, travelling on the identity papers of his dead friend. Neutral Argentina was his destination: Buenos Aires, the Paris of Latin America. But he would never make it that far.

PART FOUR

MEXICO

"Whatever is said and done or even thought, we are prisoners of this senseless world."

– *Arthur Cravan*

I no longer felt like a human being. I had been on the bus for almost three days.

And then suddenly there came a variation in the drone of the engine, and this roused me from my stupor. We were pulling into a truck stop somewhere outside San Antonio, Texas. I looked out of the window. An abandoned parking lot. A cluster of petrol pumps. A bungalow under a flashing neon "SNACKS" sign. Further off, a few flimsy, temporary-looking warehouses comprising a retail park. And beyond, *nothing*.

The bus shuddered to a standstill and the door swung open. There came the percussive sound of groans and the cracking of joints as the other passengers struggled to their feet and shuffled along the aisle. But I remained seated. I remained staring into space.

The bus had departed from Penn Station at eleven at night with a full complement of passengers. I found myself seated next to a black kid listening to hardcore on his head-phones.

In the seat in front was a grossly overweight man who fell sound asleep as soon as the journey got under way. He snored steadily and vocally. Sometimes the snoring would fall abruptly into long periods of silence and I would find myself anxious with expectancy. The silence would drag on and the agony would subside to a burning hope that his heart had buckled under the weight of his obesity and finally packed in. But without fail he would then emit a sudden, savage rip-roarer to trumpet his return to life.

As if this wasn't sufficient, sitting immediately behind there was a teenage single mother with an inconsolable baby. She whispered to it, chided it, wrested its greedy, clawing hands from the back of my seat. She tried squeaky toys, then jangly ones, and plied it with all manner of refreshments, but still it went on. Evidently the infant was spoilt half to death, and with every blood-curdling scream it emitted I came that bit closer to finishing it off.

I was kept awake for much of that night. I spent it staring deliriously at the blank exterior world, the headlights of passing cars. All the while, chiselling relentlessly into the pulpy recesses of my mind, the orchestration of snores, yawls, air-con whine and the tinny muzak coordinated itself into a discordant symphony of loneliness.

I observed the dishwater dawn light come up over the dismal wasteland of America. Thousands upon thousands of miles of interminable monotony. Sometimes the emptiness took substance from the vast billboard hoardings fringing the highway or the occasional rusting discount store that clung hopelessly to the roadside. JUNIOR'S ALL-AMERICAN BBQ, *next exit*. SURRANEE ONE-STOP CAREER STATION, *for all your Drive-Thru Career Needs*. SLEEP STORE – *Try Kingwoods Dormo-Dermatological Body Profile*. CHAMPION BURGER – *America's Finest Charbroiled Burger*. THE DIVINE METAPHYSICAL RESEARCH CENTRE, *the Answer is Here*.

Every few hours the barren scrubland would bloom into a desolate settlement, a few aluminium buildings clustered around a diesel pump, a one-storey sprawl aborted before it could become a town. The bus would drop down through the gears and crawl into a roadhouse truck stop, where the passengers would disembark in search of junk food, for which their appetite was insatiable. Once I wandered listlessly after them, hoping to purchase a newspaper or a paperback novel, anything to assuage this crippling tedium. On a revolving rack next to the burritos I found the only printed matter in existence here: a picture-book version of the Holy Bible. The passengers piled back on board with their haul of fried chicken, potato chips and supersize soft drinks, and the bus took to the pitiless road once again.

I changed buses in Tallahassee, just as dusk came on. The bus was crowded, and progress up the aisle was slow because the passengers were too fat for the space they were wedged into. Excess waist and thigh spilt out from every direction into the gangway. I sat in the first seat that I came to beside a young woman. She was petite and attractive, but the empty seat next to her was ominous. Frequent travellers of the Greyhound must have developed an instinct about where it is unsafe to sit.

When I sat down she said "Hi" cheerily. She seemed nice enough, but at the sound of her voice there was the clearing of throats, and the seats nearby creaked with the uneasy stirrings of obese passengers. She chatted away amiably about her plans to move out east with her boyfriend. The bus rolled on, darkness settled outside, she didn't stop talking, and I began to panic.

"I just love New Orleans," she was saying. "There's like cultural life in New Orleans it's like there's an acceptance of the arts which as a music-maker is very special to me because in Texas when I saw how important sports was you know compared to music it really put me off everyone's like football this and football that no one gives a damn about music and I even stopped playing for a while."

She had a lardee-dardee sing-song voice with a pertness which suggested customer-service training.

"I like to keep learning you know I think life is all about learning and if you're not learning anything new you might as well die you know so right now I'm learning the guitar and the bagpipes and I was learning the trumpet my friend was teaching me but I had to give it up because it made my nose tickle!"

She inhaled and laughed at the same time, producing a high-pitched squeal which woke the woman in front with a start.

"It did it made my nose tickle!"

The woman in front turned in her seat and looked round at us. Taking no notice, the girl carried on:

"I picked up the clarinet but I didn't like the sound and of course what I really want to learn is the drums cos it'll drive my boyfriend crazy."

Another honk of laughter that rang out across the dim interior of the bus like the stifled squeal of a dying animal.

"Just tell me if I'm talking too much my friends say I talk too much just say if you wanna go to sleep cos I'll just keep talking I can talk all night I can never sleep on these things I'm gonna be awake all night I've had too much coffee although like I always like to say *you can never have too much coffee* am I right by the way you sound like you've got an accent do you have an accent?" She asked me.

I admitted I was English.

"Oh that's funny cos like only yesterday I was watching *My Fair Lady* the musical with my daughter so she can learn the songs she absolutely adores *The Sound of Music* she's seen it like a thousand times Julie Andrews is like her idol but anyway I was showing her the beginning of *My Fair Lady* over and over so she could learn the first song you know the one when Rex Harrison is saying about all the different ways people talk all the different accents and it's so true you know?"

When she paused it was to draw breath, and she did this gaspingly so as not to leave an opening in the conversation.

"I just love the way you Brits speak I've been living in Texas too long no one speaks properly any more I mean proper English like they speak in England maybe I'm just sensitive to it you know because I'm a music-maker and all and I listen to things like really listen to things."

Briefly she paused for breath. My fingernails were biting into the plastic of the armrest.

"If you stop for a minute stop for just a minute and just listen that's all *just listen* to the sound of the world you realize how beautiful it is you know like the sound of the rain or the sound of the wind or even the sound of cars or how electricity sounds in the light fixtures or the sound of your shoes or the sound of a comb running through your hair…"

Just as I could feel the tears pricking at the corners of my eyes, she stopped talking. She looked out at the darkness of the road and wistfully shook her head.

I took the opportunity to stretch my arms in a theatrical yawn, and was about to say *Mmm well time for some sleep*, but before I could form the first word she said:

"Or the sound of your body you know like the sound of breathing or the sound of the digestive system or the sound of birds you know I could go on and on or the sound of music of course or just the sound of silence or the sound of—"

Without excusing myself, I got up and started away towards the back of the bus. Perhaps she didn't notice because I could still hear her chattering away to herself for a long while. I climbed into the toilet cubicle at the back, put the seat cover down and sat on it. I locked myself in with the reek of evacuated bowels and fell asleep to the rhythmical sloshing of raw sewage against the sides of the tank.

When I went out the next morning I found there were only a handful of passengers remaining. The majority of them must have bailed out at the last stop. Through the bus windows I saw the interminable Texas badlands rolling by as we approached the border. The only traffic on the highway was travelling in the opposite direction. A steady stream of vehicles poured past, reminding me of old B-movie scenes of inhabitants fleeing a contaminated city.

The tannoy popped with static, and the blaring voice of the driver announced that we were due to arrive in Laredo, Texas, the final stop. The driver was a wiry little man with a handlebar moustache and a whiny deep-southern accent. The announcement degenerated into a rambling ad lib.

"It's been a pleasure to have y'all on board," he was saying tonelessly. "Ah wanna say God bless each and every one of you. May God be with you wherever you're going and may He get you theya safe."

There was an *Amen* from a passenger up near the front.

"And ah wish y'all a happy holiday, Merry Christmas, and a fine New Year – may it be better than the last one. And ah say that for myself as well as for you."

A gruff voice immediately behind me shouted *Amen to that!* and then there was a chorus of *Amens* from the remaining passengers. I heard the woman in the front seat saying, "It's been a terrible year for everybody, terrible." I noticed that I had lost all sensation in my left thigh, and at the side of my head behind the left ear.

The bus turned slowly into Laredo Greyhound station, and the engine died. I staggered off with the other passengers who stepped out onto the tarmac. They stood there turning in stunned circles, casualties of long-haul transit reeling from fatigue and deprivation. In the dilapidated terminal building some of them dithered by their luggage, looking lost. I saw others wandering into the embraces of family and friends. Each of them wore the kind of dead-eyed expressions seen in the faces of prisoners of war who, after years of incarceration, have noted a strange ambivalence on their release: their newfound freedom brings no joy, their loved ones appear as strangers to them, and the reunion stirs no feeling at all.

This too is how I felt as I stood at the counter listening to the woman telling me they'd lost my luggage. There wasn't even the inkling of fury in me. I nodded and shuffled on. It seemed just another part of me had fallen away, another part of me had disappeared. It was one less thing to dispose of, that's all.

It is thought that Cravan crossed the frontier in December 1917 between Laredo and Nuevo Laredo. Today Nuevo Laredo is a breeze-block bungalow town choked with dust and tumbleweed that the authorities have all but abandoned to the rule of feuding drug cartels. Around the bus station on the Mexican side are an array of dismal hotels languishing in a haze of diesel fumes and seediness. As darkness fell, I saw the street-walkers come out to tout for business, undeterred by the rumours of another girl's body found in the desert on the outskirts, dumped there naked and mutilated, maybe a victim of the snuff-movie industry that is said to thrive on the border.

When Cravan passed through here the frontier was a lawless, cut-throat place, a no man's land controlled by the rebels. The American border towns were crawling with Texas Rangers, US Troopers, smugglers and sales reps for arms companies, as well as agents of the American oil industry trying to get secret instructions to their employees on the Mexican side.

Secret-service men haunted the railway stations looking for draft-dodgers. Every day more city slickers would arrive at the end of the line, looking for a way across the border to neutral Mexico, and sticking out like a sore thumb they'd be marked as soon as they stepped off the train. Some waited till nightfall before they tried to slip past the soldiers guarding the crossings; others hiked out into the hills in the hope of finding a way through to the Mexican desert; still more trusted their lives to racketeers in the business of people-smuggling. And every day the newspapers ran another byline about the latest deserter killed as he tried to cross the border. Rumours circulated amongst those trying to get out that undercover Rangers sometimes led slackers across the line just for the fun of putting a bullet in their back the moment they set foot on Mexican territory. The frontier was as tight as a snare, and how Cravan made the crossing alive is not known.

The opposite bank of the Rio Grande teemed with fleeing Mexicans trying to cross into the States. The Mexican insurgency was in its third year, and camps had sprung up in the brush, fed by the constant procession of refugees. Driven from the interior by the fear of the approaching rebel armies, they flocked to the border in their hundreds, exhausted and dying of thirst after an eight-day journey on foot across the desert.

The haciendas existed in a state of perpetual fear: blackmailed for protection money by the *Federales* one day, pillaged by the bandits the next, they soon lost everything that wasn't bolted down. Passing foreigners were the easiest targets of all, and many quietly disappeared in the wilderness, their "guides" stripping them of everything they carried and leaving them to die under the scorching sun. Every hundred yards along the *camino* were little heaps of stones, each of them a memorial of a murder.

As Cravan made his way to the railhead, passing amongst dead creosote bushes that rattled like diamondbacks, it seemed the towering saguaros watched him from the skyline of the desert. He didn't stop here longer than he had to, and neither did I. That evening I caught a rickety bus heading south.

Morning came up over the desert. The highway extended dead straight across the flat empty plains in distances that confound the mind. The dashed lines of the road flashed underneath us with nauseating monotony. Every once in a while I watched a town go by, a cluster of half-built houses rising from the dust and sprouting their reinforced steel wires like so much dead growth from the barren ground.

Nothing but dust. Dust everywhere. From time to time it seemed to assume the shape of thorny bushes, stunted trees, or the carcasses of broken-down pickups swallowed by dry grass. But for the most part it blew across the emptiness in gusts of stifling breeze, conspiring with the heat haze that wavered all around to blur and efface the line dividing the pale earth and the paler sky, to melt this land out of existence.

In tumbledown settlements miles from anywhere, teenage mariachi bands lay in wait for us. When the bus stopped to take on passengers, out they ran from the cover of the corrugated iron shelter clutching their guitars and beat-up violins, to start up a cacophony at the back, voices tuned to vibrato by the rattling of the chassis. Sometime later I would be woken by the feathery touch of the emaciated little boy they sent round for donations.

The highway led straight on into infinity. Once we crossed a junction with another road, equally straight, equally empty, heading in another direction. Strangely, it brought back the memory of an afternoon in the park, shortly after Cathy and I had first met. After having sex in the long dry grass behind the firebombed, graffiti-infested pavilion, we had rolled over onto our backs and lay there for a long time looking up at the sky and the criss-crossing vapour trails drifting overhead. Out of the bus window I watched this other road taper away into the haze and disappear.

All around, the landscape was hard and featureless, so that it seemed we were making no progress. Occasionally a tin-foil windmill glinted in the sun, or a lopsided cactus reared its sagging limbs, or a dirt track managed to break off from the road, leading out into nothing, to be smothered by the brush. These images repeated themselves, each exactly recalling the last until I was convinced that it was the same lopsided cactus, the same dirt track, the same tin-foil windmill rocking back and forth and glinting in the sun, the same wheelless truck propped up on oil cans, again and again and again. We passed them so many times I lost track, so many times that I no longer got the queasy turning of the stomach, or the uncanny sensation of déjà vu. Drifting in and out of consciousness, I resigned myself to the fact that I was trapped in a closed and never-ending circuit. We were making no ground, we were not moving at all.

When I awoke some time in the afternoon, the scenery had changed. The view from the window was of a landscape hatched with the vertical lines of organ-pipe cacti. Across the road ahead there lay the bare muscles of the high Sierras like a thousand backs of cattle, and as dusk fell we began the long slow climb into the mountains.

The engine of the bus reached a shrill squeal of protest as the driver dropped gears to crawl up the steep grade. When we reached the top, the range opened out below a sky scored through with lines of sunset. Darkness came on swiftly and, as we began the descent, the small man cradling a bag of fruit in the seat next to me woke momentarily to make the sign of the cross over his chest. The bus freewheeled steeper and steeper, careering through hairpin switchbacks, at every turn watched over by the Virgin of the Mountains from the tiny grottoes that flickered with candles. Moonlit darkness opened up below, safety barriers flapping loose over the sheer drop at the road's edge. I thought, *This is where it could happen…*

Mexico City is a town that exists in a state of perpetual rush hour. My first glimpse of it was from the bus window as we inched our way through the gridlock towards the terminal in the northern outskirts. The roads, four or five lanes wide in both directions, vibrated with the throbbing bass note of engines, traffic congealed around junctions and the tarmac scabbed over with dense clots of stationary vehicles. Everything was engulfed in a pall of fumes. The constipated city squatted under a shroud of bluish smog that gave it the appearance of Dickensian London.

Despite the disruptions of the railway and the almost daily ambushes by marauding rebel forces, Cravan had managed to board a train bound for the capital, finding room in a boxcar amongst the mummified remains of dead and dying victims of smallpox. The route was littered with the charred skeletons of railway coaches overturned at the track-side, the remains of journeys that had never reached their destination. On his arrival in Mexico City he was met at the station by Bob Brown, an acquaintance from New York who recorded Cravan's time in Mexico in his *roman-à-clef*, *You Gotta Live*. When Brown asked after Mina, Cravan said he had left her behind. "She was sniffling a little, like most war widows, wondering what would become of her," Cravan told him with a shrug.

Brown showed him where he might find dirt-cheap accommodation, taking him to a crumbling hidalgo mansion known as the "Slackers' Hotel". Fresh from the border, American anarchists, conscientious objectors and draft-dodgers gravitated here. The grand high-ceilinged rooms were divided into cubicles with cardboard partitions, and there were now sixty slackers in residence, as many as three splitting the rent for a space barely big enough to lie down in.

Far from the band of spirited renegades living it up in free Latin America that he had expected, Cravan found himself amongst emaciated loners with matted beards, their clothes hanging off them in rags. According to Brown, the residents of the Slackers' Hotel spent the afternoons languishing in their rooms with the window blinds drawn, playing chess and pinochle by candlelight. Once a day they might venture into the outside world, in pairs for safety, to stand in line for their mail at the Central Post Office, praying for a letter from home containing a five-dollar bill. Amongst them was an anarchist bomb-maker; an old editor of *The Masses* who had skipped bail; a communist tailor from Bleecker Street; even a French dissident who had shipped himself out of New York in a trunk peppered with air holes. The hunger pains and homesickness these men suffered in Mexico City were nothing compared to the trials they had endured in order to get there. Now they took whatever life in no man's land threw at them with grim resignation.

The place was also frequented by the more established foreigners, who lodged in the hotels and boarding houses of the old town, the cosmopolitan radicals who were in the process of founding the Mexican Communist Party. They worked tirelessly in the vain hope of reigniting the ideological flame of a revolution that had begun as a peasant uprising against the ruling classes. They came to the Slackers' Hotel to wait in line for the English-language newspaper that the proprietor passed around each afternoon, scanning it intently for news of their Bolshevik comrades in Russia.

For their connections with the German espionage services these people were kept under meticulous scrutiny by the authorities: the American State Department had sent spies to Mexico to sabotage German interests here. Then there were the agents of the Japanese, the British and the Russian anti-imperialists, all with their own agendas. These groups devoted most of their energies to spreading malicious and highly spurious stories about the others. The Russians especially were keen to exploit anti-American feeling in Mexico, and they had recently sent an agent to infiltrate the slackers' circle – he had tried unsuccessfully to recruit men for a counter-propaganda mission that involved the theft of a consignment of ink belonging to an American-backed newspaper. There was no escaping the war of insidious propaganda – even Cravan's regular bar played a dance-music radio station that interrupted songs with news bulletins reporting the utter destruction of New York, or the surrender of the British forces. Mexico City was at the centre of a great diplomatic game, with either side in the War vying for control of this pivotal territory. Hiding behind its declared neutrality, the Mexican government entertained the advances of intelligence agents from all nations: Mexico's loyalty would go to the highest bidder, to whichever power could secure its future. And for their association with the radicals of the Communist Party, the foreigners at the Slackers' Hotel were themselves under constant surveillance.

The hotel, and Mexico City itself, was uncertain territory where people were never quite what they seemed, and in which an atmosphere of paranoia occupied the creaky corridors, the mouldering stairwells. Cravan was not made to feel welcome: all newcomers were treated with suspicion. The other occupants of his room kept to themselves and didn't engage in small talk. He noticed that they lived with their suitcases packed, ready to run at a moment's notice. Here people went by pseudonyms, they were mindful never to sign their own names. Cravan managed to obtain a false passport and pass himself off as a German national: perhaps in this land of assumed names he would at last feel at home.

I was relieved to be turned away from the first hostel. The place was overrun with gap-year students with guidebooks clutched to their chests, inane twitterers milling obnoxiously by reception. What was more, the hostel was administrated with an absurd bureaucratic efficiency that incensed me. Customer service ran by a system of numbered ticketing, as might be found at a supermarket delicatessen counter. I had stood for half an hour with ticket number seventy-two, watching the lethargic desk clerk incompetently resolving a double-booking involving a trio of German lesbians. Tired of explaining the intricacies of the ticketing system to all comers, by the time he'd got to number sixty-seven he had abandoned it altogether and was attending to a mob of Americans on a first-come-first-served basis. I left in disgust.

I was directed to another hostel, which I found to be ominously tranquil by comparison. The front door stood ajar. The reception was deserted. Half a cup of cold coffee stood on the counter, and next to it the twisted remains of numerous cigarettes lay in an ashtray. On a bracket in the corner a television with the sound turned down displayed the silent histrionics of a telenovela. For a minute I stood still in the empty foyer and took in its unsettling atmosphere of recent abandonment. Then I rang the bell on the counter and a stunted watchman appeared in the doorway wearing a pair of pink marigolds and a flustered expression.

The following morning I sat on the deserted roof terrace recovering from a troubled, sleepless night. The dormitory's only other occupant had been a nervous Italian who suffered from noisy and disturbing wet dreams. The grating and the whimpering had kept me awake for some time. My bunk was next to a draughty window, and under my meagre bed sheet I had shivered with the cold. When I awoke in the morning I found that the infection had spread into my chest.

Now I was sitting across from the nervous Italian. Evidently to him it had seemed only civil to join me at the table, since there was no one else on the terrace for breakfast. After an initial failed joke about a pubic hair he had found sticking out of the butter, he made no further attempts at conversation.

We sat resolutely on in silence. I watched flies gathering on the cakes. When the end fell out of my cigarette I turned my attention to the glowing tobacco ember and the dark hole it was scorching into the fabric of my shirt. After a few more minutes had passed the Italian cleared his throat to speak.

"Excusa me…" he said, leaning forwards a fraction. Before he could continue I coughed up an almighty clot of phlegm, and he watched me spit it out onto the floor. I wiped my mouth with the back of my hand and then raised my eyebrow at him.

"Ah…" he said with a slight falter of trepidation in his voice, "canna you spare for me a cigarette?"

"Afraid not," I told him, and lit another.

Inhaling a strong current of smoke, I felt a rush of blood to the head, a sudden flare of adrenaline, and it was all I could do to stop myself informing him of the full extent of life's horrors and its fatuities. I sensed he was weak-willed, it wouldn't take much to bring him over to my way of thinking. My hand pressed against the bulge of the vial in my pocket until I felt the plastic flex inwards.

The vial was empty. I had even swilled out the residue with water, consuming every last drop. There were no pills left to take, and yet I couldn't bring myself to throw the empty bottle away. I kept it with me: it felt reassuring somehow to feel it against my body, a last defence against the loss of all control. It was a great relief when at last the Italian got up from the table and walked away.

I heard that the weekend before I arrived in Mexico City a crowd of over a million had congregated in the Zócalo to protest against the privatization of the country's electricity supply. They had massed into the vast square around the stone-lacework cathedral where the new President Carranza had stabled his cavalry during the revolution. Today the cathedral remains one of the capital's most visited tourist attractions, despite its undeniable drabness and the dilap-idated appearance given by its pockmarked plasterwork of pigeon droppings. The demonstrators apparently wore red and waved communist banners, and there were rumours amongst the travellers that the police had fired shots into the crowd, killing five.

But it was only rumours, and as far as I could see the communist movement that had come into being in Cravan's time has all but evaporated in the capital now. Back then the radicals at the Slackers' Hotel believed that communism promised a better future, drawing strength from the news of the Bolshevik triumph in Russia. They even took over Mexico's biggest English-language newspaper, using it to reprint articles taken straight from *Soviet Russia Today*. The movement was to grow and grow, winning the devotion of national icons, the artists Diego Rivera and his wife Frida Kahlo. Mexico City was even to claim a dubious distinction as the final resting place of Leon Trotsky himself.

After his path had touched that of Cravan on the trans-atlantic crossing of the *Montserrat*, Trotsky had found his way back to Russia, bringing the long, bitter years of exile to an end. Taking no heed of Cravan's warning about the futility of all revolutions, he led the Bolshevik armies to victory, over-throwing the Tsarist regime, and laying the foundations for what he hoped would be a new world order.

Having prepared the ground for Lenin to emerge from the underground to take charge of the revolutionary movement, Trotsky set about creating the Red Army to defend the Communist Government from foreign intervention.

But by 1921, Trotsky's influence had waned, and political exigencies had forced him to compromise his ideals. When Lenin suffered a cerebral haemorrhage that year, Trotsky found himself squeezed out of the succession battle by a conspiracy of his colleagues on the politburo, and the

Central Committee quickly fell under the sway of Joseph Stalin. Using the secret police to establish a hold over the administration, Stalin emerged as the new leader. Stalin abandoned the struggle for world revolution and set himself up as a new dictator, earning the moniker "The Executioner" for his systematic elimination of the other twenty-one original members of the Revolutionary Council.

Trotsky, the only survivor, fled the Soviet Union and found himself once again in exile. Drawn to Mexico and its communist sensibilities, he settled in Coyoacán, a suburb of the capital. From his town house on the outskirts of Mexico City, Trotsky watched Stalin consolidate his stranglehold over the Soviet Republic. Just as Arthur Cravan had warned him, the Red Army that Trotsky had created to protect the ideals of the revolution now became the enforcer of Stalin's reign of terror. With the ideology of the Revolution in tatters, Trotsky realized that, far from making the dream of a socialist Utopia a reality, he and his fellow idealists had paved the way for an oppressive totalitarianism that would threaten the peace of the world.

In the seclusion of his study, Trotsky buried himself in his seven-volume history of the Revolution. Before he could complete it, on 20th August 1940 a Stalinist agent who had insinuated himself into the bed of Trotsky's secretary gained admittance to the Bolshevik leader's study and drove the pick of an ice axe into his skull.

Looking for peace in neutral Mexico, having hoped to put himself beyond the reach of the War, Cravan instead found himself in a country in the throes of its own hostilities, in a town simmering with political instability and radical agitation. The long years of revolution had taken their toll on Mexico, and its capital was suffering desperate privation. The pavements had been taken over by encampments of refugees driven from their villages by the fighting. Clamorous mobs of beggars rushed after passers-by and would fight one another for the chance to grovel at their feet of a foreigner.

Cravan hadn't seen poverty like this before. Here there was no refuge to be found in the comfort of rich friends' apartments. When he went to collect his mail, Cravan stepped over the prostrate bodies of the homeless, the maimed and the destitute that lolled about the post office under a filthy brown miasma of corn-husk cigarette smoke. The place resembled a mortuary strewn with bodies laid out like sandbags on the pavements. Coddling limbs bloated from elephantiasis, they appealed with the remains of arms and legs eaten away by leprosy. As much as they appalled him, Cravan took a peculiar interest in the derelicts – perhaps because he realized that what he saw in those pinched and ravaged faces might well be a vision of his own future.

But for foreign exiles like him, this newfound poverty was the least of their worries. Cravan and his acquaintances survived in an atmosphere thick with anxiety and suspicion: under surveillance by the authorities, watched by under-cover agents, they lived in perpetual fear of being sent back across the wire. Rumours had begun to circulate that government agents were planning a raid on the Slackers' Hotel, and that its inmates were on the verge of deportation.

For Cravan, who already found its close, fetid air of penury and paranoia suffocating, this was incentive enough to find accommodation elsewhere.

For a while, it looked as if Cravan's luck was changing: he landed a job as a boxing tutor at the Escuela de Cultura Fisica. The offer of work had come out of the blue following a drunken night in a bar, where he entertained all present with wildly exaggerated tales of his achievements in the ring. He took a pokey room in the old town on the calle Tacuba near the Zócalo. For those first months in the city he lived here at number 15, in what is now a dilapidated building with a painted sign over the entrance declaring it to be a "Dental Practice". But I found that it was boarded up, its licence long revoked, its windows stoned out.

Little is known about these first months in Mexico. From what survives of his correspondence, Cravan claimed to be living a frugal, disciplined existence. He wrote that he was determined to improve himself, and to this end he spent much of his time in the library studying the classics. Acquaintances, however, remember Cravan differently: Bob Brown, for example, recalled him drinking as if he had been "baby-bottled on grain alcohol". On these nights of debauchery, he said, Cravan behaved as if "his spirit surged with the blinding cruelty of creative impulse that makes kids kill cats with lengths of gas pipe".

He had started writing to Mina Loy in New York, and the nine letters that he sent to her comprise the only surviving evidence of Cravan's activities during these early months. They are love letters, dramatic and overwrought, in which Cravan writes of his loneliness and his sense of isolation in Mexico. However, these letters are also full of contradictions and outright lies that provide the clearest of insights into the devious, perhaps pathological workings of his mind.

In the first letters, Cravan reaffirms his commitment to meet Mina in Buenos Aires. And yet, with the prospect of a living to be made as a boxer, it seems all the while he had no intention of leaving Mexico. He complains at length of his many thwarted attempts to reach Argentina: the train line had been closed; he'd heard that Argentina would enter the war; there was a problem with his passport; he could only get there by steamer via Spain. "It appears there is no other route," he claims despairingly, "You can imagine the exasperation I feel as I write this!"

Cravan's excuses grew increasingly inventive. Before long he was claiming that his parents were with him in Mexico, and that they wouldn't allow him to leave. "You will love it here," he wrote to Mina. "My mother will be thrilled to meet you. I often speak of you. If it wasn't for her I would have left by now." Cravan was fulfilling the role of the dutiful son – a role he had never played as a child. He told Mina that he was staying with his parents in a house in the suburbs; that he took them on boat trips in the floating gardens at Xochimilcho and for long walks in Chapultepec. On their return home he would make tea and massage the soles of his mother's sore feet. In his letters Cravan was eager to impress upon Mina the fact that he had changed – and this bizarre rapprochement with his estranged mother was surely the final proof that he was a reformed character. Of course his parents had never left Lausanne: it seems the story was nothing more than an absurd fabrication meant to justify his stay in the capital. Before long he was also claiming that he was succumbing to a serious illness, he could feel his life ebbing away, and somehow Mina's love was the only thing that could save him. "Forget the past," he beseeched her. "In New York I was full of lies. But now I want to live only for the truth."

Another letter, sent the following day, increased the pressure for her to join him in Mexico: "Today I should have taken the boat to South America, and I didn't do it. I would not have survived the voyage." This is a letter of studied desperation and carefully crafted confusion, in which he begs her in ever stronger terms to come to him at once. "I told you that my mind has gone," he wrote. "To take myself further from you is impossible. You must join me here or never write again... My parents won't let me leave Mexico. You and I, we will never be apart again. Ah! If you could only be my wife!"

Mina, perhaps entertaining a suspicion of the subterfuge, was obstinate in her refusals to go to Mexico. Cravan persisted, resorting to greater and greater lengths to move her. On Christmas Day 1917 he wrote to her seemingly in the grip of hysteria: "I have a terrible fear of going mad," he claimed. "I can't eat anything, and I can't sleep at all... I can't stop thinking about killing myself. If you suffered half as much as I do, you would fly to me."

Sensing her resolve was beginning to weaken in the face of this emotional blackmail, Cravan persisted on this tack. On 30th December he wrote her two letters and a postcard declaring himself at his wits' end: "I am dying for you. I was born too tender." Casting himself as a martyr for her love, he continues in the most deranged of tones. "It's my fault, I should never have left you, and I am punished terribly. I have decided that, if I don't see you, I will destroy myself. If you want, at least send me a telegram to say goodbye," he pleads darkly. "Five minutes after reading it I will be dead."

Mina held out for as long as she could, but as Cravan's reports grew more extravagant, she became more concerned about his state of mind. In a letter sent in early January Cravan claimed that he had fallen gravely ill, that his longing for her was a mortal condition. "I dare not look at your photograph any longer," he wrote. "Ah! The tears drain from me like the blood from opened veins. Sweet death!"

It was the high drama of this final letter that galvanized Mina to find Cravan in Mexico. She was moved by the strength of the feelings he professed for her, and deeply frightened by his assertion that he felt his end was not far off. Alluding to the sudden death of his tubercular friend, he declared, "Frost didn't suffer as I do. The death of the soul is ten thousand times worse than cancer. Life is a bitch."

Mina left New York at once, setting off on an arduous five-day journey towards the unknown.

It was André Breton – the Dada initiate chiefly responsible for sanctifying Cravan's memory – who, on his own travels through Latin America a decade later, declared: "Mexico is truly the land of the Surrealists." And indeed my every day in Mexico brought strange new apparitions shimmering through the stifling smog, scenes that obeyed no logic, as solid and improbable as a waking nightmare.

In a gutter I saw a tramp under a blanket filling out a lotto card.

In the grounds of the Castle of Chapultepec great hordes of schoolchildren in red tracksuits were scattered like pigeons by a runaway fibreglass tourist train. As I rested on a bench by the statue of Benito Juárez a crocodile of Japanese sightseers looked at me with curiosity as they filed past, and several of them even took my picture.

In the streets around the Zócalo I saw the morning market play out like a riot in slow motion, thousands of dead-eyed Mexican wives battering one another lethargically with plastic shopping baskets.

I saw roads liquefying in the heat of the sun, tarmac puckering around the tyres of trucks and buses caught in terminal gridlock. I saw the fumes thickening around the driver's windows of stationary cars and cabs that seemed to decay before my very eyes, rusting into the ground in this commuter's worst nightmare, this ingrowing M25 of Mexico City.

The capital's inhabitants flee underground, into the city's vast metro system, into the Inferno. Heavy, asphyxiating heat collects here in the miles of corridors between platforms, mingling the bodily aromas of the shuffling, tightly packed multitudes with the sickening reek of cooking fat from the taco stands and doughnut stalls. People accumulate on the platforms without speaking, pacified by the ghostly murmur of Glen Miller dance tunes playing over the tannoy. But when the tunnel resounds with the rumbling of an approaching train, people swarm in their hundreds to claw their way aboard with tooth and nail. The doors champ savagely at those caught on the threshold, and train after train pulls away again with rows of vacuum-packed faces pressed up against the glass staring miserably out.

I rode the metro for much of that afternoon, wallowing in the sheer horror of it. As the carriages concertinaed with a wrenching sound of fatigued metal I studied the faces of the commuters. There was no muttering, no inhaling through clenched teeth, no harrumphing sighs of outrage. When the train approached each station and careered to a violent standstill, I watched as they were thrown against one another, and compacted into a single half-living mass inside. These people betrayed no emotion, they showed only expressions of long-crumpled blankness. They clung loosely to the supports, allowing themselves to be battered and flung to and fro by the bucking of the carriage. They had fallen back into some ancestral memory of life's futility, in their eyes a placid capitulation to the endless humiliations of existence.

At the end of the line I took to the streets again by foot. I kept walking until the light began to fade. I was trying to keep ahead of the boredom, ahead of myself. It seemed like a long time ago when I had sat in the office, daydreaming about coasting down the corridor on my swivel chair, taking the lobby at a gallop, charging out of the front entrance and away. I'd imagined that I'd feel like a different person, and that Mexico would feel like a different world… But it was just the same. There was the same aching of the feet, the same insistent itch of the haemorrhoids, the same thoughts nagging at my head. And I couldn't help wondering if, when the time finally came, I would have the guts to go through with it.

By that evening I had reached the outskirts of the city, a long traffic artery lined on either side by big garages and auto workshops where grease-stained engineers hauled engine blocks around with pulleys. I turned into a side street and headed uphill. I passed a depot where city buses were parked in ranks behind twenty-foot fences for the night. The road grew steeper and steeper, finally emerging on to a hillside of threadbare grass. I stopped to catch my breath and look down over the city laid out below, the lights coming on block by block, orange pinpricks growing sharper in the gathering dusk and stretching to the distant edges of the valley.

I carried on climbing, passing through a quiet slum clinging to the hillside. I went between tumbledown houses, through the untarmacked alleys where barefoot kids played football under the drone of occasional street lamps. The way grew steeper and steeper and eventually the dwellings fell away altogether, and darkness closed around me.

I came into the wooded foot slopes of the Cerro de la Estrella. A deep silence descended all around, and as I felt my way up the dirt path, from the corner of my eye I caught glimpses of movement in the undergrowth. There was a snapping of twigs, a patter of footfalls, the pale flurry of wild dogs. My mind conjured strange sounds and visions from the emptiness, I thought I could even distinguish the bass rhythm of tribal drums from the distance.

I heard the engine when it was still far off, the dropping and revving of the gears as it tore around the hairpins. I stopped to listen. The car was approaching quickly, crossing back and forth across the hillside below me. Soon I could make out the grating of the tyres on the bends, and a dim grey light began to build through the trees. There was something menacing about the roar of the powerful engine out here, and I had to resist the urge to find a hiding place.

All of a sudden, the headlights broke over the horizon of the track and the darkness flared with a row of blinding full beams, for an instant illuminating the deadfall and the leaf litter on the forest floor, the vertical lines of tree trunks and, deep in the undergrowth, the flash of a watching eye. The big four-wheel-drive barrelled past with a surge of superchargers, and fishtailed into the switchback, brake lights illuminating a trail of dust. In an instant it was gone again, the stillness smothering the engine's growl, the darkness reclaiming its territory. As the noise of the pickup faded, the breeze carried to me the sound of beating drums from up ahead, clearer this time.

I pressed on upwards, and eventually came out onto a wheel-rutted track that circled the base of a sheer rock wall. The sound of the drums was overwhelming now, seeming to come from all directions at once, now just ahead, now far off. The summit was up there somewhere, and as I followed the track I strained my eyes towards the source of the drumming. I saw, silhouetted against the night sky, a giant crucifix jutting up from the rock.

I followed the path around the foot of the crag, past a clapped-out bus. It was parked, with a pair of sleeping feet lolling out of the driver's window. Continuing on, I began to hear the throbbing of a generator, and just around a buttress of rock I came towards a group of men standing under a floodlight. They were smoking and passing round a brown bottle. As I went past, one of them spat into the dust at his feet. I saw that the floodlight was directed up a steep flight of steps carved out of the rock.

I climbed with grim determination. The pulse of the drums, from just up ahead, had grown more frenzied. The rhythm was spiralling out of control, and drowning out even the sound of the generator. At the top of the flight I emerged onto a small plateau at the summit of the Cerro de la Estrella.

There was a handful of people standing around a small Zapotec pyramid, and on the stone platform above them whirled a quartet of bizarre figures. I saw them in outline, cast against the purplish haze of the city below, spinning madly one way, then another, headdresses of palm fronds in strange configurations splaying in the dust around them, lolling tail-feathers bobbing, legs kicked wildly into the air in a flourish of rattling shells. They moved so fast they became a blur without substance. With their monstrous headgear, their shields and grass-fringed spears thrust into the sky, they were other-worldly beings, outside of space and time.

But then, from the other side of the plateau, there came a blood-curdling yell of "YEEEEE-*HAW!*" My heart sank. I saw that it was a fat American in a Hawaiian shirt and sandals. He panned his camcorder over the scene and zoomed in on the cross-legged drummers. Re-angling his baseball cap, he yelled, "HOOOOO-*WEE!*" and stuck the thick butt of a cigar between bearded lips.

A group of women in palm skirts, with jangling bells around their ankles, were congregating around a pole on the open ground, and they started dancing, weaving ribbons around it. An old crone lit a chalice of incense, illuminating the faces of watching children. The American, grinning into the screen of his camcorder, got in there for a close-up.

The sight of the stamping women in their grass ankle-warmers called suddenly to mind a troubling memory of a leotarded Jane Fonda in an old aerobics video of Cathy's. By this time the gringo had joined in the dancing, turning clumsy circles, shouting "Yooo-*Heeeee*", his right foot pounding the dust like the hind leg of a flea-bitten dog.

That was it, that put paid to the fleeting impression that I had stumbled onto a piece of the real Mexico, something kept sacred from the grasping sticky hands of tourism. The weaving path of the dancers had taken them close to the pole now, in a frantic figure of eight, and one squat woman knocked off her headdress as she ducked under the rope. I watched her, disoriented from all the spinning, staggering after it in the dust. By now the four whirling figures had climbed down from the pyramid and were sitting on a wall. One of them had taken his mask off and lit a fag.

The onlookers got to their feet and collected sticks with cloth bundled around the ends. A woman was dipping them in a bucket of kerosene and another was attempting to set them alight with matches. Somehow the American too had got hold of one. The kerosene flared for a moment, then burned itself out. The dancers took their torches, which blackened and quickly guttered out in a cloud of acrid smoke. They tried to relight them, but the cloth ends smouldered reticently and snuffed out, so they seemed to give up on the idea.

In a flurry of palm leaves and feathers, with a chattering of bells and rattles, trailing swirls of fumes from their sputtering torches, they filed down the steps half-running. I watched them emerge onto the floodlit ground below, quickly pursued by the American with his camcorder. By the time I got to the bottom of the steps, the jangling procession was already out of sight. The men killed the floodlight and loaded the generator into the flatbed of a pickup. Then there was a whirl of backfiring vehicles, the gurgling, clapped-out bus and, bringing up the rear, the American's vast, gleaming Winnebago, satellite dish wobbling on top.

When the dust settled, I was alone again in the darkness, the jangling and the engines receding down the hillside. From the high plateau I looked out over the panorama of the city at night, the Milky Way of street lamps that lapped against the black mountains skirting the valley, the lights of aeroplanes in their landing patterns, that struggled to penetrate the smog.

I thought about taking a running jump over the side. Then I miserably followed the path back down again.

Mina's train pulled into the station in Mexico City one sweltering afternoon in January 1918. She looked anxiously from the window for Cravan. Then, waiting on the platform, she watched the crowds disperse and the dust settle and she wondered what she had got herself into.

According to Bob Brown, it was he and his wife who met Mina at the station, and they took her on a tour of the capital's bars and *pulquerias* in search of Cravan. They tracked him down to a disreputable saloon, where he had the whole establishment in thrall with a slew of dirty jokes in poor Spanish. When she walked in, Cravan spotted Mina out of the corner of his eye, and he let her wait by the door for him to finish his joke amidst an uproar of hysterics from the peons that crowded around him. Not wanting to drag Cravan away from his party, Mina spent that first night in Mexico alone in a fleabag hotel, and was kept awake until the early hours by the sounds of an industrious prostitute in the neighbouring room. It was not the reunion she had dreamt of.

In *Colossus* she claimed, "Those first days... we wandered ceaselessly arm in arm. It never made any difference what we were doing – making love or respectfully eyeing canned foods in groceries, eating our tomatoes at street corners or walking among weeds. Somehow we had tapped the source of enchantment, and it suffused the world." In running to Cravan in Mexico, Mina had thrown caution to the wind and, against her better judgement, she now surrendered herself utterly to her love for him.

Her memories of their short time together in the city are a rose-tinted dream of romantic passion that finds apt expression in her florid, overwrought prose: "After straining

our hearts for so long across so many miles... our separation... had become an entity. It laid its embodiment of our
late solitude between our bodies of flesh – thrust its aborted
mouth of nostalgia between our lips. Longing had aroused
our emotions to such crescendo it crashed the senses...
exquisite flood!"

The couple moved into a gloomy, earthen-floored basement
on the road to Guadalupe in the ordure-strewn outskirts
of the city. The only source of natural light was a window
vent at pavement level, and on weekends they looked out at
the morbid parade of the bulls passing on their way to the
arena. On holy days they might have joined the procession
of pilgrims and the peddlers of religious icons, following the
road up the hill to the basilica. Worshippers came from all
over Mexico to visit the site where the Virgin is said to have
appeared to a native Indian centuries before. Today I found
that a vast steel-and-glass chapel has been erected on the
hillside to accommodate the thousands of devotees that come
to the shrine on the festival of the Guadalupe. The families
of sick and dying children climb the flights of steps on their
knees, their faces running with sweat and tears. Perched at
the rocky summit, the ancient chapel has changed little since
Cravan's day. It is festooned with flowers and filled with the
sound of crying babies, its ornamentations kissed to a high
polish by the lips of the desperate and the devout, whilst the
figure of the Black Virgin looks on.

Their new living quarters were dark and dingy, with an
unpleasant odour that no amount of carbolic soap could
scrub away. Mina swept obsessively in a vain attempt to hold
off the dust. It is remarkable how quickly this "prototype
of the Modern woman", who had barely so much as set
foot in a kitchen, settled into her new role as a housewife.
She spent her days stooped over a charcoal stove to cook
Cravan's tortillas. She mended the holes in his socks, scrubbed
his underwear, did the dishes. Her lily-white bohemian's

hands soon grew red-raw, her fingernails frayed and her palms ingrained with charcoal. Before long, Cravan stopped bothering with the pretence of looking for work and lay in bed until lunchtime, watching Mina crawl around the flat on her hands and knees searching for cockroaches to poison with a sprinkle of Keating's powder.

From Mina's description their relationship seems to have been one of absolute and mutual intimacy, in which every thought or sensation was perfectly reciprocated. According to her, they seem to have melded into a single entity. Indeed she felt so closely and inseparably united with Cravan that she fantasized about a magnificent wedding ceremony: "We wanted to 'really' marry in a rosy Mexican cathedral... in receptive aisles splashed with the wine and gold of stained-glass windows." However, while she claimed to speak for Cravan, her delirious, love-struck musings hardly reflect the workings of his mind. He seems to have been playing a role with her, and she was happy to be drawn into his fantasy life.

Other than Cravan's known proclivities for fabrication, a further reason to doubt the sincerity of his devotion to Mina is that he was still carrying on with his Paris mistress, Renée. Not only had he been corresponding with her regularly and in secret, but barely a fortnight after he was to marry Mina he wrote to Renée begging her to join him in Mexico.

In fact Blaise Cendrars, Cravan's old friend from Montparnasse, intimates that Renée had always been more than a mistress: in his memoirs he talks of "the letters that Arthur Cravan wrote to his wife in Paris". In these letters, Cravan reportedly discussed plans to meet in Mexico, swearing that he had never stopped loving her and could live without her no longer. Whether or not the couple had been secretly married, this shows that their relationship was still far from resolved.

However, the revelation of Cravan's continued affair with Renée was not the most surprising aspect of this correspondence. According to Cendrars, Cravan poured out his soul in these writings, and their contents grew increasingly extreme. The last of the letters were "poetic masterpieces... as prophetic and rebellious and desperate and bitter as those of Rimbaud". This was a fact that Cendrars found difficult to square with his recollections of the lazy, infantile Cravan he had known in Paris. He came to the conclusion that his friend must have suffered a breakdown, that "he was being slowly overwhelmed by some terrible crisis of the spirit".

The letters offer a tantalizing glimpse into the hidden complexities of Cravan's existence in Central America. Years later, when Cendrars attempted to investigate the mystery surrounding his friend, he tracked Renée down to a tenement in Montparnasse, hoping to inspect the letters for any clues they might yield about Cravan's activities or his whereabouts. But here the trail went cold, for Renée explained to him that she had recently married and that two weeks earlier her husband, in a fit of jealousy, had burnt all her relics of Cravan. Of the sixty extraordinary letters, nothing remained.

Mina Loy, however, hadn't the vaguest inkling of this other, darker aspect of Cravan's nature. They did get married, but under the name that appeared on Cravan's forged immigration papers: they became "Mr and Mrs James M. Hayes". And, instead of a grand Mexican cathedral, Cravan took her to a registry office and collared a street urchin and a passing shoe salesman to witness the nuptials.

The realization struck me one day as I was traipsing around Tesco's with Cathy.

By that point in our relationship we had the shopping down to a finely honed routine. She would go on ahead, crossing things off the list, and I followed a few paces behind with the trolley. While she went to handle the avocados, I parked up against the shelves so as not to obstruct the aisle.

She took a ticket at the delicatessen counter and we waited. We hadn't exchanged a word for some time. I was staring off into space – in the vague direction of the man in a plastic cap who was putting a block of cheddar on the scales for a portly woman in pink leggings. But then I became aware of Cathy watching me. She put her arm around my waist and gave me a little squeeze under the ribs.

"What are you thinking about?" she said.

"Mechanically reclaimed meat," I answered.

Then our number came up and Cathy went to order two Scotch eggs and half a kilo of artichoke hearts.

The night before she'd asked me the same question. We were sitting up in bed with our books, but she'd noticed me staring off into the corner of the room. I'd told her I was thinking about Phil Marsh, ex-coach for Romford Town, and how his dismissal would affect our position in the league. It had become so easy to lie. At first it'd been small things, moment-to-moment things that you'd never think would add up to anything.

Now Cathy headed towards the canned foods and I wheeled the shopping along behind. She heaved a six-pack of dog-food into the trolley, and for an instant our eyes met. That's when it struck me: I would never let her in on the secret.

We continued on to the freezer section.

It's a ridiculous situation when you find yourself lying to the one you love and saving the rest for total strangers, but that was the only way I could keep hold of her, and keep things crawling comfortably along. Every now and then, of course, the truth had to come out, and when it did I made sure it was far away from home.

I'd go to a bar and look for someone sitting alone. It would have to be someone I was never likely to see again. Once I was loosened by a few drinks I'd strike up a conversation. I'd buy us both a few more, and then I'd let it all out.

Before long this too had developed into a well-practised routine, and I found myself deriving a peculiar satisfaction from it. I remember one evening I introduced myself to a sales rep for a health club who I'd noticed sitting by himself in a corner, stooped over a double vodka. It was such a relief to get it all off my chest. And later that night I walked away feeling exhilarated, having left him on the roof of the multi-storey, staring over the side.

In Tesco's Cathy and I proceeded on to the till. She took up her position at the end of the conveyor belt to field the shopping into plastic bags, while I waited with the credit card for the checkout girl to resolve a problem with the barcode on a bottle of Mr Muscle.

Cravan was beginning to establish a reputation in boxing circles, and was even in correspondence with Jack Johnson in the hope that the ex-champion might stage a rematch. The newspapers were running announcements that Cravan was in training for a big fight against Jim "Black Diamond" Smith for the championship title of the Republic of Mexico. The copy read, "The best praise one can give Cravan is that three years ago he faced the formidable Jack Johnson in Barcelona and lasted seventeen rounds." Evidently Cravan had once again been lying through his teeth.

The match with Smith was to be a high-profile affair, contested in the bullring, and hyped with Cravan's proven skills in self-promotion. On the day of the fight there was an atmosphere of excited anticipation in the arena. True to form, Cravan was knocked down in the second round and duly counted out. Bob Brown, who was in the audience that afternoon, recalled his friend sprawled flat-out on the canvas, "a disorganized, pulsating jelly mass of sickened, senseless man". The spectators, having paid through the nose for five minutes of deplorable boxing, held their tickets in the air, clamouring for their money back. The press concluded angrily that the whole thing had the smell of a put-up job.

Things were getting desperate in Mexico City. The hundred pesos Cravan had earned from the Smith fight didn't last long. Convinced that government agents were watching him, he was growing increasingly paranoid. The couple had been living off Mina's inheritance, but by midsummer her funds were nearly exhausted. To cut down on expenses they now missed breakfast every other day, and Mina began to root through the kitchen waste at the Excelsior Hotel, scavenging chicken carcasses and vegetable peelings, anything from which she could boil some scant nutrition. She recalled how people passing in the street would stare at her jutting shoulder blades. Once, as the starving couple walked in the town, a stranger whispered his condolences, and reassured Cravan that his wife would not live to suffer much longer. After many days without food, they could no longer find the strength to get out of bed, so they would lie clutching one another in a weakly comforting embrace for hours on end. Mina had started experiencing waking dreams in which she saw chorus lines of sarcastic cream buns and leering regiments of sausages on parade. It wasn't long before Cravan plunged into pessimism, proposing that rather than face the agony of starvation they should kill themselves. But Mina was not quite ready to contemplate suicide.

That night, as the last candle sputtered towards its end, Cravan murmured, "You have to get it into your skull: it's all over... We'll kill ourselves tonight."

And then she watched him drift into a restless sleep.

As the summer reached its peak, the needle rose in the barometer at the Slackers' Hotel and with it the mood of anxiety in the capital. It was no secret that the authorities were on the verge of deporting all foreign undesirables, and as soon as word came that a census of draft-dodgers was being taken, the slackers gathered their meagre belongings and left for Veracruz, where they planned to board a ship for Buenos Aires.

With his reputation in tatters, and having lost his job as a boxing instructor after his humiliating defeat in the Smith bout, Cravan agreed to let Red Winchester, the proprietor of the Slackers' Hotel, manage his fights. In return Winchester loaned the couple money for food, and ensured that his investment recovered his fighting form. Bob Brown described Winchester as a flame-haired, homuncular Jew who walked beside Cravan "like a keeper beside his elephant". As well as being Cravan's "impresario", Winchester would also be in charge of all bets, and in this way the pair devised a scheme to gather sufficient funds to get out of Mexico for good.

It is curious that in *Colossus* Mina never mentions Cravan's fights. Her biographer Carolyn Burke wonders if this was simply because she found it too painful to record his failures, but it is also possible that when she saw him in the ring, without the pretence and the posturing, she glimpsed a side of Cravan that frightened her. Violence was an aspect of his persona which she wilfully ignored. In New York boxing had been just another of Cravan's many spurious occupations. She'd never had to contemplate his body's potential for brute force, thinking of it instead in terms of aesthetics – "like something that had escaped from the British Museum". Turning a blind eye too to his appetite for scandal, Mina had been able to construct her own version of Cravan, the heir to Oscar Wilde and her intellectual equal. But Mexico was another world, where no one cared in the slightest about his poetry. Here boxing was no longer a game, or a Dadaist performance – it had become the blunt cost of survival.

Winchester arranged a rematch between Cravan and Jim Smith, despite hoots of derision from the Mexican boxing public. Following his defeat in their previous meeting, the odds against Cravan were twenty to one. Everyone knew he didn't stand a chance. But with the promise of a cut of the takings from the bets, Smith was persuaded to throw the fight and, sure enough, he took a dive in the fourth round. This would remain the single victory of Cravan's boxing career. Fearing reprisals, he and Mina took their share of the winnings and left the capital before morning.

The bus had seats that were supposed to recline, even though mine was jammed, and most of the holes in the upholstery had been darned. It seemed like the height of luxury after the torture of the Greyhound. Such buses, which ply routes all over Mexico, are called Pullmans, in memory of the great locomotives that once travelled this country.

The Transisthmus Interoceanic railway was once the pride of Mexico. When it was completed after years of hard labour – the five thousand miles of track painstakingly laid, the tunnels bored through the great mountain ranges – the railroad announced the country's emergence from the dark ages. Modernity had come to Mexico, and now, with one of the finest railways in the world, it had the means to rival the United States as a true world power.

Today the Pullman rolling stock – all burnished copper, gracefully curving mahogany, the hiss of steam and the rainbow sheen of dripping oil – are no more. All over Mexico the tracks lie neglected, subsiding into the dirt. Mexico's great railroad has long since died, taking the country's fortunes with it.

The departure of Cravan's train had been delayed for hours as it awaited its military escort. The train sat on a shunting line until the afternoon, when armoured cars brimful of soldiers were finally coupled to the head and rear. Railway hold-ups occurred with unerring frequency during the revolution, and as security against ambush soldiers were posted on the cowcatcher and on the roof.

The train ground uphill past Guadalupe, the engine hammering, the smokestack throwing up a towering column of soot and steam. Once the last of the suburban outposts gave way to the rocky footslopes of the Western Sierras, they were already deep into the heart of bandit territory. Here the line snaked its way amongst the mountains through a complex of tunnels that made it a perfect trap ground. It was slow going, the train dropping to a walking pace, armed soldiers sent on foot into the tunnels ahead to check for explosives on the track and to warn of ambush. The long crawl through the black tunnels was agonizing. The locomotive engulfed the carriages behind in a choking cloud of smoke and steam, and the deafening clatter of flat-wheeled cars resounded off the close rock walls.

They climbed on, passing through the mountain settlements above the snow line, and then they began the long descent to the banana plantations and cane fields, the brakes sounding a squeal of anxiety. When they reached the lowlands, the train paused for fuel and water at a ghost town in the sandhills. The adobe huts stood empty, some of them without roofs, others showing the gaping holes of cannon shot. Smoke rose into the hot still air from the embers of a burnt stockade, a sign that the rebels had passed through here recently. Later in the afternoon, as they neared the coast, there came the sudden sound of gunfire from the soldiers on the locomotive, but when the passengers rushed to the windows they saw it was only target practice with a coyote fleeing into the mesquite brush.

My bus came into the outskirts of Veracruz at seven in the morning in the tail end of a hurricane. There were pieces of tree lying across the pavements. Telephone wires dangled loose from rooftops. Huge billboards hung tenuously from the remains of steel scaffolds wrenched apart in the wind. I stepped down into a desolate bus depot amidst great clouds of dust spun into whirlwinds around me.

I found shelter in a diner around the corner. A sour-faced waitress deposited a menu in front of me and I pointed at something at random. I stared out of the window, watching the dust devils kicking dirt into the wincing faces of passers-by – the kindergarten children tossed about like litter in the wind, and the first traffic of the morning turning the corner onto the Avenida Cinco de Mayo.

The waitress plonked a dish of mashed egg and green chilli in front of me, with a plastic beaker of over-milked coffee. Almost as an afterthought she brought a side serving of *frijoles* that appeared to have already been digested. Not only was the food repellent to the taste, but it brought on a feeling of violent sickness as soon as I had swallowed it. I broke into a cold sweat, my stomach churned, my head reeled. As the wind outside threw up a great cloud of dust, flexing the glass like a musical saw, I felt the onset of a violent bout of dysentery.

I spent the rest of the day and that night down by the docks in the Santander, a cheap hotel that was deserted. The rain puddled in the room. Outside the window, wind-weary palms bent beneath the violent monotony of the storm. Between the vomiting and the diarrhoea, I slept very poorly because throughout the night there was no letting up in the wind that buffeted against the loose-fitted windows in heavy gusts, threatening to shatter them inwards at any moment. The noise of big trucks revving at the traffic lights, and the repetitive bass notes reverberating into the early hours from a disco nearby, added to the din.

By 1918 Veracruz had already gained fame in the history of the revolution. It was here that the Americans had made a play for control of the Gulf coast supply routes in the hope of protecting their business interests in Mexico. In their bid to turn the revolution to their advantage, the American planners had targeted Veracruz as the crucial staging post for their interventionist strategy. But they had not counted on such dogged resistance from its citizens: whilst US warships moored offshore raked the town with shells, their every attempt to land troops was foiled. From improvised sandbag emplacements on the street corners, bands of locals repelled the Navy's landing parties and held off the American troops with rifles for the duration of the four-day stand-off. The town incurred heavy damage and loss of life, but for preventing the Americans from gaining a foothold in Mexico, and effectively stopping US interventionism in its tracks, the people of Veracruz became heroes of the revolution.

But if Veracruz had earned a reputation as the site of one of the most illustrious moments of the insurgency, it was also to gain notoriety as the place where the myth of the great revolution finally bit the dust. It was here that Venustiano Carranza, the figurehead of the new Mexico, met his ignominious end.

When the peasant uprisings had dethroned the dictator Porfirio Díaz, it was Carranza who had risen from the ashes of the fallen regime as the strong new leader of the Republic: the bandit leaders having done the dirty work, it was Carranza's task now to draw order from the chaos and ensure the country's future. In contrast to the rough-and-ready, tobacco-chewing, sombrero-wearing rebel leaders Pancho Villa and Emiliano Zapata, Carranza seemed a model statesman. He cut a striking figure, tall and dignified, stern and yet benign of appearance with his trademark white beard and hard-set spectacles. He became good friends even with Jack Johnson when the ex-champion boxer passed through Central America in 1919. Mexicans revered the ageing Johnson as a symbol of the struggle for civil rights, and he appears with the President in postcards of the time: he and Carranza are pictured shaking hands, each of them bowing their head in mutual deference.

As the architect of the new Constitution, in which the spoils of the revolution were enshrined, Carranza himself had gained a saintlike status. And yet, as time passed it grew apparent that the peasants reaped no profit from the promised redistribution of land, and poverty continued unabated in the cities. Indeed, apart from the officials, Mexicans saw none of the benefits of the new order: the new order, in fact, was much the same as the old one. Having led his country to independence, Carranza had come to embody the idealism of the Revolution, but deep down he was just as crooked as any of Mexico's old leaders.

In 1920, with his reputation souring and the tide of public opinion turning sharply against him, Carranza's administration collapsed. In his final days in office, he stole everything he could get his hands on, stripping the presidential residence even of its gilt wallpaper. Then he and his followers loaded fifty million pesos of the national treasury into a train and set out for Veracruz, from where they hoped to flee the country.

With his enemies in another train close behind, a strange high-speed chase ensued as Carranza made for the coast. The President's pursuers gained on him whilst the "Golden Train" was held up outside Veracruz, where the tracks had been dynamited. His locomotive finally packed in for lack of water just a few miles from the port, and Carranza was apprehended and shot. His naked body was found some time later in a peasant's hut on the ranch where his assassins had discovered him hiding amongst the livestock. They had robbed him of his spectacles, his whip and all other identifying features. They had even torn his beard out by the roots.

Weeks after Carranza's disgraceful death, his friend Jack Johnson finally made his way home to the States after seven long years of exile. In June 1920, Johnson stepped across the border at Tijuana and gave himself up to the police. For the ex-Champion of the World this was no hero's homecoming: he was clapped in irons and incarcerated in Leavenworth Penitentiary on charges trumped up a decade before. He served his time, and when he was released he tried without success to rekindle his boxing career. He fought the occasional exhibition match, but soon ended up working the vaudeville circuit on a double bill with a troupe of trained fleas.

"Arrived at a new town," Loy wrote, "[Cravan] would give it a glance and assess its population, then tramp through every street, round its suburbs, along the harbours, through the warehouses on the wharves, past the shunting lines of the railways... He was looking for something of his own among all this, that something the poet always seems to have mislaid."

In the morning I emerged from my hotel room with the air of a man convalescing after a terrible accident. I found that the weather had passed and the streets of Veracruz lay in an eerie stillness. Everything was covered in windfallen debris that was slowly rotting in flooded drains. On street corners, vendors of sweets and keyrings had laid out their wares on plastic tables. The buildings here were painted in pinks and oranges, colours intended to be tropical, but which fell inert now under an overcast sky. Inert, like the atmosphere of the town, where the chiming of exotic birds in the palm trees and the sound of marimba in the empty Zócalo seemed out of place.

Cravan found that Veracruz possessed a peculiar sordid appeal. The summer was over and the Mexican monsoon was blowing in from the north, the stifling heat giving way to the first rains of the season. Humidity lay thick over the town, the salt off the sea mingling with a sickly sweet smell of rotting tropical vegetation, and there was a strange romance in this. A number of slackers were already installed here in dirt-cheap hotel rooms furnished only with a straw mattress crawling with mildew, where the tattered wallpaper dripped despondently from the walls.

I wandered through the outskirts along the highway, past disused warehouses and freight yards. From the flyover I looked down at the shanty huts that had barnacled themselves to the supports. There was an old woman gripping a goat between her knees, bending it over a bucket as she slit its throat. On the street corner a group of men sat around a pile of rubble drinking dark beer from plastic cups. They were cheering at a friend of theirs who had lost control of his wheelchair and was stuck in a pothole. Tipped over at a crazed angle, this man raised his disposable cup, then drained it. His arm fell to dangle at his side, the cup toppled out of his hand and rolled to and fro in the dust.

In Veracruz, Bob Brown recalled, the slacker population did everything from driving taxis to selling ready-made tortillas. Cravan capitalized on this entrepreneurial spirit, getting in on the illicit trade in "rubber goods". The slackers had spotted a niche for condoms in this Catholic country, and several of the shrewdest businessmen amongst them had quickly established a monopoly. Having learnt their techniques from bootlegging in the Puritan dry states of North America, the condom vendors patrolled the pool halls, the bars, the bullfights and the cockpits gathering little groups of men for a whispered sales talk. The best salesmen employed as visual aids a plantain and a peon assistant afflicted with venereal disease, and business was booming. Cravan got a slice of the action, managing to scrape together enough money from the sale of prophylactics to pay for the onward journey.

Cravan and Mina Loy had come to Veracruz because it was on the main shipping line to Argentina, and promised an escape route to South America. But they found that they were too late: passport controls had been set up at the docks and it was reported that Allied patrols routinely stopped boats in the Gulf to search for deserters. So the couple decided to continue to the Pacific coast, to what was rumoured to be the last remaining route out of Mexico.

I wandered on, walking for the sake of it, not taking anything in. My most abiding memory of Veracruz is, for some reason, a boy I saw sitting on the flatbed of a passing pickup who was holding steady a life-size fibreglass statue of the Virgin Mary.

My rickety bus left Veracruz and sank into the jungle depths. The engine whined and spluttered, the driver tore at the gears, throwing the nose of the bus into the sharp turns and switchbacks as the road followed the contour of the hill. Dense green walls of vegetation pressed in on either side, the trees sagging under the weight of parasite ferns and the strangling embrace of lianas. Splinters of branch stabbed through the open windows on the sudden bends, and the other passengers all leant instinctively away from the openings to avoid the threat of a fatal wound. The bus drove on, tearing the branches loose so that they collected in the crook of the window in a little ragged spray.

Cravan stared out of the train windows, his eyes following mysterious shadows in the undergrowth. Monkeys stared back from the high branches over the track, and occasionally a parrot mimicked the screech of the wheels. Mina's heart missed a beat at the sound of the "belching ghost-wail of the locomotive" that cut through the "sibilant silence" of the jungle.

When the train stopped at way stations to take on water, it was overrun with flat-footed Indian women who hopped on board to sell caskets of gardenias, engulfing the carriage with a sweet unctious stench that made Mina think of funerals. They padded barefoot from carriage to carriage, stepping nimbly over the bundles, bunches of bananas, babies, hair-less dogs and pulque pots that littered the aisles. Once the stokers began feeding the furnace ready for departure, and the engine sent its first shudders back through the carriages, the Tehuana women would glance nervously out of the windows, then waddle through the corridors, frantically marking down the last of their gardenias. The train made good progress during daylight hours, but once darkness fell it was too dangerous to carry on. At twilight the train ground to a halt, and the barefoot lookouts clambered down from the roof to pitch their fires along the track.

After a few hours the fat, string-vested driver of my bus pulled up next to a thatched shack perched precariously on the edge of a ravine. A little grinning man came out to meet him, and together they started pulling lemons off a tree. A wide-eyed infant watched from the doorway. When they'd stripped all those within arm's reach, the little man shinned up the trunk. From the bus the passengers watched without interest as he got up into the high, thin branches that drooped and creaked under his weight. Waiting below, the fat driver caught the lemons as they fell down to him, collecting them in the cradle of his vest. The child's attention had long since turned to an ants' nest, and he was now absorbed in the meticulous task of snuffing them out of existence one by one with his tiny fingers.

The long journey across the continent was drawing to a conclusion. Shortly after they had left Veracruz, Mina had caught a glimpse of a body hanging from a tree, a sight she took as an omen. But by the time the train approached the western settlements, where sun-bleached skeletons littered the tracks and desiccated corpses dangled from the telegraph poles, Mina realized that here death was without significance.

The mattress in the hotel room in Puerto Angel sagged in the middle when I sat on it, and wheezed a cloud of dust. It was a welcoming place where the cockroaches had bounded up to meet me like friendly dogs. The well-ruckled bed sheet smelt of stale sweat and bore the stain of a ghostly man-shaped imprint that reminded me of the Turin Shroud. I looked over the walls, scanning the intricate blood-flecked chintz of mashed mosquitoes.

I was close now, close to the ending that I had anticipated for so long. But as the bus had brought me sluggishly nearer to the scene of Cravan's final performance, I had the impression that Cravan himself was growing more indistinct with every passing day. The facts were already beginning to fragment, to dissolve in uncertainty and contradiction. It was becoming increasingly difficult to discern where Cravan ended and the fabrications began. Soon I would be joining Cravan on the shore of his last misadventure – by the time I got there, would there be anything of him left?

Puerto Angel is a picturesque fishing village a hundred kilometres up the coast from Salina Cruz. It is a peaceful, reassuringly run-down leftover from the hippy trail, as yet untarnished by the encroaching corruption of package tourism and the luxury resorts that are spreading like an epidemic from the north.

Cravan and Mina passed through here on their meandering progress towards the shipping lines going out of Salina Cruz. Mina had sewn their fare, in gold coins, into her belt, and they had sworn to touch it only in the gravest emergency. They were scraping a living from the impromptu performances that they put on in the *zócalos* of the villages they passed through. Cravan would flex the paling muscles of his torso and shadow-box for the amusement of the village children. Mina would exhibit some silent theatre for the reward of a few pesos or a crust of bread.

In Puerto Angel they came across a worn-out circus that languished outside town, and they found work here for a while. The Gonzales Brothers' circus had recently been cursed with an extraordinary run of bad luck. First it had lost its big top in a fire, and then two weeks later it lost its most popular attraction – a blind lion with jutting ribs, which had to be put down after it mauled a member of the audience. The final blow came when the circus' ham-fisted magician lost two fingers in a trick that went awry. The few remaining acts were being worked ragged in an attempt to fill the holes in the line-up. Now the mariachi band was threatening strike action, whilst the anaemic cooch dancer looked on the verge of nervous collapse. The Gonzales brothers were in desperate need of a new draw, and Cravan was an answer to their prayers. He was presented to the audience wearing a strongman's loincloth, and after he had flexed his wasted muscles and showcased his footwork, a senile bear with its claws pulled was unleashed into the ring. Cravan would attack the unsuspecting creature and grapple with it in the dust until it turned limp with fatigue. Mina provided a musical interlude dressed as a Pierrot with a penny whistle, and after her act the dwarf ringmaster would send around a decrepit, whip-sore chimpanzee to hold out its tin beggar's cup for the audience. The show had to go on, at least until the last drunken spectator awoke and shuffled to the exit.

When I came out of my room a patter of cold rain swept across the street, and then was gone. The locals were going quietly about their business as usual – business which consisted, as far as I could tell, of little more than lolling on plastic chairs in the shade of their *palabas*. I walked wearily along the street, stepping over pools of fetid mud slowly digesting plastic bottles and cigarette packets. Every now and then distorted Latino music would come wafting out of the subsiding shacks. And once or twice I became aware of a human eye watching me from the dark interior, a single eye picked out by the zebra stripes of sunlight falling from a palm-thatched roof.

I went along the seafront, passing amongst throngs of mangy dogs hanging around the gutters where they presided over chunks of rotting fish thrown out of the restaurant kitchens. They looked up guiltily from their meal as I went by, and showed me their toothless gums. Others stood further off, growling from the street corners, spoiling for a fight.

On the road that wound out of the village and around the headland, dirty blue smoke extended across my path from piles of garbage smouldering in the ditches. As the last habitations and boarded-up guest houses fell away, I continued up the hill amidst the overhanging trees and the chattering of invisible birds. Occasionally I heard the engine of a *colectivo* dropping down a gear to climb the steep grade, and a few minutes later it would crawl abreast of me and sound its horn expectantly, before speeding away. This was a well-plied route connecting the bus terminus in Puerto Angel to Zipolite, a popular tourist beach a mile or so ahead. I followed the coastal road on into the jungle, and from all around came the deep thrum of insect life, the pitching modulations that recalled voices on a fast-forwarded cassette.

All of a sudden I caught a flash of white in the undergrowth, out of the corner of my eye just a quick flurry of movement. I stared attentively into the shadowy world of the jungle that sprouted from the very edge of the tarmac. The dense vegetation shielded from view the darkness beyond, save a few brilliant squints of sunlight falling from the canopy. But as I stared I caught another glimpse of movement from deep within. As soon as I had seen it, the chaos of the jungle tightened itself again and fell still. I walked on for a long time, my eyes searching the undergrowth intently.

Ten minutes further on I came across the sun-bleached wreckage of a car overturned in the ditch at the roadside. The car had crashed into a tree, breaking it off at the trunk, and through the gap I got a clear view into the dead world of the jungle floor. There, a hundred yards away, visible for a moment in the tight-packed darkness of the trees, stood a lanky old man in a dirty panama hat, naked to the waist, gripping a butterfly net and gazing into the air above him. A long white beard gave him the appearance of an ancient druid.

I blinked and he was gone. A moment later there was a glimmer of white deeper into the jungle, and for an instant, like a single frame of a movie escaping from the shutters of the trees, I saw him bounding through the vegetation at extraordinary speed, his net raised above his head like an axe. The jungle swallowed him without trace.

Zipolite is a long, curving stretch of sand that would look at home in a picture postcard. The place itself had a strange atmosphere of unreality about it. Out on the horizon a lone surfer paddled up the face of a wave. A stark-naked man wheeled an old bicycle past me by the water's edge. The long *playa* stretched on for a kilometre, bookended with hulking rocks shrouded in a halo of spray. On the fringe of the sand was a line of sagging wooden shacks where dreadlocked youths hung limply in hammocks smoking spliffs and drinking fruit juice. Behind was a mess of flimsy tree houses inhabited by ageing gringos whose bedraggled white hair clashed against thick shoe-leather tans.

As well as sclerotic drop-outs from the hippy trail, Zipolite has been a haven for fugitive bank-robbers and paedophiles fleeing convictions in the States: between the ocean and the jungle, they have created a place that exists purely for hedonism and oblivion, a place to lose themselves in anonymity and forgetfulness.

These days, reading of its reputation as a New Age utopia, young travellers follow their guidebooks here looking for leftover scraps of Sixties idealism. Once here they find that free love remains a myth, and instead they settle for the consolation of cheap sex and cheaper drugs. You can buy it all here in the splintering bordellos hidden in the shade of the palms. And between the knocking shops, the drug dens and the juice bars, the circuit of the tourist industry is completed by the taxis that ply the dirt tracks between the habitations, scavenging for little groups of backpackers to extort.

I stopped under the awning of a bar. Tables were arranged haphazardly, the place was engulfed in marijuana smoke. It appeared to be empty, but after I had been sitting there for a while, and my eyes had adjusted to the shade, I became aware of others. Further into the darkness, there were people as still as furniture. In the corner, slumped like a fly-tipped mattress, was a hairy man in Speedos lying across a plastic sun lounger.

I lit a cigarette and looked out over the scene. Waves spilt across the beach with a troubling regularity. Balding men dallied in the froth with trophy wives half their age. The place was the closest you can come to crossing over to that other dimension: fine white sand displaces softly under footfalls, the smooth grains massaging the toes; sets of waves line up to the horizon, rising into barrels that refract the sun like cut glass, then peaking and collapsing with a great sigh and brilliant foam; the clear early evening sun casts everything in a sepia haze. For a moment it dawns on you: this *is* the soft-focus world of aspirational television advertising. A couple of girls in G-string bikinis toss back their hair and you think, *My God I've made it.*

But it's a fleeting moment. Without fail, a passing German nudist trounces your private idyll, his low-slung testicles clacking together with the monotony of an executive toy. As he marches by, those moistly flapping obscenities bring everything toppling back to earth.

Later, after it had grown dark, I was watching from behind a tree. Out on the beach there was a bonfire raging. They had built it with scraps of palm and the floorboards from a derelict shack, and now the flames licked the darkness hungrily, sending sparks spiralling into the sky. A dozen or so figures sat around it, silhouetted, the light occasionally finding a smiling face, the glint of a bottle held up to the lips, or teeth bared in laughter. A moment or so later the sound of them would reach me over the sand, distant and muffled. I watched without comprehension, as if witness to some terrible and unfathomable ritual. An hour before I had been sitting amongst them; now I was hiding behind the tree, the skirl of insect song closing in with ever-accelerating tempo. Under the potent influence of the marijuana, the sound made my head reel, made the ground beneath me violently pitch and lurch, and out of fear I held fast to the tree trunk. I was so frightened it didn't seem likely that I would be able to move for the duration of the night.

The panic had seized me just as they started to share out the chicken they were roasting above the fire. I had sat staring intently into the embers, listening to the voices trilling happily all around, willing myself to become invisible. I knew I had to get away. I was sure they were no longer laughing at me, but had grown hostile. I formulated a plan to walk calmly from them on the pretext of needing a slash but, after working myself up to it for half an hour, when the time finally came I sprang to my feet, the words caught in my throat, and I ran into the darkness, throwing myself into the cover of the jungle. That's how I ended up here, cowering behind a tree on what had promised to be such a pleasant evening.

Earlier that afternoon, sitting under the awning of a beach-side bar, I had drunk lukewarm beers and smoked successive packets of cheap Mexican cigarettes. Lone, mulleted men wandered along the water's edge, basking in the full, shrivelled glory of their waxed nakedness. Young girls in minuscule bikinis lay like corpses on the sand, sunburnt to a crisp. Up on the horizon a lone surfer rose out of the water, pulling himself upright, cutting his board into the leading edge of a great wave.

As I sat there an old man came up. He was rake-thin, with a long white beard that mingled with the single sprig of wiry white hair that garnished his pigeon chest. He wore a panama hat, sandals, denim shorts and a string of wooden beads around his neck. He dropped his satchel, propped his butterfly net against the next table and drew up a wicker chair at the very edge of the shade. He sat down heavily, immediately crossing a pair of long bony legs. There was sweat glistening on the fibres of his eyebrows, and there were streaks of dirt on his cheeks where dust had collected in the lines of his skin. A girl in a sarong brought him a tall glass of fruit juice, and he drank it thirstily until it was all gone. He crossed his legs the other way and remained there in his seat, looking around him in a discontented fashion as if he were missing something. After a time he turned to me and in a thick Bolton accent asked for a cigarette.

I handed him one, saying, "I saw you earlier. In the woods."

Taking the fag off me he nodded slowly and deliberately throughout the entire process of leaning over for the lighter and drawing in a lungful of smoke. At last he said:

"Oh yeah?"

He kept on nodding, for some reason, whilst he exhaled a languorous current of smoke. I looked out to sea and spotted the surfer bobbing into view again on the back of a wave.

"I hunt butterflies," the old man said with a nod to the net that hung from the end of the propped stick.

"Catch anything?"

He rooted in his satchel and pulled out a small Tupperware pot. He turned it over a few times in his hands and held it out to me. He tapped on the lid and said:

"There."

The box was made of opaque plastic, but inside there was the shadow of a vague shape moving. It was floundering against the walls of the pot.

"What is it?"

"Red Daggertail," he said, having another go at his cigarette.

"Is it a rare one?" I asked him.

"No, not especially. I've got seventeen of them at home. But they're elusive. You have to go into the jungle to find them. Thrill of the chase, isn't it." He swatted at a bluebottle that had landed on his shoulder.

"You ought to put some air holes in the lid, you know," I told him.

He shook his head. "It's a killing jar," he said. "When I get home I'm going to put a pin through him."

He put the box back in his satchel and picked a strand of tobacco out of his beard.

"It's like anything beautiful, you've got to kill it if you want to keep hold of it." He poked his cigarette out philosophically in a dead candle on the table. "Like anything."

I said, "Mmm," and nodded.

A sun-bronzed girl on the beach turned over onto her stomach and untied her bikini.

"Like this place. When we came here it was a paradise." His arm made a long sweeping motion over the beach, and by the time his hand reached the naturist doing yoga in front of the rocks at the far end, it had become a gesture of dismissal. "You can't imagine how perfect it was... Built a house over there behind the rocks." He stabbed a thumb in the direction of the nudist who was standing on his head and who, as I watched, overbalanced and careened tits-up onto the sand. "Married a beautiful little Tehuantepec girl with flowers in her hair," the old man went on. "Never left, though I probably should have done. *Now* look at it." He laughed, showing a cavernous ridge of devastated yellow teeth.

"Tourists have moved in, locals have cleared off. They're building luxury hotels over at Mazunte. There's muggers, prostitutes, needles wash up in the surf every morning. It's all gringos, nudists and backpackers all summer long. But when the rainy season comes it'll be dead as a doornail, everywhere boarded up like coffins. It's a crying shame."

A hacking, wheezy guffaw forced itself out of his face, and he lurched forwards in his seat coughing. He spat a big lump of phlegm onto the sand between his sandals.

"Crying shame," he said.

I saw the surfer climbing out of the water, tossing a curl of wet blond hair out of his face. He walked up onto the beach with his surfboard under his arm, and the cord tied around his ankle dragging through the sand behind him.

"And you should see the wife," the old man went on musingly. "She's a typical Indian woman – prettiest things you've ever seen... Until you marry them, and then..." Poking a long pink tongue between the stiff bristles of his beard, he blew a long, melancholy raspberry.

The surfer was coming up the beach in our direction. After waving at a couple of sunbathers, he jogged up to the shack and came squinting into the shade. He was tall, there wasn't an inch of fat on him, beads of seawater stood out over the contours of his muscles. His face broke into a wide grin when he saw the old man. The glistening blond of his hair, the radiant brown of his skin and the glinting white of his teeth gave me the fleeting impression that he was cast out of gold. He threw himself panting into the next chair.

"G'day Roger," he said to the old man, pulling back his mane. "How's it going old-timer?"

They shook hands, and then he reached over to me. "How's it going," he said, shaking my hand. "Name's Wayne." I noticed that he applied just the right balance of pressure in his handshake: it was firm, reassuring, yet without the wringing assertion of supremacy.

"How's the surf out there?" the old man asked him.

"Oh yeah," he said, catching his breath. "Seen worse. You coming out?"

The old man emitted a rasping giggle.

Wayne reclined in the seat, exuding vitality.

"Who's your friend there, Roger?"

"Don't know." Then as an afterthought he said, "Gentle-man kind enough to offer an old man a smoke when he needs one."

"Oh righto," said Wayne.

I passed the old man the pack again and offered one to Wayne.

"No thanks, mate." He pulled back his lustrous blond hair into a ponytail.

I eyed him as he came to rest, his rigid chest rising and falling rhythmically. His eyes closed, his head leant back, there was not a line on the smooth flesh of his face that would acknowledge even the faintest glimmer of pain. It was a sight that would ordinarily arouse my immediate and vehement contempt.

Wayne's nap was disturbed by the girl, who brought him a cold beer. She hung around coyly and he sat up to attend to her. He chatted her up in clumsy Spanish, intonating each word with a heavy Australian accent. Usually at this I might feel an excoriating hatred fermenting in the pit of my stomach, but his manner was so affable and laid-back that somehow it invalidated that emotion. I watched them flirting and something troublingly like gratification came over me. Then the girl went away smirking, and I managed to snap myself out of it.

Pleased with himself, Wayne took a long gulp of lager. He saw me watching him sidelong.

"How long you staying?" he asked me.

I told him: "A day or two."

"Where you headed?"

"Down the coast," I said. "Salina Cruz."

Wayne leant forwards, his face lighting up.

"Oh yeah? I'm headed there meself. Best waves on the Pacific apparently. It's like Baja down there, mate, you'll love it."

He put his empty beer bottle down on the table.

"Listen, you should hang around," he said, standing up. "We're having a barbie tonight, lighting a fire on the beach, there'll be stacksa people round, should be fun. You'll be there won't you, Roger?"

The old man nodded ponderously and said, "You bet."

"Bring your guitar along again tonight? He might be an old-timer, mate," he said to me, "but he knows how to enjoy eemself." Wayne picked up his surfboard and, calling, "Catch yous later," over his shoulder, he bounded back into the sea.

I watched him go, and it seemed the shade under the thatch roof grew darker and more desolate.

Roger chuckled and said, "Good lad."

That night on the beach there were a lot of people gathered around the fire. As I made the long approach across the wide open ground, I had resolved to walk calmly into their midst, but as it happened I ended up loitering awkwardly fifty yards from the fire, pretending to be fascinated by a dead fish that lay on the sand.

When Wayne saw me, he called to get my attention and then jogged over, beaming, to meet me with a slap on the back. Seeing my interest in the fish, he gave it a poke with his sandal and said, "Angelfish. They're better in the water, when they're still alive." He held me around the shoulder and walked me over to the fire, saying, "I don't know what your poison is, but there's some beers going round and some tequila, whatever tickles ya."

Amongst those milling around the bonfire were a handful of German nudists, some dreadlocked backpackers, fresh-faced girls, even some curious Mexican boys. There was also the occasional older couple enjoying an extramarital affair. These people chattered fiercely, without rest, and the murmur of competing voices, punctuated by laughter and shrieks of excitement, reminded me of the road from Puerto Angel, the road besieged by the jungle and reverberating with the oppressive din of insect life.

Dubiously I accepted swigs from bottles offered to me by strangers. At first I would take them hesitantly, sniff the mouth of the bottle and search these people's eyes for any sign of intent before taking a surreptitious taste. I could find nothing to account for their friendliness, and after a few swigs I gave up trying. Everyone was in high spirits, and I must say it was beginning to rub off on me. I nursed a quarter-pint of whisky someone had passed me, and followed the progress of several large joints that were circulating in my direction. I felt the warmth of the sand and the heat from the fire.

Wayne was nearby, befriending some young Mexicans, telling them an anecdote that was absurdly drawn out by rudimentary Spanish. The fire lit their grinning faces and their eyes, wide with attention. Roger had brought musical instruments and a canvas chair, and he sat with his chin nestled in his prodigious beard, consumed in an interminable guitar solo.

Wayne was now orchestrating a football match. He, a couple of backpackers and a nude German were putting together a team to play the Mexican boys. A small throng of girls cheered and whistled by the fire. Wayne tied his hair back with a piece of rag and came over.

"Who's up for some footie?"

I wondered where he found this energy that never seemed to run dry.

"I know it's dark," he said, "but your eyes'll get used to it."

The people next to me passed him the spliff.

"We need you on the pitch, mate," he said to me. "I think we can take these Mexicans." He hollowed his cheeks inhaling, then drew in sharply through his teeth. "What d'you reckon?" he said breathlessly.

"No thanks."

"Sure?" he said, exhaling a fine mist of smoke. "You can't sit on the touchline when your team's one man down!"

"I'll just watch, thank you."

From the other side someone handed him a second large spliff.

"Suit yourself, mate."

He gave me a spliff in each hand and walked off. I smoked them alternately, down to the ends, and no one seemed to notice.

The German, by the name of Helmut, was stark naked apart from a pair of white trainers that gave him a distinct air of absurdity. He joined the match with gusto, sending up rills of sand with his sliding tackles, and scoring a number of goals including one from a finely executed bicycle kick. Despite this the locals won 10–8, and when Helmut came back to the fire I noticed that all the frenzied activity, along with prolonged exposure to the Mexican sun, had brought his leathery privates into a state of glaring inflammation.

By the time Wayne came to sit next to me, the marijuana had taken hold. I could feel butterflies in my legs and a deep paranoia skirting my mind. Wayne was out of breath, the exhilaration of the game subsiding. I couldn't look away from the embers for fear of making eye contact.

"Sensible option staying put," he said. "Half-killed meself out there."

After a while he shouted, to no one in particular, "What happened to that tequila?" There came an answer from somewhere far away. "Who's up for some proper drinking, eh?" Wayne called out, and there came a chorus of hoots and wolf whistles in reply.

"How about it, mate?"

I had difficulty finding suitable words to answer, so I ended up saying nothing.

"You all right there?" Wayne asked, laying his hand on my back. "Have you dropped acid?"

I shook my head.

"Seem pretty uptight, there. If you've had some bad weed, no worries mate, you can just sit and ride it out, you're among friends here."

"Of course I haven't smoked any bad weed, don't be ridiculous," I told him quickly. "I'm entitled to sit here if I want without kicking sand around aren't I?"

"Absolutely." He took his hand away gently. "I just wanted you to know, if you feel like letting loose, having some fun, you're welcome to join us. Might as well enjoy yourself or what's the point?"

"Ah," I sneered, "a philosopher."

He shifted forwards on the sand thoughtfully.

"If there's something botherin' ya I'd like to hear it," he said abruptly, and it was as if the darkness moved in closer to the fire. "You never know, might be able to help out."

I gave a little snort of derision and instantly regretted it.

After a long time he shifted again.

"Life's a funny thing, mate," he said softly. "You've got your ups and you've got your downs. You just have to take the rough with the smooth and make the best of it."

I felt bile bubble up inside, anger pulsating behind my eyes, my brain wriggling clean out of my control.

"If you've heard it a million times before," Wayne continued, "it's because it's true."

Before I could stop myself I was saying: "*Why don't you stick to your surfing, your tear-arsing around, your footie-in-the-dark, your absurd cavorting with nubile girls and leave me to suffer my life in peace?*" The words came out of nowhere, and left me out of breath. The sensation of regret was immediate and intense, I especially hoped that no one else had heard.

"Sure thing, mate," said Wayne. "Feeling sorry for yourself's a terrible thing, though."

"What would you know about it?" I said, raising my voice.

"I've been there. You can't let it take over."

A malicious laugh belched up from deep in my stomach.

"I've had troubles in my life, too, mate."

"*Really*," I said. I was scoring deep ruts into the sand with my finger.

Wayne sat staring at me for a long while.

"I was in a car crash a while back," he said.

From the corner of my eye I could see the glow of the fire glancing off his face, but I couldn't make out his expression.

Shifting heavily on the sand, Wayne straightened his leg out and angled his knee into the light.

"See," he said.

When I looked across at it, I noticed a pattern gleaming on the surface of his skin. The muscle was misshapen and pitted with scar tissue.

"The family in the other car were killed instantly," he said, running a finger curiously along the line of the wound. "Amazing I came out of it just with this."

He folded his leg back underneath him.

"Drink-driving. They gave me three years and let me tell ya, it didn't feel long enough. Not by half."

I noticed that I was feeling a bit sick. I wasn't in a laughing mood, although there was something absurd about the whole situation, something ridiculous about the fire on the beach, the German in his training shoes, the laughing and the chatter, something woefully inane about this whole planet.

"Some things you wish were different, but you've got to live with 'em. I'm a better person now, life's all right," he said. "Look around ya, mate, it's not all bad."

In the silence that followed I did look up from the sand between my crossed legs and it felt like I was tearing myself away from something secure and familiar.

The fire was blinding, it took a while for my eyes to adjust to the light, and when they did the first thing I saw was Helmut picking sand out of his crotch.

"Not all bad, eh?" I said quietly.

"Reckon so. I mean, if there's no hope, why do we all keep on. Are we all idiots?"

I nodded slowly and plaintively.

"Righto, righto. And you know what's really going on."

"Yes."

"Well, I'd rather be in the dark."

"The penny's dropped."

"I'm sorry for you, mate. Reckon I'd kill meself if I felt like that."

I nodded at the fire.

"Can you look me in the eye and tell me straight you can't think of one good reason to be here?"

He let his question persist in the silence, waiting while I searched for a response. I couldn't think of a good way of putting it, so by way of a reply eventually I keeled over on my side, just enough to point my arse into the light. I pulled down my trousers to show him the gangrenous welts in the cleft of my buttocks. Ever since the sand had got into them, each one had swollen around the grains like a plump oyster incubating its pearl.

I gave him a good long look at them and a cheer went up from the others around the fire who hadn't been party to our conversation and had mistaken the gesture altogether.

"Righto," Wayne said. "I'll leave ya to it there, mate."

He got wearily to his feet and went to intercept the bottle of tequila. He instigated a drinking game that involved spinning around and around in circles and then running blindly into the darkness. Apart from Roger, still engrossed in his guitar-doodling, and a middle-aged American couple wearing matching white linen who sat cross-legged in mutual admiration, everybody was drawn away from the light of the fire, following Wayne's voice into the darkness, and disappearing from view. I could hear screams of laughter from different directions and the whoops of distant voices calling. It would, perhaps, have been prudent to leave at that point, but I found I couldn't yet move.

Later, from behind the tree I watched them coming back from skinny-dipping. From that distance I observed them. The paranoia had given way to an all-consuming sorrow, flaring from time to time into bitter resentment. Some backpackers were dousing the bonfire with paraffin and leaping through the flames. Wayne was lying away from the fire with a girl in a bikini, and they were talking softly and stroking each other's hair.

I stifled a fit of sobbing and spat obscenities under my breath. I wanted to charge out of my hiding place, empty the remainder of the paraffin over my head and throw myself onto the pyre, if only to dampen their enjoyment of the evening. I wanted to trounce their happiness simply because I was not capable of it myself.

Mina Loy was five months pregnant with Cravan's child by the time they came to Salina Cruz. Spread along the narrow coast of the Bahía Ventosa, the settlement is scoured by a brisk wind from the surrounding hills that blows day and night, without rest. The deep waters off the shore are said to be troubled by powerful riptides that have spawned many fishermen's tales of boats driven out to sea. As the largest of the southern ports, slackers were congregating here angling for a space on a steamship out of the country. Bob Brown recalled that, "Everyone was bound for South America, the Land of Opportunity, as Mexico had seemed only a few months before".

Today Salina Cruz is an oil town, its inhabitants clinging for their survival to the vast PEMEX refinery that looms on the headland. Huge tankers queue up to dock with the loading platforms out in the bay, and the off-duty refinery workers, with their orange boiler suits unzipped to the waist, have a reputation for hard-drinking and brawling.

I seemed to be the only customer at the Garden Palace Hotel. The woman at the desk was gutting fish into a plastic bowl when I arrived, and she seemed surprised to see a foreigner, even a little resentful of the interruption. There were a dozen tiny rooms drawn tight around a courtyard – the "garden" of the hotel's name – that was cast in perpetual shadow by the mess of overgrown weeds, their lazy tropical leaves drooping under the weight of blackfly encrustations. The room reeked of the kerosene that was used to douse the mattress for bedbugs, and as I lay on the bed staring at the intricate patterns of black mould on the ceiling, fancying I could interpret in them some omen of my future, many hours passed.

Later I walked through the shadowy colonnades of the market, past displays of fat vegetables and brightly coloured fish, as the restless hands of stall-holders brushed off the flies. I felt stared at and scrutinized by sour-faced housewives with their polythene-bag burdens and sullenly trailing infants.

Further on up the road was a traffic island that had once been the town *zócalo*, now a clutch of untended flower beds and empty benches isolated by the unremitting slew of traffic that cuts through the centre of the town. Bordering the square was a row of awnings frowning over jerry-built breeze-block shopfronts. One establishment was the closest this place came to a coffee shop, and I saw that it was deserted but for a gaunt man lingering in the shadows. Seeing that I was a foreigner, this man immediately pounced upon me. My mistake had been to show an instant's hesitation as I passed, and now the bony little man had me by the arm, manoeuvred me into a plastic chair and clapped his hands to a dead-eyed young girl by the coffee machine.

The man was edgy: it was clear to me that he suffered from an overactive thyroid. He said his name was Herbert, and he thrust a limp hand out for me to shake. As he pulled up a chair, the flimsy table wobbled from side to side on the pavement.

"I cannot say what a pleasure is it to have a human being to talk to," Herbert said, crossing bare skinny legs effeminately and drawing his packet of Marlboro Menthols nearer on the plastic tablecloth. "English?"

"Yes," I said.

"It's rare to see a tourist here." Then he turned around in his seat to stare into the interior of his shop, where the girl was dawdling by the coffee machine. He barked at her in nasally inflected Spanish and clapped his hands twice. The girl shuffled over bearing a coffee cup before her in both hands, staring at it in intense concentration so as not to spill its contents. Herbert watched her lower the cup with agonizing slowness and set it down on the table top in front of me. He spat three harsh words at her and the girl scuttled petulantly back into the shop.

"Do you know how hard it is to find a good girl in this place?" he asked. "I have nine girls in ten weeks. The last one, sixteen years old, she is happy to have the job, yes she like this, yes she like the kitchen, she want to learn the cooking... And I don't see her again, she never turn up the next day. These people! There is no work ethic here, is *unbelievable.*" He held his hand over his cigarettes as if to comfort himself that they were still there. "Unbelievable. *This* one," he said nodding at the sluggish girl standing bored by the sink, "This one is not bad. Very pretty, but she will not smile. She will do everything, but she does not know how to smile. I am having to teach her." His haggard face jerked into a grotesquely shallow grin. "Hey!" he shouted at the girl inside, turning the smile to her, his hands making little curling gestures insistently at the corners of his mouth. The girl looked back at him blankly. Then with great effort she turned up the edges of her lips into an expression that was half-sneer, while her eyes remained cold.

"They know nothing about work here," he said, rolling his eyes and fumbling for a cigarette. "Here they never have to work, fruit falls into their laps, the fish jump into the nets, it's paradise. They don't know what work is. All they do is sleep and drink. They're not interested in work. No work, no education, like *animals*. This is horrible place."

Herbert lit a long menthol cigarette and inhaled it with a look of physical pain.

"You know what they call me?" he said. "*El Mulo.* The fucking *Mule.*" He flashed a smile full of decaying teeth, and his face abruptly collapsed again into its natural expression of pained distaste.

Herbert told me the story of his life between wincing drags

on his cigarette. It seemed he was an Austrian exile who now found himself stranded in this dead-end town. He claimed that back in Austria he had made millions in the restaurant business. He had opened art galleries, owned Ferraris and a private jet, mixed with the rich and the famous, he'd had it all. But then he developed a taste for cocaine, let the businesses fall into neglect, and had a heart attack. Fearing he would suffer a mental breakdown, Herbert's family tried to get him admitted to a clinic. Herbert, however, had other ideas. He went directly to the airport and got on to a flight that would take him far away from Vienna. He arrived in Mexico with no Spanish, no money and nowhere to go.

He drifted for a year, staving off hunger by doing odd jobs in the towns he passed through. Finally he came across Salina Cruz. Here he managed to convince the landlord to let him manage this failing café, promising to transform it into an Italian eatery. In three years, Herbert declared to me, drawing menthol cigarette smoke through clenched teeth, he would have a chain of pizza restaurants here. Despite the idle shop girls who came and went, he ran the place single-handedly, busting a gut trying to ingratiate himself with the locals and wean them on to tagliatelle and Italian coffee, earning himself the nickname *El Mulo*: The Mule.

The place was dead. By the enthusiasm with which he plied me with coffee, I suspected I was the first customer he had seen for days. He had sat me out on the pavement by the swing sign where passers-by could see me. He would exchange words with pedestrians, flash theatrical smiles across his craggy face, from time to time he would wave at a passing pickup that sounded its horn or would offer a coffee, free of charge, to the old woman in the neighbouring shop, who presided over a vat of fruit juice, chin in hand, and watched us myopically through bottle-thick spectacles.

Herbert was a mass of nervous energy. He sat opposite me, twitching and demolishing cigarette after cigarette, looking

anxiously through his green sunglasses for potential customers. At the back of the shop the girl yawned.

"Life means nothing here," Herbert said after a while,
shaking his head incredulously. "You don't know where you
have come…"

A couple of barefoot kids came to the stall next door and
watched us curiously as the old woman served them a plastic
bag of fruit juice with a straw sticking out.

"This is horriblest place, *really*. They are like animals."
He eyed a couple of beautiful young girls amble by, hand in
hand with squat older men with slicked-back hair. "The taxi
drivers, the truck drivers, they keep a score sheet in their cars:
'Yesterday I kill five dogs, six dogs today'. I am absolutely
serious."

Across the road on the traffic island I saw a sleeping,
mange-ridden dog lift its head, cast its eyes over its surroundings and then sink back into the dust again.

"When I drive I have to be careful," Herbert was saying.
"They think I'm American. They see white skin you must
be gringo, you must be rich. Women throw their babies
in front of my car because it's worth to lose one baby for
nine hundred pesos." His face cracked a look of grotesque
disbelief. He nodded.

"Fathers, grandfathers fuck girls fourteen, fifteen years old.
It's absolutely *horrible*. I hate hypocrisy. One man comes
here, he points at this painting: 'You have got to take down
this picture, is prostitution. Disgusting.' Five minutes later
he says, 'I want to fuck your waitress.' Fourteen years old. Is
horrible. I hate hypocrisy and here is the absolute *worst*."

He pecked his cigarette end out in the ashtray and said,
"This place is the end of the world."

I came back to Herbert's café that evening to get something
to eat. Sitting at the plastic table by the entrance was a
Mexican in a hat making thumbnail sketches on serviettes,
and next to him a rotund woman with a bumbag and big

drowsy eyes. Herbert steered me to the adjacent table and, with a restaurateur's knack for showmanship, dashed off the seat for me with a tea towel. When I sat down, the woman seemed to rouse herself from some far-off place and picked up her basket of cakes and biscuits decorated with red ribbons. When I said *no gracias*, she let the basket drop and settled back into her lethargy.

The man was a dishevelled local artist known as Miguel, with a hangdog expression and heavy five-o'clock shadows creeping up towards his tired eyes, and the woman seemed to be his muse. They sat in silence, she staring off into space, he listlessly doodling on the table top. Occasionally he would venture forth with a comment or a question, and she would nod or shrug without interest.

I had come hoping to get a sandwich, but Herbert wouldn't hear of it.

"This is an Italian *restaurant*," he enunciated deliberately. "I am trying to introduce to these people the idea of Italian *eating*. It is plate followed by plate. Quality ingredients. Real flavour. All they're used to is tacos tacos tacos tacos, they have no *idea*." His face crumpled in a rictus of displeasure. He exhaled a long skein of menthol smoke.

"Do you trust me?" He said at last, giving me a level look. "Then I will make for you a real dinner."

He immediately set to work behind a flimsy partition, banging pots and knives in his makeshift kitchen. Miguel raised his eyebrow and shrugged at me, then went back to his pencil sketch. Some people wandered by on the pavement, looked in curiously, and carried on past. From the kitchen there was the sound of clattering utensils, whisked ingredients, the roar of a gas stove.

A few minutes later, Herbert came quickly out of the kitchen, mired in perspiration. He set down a dish before me.

"Cream-of-zucchini soup," he announced, then turned and resumed the cacophony of spatula and rolling pin. Although the soup had a primordial look about it, it was good. I was quite satiated by the time he came out again, carrying another dish. He took away the soup and thrust in front of me a salad of tomato and mozzarella.

"With Italian white-wine dressing," he said.

Miguel gave a show of delicate applause like an opera-lover.

Before I had a chance to finish the salad, Herbert burst out of the kitchen to replace it with a plate of tagliatelle. He slammed the plate down, then cracked an egg against the rim, and dropped the raw yolk onto the pasta, stabbing it a few times with the prongs of a fork. He went this time without saying anything. The sound of ringing steel went up in the kitchen again, more violently this time.

I ate less enthusiastically now. I had lost my appetite, and the roof of my mouth was coated with raw egg. Miguel and his corpulent companion watched me without expression.

A short, sharp scream of pain came from the kitchen. It was a heartfelt, high-pitched note that resounded off the walls of the café and seemed to hang in the air for a long time. After that I ate slowly, listening with trepidation to the clatter of kitchen equipment and the sound of vigorous frying.

Whipping his tea towel over his shoulder, Herbert came out of the kitchen again. I noticed that his hand was heavily bandaged in bloodstained tissue paper. There was no longer any attempt at ceremony. Each time he emerged he seemed to have picked up more speed, whilst with each course the food in front of me seemed less inclined to leave the plate. Each mouthful slid down less willingly, catching in the throat with the accumulation of fat.

I was still chewing a potato sautéed in tarragon when he deposited a dish of fried calves' livers in front of me. He was gone again before I could stop him. I stared at the softened livers for a few minutes, my stomach curdling. I offered them to Miguel and his girlfriend, and they just looked back at me without interest. The livers were dense and rich, fried in brandy, they puréed under the tongue and solidified before I could work them to the back of my mouth. A cold sweat had broken out across my brow, and my head throbbed with a dull ache. I looked across towards the kitchen and caught a glimpse of Herbert scooping a great lump of double cream into a frying pan. My oesophagus tightened with nausea.

After the meal I sat there feeling bloated and queasy. Herbert made a great show of the washing up, breaking one plate and swearing bitterly in Spanish. I was dimly aware of Miguel, paying me close attention and making a careful sketch on a serviette. His girlfriend stared forlornly out on to the dark street. Eventually Herbert came out of the kitchen, fell into a seat at the table and mopped the sweat from his face. He still had the tissue-paper bandage clenched tight over his left hand, the dark spot of blood slowly expanding across it. Wincing with exhaustion, he lit a menthol cigarette and leant back.

"What do you think?" he asked. I noticed a small convulsion in his eyelid.

"Mmmm," I said, feigning a look of sleepy contentment.

"It is something special to be appreciated. These people do not appreciate good *food*, they do not recognize *quality*, they know nothing except *tacos*." He gave a pained smile.

Miguel put his pencil down and leant back from his sketching. He looked out at the street.

"Miguelito here, he thinks I am crazy."

The artist shrugged. "Herbert tries to change the world," he said. "But he cannot change the way Mexican people eat. You cannot change the way people think." He made an apologetic moue at Herbert. In response Herbert gave a sharp hacking laugh.

"Well," I said, to break the silence. "It's a big task you've set yourself, but you're getting there slowly."

Herbert gurned a dubious assent.

"You have some good friends, at least," I ventured.

At this, Herbert's face cracked open in an expression of outrage in high camp.

"I *have* no friends," he exclaimed. "Not one!"

Miguel went back to his sketching, as if he hadn't heard. Herbert gave his menthol cigarette a vicious pull through gritted teeth. The big woman got to her feet wearily, collected her basket and went off down the street.

"You have come to another *world*," Herbert said, exhaling smoke with a sharp hiss. "Here there are no friends. No morals. No ethics. Here there is…" – he raked his sinewy hands through thin air – "…*Nothing*."

Herbert's face cycled through new grimaces.

"Oh yes, everyone smiles at you, *buenos dias* smile smile," he pulled a series of grotesque Disney smiles. "But when you need something, they run! Believe me, I've seen it when I had…" – he pronounced it slowly and with distaste – "… *Nothing*."

His face cramped in bitterness.

"All they care about is *dinero*. Money. For them there's nothing else."

He turned back to his cigarette, which he took apart with short, angry little tokes, a far-off look in his eyes. Miguel got up heavily from the table and went towards the toilet.

Herbert leant over to me confidentially. *"There's no one in this town I can trust,"* he whispered sharply. *"Not one."* He gestured over his shoulder towards the toilet door. "This one," he said, "I saw him in the street two months ago when I had five pesos, and he wasn't interested." He pouted and then winced. "And now I have a bar and a café he's here every night. He's not my friend."

Leaning back, he flashed me a camp smile, all brown teeth and bloodshot eyes, half defiant, half defeated. He shrugged, and his body collapsed perceptibly. He had been working seventeen-hour days, seven days a week. Tomorrow they would cut off the water supply, next week perhaps the electricity.

"Today I work hard for *poco*, *poquito dinero*," he said after a time. "Tonight I won't sleep. When I turn out the lights, I start to worry. I have to keep working working working, as long as I'm working I don't *think*." He shook his head and then turned to me with a terrible grin that split his face from ear to ear.

I asked him how much I owed him.

"Whatever you think," he said, wiping the perspiration from his forehead with the back of his arm. "Whatever is *fair*."

How much is a last supper worth? I unscrewed my last hundred-peso note and pressed it into his hand. His fingers closed around it and turned white at the knuckles. I thought it was very generous, but Herbert took the note in silence with a grudging nod. As I left, I heard the clatter of pots and utensils resume behind the partition, the melancholy ring of tin and aluminium.

The streets of Salina Cruz were deserted, and they seemed to writhe beneath my feet and flinch away from my foot-falls.

Lying on my bed, I watched the inscriptions of black mould slowly spreading across the ceiling, inching down the walls towards me. Then I knelt by the toilet and wormed a finger down my throat to make myself sick.

A sizeable group of slackers was already occupying the finest flop-house in Salina Cruz. They spent their days at Otto's, a ramshackle bar knocked together by a ship's carpenter who used his connections in the merchant navy to keep the place stocked with German beer. Pink insect netting drooped over the doors and windows, for decorative purposes more than anything else, for it provided scant protection against the merciless advance of the mosquitoes.

The proprietor, armed with a rag and a stiff brush, expended his energies in tireless defence of his territory from the incursions of poisonous animals and from the fine dust that seeped in through cracks in the boards, replenishing itself as quickly as he could sweep it away. Bob Brown recalled that from time to time Otto's eyes would turn glassy, focusing somewhere in the air beyond his customers, then he'd vault the bar, bring down a scorpion from the wall with his dishcloth and dance it to death on the floor. This was the extent of the entertainment in Salina Cruz.

Skirmishes between the rebels and government forces ground on up in the surrounding hills. The inhabitants of the town were gloomily accustomed to the fighting. At the first volleys of gunfire they would withdraw solemnly into their houses, pulling steel shutters over the windows. As the crack of distant gunshots resounded off the hillsides and the wind brought in the smell of cordite, as the streets fell silent and dust settled on the pavements, Salina Cruz became a ghost town. In Otto's bar the foreigners hunkered down, pouring another drink to numb the fear of the occasional shell that screamed close over the tin roof.

Cravan and the other slackers were worried that the secret police knew about their plans to get to Argentina, and that any day they might be apprehended. Over a bottle of whisky at Otto's they planned their escape routes. Brown and his wife would cross the frontier by train, whilst Cravan and Winchester – who couldn't risk the border control without passports – would make for Chile by sailing boat. Cravan told Mina that the crossing would be dangerous, that for the baby's sake it would be best if she made her own way by steamer. She was reluctant to be parted from him, but with the Browns' reassurance she finally agreed. "We would all meet again at the foot of the towering Andes," Bob Brown hoped, "under better conditions."

The following day Cravan took up a collection for a small boat. He didn't wait for the monsoon to pass before he began the search for a suitable vessel; sometimes he would set out for the docks at the height of the storm and not come back for days. Cravan was gradually succumbing to the same blind panic that had driven him to desperate action three years earlier, and set him on this dwindling path.

He soon fell ill and, overtaken by fever, was confined to his bed. Mina patiently nursed him through his sickness. She lugged in buckets of cool water from the well along the road, she wrung out cloths to lay over his burning forehead. Cravan was seized by waking visions of imprisonment, he dreamt of Mina as his jailer, pinning him down. Listless, exhausted with fever, he lay on the floor of the room watching her shaping flaccid tortillas like a tawdry housewife.

One afternoon, while Mina went to buy fruit and vegetables from the market, Bob Brown paid him a visit. Brown was struck by how swiftly his friend had deteriorated. Cravan had lost weight, his hair was thinning, he was barely recognizable. His twisted face was a morass of hostility, he exuded resentment as thick as the sweat pricking at his forehead. The inclinations that Brown had often glimpsed in Cravan on nights of excess were now laid bare.

That afternoon, Brown recalled, Cravan lay in the throes of delirium, railing bitterly against his wife. He complained that "She is too much the long-suffering heroine for me. I want to be alone, I tell you." He lay still and limp, sweat standing out on his chest. His lips were contorted with loathing, his eyes stared up at the ceiling with an expression of feverish clarity. "I want to get a boat and sail off all by myself somewhere," he whispered. "Get away from all these savages, draft-dodgers, everybody, get away to South America, Tahiti, anywhere. I'm sick of anything in skirts."

At that moment, Mina returned with a basket of *zapotes*. Cravan let out a deep sigh of exasperation and rolled over to face the wall. Gradually, under Mina's unrelenting care, his health improved. A week later he felt strong enough to walk, and she led him by the arm to the beach. Soon Cravan resumed his search of the harbour and the breakers' yards, until he found a fisherman with a small boat for sale. "Because of a hole in its hull," Brown recalled, "he bought it cheap." Cravan threw himself into the task of repairing the boat with renewed vigour, impatient to leave Mexico. An idle ship's carpenter helped him patch the hole, and then he had the vessel towed to a small private pier a mile from town at La Ventosa, where he began work to refit it.

"I must get away," Brown had heard him whisper, and at the time he had dismissed Cravan's words as nothing more than delirious ravings. But given the course of events those words came to resonate with an ominous significance.

It was a long drive out of Salina Cruz along dusty, potholed tracks through arid scrubland. Wind trapped in a steep-sided valley was spewing up a vortex of dust, incandescent in the sun, the silhouettes of vultures circling around it. The engine of the antiquated taxi stuttered on the inclines into the hills, and occasionally gave a roar of displeasure when the driver missed a gear. On the windscreen was a faded sticker of Jesus weeping.

The car pulled up by some vertiginous steps that disappeared between derelict whitewashed buildings. When I offered him the coins, the driver turned on me, cursing in incomprehensible Spanish. We had agreed a fare of ten pesos, but now he claimed it was ten *dollars* I had promised him. I drew in breath to argue, but then let it sigh out of me again, in disgust. The driver rolled his bloodshot eyes back into his corpulent, sweaty face, and I noticed the sharp barbs of white stubble that grew from the base of his neck up to the forehead and gave him the grotesque appearance of a plucked goose. Defeated, I looked into my wallet, which was empty. I found a battered fifty-peso note in the bottom of my pocket and showed it to him, gesturing that he would get the rest after he took me back into town. He rolled his eyes again and said *Quanto tiempo*. I told him I would be one hour. He spat out of the window and shouted more phrases that I didn't understand, although I think I caught the general gist. I handed over the note and slammed the door. With him still shouting after me, I sloped away from the car and started down the narrow steps, watched from all sides by grubby, skinny boys in ragged shorts.

I allowed myself a smile at the thought of the taxi driver sitting up on the road all afternoon. As I was dragged under, never to resurface, he'd still be sitting there, his meter ticking up a vast sum, waiting interminably, the spray kicked up from the sea slowly rusting his car to the road. The thought of it gave me one last stir of satisfaction.

I hadn't slept the night before. I had lain in bed, listening to the high-anxiety whine of the mosquitoes as they prepared for their onslaught. In the back of my head the thought of Cathy had lingered like a tumour, and in the darkness I thought I could even make out the lines of her face in the patterns of mould on the ceiling. There too was the face of my dead father and the curled form of the child that would soon see life. And Cathy, always Cathy... I understood it was the loneliness playing tricks on me, but that didn't make it any easier to bear. I burned to hear the sound of her voice one last time.

The thought persisted all night, growing starker, more insistent, until I couldn't resist it any longer. I went out into the courtyard, amongst the wilting angular plants poised like desperate figures in the early morning light. I went out into the empty street to the payphone on the corner. I would say nothing, just listen, and then hang up. She would be right there, at the end of the line, just for an instant. She wouldn't have to know who it was, it would change nothing. But it might be enough, just enough to carry me through. I lifted the receiver. I dialled the number.

That telephone was broken, so I found another kiosk further down the street. When I dialled this time, I heard the chattering of the line connecting, the deep hiss in the cable that reached across the great distance that separated us. The ring tone sounded. Once. Twice. Three times. The interval between the tones expanded each time closer to infinity. In the space between I could hear the blood rushing in my ear, the white noise of thousands of miles of static.

The telephone rang on and on. I pictured the white plastic phone on the wall in the hall, the twisted wire hanging towards the floorboards, the dust in the runnels between them, the junk mail scattered beneath the letter box. The sound as it rang reverberated between the close walls, touched the calendar hanging by a nail, now turned to the page marked with an excited cross, the end of the nine-month term.

The phone rang and rang. It sounded off the panels of the cupboards in the kitchen, trickled through the leaves of the spider plant that spilt over the table, past the little basket containing forgotten odds and ends, pebbles, pine cones, unwanted key rings and other useless things never quite discarded. The ring of the phone had woken the dog, and it barked from its cushion by the wall, but couldn't quite be bothered to move. The sound glanced off the fridge door, running softly across the photograph of Cathy and me in a park that was held in place with a carrot-shaped magnet, and that had accumulated over time a patina of grease and dust. The sound moved on into the bedroom, brushed over the surface of our bed that had once been ruckled with our imprint and infused with the smell of us. It found its way beneath the bed, over the edge of the matted sheepskin rug into the indistinct territory where the Hoover never quite reached, to disturb old bus tickets, bits of tissue, long blonde hairs, and perhaps an ancient plaster shrivelled by time to resemble a cornflake and bearing the rusty trace of a forgotten wound. It seeped into the wardrobe through the crack in the door, rummaged amongst Cathy's assortment of shoes and fallen clothes and the strange knotted plastic bags of baby things waiting at the back. The sound of the ringing telephone slid across the walls and the previous tenants' wallpaper that we had never liked, but never got around to stripping. It tangled with the legs of the high chair in the corner, a hand-me-down from her sister, whose children had now outgrown it. And the sound crawled across the sill, past the corpse of a bluebottle with its legs in the air, coming to rest by the window, pressed up against the glass, the beads of rain and the view over the gasometer.

The phone rang and rang in the empty flat and eventually I hung up.

Late in the morning I came out of my room, and left my key at the desk. On my way I passed Herbert's café, and for some reason I stopped by to say goodbye.

I found Herbert manic and overworked. There was a single customer sitting at one of the tables, and he didn't look in any immediate hurry. Herbert, however, was sweating blood, racing around the tiny kitchen, savagely stirring pots, slamming pans onto the gas, measuring drops of sauce from bottles, his face twisted with bitter exhaustion. I stood there for several minutes waiting for him to see me, and when he did catch sight of me, he pretended not to have noticed. He plucked a pot from the stove and slopped its contents artfully onto a plate, which he snatched up in his hand. He came round the partition, shouldered past me and set the plate down at the customer's table. On his way back he acknowledged me with a nod.

"Nothing but foreigners today," he muttered. "There was even an Australian this morning."

And he set about slamming and knocking things about again in the kitchen.

"What do you want?" he called to me. "Italian coffee?"

"No thanks. I just came to say goodbye."

He flinched away from a flame that went up as he flash-fried something.

"You're leaving?" he said. "Okay, goodbye."

"Bye," I muttered, but didn't move.

After a while longer of pot-juggling and the loud, angry chopping of vegetables, he caught sight of me out of the corner of his eye and, surprised to see that I hadn't left, he stopped what he was doing and raised his eyebrows. I had nothing to say, so I drained the mucus from my nose into a serviette.

"Be sure to tell your friends about the Swiss Donkey," he said. Then the kettle started whistling, so he turned back to the coffee and paid me no further attention.

Throughout my childhood, Saturdays used to be a source of particular dread. The other boys at school would go with their dads to see the Arsenal or Crystal Palace. My Dad would take me on a two-hour drive across the city to see Romford Town FC.

Wearing matching green anoraks, we'd sit on the deserted, rainswept terraces at their home ground for ninety minutes of Romford being trounced by one of its mediocre rivals in the second division. The drive home would be an interminable trial of melancholy silence. I often wondered why he insisted on this morbid pilgrimage every other week. Romford had lost or drawn twenty-seven games in succession, and the club seemed to persist only with the stubborn nostalgia of lifelong supporters unwilling to lie down and die.

One afternoon – I remember it vividly – the team won one–nil after an own goal from the Sunderland fullback, and on the final whistle the sparse crowd erupted in a maelstrom of jubilation. Singing ecstatic Romford anthems that hadn't been aired for years, they emptied the ground in a conga. But driving back into the city, Dad's car was saturated with the same morose silence that he exuded every weekend. Watching sidelong, I wondered at him bent over the wheel with the same stolid expression, the same dead set of the eyes. He stopped at a petrol station on the way back, and curiously I stared at him in the wing mirror as he filled the tank.

It didn't strike me at the time as strange, but when we got home that particular weekend, Dad drove the car into the garage and then closed the door, shutting us both inside. He put an arm around my neck, but it was a little too tight to be wholly comforting, and we stood like that for a long time. Perhaps it was the match, the flush of victory, that had spurred this rare show of affection. It was an awkward, slightly constrictive hug, but I was sure it was a hug none-theless, even though I had never received one before. We clung on to one another like that for a long time, and I began to feel happier than I could remember.

I assumed that on the journey back from Romford he had heard something in the engine that troubled him, and that was why he left it running. I stood by him there in the dark for what must have been half an hour, without daring to move. I didn't want to disturb the moment, I didn't want it to end. We stood together, listening intently to the purr of the motor. I waited, watching condensation dripping off the exhaust pipe.

Finally, seeming to grow impatient, he emitted a sigh and reached in through the driver's window to turn the key in the ignition, and the motor spluttered out. Then he swung open the door and daylight flooded into the garage. I followed him into the house, where he sequestered himself in his study with a bottle of wine for the rest of the afternoon, as he did every weekend without fail throughout the course of the recession, to pore over the *Financial Times* and check the rate of decay of his investments.

The flat expanse of La Ventosa spread out before me. Featureless, scoured by a deafening wind. Stark brown sand ebbing into thick brown water, the enormous wingspans of pelicans tipping and twitching in the gusts overhead. Along the shore was a collection of what may have once been restaurants, now abandoned shells peeling paint and dissolving into the beach. Beyond, on the north side, was a landscape of dark boulders, overcast by a plume of dirty-blue smoke billowing out of a bonfire above. Everywhere in the sky, the angular specks of frigate birds pointed in one direction to brace the wind. And further out, bristling amongst the treacherous tides, barren crags of rock dwindled gradually towards the flat line of the ocean horizon, infinite and empty. This is where Cravan was last seen by human eyes. This was the jumping-off point, the place where he finally disappeared over the edge.

I stepped into the remains of a café eroded by the blistering wind and subsiding dramatically into the sand. Outside, a wave threw itself headlong into the rocks and broke apart. A fat woman with sunken eyes placed a menu on the plastic table top, and immediately the wind tore it away, sent it cartwheeling across the sand. I ordered a Pepsi, it was to be my last. She brought it with a serviette in a plastic palm-frond stand, which was snatched by the wind as soon as she set it down and tossed over the side towards the water. Here even inanimate objects, anything that wasn't weighted down, had the tendency to dash themselves against the rocks or plunge despondently into the sea. I couldn't imagine what had prevented the rotund proprietor of this sorry establishment from doing the same long ago.

I watched the woman shuffle defeatedly after the menu, saw it fling itself out of reach when she tried to grab at it.

I lit a cigarette, and before I could take a drag, the wind whipped it away. The bottle of Pepsi toppled, emptying over the concrete floor in a muddy welt of foam. Across the other side of the terrace a middle-aged couple hung together in a hammock that was pitching from side to side. They were clutching on to one another for dear life as if they expected at any moment to be torn asunder and catapulted into oblivion. Up on the rocks a throng of shirtless boys squatted by the bonfire tossing scraps of desiccated scrub to feed the flames.

For the last time I looked long and hard at the passport photo of Cathy. Then, unpinching finger and thumb, I let the wind take it. It fluttered once in the air, and then plunged in a long arc towards the water.

Half a dozen of the slacker crowd at Otto's had been picked up in a raid by the authorities, and the remainder now dispersed, making a retreat into the Mexican interior or hazarding a last doomed run for the border. It seemed there was no escaping the War, no sating its appetite: it would consume all in its path.

Cravan and Mina moved out to La Ventosa, and now they even stopped going back into town to sleep. They spent the nights here on the beach, so that Cravan could give the boat his full attention. While he hammered and sawed without rest, Mina settled in the shade of a low tree nearby. She spent the days preparing his meals, stoking the fire for the stewpot and sewing the sail. Red Winchester sometimes stopped by to help with the heavy work and to check on the vessel's progress.

One evening, as they expected Winchester for dinner and the stew bubbled over the fire, Cravan threaded the sail and raised the mast. The boat was ready at last, and he couldn't wait to test it in the water.

"What, right now?" Mina called. "Hadn't you better wait till Red comes to help?"

"I'll just go a little way out," Cravan shouted across the sand. "I'll get the sails working and then I'll tack back and pick you up."

Mina watched from the beach as the sail fattened in the breeze and pushed the boat out to sea. When Winchester arrived, the two of them stood together for a long time watching the boat dwindle to a speck on the horizon, until finally the sail dropped out of sight altogether.

Six years later it was to reappear in the form of a folded-paper boat adrift over Paris rooftops in René Clair's surrealist film, *Entr'acte*. Shot by Cravan's acquaintances, Francis Picabia, Marcel Duchamp and Man Ray, the film is full of hidden references to his disappearance. Disembodied boxing gloves cuff the darkness; ghosting over the image, the enigmatic upturned profile of a man's chin; Picabia and Duchamp playing chess on a precarious ledge high over the city; a sudden torrent of water washes the pieces from the board; and most haunting of all, the recurring image of a woman's staring eyes superimposed over the relentless churning of ocean waves. In the final scene, mourners in top hats hop absurdly after a runaway funeral cortège, before the coffin rolls to a standstill in the middle of a field. The corpse prizes off the lid and then makes the onlookers disappear one by one before willing himself to blink out of existence.

It wouldn't have been difficult. Cravan had, after all, been slowly killing himself for years: his whole life had been an experiment in self-destruction. This was the end of Arthur Cravan: now he obliterated him once and for all, as surely as if he'd poked a gun in his mouth and pulled the trigger. The last, biting irony of Cravan's story was that the armistice was to bring the Great War to a close mere weeks after his disappearance.

At La Ventosa that night, Mina refused to go back to the hotel, staying on the beach until dawn. Wrapped in Cravan's enormous coat, with its sleeves drawn tightly around her, she squatted there by the dying embers of the campfire, and waited.

The little boat had been sighted by a steamer just as it grew dark that evening, reportedly holding a steady course into the open sea. Mina waited on in Salina Cruz, certain that her husband would return. Her hair turned white within a week, and soon she felt the first kicks of the baby. Since she found that Cravan had taken with him the precious money-belt containing the last of their savings, she relied on the Browns to pay for her passage on a Japanese hospital ship bound for Argentina. She gave birth to Cravan's child, a girl, in Europe. Mina named her Fabienne, after her father, to whom she was said to bear an unsettling likeness.

I was standing stark naked at the water's edge, shivering in the unrelenting wind. The transparent, anaemic husk of a half-eclipsed moon hung over the horizon. A pelican skimmed the wave tops, then pitched suddenly and crashed into the water.

I had walked around the headland a little way to this deserted stretch of sand, a place where I would not be overlooked. Tattered black vultures wheeled overhead, descending on some dead or dying thing across the sand. Further out the vast refinery loomed, with its rank upon rank of coiling pipes and towering chimneys like the ribs of a monumental carcass rising half-buried from the mud.

I noticed that the ragged boys had come down from the rocks to collect in the surf two hundred yards along the beach. First I thought they had come down to watch me, but then I saw that they were pointing at something out to sea, where the waves reared up. Their presence was putting me off. I took a few deep breaths and tried to put them out of my mind. I was halfway to regaining my composure when I caught sight of what they were pointing at: far out in the bay a great wave lifted a figure into view. The figure rose up on the face of the wave, paddling and then heaving himself to his feet.

Even at that distance Wayne was unmistakable. His sodden hair whipped behind him as he carved his surfboard, clinging to the sheer face of the wave. Watching from the beach, the boys in their ragged shorts were jumping and hooting with excitement, some of them mimicked the surfer, poised, crouching on flaps of driftwood.

I laughed, but there were tears in my eyes. I couldn't quite believe it: the golden-boy surfer from Zipolite, here to meet me at the end of the road. I looked up at the sky and shook my fist at it lamely. This was the final proof of the existence of a malign god.

I would have to go through with it, there was no turning back now. It wouldn't work to put it off until tomorrow: I knew it was now or never.

So this was the punchline I'd been waiting for all my life, was it, for this practical joke's dismal duration? How compelling the gut instinct for survival, even as every reasoned thought points the other way.

This was the moment I had been living for; for years this was the place I had dreamt of: everything was focused here. But now even the fibres of my body were conspiring against me. My legs were cramped with fear, I had a terrible urge to turn and run. And yet it was turning back that terrified me the most, because then there would be no telling what I might do.

I saw Wayne again, scything his board below the horizon, merging with the crest of the wave. If only I could hate him, perhaps I could find it in me to plunge after him into the sea and drag him down with me.

The tricks the mind plays. The straws it grasps at. Just as my grip began to falter, the thought of Cathy chose its moment to flutter into my head. All of a sudden her face came back to me, vivid, the way it had been that morning nine months before. In bed, her face held close to mine, the colour high in her cheeks, the sweat starting where our skin pressed together.

Trembling there at the water's edge the longing was so intense it was almost physical. It was an actual pain, a churning sickness in the belly, a dizzying gravity that accelerated me backwards. With her face, I remembered the scent and the feel of her, and the strange joyful feeling when she told me how much she loved me.

The mind will try anything to make life seem worth the trouble, and of all its tricks, love is the most dangerous. Now my resolve had abandoned me, and my head reeled with doubt. I began to sob like a child does, with a heaving chest and a string of snot caught on the chin. "It isn't too late," I was muttering. "It's never too late to turn back."

Goose pimples stood out all over my body. My teeth were beginning to chatter. I looked around from the water, and through the tears I could see my footprints leading back across the sand.

The shame of it, to bottle out at the very end – after all this time, after all the years of waking dreams over an office desk, after the plans made in the secret fever of so many nights of insomnia, after a lifetime spent travelling towards this single point.

My eyes followed the footprints away from me, back onto the beach. There, ten metres away, were my clothes, neatly folded in a pile, one shoe laid on either side. That was the way I had always left them every night at home before I went to bed, and the recollection of it cut through all my vacillation. It brought me back, suddenly, to my senses.

This was a habit, ingrained since infancy, something I'd caught off my father. As a child he had shown me how to put myself to bed, and it became second nature. I didn't give it a thought until he had put himself to bed that final time and I noticed his tidy mound of clothes set meticulously aside. And the true purpose of that odd ritual only became apparent all those months later, when the nurse handed me his personal effects, ironed and folded with a consolingly clinical crispness. Creased and inserted into their sterile paper envelope they were not clothes shrugged off the back of a dead man – they were the self-fulfilling prophecy of a life that was stillborn, that had never quite come into being.

I held that thought in my mind, and the recollection seemed to galvanize me. At that moment it all came together, and I remembered what I was here for.

My body stiffened, the knots of my muscles straightened out. The anger flared up inside me like a chip-pan fire. The surf came to meet my ankles, and it all came flooding back: *My God I'm a wanker.*

That was enough, stronger even than the strange attachment to life.

I recalled all the dogs I'd sent squealing with a kick, all the creatures on the road at night that I'd steered into. I recalled my perpetual scowl, the look I used to wither strangers passing in the street. I recalled the scoffing exhalation through the nose that I called laughter, as mirthful as a bicycle-pump wheeze. I remembered all the conversations I'd killed, all the pleasant atmospheres I'd soured, all the bubbles I'd done my best to burst.

I thought of Cathy. I thought of her going into labour alone. Most of all I thought of the child.

I waded quickly into the foam of the breakers. I felt only the cold of the wash sucking at my knees.

I began to swim with wild convulsions, gasping. I put everything into it. I swam fiercely, desperately, with every stroke clawing myself further from land, and further from life. I felt a great void opening up beneath me, a great distance unravelling, a horrifying solitude drawing me in.

The violent pitching of the waves hiked me up and swooped

me down again. I swallowed great salty gouts of seawater, it filled my gullet and burned the lining of my sinuses.

By now I must have swum a hundred metres out. It occurred to me that the survival reflex could not bring me back from here: I had gone past the point of no return. With this thought came an odd surge of triumph: killing myself wasn't as difficult as I'd thought.

My muscles seized and my legs froze. I flailed my arms, but there was no strength left in them, and they sagged heavily against the waves that lifted me backwards. My throat was clotted with phlegm, my breath burst out of me with a note of hysteria. And I gave in to it, just like that.

Everything stopped, I let myself go limp, let the current take me. I remember hoping that my life would not flash before my eyes: I'd sooner not be reminded of it.

I was still except for the occasional jolt of my stomach as it cramped. It wouldn't be long now. When my head went under again, I listened to the great roar of the sea; the rush of blood in the ears; the reverberation of an empty motorway; the static over a disconnected telephone line; the sound of words breathed by a cadaver.

Another surge dragged me backwards, turning me away from the open sea. My face broke the surface and through searing eyes I caught a sudden glimpse of the shore. A heavy wave broke across my back and thrust me forwards. Then I felt my shoulder dragging through sand, and with a faceful of kelp I was deposited back onto the beach.

Cravan's death was as confounding and inexplicable as his life. In fact it was an end so larded with irony and ambiguity that it seems inconceivable that there was not an element of design to it. Of course he had never quite existed in the first place: "Arthur Cravan" had been no more than a persona, a pseudonym. As Bob Brown observed, "He was a great melodrama to himself, and the leading actor in it." Even

Mina Loy came to understand that the ease with which he now flickered out of existence was due to the fact that Cravan had always lacked substance: he presented "an unreality of himself to the world," Loy said, "to occupy itself with while he made his spiritual getaway."

Now he made the final transition into fiction, disintegrating into a plethora of tall tales, leaving his bones to be picked dry by the starved imaginations of biographers. For them his disappearance was a gift, an invitation to give free rein to their fantasies. From Salina Cruz the legend veers wildly in contrary directions, sprouts myriad apocrypha, gives way wholly to conjecture, and all seemingly encouraged by Cravan's own proclivities as a fabulist, his knack for disappearing acts and for exaggerating the news of his own deaths. Over the next thirty years Cravan was to resurface in numerous guises, in numerous corners of the world, only to disappear again without trace.

Blaise Cendrars vaguely recalled that in the last of the mysterious letters that Cravan sent to Renée in Paris he talked about time spent adrift in the "godforsaken wilderness" of central Mexico. He headed for Durango, where the abandoned mines were said to glisten with gold, but he found that they had been dynamited by the fleeing prospectors. Cendrars remembered little else of the letter, other than a passage praising the primitive ways of the native Indians.

A few months after the events at Salina Cruz, a newspaper report mentions an English boxer fighting on the border at Nuevo Laredo. The article described an enigmatic man who turned up just as the fight was due to begin, and gave no name. But the crux of the article was not the riddle of the man's identity, but his incompetence as a boxer: under the headline 'KOed Twice in One Night', it reported that the man was knocked unconscious in the very first round of the fight. Around midnight he was spotted again, drinking in the rundown saloon where the boxing crowd retired after the fight to mingle with the cattle hands, the Yankee drifters and the wealthy Texans who had crossed the border for a toss with a Mexican whore. Here he got into a drunken altercation with some locals and – to roars of jubilation amongst the spectators – the man was once again laid out cold.

Soon afterwards an old acquaintance from Cravan's Paris days thought he recognized a description of him in a byline in the *Paris Soir* newspaper, a story about a band of outlaws shot at by border guards after a pursuit across the Rio Grande del Norte.

Inconclusive evidence suggests that Cravan appeared the following year in the United States as a poet-vagabond going variously by the names James M. Hayes and Dorian Hope. A book collector who crossed paths with Hope was less intrigued by the man's poetry than by his curious demeanour. He recalled that Hope had the air of a ruined aristocrat, combining the clipped diction of an expensive education with the coarse language of a boiler-room stoker or a guttersnipe.

Three years later, sailing under the name Sebastian Hope, he is thought to have turned up in London. Here he passed himself off as a friend of Oscar Wilde, staying long enough only to sell a number of Wilde manuscripts to a bookselling firm for an undisclosed sum. By the time the manuscripts were revealed to be skilful forgeries, Hope was long gone.

Cravan is also linked to a similar scam perpetrated against the Dublin booksellers Hodges, Figgis & Co. by a certain Dorian Hope in the 1930s. The man claimed to be André Gide's secretary, and it struck the book dealer as peculiar that he didn't remove his dark glasses or turn down the fur collar of his overcoat when he entered the shop.

It has even been suggested that Cravan never left Mexico, but reinvented himself as a reclusive writer under the name B. Traven. In 1946 a newspaper reporter claimed to have traced Traven to a bar in Acapulco, but when confronted the man sought to deny his identity with a remarkable

series of explanations: Traven was his cousin; Traven was a
woman; Traven was dead; Traven was alive in a sanatorium
in Switzerland. Although his identity remains a mystery, this
– the only recorded encounter with Traven – seems an apt
postscript to the story of Arthur Cravan.

Mina Loy shared the cruel fate of many war widows whose
loved ones never returned from the front. Strung along by
rumours of his survival, for almost a decade she refused to
give up Cravan for dead. Stories reached her that he had been
sighted boarding a train at Valparaiso; he had applied for a
visa at the Russian embassy; a man of his description had
undergone treatment for amnesia at a military hospital. Her
hopes were revived even by the malicious gossip circulating in
New York that Cravan was alive and well in the Pacific islands,
having escaped to Tahiti for a tryst with a former lover. For
years after Cravan's disappearance these stories spread like
Chinese whispers, denying Mina the chance to grieve.

Decades later, as Mina lived out her last years in Aspen,
Colorado, Cravan even haunted her senility. She would bring
the familial chatter of Thanksgiving dinner to an abrupt
standstill with the doleful interjection, "Why was I never able
to find him?" She had indeed followed every lead tirelessly,
all to no avail.

Hoping that secret-service surveillance might shed light
on his whereabouts, she had succeeded in tracking down a
British agent who had operated in Mexico during the War.
The spy could tell her nothing about Cravan, but his claim
that many draft-dodgers, having been incarcerated without
trial, still languished on, forgotten, in prison cells, enlivened
her interest. She returned to Mexico in 1922 and searched for
Cravan in all the crumbling jails of Central America in vain.

Until the end, Mina remained unsatisfied. The version of
events that she liked the best was suggested by a Christian
Scientist who had heard stories of a man stabbed to death in
Mexico by bandits. This was the explanation she often gave

people. Perhaps she clung to this because it proved he hadn't tried to leave her. Secretly, though, Mina always hoped that he would come back into her life again, out of the blue. In an interview she gave shortly before her death in 1965, she was asked about the happiest times and the saddest times in her life. "The happiest?" she replied. "Every moment I spent with Arthur Cravan. The saddest, all the rest."

It wasn't surprising that Marcel Duchamp should be the first to write him off, although it was nearly thirty years before he made this sworn testimony: "I, the undersigned, Henri Robert Marcel Duchamp, artist, hereby affirm that I knew about Fabian Lloyd whose disappearance, in 1918, caused a flutter in the art world. We expected a great deal of his poems, the manuscript of which was lost with him. I knew him well, and only death could be the cause of his disappearance. New York, March 1946."

Cravan's body was never recovered. That no one should sign his death certificate, that he should become a figment of the fervid imagination of others, that his ending should throw his entire existence into question, is exactly as he would have wanted.

A bitter wind brought the first pinpricks of rain from the dark clouds over La Ventosa. I lay there at the water's edge, feeling the wash rocking me back and forth. I stayed like that for a long time, numbed by the tremendous weight of disappointment.

Then I made a half-hearted attempt to choke myself with sand, but succeeded only in making myself dry-heave. The sensation of defeat was absolute.

At last I dragged myself to my feet and began the sullen exercise of putting on my clothes. I had pulled my underpants up to the knee before I realized I'd put both legs through the same leg hole. It was a struggle to rethread them, and I fell on my face several times.

I walked back along the beach, past the half-naked kids. They were still staring out to sea, but they were more subdued now, without the jumping and the squealing and the excitement. Further on, a couple of them were up to their waists in the water, collecting pieces of a broken surfboard. There was no sign of Wayne.

As I crossed the final stretch of sand, I watched the passport photograph skitter back into my path in a little whirlwind of dust and dried seaweed. I stopped and stared, and the image of Cathy twitched back at me persistently in the breeze. Stooping to retrieve it from a snag of netting, I grasped it tight in the palm of my hand.

I picked my way up the mound of rubble to the road. There I found the taxi driver snoring in his car, drool idling through his stubble. He greeted me with a contemptuous grunt and demanded fifteen dollars to drive me back into town.

Acknowledgements

Like all Cravan enthusiasts I am indebted to Jean-Pierre Bégot for the wonderful and wide-ranging sources that he has collected in Arthur Cravan, *Œuvres: poèmes, articles, lettres*. As well as Cravan's own writings and correspondence, this volume reproduces numerous newspaper reports and testimonies by people who knew Arthur Cravan (aka Fabian Lloyd, *b.*1888), and has provided me with many of the quotations contained in this novel.

Among the other primary sources that have proved invaluable for forming my image of Arthur Cravan are the vivid and entertaining reminiscences of Blaise Cendrars in *Le Lotissement du ciel* and *Blaise Cendrars vous parle*. I have also gleaned much about Cravan's life and character, and about the avant-garde milieu, from the memoirs of Gabrielle Buffet-Picabia in *Rencontres avec Picabia, Apollinaire, Cravan, Duchamp, Arp, Calder*.

I owe much to Maria Lluïsa Borràs whose *Arthur Cravan: Une strategie de scandale* is a mine of information and remains by far the most comprehensive study of Cravan's life. Borràs's commitment to rigorous research ensures that hers is an account of Cravan the man rather than Cravan the myth, and this biography has provided me with a thorough grounding for my own tale, although I have occasionally adapted the original material. I have frequently drawn on the excellent collection of sources that Borràs has uncovered – especially the Lloyd family correspondence and the Catalan newspaper reports on Cravan's boxing career in Barcelona. Borràs's contribution in *Paris-Barcelone de Gaudí à Miró* was also a key source when I came to research the Barcelona avant-garde during Cravan's stay there.

I owe a deep debt to Roger Lloyd Conover, who in his capacities as Arthur Cravan's biographer, Mina Loy's editor, and literary executor for the estates of both Arthur Cravan and Mina Loy has devoted much of his life to researching and encouraging others to research their lives and works. Through his own witty and imaginative writings over several decades, as well as his discovery of original Cravan documents and primary source materials, Conover has nuanced the lives, enriched the evidence and complicated the legends of Loy and Cravan. Conover's reconstruction of events, presentation of texts and speculations about meanings and motives in a number of difficult-to-find but extremely rewarding books – including *Arthur Cravan: Poète et Boxeur*, *4 Dada Suicides*, *Boxer* and *The Last Lunar Baedeker* – have been sources of many of the ideas and insights of this novel.

Isaki Lacuesta's documentary *Cravan vs Cravan* is the best-known film treatment of the Arthur Cravan story. A brilliant and entertaining take on the subject, it has also provided me with numerous gems of information – not least of which is the evocation of Cravan in René Clair's surrealist film, *Entr'acte*.

Mina Loy's *Colossus* and *Arthur Cravan is Alive!* have been rich sources upon which I have drawn heavily for my understanding of her relationship with Cravan. *Colossus*, which has never been published in its entirety, is a particularly valuable resource and notoriously difficult to get hold of – so I am indebted to Jean-Pierre Bégot and Roger Lloyd Conover for the precious extracts they have reproduced, respectively in *Œuvres* and *New York Dada*.

The "book about suicide" that introduced the narrator to the story of Cravan was in reality *The Savage God* by Al Alvarez. This book, together with Hans Richter's *Dada: Art and Anti-Art*, has been influential in shaping my portrayal of Dada, as well as the philosophical underpinnings of my tale. Ruth Brandon's *Surreal Lives* is another erudite and engrossing account of the extreme fringe of the Modernist era, and these texts have done much to enlighten me about the complex and interlocking stories of the leading figures of

312

Dada and Surrealism. My understanding of the movement's meaning and impact has been greatly enriched by Greil Marcus's extraordinary take on twentieth-century history in *Lipstick Traces*. I have also quoted extensively from the manifestos, memoirs and commentaries collected by Robert Motherwell in *The Dada Painters and Poets*, a definitive text which has proved indispensable.

Carolyn Burke's wonderful biography, *Becoming Modern: the Life of Mina Loy*, has formed the basis of my understanding of Loy, and I have drawn on it frequently for my portrayal of her relationship with Cravan, as well as the course her life took after his loss. I have also relied upon the exhaustive bibliography compiled by Marisa Januzzi in *Mina Loy: Woman and Poet*, as well as the extensive collection of materials contained in the book – including the transcription of Paul Blackburn and Robert Vas Dias's interview with the poet. Natalie Barney's *Aventures de l'esprit,* Virginia M. Kouidis's *Mina Loy, American Modernist Poet*, and Gillian Hanscombe and Virginia L. Smyers's *Writing for their Lives: American Modernist Women,* have also yielded valuable insights.

To reconstruct the charged political atmosphere of Manhattan on the eve of the War, I have drawn on the writings of John Reed compiled by James C. Wilson in *John Reed for the Masses.* Meanwhile, *Victor* by Henri-Pierre Roché, *Republic of Dreams: Greenwich Village* by Ross Wetzsteon, and Calvin Tomkins's terrific *Duchamp: A Biography* have shed light into the Arensberg circle and New York bohemia.

In order to reconstruct Cravan's time in Mexico, I have depended primarily on Bob Brown's *roman-à-clef, You Gotta Live* – from which I have also taken the imagined circumstances of Cravan and Loy's separation. To render the slacker experience south of the border, Brown's evocative and hilarious novel – full of the sights, sounds and smells of revolutionary Mexico – has proved a rich source, as has John

Reed's *Insurgent Mexico*, with its shrewd and compassionate account of the country's people and politics, as well as T. Phillip Terry's colourful descriptions in *Terry's Guide to Mexico*. My grasp of the complex nature of the country's neutrality and the consequent espionage activities owes much to Friedrich Katz's *The Secret War in Mexico: Europe, the United States and the Mexican Revolution*.

To conjure up the afterlife of Arthur Cravan I have drawn on Henry Lethbridge's astute detective work for his article 'The Quest for Cravan' in *Antiquarian Book Monthly Review*, which I was led to by reading Roger Lloyd Conover's comprehensive summary of Cravan's posthumous existences in his introduction to *4 Dada Suicides*. I have also taken inspiration from Albert J. Guerard's imaginative speculations in his beautifully nuanced novel *The Hotel in the Jungle*.

Other sources that I have drawn upon are Jack Johnson's autobiography, *In the Ring and Out*, Tony Van der Bergh's *The Jack Johnson Story*, Joyce Carol Oates's *On Boxing*, Donald O. Chankin's *Anonymity and Death: The Fiction of B. Traven* and Janis Mink's *Marcel Duchamp, 1887–1968: Art as Anti-Art*.

I would like to thank Seb Barwell for his advice. Thanks too to Sam Hopkins for the loan of the Praktica, and apologies for breaking it. I am most grateful to Tim Bates and Joan Deitch at Pollinger for their enthusiasm and their belief in this project, and to Alessandro Gallenzi, Elisabetta Minervini and Mike Stocks at Alma for their support, good advice and patience throughout the long process of bringing this book to fruition.

– David Lalé, 2007